Praise for the Darkwing Chronicles

"Exciting, fast-paced . . . it has everything."
—Huntress Book Reviews

"Savannah Russe [lets] us know that there is more than one way to tell a good vamp's story."
—Victoria Laurie, author of *Demons Are a Ghoul's Best Friend*

"Exciting . . . superior supernatural suspense."
—The Best Reviews

"Wonderful . . . with a sharp bite."
—*Midwest Book Review*

Dark Nights, Dark Dreams

SISTERHOOD OF THE SIGHT

Savannah Russe

A SIGNET ECLIPSE BOOK

SIGNET ECLIPSE
Published by New American Library, a division of
Penguin Group (USA) Inc., 375 Hudson Street,
New York, New York 10014, USA
Penguin Group (Canada), 90 Eglinton Avenue East, Suite 700, Toronto,
Ontario M4P 2Y3, Canada (a division of Pearson Penguin Canada Inc.)
Penguin Books Ltd., 80 Strand, London WC2R 0RL, England
Penguin Ireland, 25 St. Stephen's Green, Dublin 2,
Ireland (a division of Penguin Books Ltd.)
Penguin Group (Australia), 250 Camberwell Road, Camberwell, Victoria 3124,
Australia (a division of Pearson Australia Group Pty. Ltd.)
Penguin Books India Pvt. Ltd., 11 Community Centre, Panchsheel Park,
New Delhi - 110 017, India
Penguin Group (NZ), 67 Apollo Drive, Rosedale, North Shore 0632,
New Zealand (a division of Pearson New Zealand Ltd.)
Penguin Books (South Africa) (Pty.) Ltd., 24 Sturdee Avenue,
Rosebank, Johannesburg 2196, South Africa

Penguin Books Ltd., Registered Offices:
80 Strand, London WC2R 0RL, England

First published by Signet Eclipse, an imprint of New American Library,
a division of Penguin Group (USA) Inc.

First Printing, December 2008
10 9 8 7 6 5 4 3 2 1

Printed in the United States of America

To the courageous men and women
of America's armed forces—they give their all.

I dream, therefore I am.
—August Strindberg

He who does battle with monsters
needs to watch out lest he in the process
become a monster himself.
—Friedrich Nietzsche, *Beyond Good and Evil*

1

THE embassy's thick walls didn't block the sound: a hollow bang followed by ominous silence, then, a heartbeat later, another bang. *Mortar fire,* Sam thought, *122mm, Katyusha rockets, maybe. People are dying out there.*

It wasn't a guess. Sam knew they were dying. The images came to her as vividly as if she were witnessing them with her own eyes. A little boy, perhaps ten years old, lay motionless in the street, blood becoming a puddle beneath his small body, his blue bicycle twisted and ruined near where he had fallen. His mother, screaming his name, emerged from the doorway of a nearby house and rushed toward him.

Sam felt the woman's anguish wash over her. She wished she didn't hear, didn't see such things, but she didn't know how to shut them out.

Pushing the disturbing scene into a dark corner of her mind, Sam sat down at her desk, took a deep breath, and turned her attention to the letter that had just arrived in the diplomatic pouch. She ran her index finger across the smooth surface of the white business envelope. On its front her name was printed in a plain font: SUSAN ANN MARIE CHASE. Stamped in red in the lower right corner, like a smudge of blood, was the warning: EYES ONLY.

The flap had been glued shut on the reverse side of the envelope. Then, for added security, an official wax seal had been added. She thought this was odd, old-fashioned, really. Quickly she used her fingernail to crack the irregular blob of carnelian in two, making it look like a broken heart.

A wide smile released the tension in her face as she pulled out the sheet of official stationery and unfolded it. She had been waiting weeks for these orders. The delay had been driving her crazy. Back in May she had heard from reliable sources that she was being posted to the embassy in France. Since then she had daydreamed about sitting in a Left Bank sidewalk café, sipping wine, a gorgeous man lounging in the chair opposite her.

Her dream man was always the same. He would be urbane, well educated, and smartly dressed. He would never have saluted, marched, or held a rifle. He would read Sartre and have arguments about modern art until three in the morning. And he would be crazy for her.

Then she began reading the letter she held in her hand. Her smile faded. This wasn't what she had expected. She flicked her eyes away from the words and thought, *What a fool I have been. A victim of vain self-delusion. A stupid woman who believes in hope instead of truth. If I had been going to Paris, there would have been no delay, no lame excuses about a glitch in the paperwork while I stayed in this abattoir, doing my best not to get killed.*

Suddenly the anguish she felt was entirely her own. She let the sheet of paper slip through her fingers onto the desk. Why hadn't she seen this coming? What happened? What went wrong? Paris was going to change everything. Now it was . . . what? Just another dream that died.

Paris absolutely wasn't in the picture anymore. Her orders were clear: She was to report to CIA headquarters at Langley in McLean, Virginia. She frowned, making an angry line appear between her eyes. *Why?* she thought. Going back to the United States made no sense. If the agency wanted to recruit her, as they did routinely with employees of the foreign service, a handler could have contacted her here. Or in Paris.

No, something had gone fundamentally wrong with

this transfer. Somebody wanted to screw her out of the posting she deserved. It wasn't fair. She had worked so hard to excel, yet . . . No, she didn't want to even consider that someone could have found out about her, about the things she hid.

Sam's eyes, as golden as Baltic amber, filled with unshed tears. She glanced up at the early-morning light leaking through the thin, vertical window. Another thought skated along the surface of her consciousness: *The same kind of windows are used in prisons.*

Through that narrow opening she saw a slice of sky, not blue, but a rusty orange, filled with the sand of an approaching storm. "Sam," a high school nickname that came from S. A. M., her initials, knew exactly how hot the day would soon be: 112 degrees Fahrenheit in the shade, not unusual for July in one of the hottest and most dangerous cities in the world.

That city was Baghdad—just another word for pure, unmitigated hell.

She heard the mortar fire again, closer this time, but still not in the Green Zone. Most days insurgents lobbed four or five shells at Baathist houses and shops before scurrying away like rats into the ruined buildings along the streets. The *whump* and *thwack* of the mortars were psychologically disturbing. But the shells—not much more powerful than hand grenades—posed no threat to anyone working inside the new, heavily fortified, $2 billion U.S. Embassy compound.

This thought had barely registered in Sam's mind when she felt a tingle, like an electric current, surge up her spine. Beneath her honey-colored hair, pulled as usual into a severe chignon, her scalp began to crawl. Then she heard a voice speak inside her head: *Get out.*

Her heart began to race. She immediately pushed away from the desk and hurried through the office door into the hallway. All was still. The long corridor lay silent and empty under the glare of fluorescent lights. Most of the people working on this floor hadn't arrived so early in the day.

Run. Get out, the voice commanded.

Sam didn't hesitate. She hiked up the skirt of her

boxy blue business suit and sprinted toward the exit. She didn't know why she had to run, but each time the voice had commanded her to do so over the past months, what Susan Ann Marie Chase had been fleeing was death.

2

BEFORE exiting the embassy's cavernous lobby through the huge outer doors, Sam yelled to the guards by the entrance's metal detector, "A bomb! Run!" She didn't wonder about how she knew there was a bomb. The thought had come into her consciousness, and she understood it was true.

The two MPs, their uniforms crisp, their faces clean shaven, and their eyes very young, stared at her with puzzled looks. They stayed unmoving at their posts. Sam didn't stop to argue or explain. She yelled once more, "Run, you fools!" and continued her headlong dash outside.

A haze of heat encircled Sam as she stumbled and nearly fell when her feet hit the cement walkway between the buildings. The parched ochre dust in the air made it hard to breathe, but her legs kept churning, carrying her away from the building she had just exited.

A thin young woman and a man carrying a briefcase, newcomers to the foreign service, were walking toward the embassy. Sam knew them both and cried out as she ran, "Amy, Tom, turn around! Run! A bomb!"

The woman's face registered surprise, then fear, but she got the message. She turned and ran too. The man did not. He remained standing on the sidewalk, gazing in bewilderment at the fleeing women.

The voice inside Sam's head came again: *Go there. The armored truck.*

Sam spotted the fifteen-ton Mine Protected Clearance Vehicle, or MPCV, parked a hundred feet away. A U.S. Marine officer in a camouflage-print uniform crouched in the open rear door. He was intent on tying his right combat boot.

Sam rushed desperately toward him. "Let us in!" she screamed. "A bomb's about to explode!"

The man jerked his head in the direction of Sam's cry, then moved swiftly to the edge of the sand-colored vehicle. He yanked Sam up by her outstretched hands. As she scrambled into the blast-protected interior, the soldier grabbed the other woman's arms and swung her up too, then pushed her in front of him into the steel-encased truck. He slammed the door shut, and barely a second later the vehicle rocked violently as a massive explosion roared outside.

The three of them sat there in silence, their faces eerily green from the light penetrating the thick tinted windows. For a moment nobody spoke. Then the woman called Amy whispered, "Tom. He's still out there." She started shivering violently despite the heat, her legs trembling, and her hands shaking like aspen leaves in the wind.

Sam did not shake. She did not quiver. She appeared calm, her face placid. Pressing her lips into a hard line, she quashed her emotions down far inside her and pressed her palms together to make sure a tremor didn't reveal the turmoil roiling through her gut.

Soon the rumbling of the explosion faded away into no sound. The dark-haired marine, one elbow resting heavily on his knee, the shoelace of his boot still untied, looked at Sam and asked in a soft South Carolina drawl, "Just what happened back there, ma'am?"

Sam's voice held a convincing sangfroid. "A bomb went off inside the building."

"Do you think it was a suicide bomber?" The other woman could barely whisper the question.

"No. The explosion was much more powerful," Sam answered without thinking, a scene coming like a dream into her mind, her words revealing facts she didn't even know she possessed. "I saw a fuel delivery truck pull into the service road. Early, around seven, when I got here. The tank had a false bottom that was rigged to—"

Sam stopped herself abruptly and shrugged, dropping her eyes. "You know . . ." she finished feebly.

The marine, who wore a second lieutenant's gold bar on his shirt, stared hard at her now, his eyes filled with questions. "Pardon my asking, ma'am, but just how do you know that? And how did you happen to know when this here bomb was going to go off?"

"I . . . I . . ." Sam felt her face getting hot. "I got a tip, a call, to get out of the building," she lied, still avoiding his eyes. Then, making her face hard, she coldly met his gaze. "I can't tell you anything more, Lieutenant. It's classified. I shouldn't have said anything at all. I trust you can keep your mouth shut."

Her words, sharp and condescending, clearly held authority. "Now, I'd better get back out there and find my section leader."

The marine was polite toward the women, as boys raised in the South are taught to be, but his suspicions had put anger in his tone. "Well, before you do that, ma'am, may I get your name? And yours." He nodded toward the other woman, who had collapsed into herself, becoming as small as a frightened mouse.

"Susan Chase," Sam replied, raising her chin, her nose pinched in with hauteur. "Perhaps you know of my father, Brigadier General Hilton Chase?" Sam grew up around soldiers. She knew how to pull rank when she had to, and to keep this marine, who was probably ten years older than she, from questioning her further, she intended to pull rank now.

"Well, ma'am, I guess just about everybody in the corps knows of General Helldog Chase," the marine said, his belligerence ebbing. "Shame he had to retire when he did. Guess your being his daughter explains it."

"Explains what?" Sam asked, arching an eyebrow.

"Why you're such a cold-blooded SOB, ma'am. No offense," the marine said without rancor, and flung the truck door open into a world strewn with rubble and echoing with screams.

Emerging from the MPCV, the first thing Sam saw was an arm. It lay in the road maybe fifty feet away, and it still held a mahogany calfskin briefcase clutched in its hand. A shoe, a bloody foot inside, sat undisturbed on the sidewalk where Tom had once stood.

Sam squeezed her eyes shut for a brief moment. She choked, then coughed as she climbed down from the huge vehicle. A fine grit covered every inch of her bare skin and got into her hair. She could taste salt from dried perspiration on her lips. Her suit was wrinkled and her low-heeled pumps were scuffed.

She didn't even consider searching for the rest of Tom. There was no point. He was dead, the arm probably the largest piece of him left.

Barely glancing toward the damaged embassy, she walked quickly away from the MPCV toward her apartment on the far side of the huge embassy compound. Despite what she told the lieutenant, she had no intention of finding anyone or explaining anything. As soon as humanly possible, she planned to get her clothes off and stand under the shower until her fingertips wrinkled. She imagined she would be happy to stand there, the cool droplets striking her face, for the next couple of years.

3

SAM never spotted the two men in black when she exited the elevator on her floor. Before she knew what was happening, one was on either side of her, their hands on her arms, moving her down the hallway. Anxiety squeezed her heart hard. She knew about the SAP, the Pentagon's Special Access Program, and its top secret commando units that kidnapped men and women off the streets of Baghdad without worrying about the Geneva Conventions or rule of law.

But what would they want with her? "Who are you? What do you want?" She tried to keep any trace of fear out of her voice.

"Shut up and settle down. We're just taking you to the airport," barked one of the men, who had a thin face and pockmarked cheeks.

"The airport? Why? Where am I going?" she demanded. Her heart raced, but she squared her shoulders and set her face in hard lines.

The commando didn't answer her questions. In seconds they reached her apartment, and he opened the door as easily as if she had never locked it.

Sam balked. "Wait! What's going on? Am I under arrest?"

"Do as you're told," the same commando said with ice in his voice. He added that he would put her in restraints if she continued to resist. He went on to tell her that she had fifteen minutes to pack a carry-on bag. No, she didn't have time to shower. No, she didn't have time to change her clothes. No, she couldn't make a phone call. Yes, they needed to observe her at all times.

Yes, her possessions would be boxed and shipped to her in the States.

"Why?" she insisted again. A small, hot flame of fear had begun to burn in her stomach. "I'm not a criminal. I haven't done anything wrong. I'm a member of the foreign service. What is this about?"

The commando, who also had cruel lips and humorless eyes, repeated that she needed to pack her carry-on *now* or he would remove her by force. Then the two men stood silent and still, their arms folded across their chests.

After that, Sam didn't bother to argue or ask anything else. She didn't bring up her father. She had played that card once already today, and frankly she doubted whether his influence could help. She realized she was caught up in something serious, something she didn't understand at all.

The vast interior of the C-130 "Herky Bird" held no other passengers when Sam and the two soldiers entered. The clink of metal from the commandos' belts against their weapons echoed in the emptiness, like a Sanctus bell in a cathedral. Sam wondered why the huge plane contained no other passengers or cargo. Fifteen minutes later she wondered why they were still on the ground, not moving to the runway, the engines revved, making a din that had already given Sam a dull, throbbing headache.

She finally let go of what she couldn't control. The commandos hadn't hurt her. She was in a standard military plane. She seemed safe enough. She resigned herself to waiting without knowing what she waited for. She stared out the window at the desolate landscape of Iraq, a wasteland blasted by wind and stained with death and sorrow. She had survived this place and this soulless war, but she wondered if the times she had known things were going to happen had attracted more attention than she had realized.

She laughed to herself without mirth. If anyone asked whether she was psychic or something, she would have said no. Sure, she heard an odd voice in her head. The voice belonged to a woman, she sometimes thought—but it was definitely not her own voice. In a rushing like wind or a roaring like ocean it whirled into her mind to warn her about danger, and sometimes intruded on her decisions and choices, even about small things, such as which way to turn at an unfamiliar crossroads.

Sam had tried to stop the voice. She had tried to ignore it. She had never been able to do either. The voice would insist she listen, and if Sam didn't obey, it moved her as surely as if she were a puppet and it the puppeteer. The voice had never brought Sam harm or made her do anything evil, yet to Sam it was an intruder into her life that came unbidden and unwanted, something or *someone* that she wanted to escape, not embrace.

As if the voice weren't enough of a torment, she experienced times when she seemed to dream while wide-awake. Like the rolling of a movie trailer, live-action scenes played out in her head, bringing visions of terrible things that were happening or about to happen, often far away from where she was. Then the vision would be gone, as if the director had cut away and faded to black. Only the haunting memories—like that of the bomb killing the little boy on the bicycle—remained.

The irony was, Sam realized grimly, that she couldn't see her own future at all. Her situation fit the old witticism, "Why don't you ever see the headline, 'Psychic wins the lottery'?"

Yeah, why don't you? she thought. She felt like the victim of a great cosmic joke, one being played on her.

She shivered when she thought about the possibility that her oddity might be discovered and she would have to go through life branded as a psychic. She wanted only to be "normal" and accepted. The label of *medium* or *empath* or whatever those misfits and charlatans purported to be would make her a freak. It would make her forever different.

Now, since she had kept her secret well, it just made her lonely. She had never confided in her friends, and she certainly had never disclosed her inner voices to her employer. They'd never believe her. They'd think she was crazy. She'd probably be referred to a psychiatrist, who would want to put her on Thorazine or something.

And, strange as it all was, Sam Chase knew without a doubt that she was not mad. She had known since she was a small girl that this "gift"—or this curse—was real, and that it had been passed down with her genes.

When Sam was five years old she had tugged at her father's sleeve after he had lit his nightly cigar and sat down with the *Baltimore Evening News*. She said to him, "There's a lady who talks to me in my head, and she told me you should get your heart checked, Poppy."

Her father's face turned angry. He took the cigar from between his lips and glared at Sam. "It's just your imagination. I don't want to hear anything more about it." He turned away and opened the paper to the sports section. He never brought up the matter again—even after he had his first heart attack later that year.

But that same night her mother, Beth, had gathered Sam onto her lap and whispered that the voice and "the sight" were real. Then, with her words low and hushed, she told Sam what Poppy's own grandmother, Nana Mary Sullivan, had confided the night Beth and Poppy had gotten engaged. Nana Mary, a stout woman who liked to dress in lilac and carried an ebony cane with a silver handle—given to her father by Jefferson Davis himself—was an FFV, one of the First Families of Virginia, just like Mama's own family, the Bridgers.

"But what Nana Mary told me," she whispered as she rocked Sam, "was that the Sullivans hear voices. They see things too. It's in their genes."

"Does Poppy see things?" Sam asked, turning her head so she could look up at her mother's soft gray eyes.

"Shhh. No, he doesn't." Her mother's cool hand brushed tendrils of hair away from Sam's face. "It's nothing to be ashamed of, punkin, but it won't do to talk about it. It's a family secret. You know what a secret is, don't you?"

Sam nodded and ran her fingers along the satin edge of her mother's cardigan. Her mother kissed the top of her head and went on talking in a quiet tone that her father couldn't hear: "Pay attention when you see something, little punkin. Or if you hear a voice. It belongs to a spirit, you know."

"What is a spirit, Mama?" Sam had asked in a very tiny voice.

"Something like a guardian angel, I believe. The spirit watches out for you. And someday it might save your life."

That was true. This unwanted "guardian angel" had kept Sam in one piece, alive and kicking. Hell, if she hadn't listened to it during the year she had been in Baghdad, she'd be going home in a body bag.

Sam stared out the window again and spotted a herd of camels in the glare of the desert sun beyond a line of concrete blast barriers. She didn't regret leaving Iraq, although she would have liked to say good-bye to a few people. But in the main she had avoided getting too close to her colleagues. She had never dated anyone, although she had been asked out a few times. She had simply crossed days off the calendar and endured her time here alone.

An hour later, the long-unexplained delay still unexplained—just one more mystery in a day of mysteries—the big plane began to taxi to the runway. Bulky in the protective vest all passengers had to wear, Sam got as comfortable as she could on the side-facing webbed seat. The commando with the lean and hungry look sat on one side of her. The mute one sat across from her. She ignored them and pulled a book of sudoku puzzles out of her brown shoulder-strap purse. If she could concentrate at all, these would help her pass the long hours of the flight home.

Sam still didn't know why she was being escorted back to the States almost in handcuffs. The voice in her head wasn't telling her anything. But she could read the handwriting on the wall. She was in a pile of trouble. She didn't know how deep. But she knew her old life was over.

4

BIG, hard-muscled, and a hard-ass too, Lance "Bear" Rutledge used one key to open the iron gate covering the front door of his Georgian-style row house. The front windows were covered with iron gates as well. In this neighborhood he needed the extra security. A boom box blasted away on a stoop a few doors down. He heard the *crack-crack-crack* of a gun going off, but not close. Maybe a couple of blocks away. A guy was shot in the head last week near here because some punk wanted his Nikes.

Bear looked intimidating enough that he rarely got bothered. He was carrying, so he didn't worry much about getting mugged. But this section of Washington, D.C., could be dangerous. The neighborhood was integrated, but still remained mostly black and poor. A white man—hell, any man—had to be on guard.

He took a different key and unlocked the newly painted front door itself. He stepped into the hallway he had renovated over the past couple of months. He looked with pride at the black-and-white checkerboard marble floor and rosewood-paneled walls. He hit a light switch and a crystal chandelier came on over his head.

The decor was too rich for his blood, and maybe he'd never get used to it, but he liked it.

Not too shabby for a kid who grew up in a trailer park, he thought. *I came from nothing,* he reminded himself, as if he needed to. *Everything I have I earned with my own two hands. I came from nothing,* he thought again.

And he had. His father had killed himself when Bear was nine. His mother self-medicated with gin. By thirteen he was on his own, working when he could and running wild the rest of the time. Finally, a week away from his eighteenth birthday, he was busted for stealing a car. A county judge told him he could join the service or go to jail.

Bear chose the army and stopped screwing around. He took courses in criminal justice and discovered he liked forensic science. Along with plenty of street smarts, honed to a sharp edge by the criminals he had hung out with as a teenager, he found out he had a knack for investigation.

A bum knee got him an honorable discharge, and a helpful mentor, Col. George Allen, who had left the army and gone over to the inspector general's office at the Department of Defense, made Bear what he was now—a civilian, living in Washington, D.C., and working for Colonel Allen as a forensic expert for the DOD.

Never a big spender, Bear soon saved enough to buy a run-down house in a ghetto neighborhood fast being gentrified. Cut-Ups, a black barbershop, and Leroy's Carryout, where Bear just bought barbecued ribs for his dinner, still sat on the next corner, but a Starbucks had already appeared two blocks away. In Bear's own eyes he had made it. He had gone from nothing to something pretty damned good. If he weren't so lonely he might be content.

Bear walked down a narrow corridor that ran past the formal living room and led to the kitchen at the rear of the house. He put the Leroy's bag and his keys on the granite counter and noticed that the message light was blinking on his wall phone. He hit the play button.

"Bear, sweetie, why aren't you answering your cell? I've been calling and calling. I don't know why you got so mad. I was going to tell you I saw Chris when I was up visiting my parents last weekend. It didn't *mean* anything. Come on, Bear. Call me, please. I made a little mistake, that's all. I'm sorry. Is that what you want me to say? I'm—"

Bear's index finger smashed into the delete button. Sheila, his fiancée for the past year, hadn't just "seen" Chris. She had spent the night with his head between her thighs. Of course, she might not have known the bum was married when she did. But Bear knew all about the guy—a background check was pretty damned easy to run. It hadn't been much harder to find out why Sheila started going to see "her parents" a couple of times a week. All it took was planting a tiny microphone in the wristwatch he gave her.

Bear shrugged and tried to ignore the pain that felt like a hungry wolf gnawing away at his heart. Sometimes being an investigator meant you found out things you'd rather not know. But Bear figured that knowing was better than being played for a fool, even if it did hurt like hell.

It crossed his mind that maybe Sheila was sincerely sorry, but it didn't matter. He held others to his own high standards—no mistakes, no slipups. Bear didn't trust easily from the get-go. Once betrayed, he didn't give second chances. Bear opened the cabinet over the counter. He took out the pink mug that said HERS and tossed it in the trash.

Suddenly his breath came hard. He felt as if he were suffocating. *Must be this heat,* he thought, and turned on the air-conditioning. For nearly a month the weather had been Washington's signature "best"—stifling hot with a hundred percent humidity that did some kind of synergy with pollution and choked the breath out of a person.

In Bear's experience, seeing what he had seen of psychopaths and murder, summers like this made people do crazy things. Those urban riots of the 1960s didn't happen in the winter for a reason. In Bear's opinion it took hot sidewalks and sizzling temperatures to make the blood boil and men run wild.

With that sobering thought, Bear picked up his greasy carryout bag and went into the family room. He numbly clicked on the plasma TV, ignoring the emptiness inside himself as he watched the evening news and started eating the ribs.

In a couple of minutes the news annoyed him to the point that he mentally tuned out. Wars, violence, ethnic cleansing—if you asked him, Bear thought the world was getting worse. The new case involving Arlington National Cemetery that had landed on his desk today proved it. He didn't know what to make of this kind of sick stuff. And he sure didn't know what to think about this bizarre crime and his being ordered to look into it.

Something dark twisted in his gut. A bad feeling grabbed hold of his insides. He didn't like anything about this case—especially the unexpected note clipped to his file. It said he was supposed to liaison with some spook over at Langley. Even though he rarely rocked the boat and usually did exactly what he was told, Bear made up his mind to talk to Allen, his boss, tomorrow about what the hell was going on. He just didn't "get it."

In fact he didn't "get" anything about the investigation. He hoped Allen could give him some answers. For one thing, the cemetery lay in the U.S. Park Police's jurisdiction. He could stretch a point and see why the Department of Defense was handling the problem—after all, it was a military cemetery. But what the hell did the CIA have to do with Arlington? Nothing, that was what.

Bear's suspicious nature blossomed into paranoia. First thought—he was being set up, because if the CIA had their hands in this, they had a reason. Why didn't they just grab the whole pie? Why was he still involved? No, he just didn't get it—but he knew he didn't like it.

His thoughts began getting stuck in a repeating loop, like a Möbius strip with no beginning and no end. He forced himself to stop his inner conversation and focus on the TV. The newscaster finished reporting about a macabre voodoo ring in Haiti that was scaring the bejesus out of the locals and moved on to a story about a corporate power struggle for Middle Eastern oil.

By then Bear had had enough of the nightly doom, gloom, and greed. He grabbed the remote and clicked on an episode of *Leave It to Beaver* he had TiVo-ed.

He smiled when he heard the familiar theme song. He soon recognized this particular story as the time the Beav gave his mother the silent treatment. He had seen every episode more times than he could count. Of course, Bear never saw the original airings of the series. He wasn't even a gleam in his father's eye from 1957 to 1963, when the old hit was on television.

And Bear sure never sat down at the dinner table like the Beaver and Wally to find his father wearing a suit and his mother wearing pearls. The few times Bear could remember them all eating together brought back memories of empty beer bottles on the table next to the catsup and the platter of Hamburger Helper and oven-heated French fries that his mother made nearly every night. His family's dinner conversation usually went something like, "Is this slop all you know how to cook?" followed by, "Slop's good enough for a pig like you, ain't it?"

But Bear liked watching the classic TV show. Maybe real-life families never resembled the Cleavers, but all in all it looked to him like the 1950s had been a much better era to live in than now. He let his mind wander, and a smile danced around his lips as he thought about what life back then must have been like. He wished he had Doc Brown's DeLorean from *Back to the Future*. He'd time-travel back to postwar America and settle in the burbs. As nice as his row house was, what he really yearned for was a house like the Cleavers'. Sadness stole over him then. Bear had to admit that it wasn't just a house like the Cleavers' that he dreamed about. It was a home like theirs, one holding a family and love within.

His eyes were just beginning to slide shut when he heard a faint noise at the back door. He knew what it was. He heaved his large frame out of the recliner and went to let in the cat.

It wasn't really his cat. The small white female with a tabby-striped patch on her head and a striped tail was a stray he had started feeding a couple of months ago. The past couple of weeks the food hadn't been all she wanted. She had darted through his legs when he opened the door and dashed into the kitchen.

Her behavior didn't bother him. He admired what she did; he thought she had guts. This alley cat had been tossed out to face the world on her own, but she was a survivor, just as he was. And as he did, she came from nothing. That was why he started calling her Nada.

Bear lumbered back to the recliner and sat down. The cat took a few minutes eating the Fancy Feast that Bear had left on a paper plate on the kitchen floor. Then she stood by the side of his chair and meowed. When he nodded, she hopped up into his lap. She "made bread," rhythmically digging her claws into his T-shirt for a couple of minutes, then settled down next to his chest and started to purr. A few minutes later the big man and the small cat were both asleep.

5

THE C-130 transport plane had flown from Baghdad to Kuwait International Airport. Once it landed, the commandos, showing some humanity after all, allowed a weary Sam to use an airport ladies' room. She peeled off her blouse in front of the mirror. Then she pumped out a blob of shiny soap from the sink's dispenser into her hand. It had a disinfectant smell. Wetting down some of the scratchy brown paper towels, she gave herself a whore's bath.

Once she had removed the worst of the travel grime, she stared at herself in the mirror. Her eyes looked back at her, bloodshot and worried. Her mouth wore a pinched, aggrieved look. Her hair, now loose and tangled, had become Medusa's snakes. When she gathered it together in her hand, she felt that it was full of sand. She twisted the long strands into a rope and refastened the chignon as best she could.

Then she ducked into a stall and pulled clean underwear, a yellow pullover, a pair of khaki slacks, and a short jacket from her carry-on. Her spirits felt lighter after she stripped down and put them on. She thought for a moment before dumping her dirty clothes into the trash. But, making up her mind, she stuffed everything she had been wearing into the garbage, even the blue Neiman Marcus suit.

Screw it, she thought, *I don't care.* In truth, she did care, because she intended to leave as much of Iraq behind as possible.

When she emerged from the ladies', the waiting soldiers in their black uniforms took a position on either side of her. Sam expected them to go to a departure gate and board a United Airlines flight to Washington, D.C.'s Dulles International Airport, just like everyone else headed stateside. Instead her escorts marched her down to the very end of a long corridor to an exit where no other passengers waited.

Neither of the dour young men responded to her questions about where they were going. They hustled her through a chrome-and-glass door, hurried down a flight of stairs, and pushed through another set of doors into the open air. Suddenly Sam found herself standing on the paved surface of the landing field. The sun blinded her, and a hot wind whipped her hair loose again.

At this point, Sam's mood swung back and forth like a pendulum, from worried to just plain pissed. The commandos marched her a short way across the pavement to a sparkling white Gulfstream V turbojet. Its tail carried the number N379P painted in green, but Sam could see no national identification or airline name—telling her this was a private aircraft, not a commercial one.

It also told Sam something else that made her stop in her tracks. She knew what this was—the very type of plane the Counterterrorist Center used to take suspects to the black sites, the secret prisons only the agency knew about. She had heard about the Salt Pit in Afghanistan and the men who entered there and never came out. A sick wave of fear overtook her. She balked at the bottom of the passenger boarding stairs.

The hard fingers of the commando tightened on her arm, but she couldn't make her feet move forward to get onto an aircraft that might be taking her to one of those dark, hidden jails, where she'd disappear for weeks, years, or even forever. She waited for the voice in her head to speak. For once she desperately wanted to hear it. She silently pleaded, *Tell me what I should do.* But silence, the same mental silence that had prevailed since the commandos showed up at her apartment, offered her nothing except despair.

When she didn't move, but merely stood there uncertain, the whip-thin soldier holding her upper arm roughly shoved her forward. She grabbed the railing with one hand to keep from stumbling and whipped her head around to give him a furious glare.

"Get moving," he snapped.

The roughness of the man felt like a violation, an assault on her person. She dropped her carry-on and it rolled over, distracting his attention. Sam jerked her arm from his grip and expertly used her forearm to block his attempt to grab her. Sam had studied tae kwan do since she was ten; she had earned her black belt at fifteen. Now, quick as a striking snake, she reached out and snatched the man's hand. She twisted his fingers backward. The guy's eyes widened in shock and pain.

Sam's next move would have been to slam her knee upward into his crotch. But she saw the other commando raising his gun. She had nowhere to run, no way to escape. It would have been futile to fight. She released the MP nearly as fast as she had struck out at him. The whole exchange had lasted seconds.

Now she glared at him, daring him to touch her. When he didn't, she picked up her carry-on. "Fuck you," she said. She turned her back and ascended the metal stairs, lugging her bag behind her. A harsh wind tore at her clothing, and she blinked fast to stop the bright glistening of welling tears.

In the instant when Sam began to fight back, she'd wanted to kill that soldier. Catching him off guard as she had, she could have done it. Then it would have all been over—her future, her life. Now, fuming, she wanted to chew somebody's head off, preferably whoever had engineered her being detained and transported like a criminal.

At the top of the stairs Sam ducked through the Gulfstream's hatch. What she saw erased her fear that she was headed for a secret CIA prison. Inside the plane was no austere cell. No shackles. No bars. Instead she looked around in wonder at an elegantly appointed cabin. Two well-upholstered beige leather seats with a table between them sat directly in front of her. The table held a stack of file folders, a carafe, and two coffee cups.

A cool draft from the air-conditioning moved gently across Sam's cheek. She had gone from irritating dust and blistering heat to a protected, comfortable world. Beyond the two seats and a pretty partition, the rest of the fifty-foot cabin contained a velour sofa with colorful throw cushions and two four-place conference groupings of seats and tables. She blinked. Yes, she really did see a vase containing smooth white calla lilies. A large plasma TV hung on the farthest wall toward the plane's tail as well.

As Sam's dusty shoes sank into the deep pile carpet, she wondered if the plane perhaps belonged to a Saudi prince, or a billionaire like Warren Buffet. It surely wasn't government-issue or a CIA transport. Confusion held her immobile. Her thoughts slowed down and stuck in a sticky tar of incomprehension.

A thud behind her made Sam jump. She whirled around. The commandos had vanished and the hatch had slammed down, closed from the outside. She stood alone in the brightly lit cabin, not knowing why she was here or where she was going.

A voice came over the intercom. "Please take a seat, Ms. Chase."

Obeying, she moved to the seat nearest her, which faced toward the tail. She sank into the deep cushions and felt the soft leather embrace her. She fidgeted. The cabin was empty except for her. All was silent. She had no idea what was going to happen to her next.

6

SAM sat waiting for a few minutes, not knowing what she waited for, until a door in the rear of the aircraft beyond the plasma TV opened.

A tall woman emerged. She wore a conventional black power suit. A Bluetooth device hugged one ear. Her translucent skin had a color somewhere between the watery blue-white of skim milk and glacial snow. Her features were bold and strong. Her nose had wide, flaring nostrils. Her lips looked like a slash of red across her face. But dark, amber-tinted lenses hid her eyes. The hair that formed a cap of tight curls around her head was pale, like bleached straw.

Sam recoiled. With her rational mind she realized the woman must be an albino, perhaps of African-American heritage or mixed-race. But in contrast to the whiteness of her form, the woman's aura was dark, like a shadow hovering in the air. Sam's instincts screamed that this woman was dangerous.

The woman strode the length of the plane and stopped in front of Sam. She gave Sam a small nod and spoke in a voice as cold as if blown across a block of ice. "I am Ms. Z, chief of the agency's Alternative Investigations Unit."

The agency? The words were a match lighting the short fuse of Sam's anger. Without thinking, shaking with rage, she sprang from the seat. She grabbed the woman by the arm, hard, while the words flew from her mouth. "The agency! What the hell is this? I demand an explanation."

The strange-looking woman stiffened slightly but didn't

pull away from Sam's hold—and it took a person capable of exquisite self-control not to react. Instead, she appeared to be listening to a voice speaking in her Bluetooth. Answering the invisible person, she said out loud, "No, no problem. I can handle it."

Eyes barely discernible behind the tinted lenses, red mouth forming a smile, Ms. Z put her cold hand gently atop the one of Sam's that gripped her arm and, to Sam's discomfort, wrapped icy fingers around hers. "Ms. Chase, I will be glad to answer your questions. But I can only do that if you let go of me and sit down. We are preparing for takeoff."

The woman waited. Sam realized cameras must be watching her every move.

"It will be easier for both of us if you cooperate," Ms. Z added with the barest hint of a threat in her voice.

Sam had no alternative. Resistance would accomplish nothing at this point. She needed more information before she made any decision about what she could or couldn't do to take back some control of the situation. She released the woman's arm, gratefully escaped her frigid touch, and lowered herself back into the seat.

The woman sat across the table from her. "Please fasten your seat belt," Ms. Z's voice instructed with no emotion and just the barest hint of a Boston accent. The jet's engines came alive. The plane taxied onto the runway, and, without any further delay, the white Gulfstream with its cryptic green numbers thrust into the cloudless azure sky.

Ms. Z said nothing until the aircraft stopped climbing. Then she picked up the carafe with a hand the waxy white of an Easter lily. "Let's get off to a better start, shall we? Coffee? It's American, Starbucks, actually."

Sam glared at Ms. Z. "Tell me why I'm here. What game are you playing? What does the agency want from me?" Her chin thrust forward, and she bristled with belligerence.

Ms. Z again ignored Sam's outburst. She poured the coffee. Steam rose from the cup she pushed toward Sam. She smiled while she did this, showing teeth bleached like dry bones. "What does the agency want from you?

Quite a lot, actually. And we're not playing games." She raised her eyes behind their amber lenses to look squarely at Sam. "Is it or is it not true that during your tour in Iraq you had a number of close calls?"

Sam's eyes snapped open wide. "Of course. Doesn't everybody who's there more than ten frigging minutes have them?" Her heart began to speed up. She didn't like where this was going.

"Perhaps. But your close calls weren't like those that happen to *everybody.* Let's see." She took one of the manila folders and opened it, peering at its contents. "On December twelfth, you were in a Humvee on the road to the Baghdad airport, riding with the ambassador, who was leaving for Germany. According to the Humvee driver, you were within the city proper when you ordered him to stop.

"He said, and I quote, 'All of a sudden, the pretty young lady from the embassy started screaming at me, "Hit the brakes!" What did I do? I sure as hell hit the brakes. I just did it. And if I hadn't we'd all been dead.

" 'You're asking me why? 'Cause a motherfucking IED landed fifty feet ahead of us and exploded in the road. But that wasn't the end of it. This lady started yelling at me, "Reverse! Go in reverse!" Shit, I backed that baby up as fast as I could, because right after the words were out of her mouth the towel heads was shooting at us from every goddamned direction.' "

Ms. Z closed the folder. She took off her dark glasses to reveal eyes with irises so pale a blue as to be nearly silver. They were hard and cold as metal, with no warmth, no kindness there. "Now, Ms. Chase, according to the driver, when the vehicle and its passengers were no longer in danger you explained that you 'saw something' that made you cry out. But the driver said he hadn't spotted anything along the road before the IED exploded. So he had to wonder how in hell you could have known what was going to happen.

"I think the Humvee driver asked the critical question. *How could you have known?*" Ms. Z tapped the folder with a manicured fingertip. "I have reports here regarding five incidents where you escaped an attack by insurgents or a hidden explosive device. How did you do that?"

Sam's tongue felt clumsy in her dry mouth. "Luck. I guess I'm just lucky."

"I don't think that 'luck' had anything to do with it," Ms. Z said sharply.

"What are you insinuating?" Sam's voice took on an edge.

"That there is a logical explanation for your foreknowledge of these deadly attacks. You have been in contact with and/or are working for the enemy."

Anger darkened Sam's eyes. "You're calling me a traitor?"

Ms. Z spread open her palms, white as clamshells. "It's a reasonable explanation for your escapes."

Sam opened her seat belt in a flash, rose to her feet, and leaned forward across the table. Spittle flew as she spat out her words. "That's a goddamn lie and you know it."

Ms. Z lifted her eyebrows, so pale as to be nearly invisible against her skin. "How could I know it's a lie? It makes perfect sense that someone was giving you information about planned attacks."

"You'd know it, *Mizzy*, because your people obviously had me under surveillance for some time. You probably monitored my calls, my mail, and my movements. So you know I did not consort with the enemy."

Ms. Z raised her pale hands in acquiescence. "Yes, that's true. So do sit down, Ms. Chase. As a matter of fact, we found no proof of your disloyalty. But we did verify something else, something very interesting, by the way."

Sam's face went hard as stone. "What?"

"You see things. You hear things. You know things. *Before* they happen."

Thoughts raced through Sam's mind. Should she deny it?

Before Sam could utter a word, Ms. Z said, "You do. Don't bother denying it." Her voice turned gentler, kinder. "It's time to come clean. No more secrets, Ms. Chase, or can I call you Sam?"

"Call me whatever you want. It's your party."

"Yes, it is. So listen to me carefully. Your gift is very valuable. And we'd like to help you use it."

"No!" Panic wiped out the last of Sam's rational brain synapses, and she could barely breathe. Her eyes looked wildly around, but of course there was no escape. Her fingers gripped the arms of the seat so hard they became bloodless.

"Excuse me?" Ms. Z asked.

"No! What part of *no* don't you understand? I won't. I can't."

Ms. Z didn't move, didn't get mad, didn't react. She lengthened her neck, sucked in her cheeks, and narrowed her metallic eyes. She said in an übercalm way, "You will and you can."

Sam wanted to fly off the leather seat and smack her. Wanted to, but didn't.

"Let's not get into a 'make me' game," Ms. Z continued, "because I can *make you.* You can work with us or . . ."

Sam stared, her heart pounding, not breathing, not wanting to believe this was even happening.

". . . or you will be charged with treason. And wouldn't your father be proud of you then?"

7

THE words hit Sam like a bucket of cold water. Her eyes darted around the room. She saw no escape and could think of no course of action to buy time. In complete desperation, she mentally cried out for divine intervention and asked her spirit guide for help. *What do I say? What do I do? How can I get out of this?* she asked. No sound of wind. No rush of water. No voice replied. No help came.

Finally, her body tight, her breath shallow, realizing she had to say the words that would seal her fate, Sam answered Ms. Z, "Okay, what do you want me to do?"

Ms. Z widened her bright red lips into a smile, pleased at the answer. "You'll be part of an important new project the agency has put together. AngelWay. That's what we're calling it."

Sam felt uncomfortable, uneasy. She moved her eyes toward the window. The sun was gone. The sky had become dark. She saw only blackness. She thought for a while before she returned her eyes to Ms. Z and said, "What is this AngelWay? What's the purpose?"

Ms. Z's face got softer, her voice turning friendly. "It's a project that will let you use your gifts to help this country. It will make you a true American hero. Your father will be proud."

Sam leaned forward, her voice strained. "My *gift* cannot help this country. You obviously do not understand one thing about it. Or me."

Ms. Z gave Sam another toothy smile. She looked like a hungry shark. "We understand you very well. We've watched you for years, Susan Ann Marie Chase. Did you honestly think, your father being who he is, that we wouldn't?"

A terrible feeling came over Sam then, as if she were standing on the other side of the looking glass. Her stomach churned with acid, and a sour taste came into her mouth.

Ms. Z. reached out and patted her arm. Sam looked down at the fingers touching her as if they were the legs of a venomous spider. "We have every confidence that you can make AngelWay a great success."

Sam abruptly moved from beneath Ms. Z's hand. She felt as if her outer skin had been ripped away and her guts were showing raw and bloody. That was not acceptable to Susan Ann Marie Chase. She sat up ramrod straight in the glove-leather seat.

"Look, Ms. Z." Her affect was flat. A dark vibration was barely audible beneath her even voice. "You've gone to a lot of trouble for nothing if you believe I can do that. I can't look at a map and predict future terrorist attacks. I can't provide the military with information about the enemy. It's not that I won't. I *can't*. My *gifts*, as you call them, just happen. I don't direct them."

The rug had been pulled out from beneath Sam's feet, but she refused to fall.

"Understood," Ms. Z countered. "However, we believe that with training, even some very basic exercises, you can be more directive with your abilities. You have never really tried, have you? You've spent your whole life trying to suppress them. Am I not correct?"

Sam mulishly refused to answer.

Ms. Z continued. "In any case, let me tell you why your joining AngelWay is so important." She put her hand atop the stack of manila files on the table. "Each of these files represents an unsolved crime with national security implications." She looked through the pile and peeled off the top ten or twelve folders. "And each of these contains a crime that is not only unsolved, but particularly baffling because"—she looked at Sam intently—"it has no logical explanation. But it does, potentially, have an illogical, seemingly impossible cause—in other words, a paranormal element, be it magic, witchcraft, werewolves, extraterrestrial activity, or something else. That's why it comes to the Alternative Investigations Unit.

"Quite frankly, no staff members in our agency have been able to successfully deal with those elements. We needed to recruit a team of specialists to address the crimes that will be this project's caseload."

Sam's eyes widened with incredulity. "You're asking me to be a psychic detective for weirdo stuff like UFOs?"

"Not *asking* you. *Assigning* you, along with the others handpicked to work with you."

"What others?"

"You'll meet them soon enough."

At that point the Bluetooth commanded Ms. Z's attention again. She held up an index finger toward Sam to indicate she'd be a minute.

Sam's thoughts turned inward. Ms. Z's revelations had cracked the facade of her public face, had torn away the mask she had always worn. She was being carried on a riptide toward something called AngelWay. AngelWay? Was it like the old StarGate program that used psychics? Woo-woo national security. Would she be pulled unwillingly into this and see her life destroyed? Her mind raced.

While Ms. Z listened to her Bluetooth, the jet flew onward. *But to where, and why?* Sam thought. She wound her fingers together in her lap. She was as helpless to control her fate as she was to determine the direction of the jet she rode in. But she had questions, and she needed answers.

Speaking to her invisible colleague, Ms. Z finished up the conversation by saying, "Right. Got it. We're on schedule."

Sam waited until Ms. Z's eyes returned to hers before she voiced what was on her mind: "You ordered me to report to Langley. This meeting could have taken place there. What is so urgent that you had to meet me in Kuwait with a private jet?"

A shadow of fear moved across Ms. Z's moonlike face for the briefest instant. "I met you to save precious time. Something, a situation, has occurred—a crime with . . .

with disturbing implications for the future of America, for our way of life. We have judged that these *implications,* if they are what we think they are, pose a clear and present danger not just to our nation, but perhaps to the world—unless we act quickly." Her silvery eyes, so adamantine and cold, bore into Sam. "Before you ask me if its cause is paranormal, let me tell you without equivocation: It is. It must be. We can find no other explanation."

Sam wanted to ask another question, but she never got a chance to speak before Ms. Z took the top folder from the pile, opened it, and pushed it toward Sam.

"Read this," she ordered. "It's only a summary of the crime, but it will give you something to think about."

Sam picked up the top sheet of paper. CLASSIFIED had been stamped on the page. She started to read background information on Arlington National Cemetery. Once she hit the paragraph that began to talk about a grave that had been opened in the cemetery, she felt confused and ultimately baffled by Ms. Z's sense of urgency. She was beginning to think she had the wrong file, or maybe pages were missing. Just then Ms. Z interrupted her: "One more thing . . ."

Sam looked up.

"You'll be working with one of your new colleagues on this. Her name is Rina Martus. A crime-scene expert. Really quite extraordinary. She's consulted on homicides throughout the country. She's cracked the case in about seventy percent of them."

Sam nodded and started, "But this isn't a murder—" when Ms. Z interrupted her again.

"A Department of Defense specialist will also take an active role in the investigation."

A tingling shot up Sam's spine. Goose bumps broke out on her arms. She shifted in her seat, not knowing what had caused her gut reaction to Ms. Z's latest disclosure. Her mouth was suddenly parched again when she said, "Is this specialist going to take us, two psychics, seriously?"

Ms Z's eyes flashed. "As far as the DOD is concerned,

you, as a psychic, don't exist. You and Rina work as investigators for the agency. Do you understand?"

Uneasiness tightened Sam's throat. Nerves danced around her eyes, and she felt her eyelids quiver. She kept waiting to hear a voice inside her head, but again nothing came into her mind but a disquieting silence.

Ms. Z didn't seem to notice Sam's discomfort. Her icy voice repeated the question: "I asked if you understood?"

Sam shot back, "No, no, I don't. What if he runs a background check on me? He'll find out I'm no investigator. And I can only guess what he'd turn up on our so-called crime-scene expert."

Ms. Z paused, then put authority back in her voice. "This man already has the highest security clearance. We'll make sure that whatever he learns about you will remain classified. He'll keep your secrets."

I don't know about that, Sam thought. *I have the strangest feeling about him.*

"You'd better try to get some rest," Ms. Z said, breaking into Sam's musing. "We're going directly to the crime scene as soon as we land."

8

BEAR Rutledge shifted his weight from one size-thirteen foot to the other as he stood in a reception area of the service complex off Columbia Pike on the south side of Arlington National Cemetery. He had already been waiting around thirty minutes. The CIA guy had yet to show.

Annoyance fueled Bear's growing impatience. Bear got a hair up his ass when people were late. His own philosophy echoed that of the great Michigan football coach Bo Schembechler: *Early is on time. On time is late.*

Bear had come into the building carrying his only summer sports jacket, a blue blazer he had bought from a big-and-tall-men's catalog. Once he hit the air-conditioned interior he put it on, but after a moment's consideration he didn't take the tie out of the pocket where he had stashed it. The top of a bottle of Deer Park water stuck out of the other pocket.

A dull ache started behind his forehead. He recognized the beginnings of a headache. Maybe it came from his getting aggravated. Maybe it was the heat. Just walking in from the parking lot he had started sweating like a pig. He wasn't surprised. The weather report was again calling for temperatures topping one hundred, with high humidity: Washington had been a furnace this summer, stoking crime to record high levels and driving passions into the red zone.

As planned, Bear had gone to talk to Allen, his boss, first thing that morning. He told the crusty old army colonel that he had concerns about working with the

CIA. He said flat out that he didn't "get" what was going on.

At first his mentor didn't look up, keeping busy signing some papers. Finally Allen put down his pen and pushed back from his desk, resting his hands atop the small bulge of his belly. He gave Bear a hard stare over the top of his glasses.

"Okay, Rutledge, let me be honest with you. The CIA doesn't want you over there. I do. I need you to be my eyes and ears. I want to know every last damned move they make in this investigation."

Bear nodded. "Sure, but what exactly is going on here? Why the CIA at all? Why the tug-of-war?"

Allen sat up abruptly and threw his pen down on his desk. He spat out his words. "This case is not in their jurisdiction. It's mine! They have no goddamn business poking around in this!" Then he stopped, seeming to catch himself. He pulled his chair close to the desk and leaned his elbows on the surface. His voice was filled with emotion when he spoke again. "Rutledge, those are *our* men, our *brothers*, buried out there. This case is *our* responsibility."

Suddenly his eyes sparked with anger. "But these damned spooks start yelling 'national security'; then they drop their trousers so everybody can kiss their asses."

"You got that right," Rutledge said. He never had experienced one good moment with any of those strange ducks over at Langley.

Allen went on, his voice conspiratorial. "Rutledge, listen to me. I don't trust these people. I think they want this case to just go away. Maybe they even had something to do with it in the first place. I don't know. I had to call in some favors to make sure the DOD stayed in on this. Langley finally agreed to have you, but watch your back. They'll try to stonewall you or lead you down some garden path. Don't trust them. Don't trust whoever it is you have to work with. And I want to know everything. You got that?"

Bear got it loud and clear. He was going to spy on the spies, infiltrate their house. He also knew that Allen wasn't telling him everything. So yeah, he had to watch his back.

Bear Rutledge figured all that out on his way to Arlington in his government vehicle, a no-frills white Dodge Stratus with the air-conditioning going full blast and still not doing enough to cool the air. He drove down Constitution Avenue to the Lincoln Memorial before crossing over the Potomac on the Arlington Memorial Bridge. It was before nine a.m., and navigating through morning rush hour in downtown D.C. gave him ample opportunity to decide on his strategy. He'd ooze with charm and cooperation, but all the while he'd investigate on his own, in his own way. He'd be the one to crack the case, not the agency. He had made up his mind about that. And when Bear Rutledge made up his mind, he didn't change it.

By the time he pulled into the cemetery's parking lot, he had also come up with a theory about why the agency agreed to his being there at all. Allen had pull, yeah, but the agency held a lot of trump cards. He figured the agency *was* connected to the victim or to the crime. They had information about the case that Allen didn't. But they didn't want any visible ties to the investigation. With Bear aboard they could hang back in the shadows while he walked point, out in front, right in the line of fire. If things blew up in everybody's face, he'd be out there twisting in the wind, the one to blame.

He almost admired the CIA for that. It was the smart thing to do. The case was messy. It was macabre. It was a public relations nightmare if the press ever got hold of it. He hoped the agent he was teamed with wasn't some asshole, or worse, a newbie. He didn't have the patience to babysit anybody. He couldn't take the time to make sure this guy didn't get himself killed. He hadn't even met the guy, but he didn't like him on principle. This spook needed to pull his weight on this or get out of Bear's way.

9

A black Lincoln Town Car, its windows tinted so dark they looked opaque, had been waiting for Ms. Z and Sam at the Dulles arrival terminal. Now Ms. Z sat up front talking endlessly into her Bluetooth. Sam reclined alone in the backseat and stared out the window. She savored the familiar sights, which suddenly felt unbearably dear to her: the dazzling white monuments, the government buildings adorned with bronze, the bright restaurants and gaudy tourist kiosks, the scurrying people rushing to their workplaces. A feeling of love for them all, nearly painful in its intensity, washed over her.

After the rubble- and garbage-strewn streets of Baghdad, the unchanging brown of the flat desert, and the red sky full of dust that Sam had seen for months, Washington looked extraordinarily alive—and green. Lawns, trees, shrubs, all were saturated with color. Greenness washed over Sam like seawater, replenishing her soul. Greenness turned the desolate landscape of her heart into fertile soil, reviving its dry ground and bringing her hope like sweet, furtive kisses.

She sighed. The anxiety that had been her constant companion in Iraq cast free from its moorings within her, drifted away, and disappeared. Sudden death was not going to explode the world beneath her. Where the fear had been now came a euphoric, unrestrained joy at being back in the United States, at being home.

But the good feelings didn't last. As soon as the Lincoln pulled through the arch over the long drive that approached the cemetery, Sam's anxiety returned with a vengeance. She squirmed in her seat, wondering what was happening. A heaviness weighed on her chest, making it hard to breathe. A feeling of sadness so overwhelmed her that she felt as if an unseen hand had shoved her to the ground and was holding her down.

When the long black car pulled to a stop in a parking lot, the sound of crying began, softly at first, then increasing to a terrible wail. It was the voices of the dead. She put up her hands to cover her ears, but that was futile. The noise didn't abate. It ebbed and flowed like a siren. Sobbing from a thousand throats throbbed like a drumbeat. And amidst the wordless sounds of grief Sam began to hear a refrain, the words overlapping and repeating, calling to her: *Come here come here come here.*

Come here? Sam trembled. She didn't want to leave the safety of the car's interior. Even more, she wanted the car to start moving again and take her away from these beseeching voices. She shrank back against the upholstery, but just then the driver, who had exited the vehicle, opened her door. Sam gave him a terrified look, but he waited, not understanding her fear.

He extended his hand. Reluctantly Sam took it and emerged from the Lincoln to be smacked with a blast of heat rising up from the asphalt parking lot. But in a heartbeat the air changed. The temperature fell quickly. Gray shadows flickered through the air all around her. Sam shivered as the unnatural cold ran bony hands across her cheeks and embraced her neck.

Then she felt something else. She became motionless, like a wild thing sensing danger. She looked around and found a tall young woman regarding her with a disturbing stare.

The woman's angular face reflected the suffering of a Depression-era farmer's wife in a Walker Evans photograph, as if life's troubles, harsh and unforgiving, had sucked the marrow from her bones and left behind only flesh and sinews. Her straight chestnut-brown hair had been bobbed severely to brush her jawline. Her arms were long and tanned. A faded beige tank top clung tightly to her flat, boylike chest, and her light gray cotton pants, shapeless and well-worn, had been tied carelessly with a drawstring to hang on her bony hips, revealing a band of tanned, nearly concave belly.

But the woman's eyes, blue and defiant, glittering and wary, revealed this woman's inner mettle. She would not be the one to blink first. She would not back down.

And as the woman stared Sam felt a wave of pain, like that of a wounded animal, wash over her. Something had hurt this woman, and hurt her deeply.

At that moment Ms. Z exited from the front of the vehicle and acknowledged the lanky stranger. "Glad you were able to get up here this morning, Agent Martus." Ms. Z then glanced from one woman to the other. "Agent Chase, this is team member Rina Martus. Agent Martus, this is Susan Chase."

Rina nodded at Sam. She didn't extend her hand. And suddenly Sam froze. Where Rina stood, Sam no longer saw the young woman. Instead she found herself looking at a light brown serpent standing on its tail, its head weaving back and forth, and in its flat, diamond-shaped head the eyes were blue. Sam blinked, and Rina the woman appeared again. The only thing that remained from Sam's vision were Rina's electrifying blue eyes.

Adrenaline coursed through Sam's blood. Her reaction was visceral. This Rina wasn't "normal," and she was one scary bitch.

And just then the coldness vanished. The heat returned and wrapped Sam in a cocoon of air so hot and thick that a slick of perspiration instantly coated her skin. Ms. Z had begun heading toward a nearby building. She stopped and turned as if to ask why Sam wasn't coming. On shaky legs Sam forced herself forward and followed.

10

MS. Z walked into the waiting area of the service complex at Arlington and marched over to some big guy. Sam, her mind reeling from the unremitting screams and moans that had assailed her, had come through the door right behind her. To her relief, once she was inside the sounds of the dead stopped, as if someone had turned off a radio. She squeezed her eyes shut, filled with relief. She silently gave thanks for the air-conditioning too.

Rina had entered a few steps behind Sam. Her eyes had become huge and haunted. She remained near the door as if ready to flee.

Sam turned her attention to the waiting man. She watched as he looked at the three women with shock, incredulity, and then confusion. Sam summed him up at a glance: military or ex-military—his posture and the "at ease" stance were a dead giveaway. Timex watch. No wedding ring. His clothes said he grabbed something off a rack and if it fit, he bought it. Sam made a guess that he drank beer, not wine, went to NASCAR races, not the Kennedy Center, and would probably take a date to the Olive Garden for dinner for a big night out.

She took a second, even longer look as the man spoke to Ms. Z. She had to admit he was good-looking: dark hair, a really nice cleft in his chin, a truly great body. Despite his physical attractiveness, or maybe because of it, hostility flooded through her. This was the kind of high-testosterone male she avoided on principle, who irritated her before he even said a word.

Ms. Z turned and motioned for Sam and Rina to come over.

When they did, she said, "This is Lance Rutledge, the DOD representative. Rutledge, this is Agent Chase and our crime-scene investigator, Agent Martus."

The man broke into a smile and shook Sam's hand. She felt a current pass between them and let go quickly.

Then he extended his hand to Rina, but the thin woman looked away and didn't take it. His face registered no reaction, He kept his smile and said to them all, "Call me Bear, since we'll be working together. I spent ten years in the army; now I conduct investigations for the inspector general in the Department of Defense. This case is, well, out of the ordinary. I hope our cooperative effort will produce some answers faster than I could do it alone."

Sam was surprised at his congeniality and wondered if his comment about cooperation was genuine. In her experience a man like this always wanted to be the boss. "And you can call me Sam," she replied, her natural politeness taking over.

Rina Martus stared past the man's shoulder at a far wall and didn't say anything.

"Agents Chase and Martus have read a summary of the case. They were both just called in this morning," Ms. Z said.

Bear gave Ms. Z a lazy smile. "Well, yeah, I was brought in yesterday myself. I read the file. I have a couple of questions. I'd like to make sure we're all on the same page."

Ms. Z paused, her face looking as if she were sucking on a lemon. "Okay, then." She looked around the reception area. They were the only occupants. Cheap white plastic patio chairs, the kind sold every summer at Wal-Mart, surrounded a well-worn coffee table. It was obvious the public never came here, only salesmen and maintenance personnel. "Let's sit in here. I'll do what I can to brief you further; then you three can get out to the crime scene. I don't have much time. I have an appointment to get to."

Bear sat on a chair next to Sam. The flimsy plastic wasn't made for a man his size. He tried to get comfortable. He put an ankle across one knee and held it there with a large, wide hand.

Sam became acutely aware of his presence. She felt a tingling across the skin of the arm that was nearer him. She smelled his aftershave mixed with his sweat. She fought to keep her eyes from sliding in his direction and staring at him. As it was, his knee was only inches from hers, and she could see that the hard muscles of his thigh were clearly defined beneath his khaki slacks. She told herself she had no interest in him, but her body didn't seem to know that she had written him off.

By this time Ms. Z had opened a manila folder and pulled out a computer printout. Sam forced herself to focus on what Ms. Z was saying. Fatigue was catching up with her, and the sounds of wailing dead had drained her energy to the point of making her feel physically ill. But with Ms. Z's first words she forgot her tiredness and tried to make sense out of what had happened in this cemetery two days earlier.

"As you know, this case—on the face of it—concerns a body stolen from a grave. The body of a Congressional Medal of Honor winner, in fact," Ms. Z recited without emotion. "The incident was reported by a U.S. Park Police employee, one Rodney K. Smith. He's waiting up for you at the grave site to show you the crime scene. We've already taken his statement. It's here in this file, along with the other information on the case." She stated the obvious, her voice becoming impatient, as if that were all there was to say.

"I suppose I'm meaning to ask him a few questions myself," Bear said as he rubbed the fabric of his pant leg between his fingers and thumb. Then he raised his eyes and said in a lazy way, "I have a couple to ask *you* before I see him, though."

"As you wish," Ms. Z said. "What are they?"

"Well, first of all, what's your interest in this case?" He looked at Ms. Z with innocent eyes. "What's the agency doing mucking around in a grave robbing, admittedly with some demented desecration of a grave site? Because that's all this looks like to me."

"We don't believe this is a simple grave robbing, Mr. Rutledge—Bear. We believe it's . . . well, let me not theorize here, but stick to the facts. The circumstances of the removal of the body are inexplicable. And what was left behind in the empty coffin was . . . sick, disturbing. We call this a threat to national security."

"A threat to national security? What kind of a threat?"

"I can't go into details," Ms. Z replied.

"Okay, just give me something general. Help me out here, Ms. Z." Bear sat, immovable as stone, waiting as if he were willing to wait for centuries.

Ms. Z gave him a hard look. "All right, the missing corpse, Col. Michael X. Barringer, was one of ours. He had been working closely with members of the Iraqi government on a highly sensitive and very important mission when he was killed."

Bear nodded his head as if he were beginning to understand. "So you're saying this 'sensitive mission' is connected to his body's disappearance?"

"I didn't say that," Ms. Z snapped.

During this exchange, question after question formed in Sam's mind. A frisson of electricity was dancing up her spine, making her feel uneasy and on the alert. She didn't know why, but she was sure something was very wrong with the case. Something really horrific had to be missing from the short account of the body snatching she'd read earlier, something only hinted at in what Ms. Z was telling them now. "I'd like to ask something," Sam ventured.

Ms. Z gave her a look as if to say she had talked out of turn.

Sam went on. "The report I read said 'organic remains' were recovered from the coffin and were being submitted to tests. You just described them as 'sick' and 'disturbing.' The body was gone, so what exactly are we talking about?"

Bear's eyebrows shot up. "What the hell! Christ, didn't they tell you? Barringer's body is gone, but his heart and brains were left behind."

A shiver coursed through Sam's body, but before she could respond Ms. Z broke in: "We do not know if the . . . the 'objects' belonged to Barringer. They're being tested for his DNA."

Sam found her voice. "But still . . . they had to be left there for a reason. Did the colonel have personal enemies who would want to distress his loved ones or desecrate his corpse?"

Ms. Z held up her hand. "At this time we're looking for facts. We have no obvious motive for the theft. We have no list of suspects. No footprints, fingerprints, or other physical evidence have been recovered from the scene. No tire tracks were found in proximity to the grave. On-site cameras picked up no vehicles in the area after the cemetery closed on Saturday night. No entrance to the park had been breached. We don't know how the perpetrators removed the body from the site."

Rina didn't move her eyes from their upward gazing as she suddenly spoke: "The dead don't always need help to leave their graves."

Bear turned his head toward her and snapped, "You can't seriously think Colonel Barringer, after being dead a couple of months, opened his own coffin, dug himself out, plucked out his own heart and brains, and walked away?" Annoyance more than outright derision colored his voice.

Rina turned her startlingly blue eyes on him. "I didn't say he did. I simply, as Ms. Z suggested, stated a fact."

"A fact? The dead don't walk around like zombies in a horror movie. You have got to be—"

Ms. Z interrupted before Bear could finish. "Rina Martus is an authority on voodoo practices."

"Yeah, I guess when you own a hammer, all problems look like nails." Bear threw the words down. "Personally I'm a long way from grabbing at any *alternative* explanation. What's the mystery here? There have to be at least two or three ways the body could have been gotten out of the grave and the cemetery without detection. We can do a computer search to see if any bodies have been stolen previously from this cemetery—or any others.

Were body parts ever left behind? That's the kind of information that can help us." He glared at Rina. "We need to start our investigation in the real world, with all due respect, ma'am."

Rina turned away from the man and didn't respond.

Sam let out a long breath and gently shook her head. The exchange had given her a pretty good idea that this guy wasn't going to jump up and down and shout yippee if he found out he not only had to contend with a voodoo expert, but herself, Sam Chase, a woman who received messages from an invisible spirit guide and saw visions. For sure he wasn't going to be thrilled.

Right then Sam decided how she'd deal with this Lance "Bear" Rutledge: She'd appease him to his face and stroke his ego; then she'd work behind his back.

11

IMPATIENCE started getting the best of Bear. He didn't like sitting, and he liked sitting around getting nowhere even less. The only new information he had gleaned from this meeting was that the victim, if you could call a corpse a victim, was a CIA agent. That might help with establishing a motive—maybe. Only maybe. It seemed to Bear this crime could involve a personal grudge or some kind of revenge motive. Leaving behind the heart and brains was a message. Saying what? He didn't know yet.

And what about the threat to national security? He agreed that this was a sicko's crime and a desecration both of an America hero and of America's most sacred ground, but what was the larger picture? There had to be one. Bear's gut told him he was on target about that. And it worried him.

Right then the nice-looking woman sitting next to him leaned over and whispered, "I for one want to hear your theories on this."

Bear liked the way her breath felt against his cheek.

"Sure," he whispered back, giving her a smile. Their eyes caught for the briefest of moments. He noticed hers were unusual, so light brown they were almost golden. Then he turned his attention back toward the steely voiced, chalk white woman who was running the show and asked another question: "What other information do you have on the case that the DOD doesn't have?"

"That's all we have in the file," the ghost-pale woman replied, not really answering his question.

He tried again to get a read on what was going on.

"Did you put together an interview list? I figure we have to talk to this guy's family first, particularly the wife."

"No. That's no to interviewing Barringer's family, *particularly* the wife. They are not to learn of this situation. They've had enough grief to cope with. The press is also not to find out, and we are emphatic on that. What you and the agency team need to do is locate the body, apprehend who took it, and return it to the grave. We want this taken care of as quickly and quietly as possible."

"Begging your pardon, ma'am"—Bear's voice had a bite to it—"but to find out who took the corpse, we have to find out who would want it—and that means investigating Barringer's associates. His family is the shortest route to that. I'd also like to know more about what he was working on when he was killed—"

"Sorry, it's classified."

Bear's face started to redden. He felt himself losing hold of his temper. "This is crap. You're tying my—our hands."

Ms. Z shrugged. "Only nominally. You have the resources of two agencies at your disposal, Mr. Rutledge, along with the help of two very talented investigators."

She slapped the file folder shut and stood up. Her face was set in hard lines; her body was stiff. Bear rose out of his chair as well. They faced each other. Despite the intimidation of Bear's physical size, the CIA woman knew she called the shots, and she didn't yield one iota of control.

"This briefing is over," she stated. "I have to get back to Langley." She looked over at Sam. "I'll send a car later for you and Martus." She turned back to Bear and glared at him. "Now you need to get busy. We've spent enough time on talk."

Bear felt as if his head were going to explode. He intended to interview Smith as well as other employees on the grounds. He wanted to see exactly what the cameras had recorded, even if it was nothing. Maybe especially if it was nothing.

But he didn't like being *told* to do it. He also wanted to voice a few choice words about her piss-poor ideas on how to run an investigation. But before he blurted out something he might regret, the woman called Sam walked over and stepped between him and the black-suited ice queen.

"Excuse me, I need a word with you," she said to the older woman.

Bear backed off and let them go at it. From their body language he could see the younger woman was asking questions and not liking the answers.

He took the opportunity to really look at this "Sam" Chase. Her hair was all blond tendrils around her face. She was slender but had some shape to her, real curves. Those dark smudges under her eyes suggested she was short on sleep, but she held herself like a racehorse, all shine and pride. She was a beauty, and she probably knew it. She had class, no doubt about that.

Then a spike of annoyance hit him. This woman had class and looks, and if he were looking for a date, he'd be interested, damned interested. But he was supposed to work with her. She had all the potential to be a dangerous distraction, but he couldn't see her being any help.

Christ, he thought, *this situation could turn into a nightmare, what with warnings about sexism and sexual harassment suits in every other damned government memo I get. I'll have to watch every word I say. And keep my distance. Most especially keep my distance.*

Bear figured that he had to act like a professional and expect her to do the same. He just couldn't think of her as a woman.

Sam glanced over then and caught him staring. She lowered her eyes, but a little smile played around her lips. For all his high-minded vows, he got a funny feeling right in the center of his chest when she did that.

Distracted, he jerked in surprise when a harsh voice came from right behind him and asked, "Can we get the hell out of here?"

He turned his head to find flashing blue eyes inches from his. He never heard Rina approach, but she had moved so close she was invading his space. That surprised him. He had seen that she kept her distance from him and everyone else. Now he almost felt as if she had come close for a reason, to make a point that she wasn't afraid of him, maybe. She wasn't a bad-looking lady, but he didn't know what to make of her. She made the hair stand up on the back of his neck.

"Yeah. I'm ready." Bear backed away and put his hand on the door handle. "Go get your partner and let's take a walk."

12

"YOU'RE not a very good conversationalist, Colonel Barringer."

Tickled by his own wit, the older man laughed, a dry sound that turned into a phlegmy cough. He reached for another cigarette. He lit it and inhaled deeply. The nicotine acted quickly and his coughing stopped. His lung problems didn't come from his tobacco use. No, the fumes he had inhaled so many years ago had scarred them. Damn the military and their stupid experiments.

Now cigarettes were the only thing that soothed his throat when the hacking started.

A balding man with thin wisps of white hair like dandelion fuzz and a face ruddy from high blood pressure, he didn't look dangerous. In fact, he looked harmless, with his sunken chest and paunch. That was to his advantage. Evil should always look banal, he believed. It lulled the opposition into making mistakes.

At the moment he sat in an old maple chair, the kind with a cushion tied on the seat with strings. His hands were folded by his waist, and he was smiling as he stared at the body that lay on the bed in his spare bedroom.

"Who would have thought the whole scheme would really have worked? Not you. Oh, no, not you. But then, you thought that double-crossing your friends was smart.

"Getting killed wasn't smart, now, was it, Colonel?"

The body, which smelled of formaldehyde, remained motionless and unresponsive on the bed.

"I suppose your having the ability to speak would require a great deal more effort than the Bokor wanted to make. Perhaps for another payment? But then what would you say to me anyway, my dear friend? My dear *former* friend. You would say 'Yes, sir,' that's what you'd say, for now at last you have to follow my orders."

The balding man rose from the chair and picked up a folded sheet he had brought in from the linen closet. He moved close to the bed. He unfolded the sheet in his soft little hands and shook it out.

Still smiling, he bent over the body. "I am going to cover you up now. It's really for the best. You aren't a pretty sight anymore. But the ladies used to love you, didn't they? Or at least you thought they did, especially your pretty wife and the girl Fatima. Oh, that vixen. She liked my American dollars so much more."

He drew the sheet over the body. "Until later. Ta-ta," he said, and laughed with a wet, choking sound.

He left the spare room quickly. He had had his little fun. Now he had an appointment with the men he called his board. He wanted to shower first and put on a clean shirt. He favored those Hawaiian ones in fashion right now. They were so comfortable. He would wear the one with the blue parrots. It pleased him enormously. No one would ever suspect that a man such as himself would be wearing blue parrots, now, would they?

He smiled, showing yellow teeth as he went into his bathroom. He opened the medicine cabinet and peered inside.

Let's see, the verbena soap would be a good choice for this momentous occasion, he thought. *It is one of the thirty-eight Bach flower recipes, of course. Prescribed for "overenthusiasm." Ah, yes, that is exactly right.*

The man knew how important the sense of smell was. He had studied how aromas affected the subconscious. They regulated mood. They had special energies. They were so much more important than most people guessed.

In fact, they unleashed some very potent magic.

13

We are the dead. Short days ago
We lived, felt dawn, saw sunset glow,
Loved and were loved, and now we lie
In Flanders fields . . .
—"In Flanders Fields," Lt. Col. John McCrae,
May 3, 1915

THE instant Sam stepped outside the service building into the grassy expanse of the national cemetery a buzzing began within her skull like a thousand bees, and the wailing of the dead started again, louder than ever. Then a tingling darted up her spine and made her scalp crawl. It was as if something, *someone* jabbed her in the middle of her back with an electric prod. She suddenly felt light-headed, the ground heaving and uncertain beneath her feet. She was afraid she'd faint.

She stopped in her tracks and closed her eyes. She could barely breathe with the heaviness of the air. *This is too much,* she thought. *Too much.*

She had been to cemeteries before, but being young, she had not been in so very many. And this place, Arlington National Cemetery, with its white grave markers stretching endlessly as far as she could see and filled with thousands upon hundreds of thousands of fallen soldiers, was like nothing she had ever experienced. Not even the dead of Iraq had called to her this way—in waves of energy rising and falling like emergency sirens.

She put her hands over her face and stood still, swaying a little in the Southern summer heat and the thick, oppressive air, hoping to find a way to shut out the sound obliterating everything else—the sound of the dead.

The big man who called himself Bear appeared close to her. "What's wrong?" His voice sounded impatient.

She dropped her hands. "Just give me a minute—" she had begun to say when she heard Rina Martus cry out, "I'm coming!"

Sam raised her eyes and saw Rina running down the path.

She and Bear exchanged puzzled looks. They both began to follow, but Sam no sooner started forward on the stone walkway than her knees turned weak and she stumbled.

"Oh, Jesus!" she heard the big man mutter as he stepped in front of her, hesitated for the briefest second, then took a firm but careful grip on her arm. "Are you going to faint?"

"No . . . yes . . . I don't know. It's the heat, this terrible heat," she said apologetically, but of course it wasn't.

The man looked at her for a moment, his hard features softening a little. "You don't have to apologize. Going from air-conditioning into these kinds of temperatures can screw you up. Here." He pulled a bottle of water from his jacket pocket, opened it, and passed it over. "It's not very cold, but it's wet."

Sam took it gratefully and drank. Water dribbled down her chin. She wiped it with the back of her hand. Bear watched her every move.

Then, while she took another long drink, he took off his jacket and folded it over his arm. "It's a scorcher out here," he said. "You still shaky?"

"I'm afraid so."

"You had enough?" She nodded. He took the bottle back. "Just let me know if you need more." He regarded her for a moment. "You know, you'd better hang on to me until you get your sea legs."

"You're probably right," Sam said, realizing it was true. She tentatively reached for his arm. He slipped her hand into the crook of his elbow politely, like a nineteenth-century gentleman. The feeling of his skin beneath her fingers sent a quiver up her arm. She felt his hard muscles and his strength. His aliveness seemed to quiet the noise the dead were making.

Sam and Bear moved ahead cautiously for a few paces, then quickly moved in tandem in the direction Rina had gone.

A few hundred feet ahead of them, Rina's rangy, colt-like figure had left the service road, hopped over a low chain, and sprinted between the rows of graves. By the time Sam and Bear reached her, she was standing in front of a headstone. She was shaking her head back and forth as if saying no.

"What are you doing?" Bear's voice demanded. "This isn't the crime scene."

Rina pointed toward the grave marker in front of her. It wasn't recent. It said Maj. Marvin Barrow had died on January 21, 1968, in Vietnam. He had been twenty-six years old. He had earned a Silver Star for valor in 1967.

"This man called out to me. He insisted that I listen to him. He thought I could help. He was found in a bunker during the siege of Khe Sanh. Shot in the head. Nobody knew what happened, but"—the words ripped from her throat, jagged with sorrow—"but his family was told he had taken his own life."

Rina turned eyes filled with pain toward Sam. "He's terribly upset about that. He said that wasn't true! He was murdered. Another American killed him. He told me the man's name. He wants justice. He wants the man arrested. I can't help him. It's too late."

Bear looked bewildered. "I don't get what's going on here."

Rina responded angrily to his comment, her face, with its high cheekbones and sharp angles, defiant. "Are you deaf? Didn't you hear me? This man told me he was murdered. He told me who did it."

Bear glared at her. "But he's dead. He can't talk to you or anybody."

"That's what you say." Rina put her hands on her narrow hips and defied him. "Look, believe what I tell you or don't believe it. It doesn't matter to me. I know what I know."

"And that is?" Bear shot back.

"Agent Martus!" Sam broke in, fearful that she was seeing AngelWay being compromised and going to hell before it even started. "Leave it be."

Bear looked back and forth between the two women. "What's going on here? I just don't get it."

"Nothing. Nothing's going on," Sam said. "Let's go." She took her hand from Bear's arm and started to move away.

Bear stood his ground. His body had again become a rock, solid and immovable. "Hold on a minute. I want to get something straight." He turned his attention to Rina. "I thought you're supposed to be a crime-scene investigator. Then your boss says you're an expert in voodoo. Now you're talking to a tombstone. One of us is nuts, and it isn't me. I asked a question. What's going on here? I want an answer."

Sam looked at Bear with anxious eyes. "Can't you just leave it, both of you?"

"No," Bear said, digging himself into a position.

"Rina . . ." Sam tried again to caution her.

"No," Rina Martus said firmly. "With all due respect, Agent Chase, I tell what I know, whether people want to hear it or not. I'm not going to start, even now, hiding who I am and what I do." Her face had turned very white. For the briefest of moments she looked impossibly young, almost vulnerable, before she tensed, her back straightened, and like Walker Evan's Appalachian wife she stood there, her history of suffering showing but her chin high. She glared at them both.

"Chase, Rutledge, here it is plain as I can say it: I *am* a crime-scene expert. A damned good one. What makes me so good? I hear the truth from the dead—if they decide they want to talk to me. I hear them crying out from the place where they were murdered, or buried, or chopped into little pieces.

"The cops I have worked with all around this country know I can come up with the names of suspects, descriptions of the crime, and all kinds of evidence. They don't care how I do it, as long as I help them find the perp. Oh, please, get that look off your face, Mr. Rutledge.

You want cops' names? You want phone numbers? I'll give them to you, but I won't waste my time trying to justify myself to you."

Rina moved her blue stone eyes from Bear to Sam. "I'll call Major Barrow's family later. That's all I can do for him. He says he understands. The grave you are so anxious to see is up there." She gestured with her pale hand toward a knoll on the other side of a small brook. Sam could see temporary green mesh fencing. A blue service vehicle was parked on the road nearby.

Rina started to walk past Sam. Impulsively Sam reached out and gave the young woman's thin arm a reassuring squeeze to tell her she understood.

Too surprised to jerk her arm away as Sam thought she might, Rina stopped. Her eyes met Sam's for a second and held. Then Rina nodded just the slightest bit and whispered to Sam, ignoring Bear, "I already know everything I need to about that place. That dead man isn't going to talk to me. And I can feel bad mojo. I can even see it like a sickness in the sky. But you need to find out for yourself. I'll meet you there." She moved on.

"You still need some help?" Bear's words were gruff. He now walked at a distance from Sam, but shortened his stride to match her slower pace.

Her legs felt strong again, her steps steady even though the path they had chosen started to ascend a small hill. She didn't need Bear's arm. But she had to admit she had liked the way it had felt, even though she didn't much like Bear.

She shook her head. "I'm fine. I have to get used to the humidity, that's all." That much of what she said was the truth. The morning heat was spiking higher as the hours rolled toward noon. Her sleeveless yellow pullover felt damp, and she had long since taken off the light jacket. It didn't help. Her discomfort had intensified. She felt hot and miserable.

"Good. Glad to hear that," the big man muttered, and looked at her as if she were a burden he had to bear. She resolved to hide her feelings as best she could. She watched him gaze up the path at Rina's thin shape, almost wraithlike, in front of them. "She was kidding, right?" he said to Sam. "Or is she crazy?"

Sam took a deep breath before she answered. For her, the voices of the dead were an indecipherable clamor. None of them called out to her in the way the man called Barrow had to Rina, but she didn't doubt Rina had heard what she said she did.

And although the dead still wailed and moaned around Sam, she was getting used to their presence and able to ignore it, like white noise in the background. She exhaled. She knew Rina had said far too much. If Ms. Z found out, well . . . Sam just hoped she wouldn't. Meanwhile, Sam made up her mind to repair the potential damage of Rina's extraordinary statement the best she could.

She put strength in her voice, the way her father did when he spoke, and lifted her chin. "I just met Agent Martus today. I can't say whether she's crazy or not. I can say she came highly recommended. I wouldn't ignore what she tells us. She's not kidding. I know that much."

"So you believe this stuff about her being able to talk to the dead?" Bear's sarcasm was audible.

Sam kept moving along the stone pavers. She looked straight ahead, and her answer was measured, carefully phrased. "What I believe doesn't matter. If Martus is as good as she's supposed to be, if she provides information we can use to solve this case, I don't care how she gets it. So what if she says the dead tell her things? Maybe she spots something at the scene others overlook, or decides to look for DNA where nobody else does, or puts facts together in a new way and comes up with a breakthrough. Maybe she processes information so fast it's all on a subconscious level. Maybe to her that's the dead talking—just like they can talk to all of us if we know how to hear them."

Sam could distinguish the big man's footsteps now above the noise of the dead. She heard a robin start singing on a tree branch arching over the path. She and Bear were almost at the crime scene, which had been made to look like a temporary construction area, with green mesh fencing stretching between tree trunks and encircling a black metal sign that said SILENCE AND RESPECT.

Fifty feet away from the flimsy fence a U.S. Park Police employee stood next to the driver's-side door of a blue pickup truck.

"Yeah, well, you might have a point," Bear conceded after a few moments of silence. They reached the crime-scene area. Rina Martus had already squeezed through the temporary fence and was standing beneath a tree, indistinct in the shadows, with her brown clothes acting as camouflage. Bear looked in her direction, then glanced at Sam. "But she's one strange cookie. I've never met anybody like her."

Sam looked up at Bear's handsome face. Something twisted inside her. Without thinking she smiled at him. "I'll second that. Let's go talk to Mr. Smith."

14

A man of middle age and café-au-lait complexion, Rodney K. Smith, longtime employee of the U.S. Park Police, was sucking on a lollipop and jingling the change in his pants pockets when Sam and Bear walked up to him.

"Mr. Smith?" Bear asked, and approached him. Sam went too, but when they both stopped she took a pen and the only paper she had on her, a pad of yellow Post-it notes, from the small purse with the shoulder strap that she had brought with her from Iraq a lifetime ago. The square pad of Post-its wasn't very professional-looking, but it would have to do.

Rodney Smith quickly removed the sucker from his mouth, stuck the cherry-colored candy back in its wrapper, and put it in his breast pocket. He stayed next to the door of the pickup and looked at the big man and pretty woman who had come up the wide path with its stone pavers. "Yeah, that's me. I guess you're the folks looking into this."

Bear put out his hand. "I'm Rutledge. This is Agent Chase. Agent Martus is the woman over there."

Rodney Smith's eyes darted toward Rina but didn't linger. "Well, I got to tell you I don't know anything, and I mean I don't know anything more than I told that feller day before yesterday. And I'd appreciate it if you can ask me anything you need to right quick. I'd like to get back in my truck."

"And why is that, Mr. Smith?" Bear asked.

Sam could feel the fear rolling off the park service employee. She had a pretty good idea of why he wanted to leave. The place had a dark and shadowy feeling and an atmosphere thick with sorrow. She wasn't having good feelings about being here herself.

"Why? Makes me nervous to be up here. I keep seeing— Anyway, I haven't slept since I found . . . you know. It's like anything else. You see something like that, you want to start smoking again." He reached into his pocket and pulled out the lollipop he had put back in the wrapper. "That's what these are all about. I quit smoking five years ago, and Patricia, that's my wife, is watching me like a hawk. She bought me a big bag of Tootsie Pops. I must have gone through a hundred since Sunday." His hand trembled as he held the stick.

"I see. It really shook you up then?" Bear sounded sympathetic and friendly.

"Shook me up? Hell, I still have the shakes. Patricia wants me to take some time off. Get away from here for a while. I'm talking to my supervisor this afternoon. My doctor said he'd give me something. Pills for my nerves. They're shot all to"—he glanced at Sam—"crap."

"Okay," Bear said, still friendly. "Let me ask you what happened that morning—what was it, Sunday?"

"Sunday, yeah. The park opens at eight a.m., you know, and that's about when I picked up my service truck from the warehouse and ground maintenance building at the north end of the cemetery. I was headed down Eisenhower Drive, same as I do every morning."

Bear nodded. "Can you show me where you were when you first saw something that raised a red flag?"

Rodney Smith pointed up the road past the rear of the blue pickup. "Back there maybe ten, twenty yards. No more than that. I saw something brown, the dirt, you know. Now, there shouldn't have been no piles of dirt in that area even though this is Section Sixty where they bury the new war dead. But there it should have been only grass. So I stopped the truck. Right here I stopped, just like now."

Bear nodded. "Okay. Do you think you can walk us over to the grave site, just like you did that morning? Stepping pretty much where you stepped then?"

Rodney Smith's café-au-lait skin turned ashy. "No, sir. I don't want to do that. I surely don't. I'll show you where I went, but I ain't going back there. No, sir, I ain't go anywhere near that there grave."

Rodney Smith's face went grim and hard as he moved from the road to the grassy lawn. He ducked through the fencing and went to the tree where Rina was standing. Rina nodded at the man, but didn't speak.

Smith stood at the beginning of a line of gentle mounds between two rows of headstones. "I walked straight down here. I didn't go nowhere else. Just went across the grass, tried to avoid stepping on the graves themselves when I could. It was real wet that morning. Lots of dew. You could see the water on the grass, silver-like, and I could see the footprints where I stepped when I came back—came back exactly the way I went in, but faster."

"And you didn't notice any other marks in the grass? Footprints? Wheel marks? Tire tracks?"

"No, sir. 'Cause there weren't none. I know that for sure, 'cause I felt spooked. Felt like somebody was watching me, you know. So I looked all around the grass near the empty . . . place. Nobody had been there. Not after the dew fell, anyways. I was the only person in this section that morning. No doubt about it."

"So you got to the grave . . . what happened then?"

Smith swallowed, and his Adam's apple bobbed up and down. "I looked in it. The hole. That's when I seen what was there and what weren't."

"Which was?"

"The coffin was in there, wide-open. You could see the white satin inside real clear. The body was gone. There was . . . there was things in that grave, though. Still makes me sick to think about it. Let's leave it at that."

"I understand you're upset. But I still need you to describe what you saw." Bear had become impatient again, and his voice conveyed his annoyance.

Anger flashed across Smith's face. "You *don't* understand." Sam saw the man's hands tighten into fists. He glared at Bear for an instant; then something in his eyes got flat and surrendered. Smith let out a deep sigh. "Guess it don't matter if I talk about it. I keep seeing it anyways. So, okay. I seen two things down there in that coffin.

"One thing, I say it was a heart. It was all red and running blood. Not like anything that's been dead long. More like a heart just ripped out of a man or a beast. It throbbed. It still throbbed." His voice got loud. "You hear me? It weren't anything normal! A heart beating like that! And there was a pile of gray stuff. I thought it must be brains, but they was moving too, slithering around like a pile of worms." Smith's face started to look green. His eyes sought the ground. "That's all I got to say about it." He pressed his lips together.

Sam had nearly stopped breathing while Smith spoke. This wasn't in the CIA's report. The new information had upped the ante. Suddenly the case sounded like a lot more than a grave robbing to her—and it had to be paranormal. But even as her own excitement grew, Bear was having a different reaction.

"A beating heart? Squirming brains?" Bear spoke with obvious disbelief. "Tell me, Smith, how much light was there at the bottom of that grave that you could see so much?"

Smith balled his hands into fists again; his voice became challenging, angry at his not being believed. "They was lying on white satin. It didn't take much light to see what I saw. And I saw it. I'm no liar. You calling me a liar?"

Smith appeared as if he were about to throw a punch. Sam didn't hesitate. She stepped in front of Bear, forcing him to move away. She kept her voice calm and polite. "Take it easy, Mr. Smith. We're just trying to get the whole story here, as clearly as we can. I wrote down exactly what you said. I know you meant every word. Now, what did you do at that point? After you looked into the grave?"

Smith's face flushed. He glared at Bear for a moment more.

"Mr. Smith." Sam's voice was gentle. "Please tell me what you did next."

Smith tore his eyes from Bear and looked at Sam. His voice quavered. "What I do? What I do? I tried not to lose my breakfast, that's what. I run back to my truck and called my supervisor. He told me to stay up here until somebody came. Maybe fifteen minutes later a bunch of cars drove up. Black cars. The men asked me questions. I told them just what I told you. We through now?" He stared past Sam to give Bear another angry look.

"Just a few more questions, Mr. Smith." Bear had gotten Sam's message to back off. His voice had become neutral again. "Tell me, were you working here in the cemetery the day before this happened?"

Smith directed his answers back at Sam, ignoring the big man. "I work Saturday through Wednesday. I get a Sunday premium for coming in on the weekends. Patricia don't mind me not being home on Sunday, so I do it."

Sam took up the line of questioning. "Would you think back to Saturday? Did you come by this area at all?"

"Sure I did. I always park my own car by the warehouse and ground maintenance building. That's up past the visitors' center on the north side of the cemetery. I sign out a vehicle and drive down to the service complex. I see my supervisor. Know him a long time. We're both vets. Persian Gulf War, you know. We both been working here a long time. He's in the office down there. We have a coffee together, and he lets me know if there's anything I need to do special. Like if there's an interment, he tells me when to get down to the gate and let in the funeral cortege. That kind of stuff."

"What's his name?"

"John. John Bartikowski."

"B-a-r-t-a?" Sam kept her pen poised over the Post-it.

"B-A-R-T-I-K-O-W-S-K-I," Rodney Smith corrected.

Sam wrote the name down.

"So you went right past this area that morning, Saturday morning," Bear broke in. "Did you notice anything?"

"Wasn't anything to notice. Nothing different anytime

I went past here all that day. I'm sure about that. I would have spotted it, same as I did Sunday morning."

"What about any unusual people hanging around?"

"Unusual people?" Rodney Smith let out a humorless laugh that was more like a snort. "You know how many visitors go through here on a Saturday? They're like ants at a picnic; they're everywhere. Busloads of people, all ages, come in here. We get Amish, we get Japanese tourists, folks in wheelchairs, more *unusual* people than you can imagine. Hell, there's all kinds come here. I don't know what's unusual anymore. I see it all. Let me tell you, I see it all."

Sam took over again. Smith's hostility to Bear hadn't abated. "Would you think hard for a minute? Was there anything different happening on Saturday, or even during the few days before that? Somebody carrying something that caught your eye? Somebody acting different from the usual visitor?"

Smith cocked his head; he squinted his eyes. "Let's see . . . there may have been something. I didn't think about that previous week before you just asked me. Seems to me . . . Yeah. Wednesday a camera crew was in here. That's not so unusual. But they're usually setting up by Kennedy's grave, you know? Or at the Tomb of the Unknowns. They like to film the changing of the guard up there. That's what caught my eye."

"They were at the Tomb of the Unknowns?"

"Nah, what got my attention was that these guys was mostly right in this area, yeah. They was filming in this section, Section Sixty. Later I saw them over closer to Section Sixty-one. And, you know what? There's nothing there at all. Joe Louis, now, he's over near the amphitheater, Section Seven-A. Audie Murphy's in Forty-six. Section Sixty-one is mostly empty.

"And let's see . . . oh yeah—something else. There was three of them. Lots of cameras and equipment. But one of the fellers had flowers with him."

"Don't a lot of people bring flowers? What made you remember this?" Sam thought it was an odd thing for Smith to bring up.

"People bring flowers, sure, usually the same kinds

of flowers, depending on the season. Christmas, there's poinsettias, of course. During the summer? Look around. You see mostly yellow or pink, maybe white flowers. I don't know what kind, carnations? Something like that. So that's why I noticed this guy's flowers—they was weeds. Least they looked like weeds to me.

"I thought to myself, 'That cheap bastard. He don't look so poor he couldn't afford to buy something nice.' I could see there were some little purple flowers in what he carried, but hell, it was mostly leaves."

Rina spoke then. "Vervain. Purple-top vervain." She didn't even seem to have been listening to the questions they were asking Smith. The whole time she had been staring out across the cemetery, and she didn't turn her head now to look at Sam or Bear or Rodney Smith. "A conjuring herb," she added. "Calls the dead."

Bear shot Rina a useless annoyed look—useless because she wasn't paying any attention to him.

Rodney Smith's eyes opened wide to show the whites all around. "I don't know nothing about that. The dead never caused me no problems in here. People, that's something else. They do the damnedest things. But this . . . what happened. I never thought people could be so sick."

"Yeah, well, like you said, people do the damnedest things," Bear said. "Tell me more about the photographers. What were they doing?"

Smith's voice got hard again. "Taking pictures of graves, that's all. Shooting mostly the grave markers, come to think about it. I figured they must be filming a documentary about the Iraq soldiers. A lot of them are buried right around here."

"Were they old guys? Young? What did they look like? How were they dressed?"

Rodney Smith bristled. "I don't know. I didn't take notice. Late twenties? Thirties? White guys, far as I could tell. Nothing special about any of them. Dressed okay, not half-naked like some folks. And yeah, they all wore visor caps. Black or navy blue, I think. A million people dress like that. I didn't notice nothing different about them."

Sam chimed in again. "Would a camera crew have had to sign in someplace? Would there be a record of those men filming here?"

Rodney Smith felt more comfortable talking about this, about something normal and everyday. The fear left his face for a moment. "Yeah, there should be a record. You're supposed to get permission to film on the grounds. You can't just waltz in here with lots of equipment.

"John McCain, when he was running for president? He had a crew filming him while he walked through here and got himself in a heap of trouble. Later, he said he was visiting his father's and grandfather's graves. They're both here, you know. But he made some kind of political ad out of his visit. Against regulations to do something like that."

"So these guys couldn't have gotten in without getting permission first?" Sam asked.

Rodney Smith's eyes looked at the ground for a moment, and he shifted his shoulders uncomfortably. "I don't know about that. It's summer and it's real crowded. These three guys might have just walked in through the visitors' center. Sure, they was carrying cameras, but most people have a camera. And maybe they came in one at a time, so they'd be less noticeable."

He looked at Sam as if a light had dawned and he understood. "Yeah, they'd be taking a chance they'd get stopped when they set up their equipment. But did any of us approach them? I didn't. I can't say anybody did. Bush cut our budget. We've got fewer people than we used to."

"If they did get permission, who would have granted it?" Sam got her pen ready.

"The media coordinator. Ms. Terrell. She's up in the administration building. That's right next to the visitors' center. You about done? Don't like to say nothing, but my stomach don't feel too good. I'd like to get back to the grounds building."

"Go ahead, go," Bear said. "But I'd like to you to be present when we look at the surveillance footage from Sunday. And Wednesday's too. Where do they store the memory cards or video disks?"

"Well, I'm not sure what they use these days. Not tape no more, I know that. But it would have to be down in the security office. In the administration building, the place I just mentioned. You can probably get Wednesday's, but you ain't going to find anything from the weekend there."

"Why not?"

" 'Cause the men in the black cars took them. Practically was the first thing they asked me about when they showed up."

Bear snapped at Sam, "You know about this?"

"Hey, I just came into this. Rina too. We don't know anything more than you do."

Bear looked back at Rodney Smith. Sweat ran in rivulets down Smith's face, and he was jingling his pocket change more furiously than ever. "Go on, get out of here. When we're going to look at the video, I'll let you know. How will I reach you?"

Before the words even got out of Bear's mouth, Rodney Smith had started moving toward his truck. "Just call the main number. They'll track me down."

15

"COME on. Let's go look at the grave site for ourselves," Bear said to Sam. They started walking on the grass between the rows of grave markers. "You coming?" Bear called back to Rina, who still stood leaning against the trunk of the tree.

She pushed herself upright. "Guess I should. It's not going to be a lot of fun, though."

It wasn't fun. Sam felt more and more uneasy the closer the three of them got to what finally proved to be just an empty hole. But no familiar or even unfamiliar voices spoke to her. She wasn't getting any messages from "beyond" except for the wailing of the dead, and she was doing better at tuning them out.

Bear went to the edge of the open grave. Sam came up next to him and stood with her toes just short of the void before them.

"Where do you suppose the casket is?" Bear didn't seem to be asking anybody, just voicing his thoughts.

"Must have been taken away by the first responders, like the surveillance video," Sam answered. She noticed the signs of a lot of activity. "The lawn's got tire marks in it. The grass on that one end of the open grave is ripped up too. They must have pulled the coffin out there and had a cart of some sort to take it away."

Bear made a sound of disgust. "Place is torn up pretty good. You see any pictures of what Smith saw? Any crime-scene photos in the file you looked at?"

"No, nothing. I'll find out who has them. I'll make sure we get them." She too was feeling frustrated at the material Ms. Z had withheld. She wondered what else they weren't being shown or told about.

Bear nodded, but he had turned his attention to Rina. Sam followed his gaze. The young woman's eyes were staring at the sky. Her body was visibly shaking. Rina appeared to be in some sort of trance. Bear started, "What the—"

Sam put her fingers to her lips to keep Bear from speaking. As they watched, Rina began to sway, and her hands jabbed at the air as her head bobbed back and forth. She was making little moaning sounds, like, "Ahhh, ahhh."

"She puts on a good show," Bear whispered near Sam's ear. It had occurred to Sam that Rina was performing for their benefit. It could be all part of an act, like raps on the table during a séance.

When Sam heard her spirit guide's voice, it spoke in her mind. Her body didn't jerk or twitch; nor did she look skyward, as if an angel were making a holy pronouncement. But Rina was bobbing to and fro, almost like a snake striking.

Then, abruptly, Rina stopped what she was doing. She turned to Sam. "He's not dead," she said.

"Who's not dead?" Bear demanded.

Rina sounded exasperated. She frowned, making a single crease between her eyebrows. "Barringer. The missing body. Who else are we talking about here?"

Bear let out a hard breath, clearly disgusted. "The guy was *buried* for months. He has to be dead. What do you mean?"

Rina stretched out her thin arms, her palms turned upward. "His soul isn't here. I don't know if it's anywhere. And this whole place . . ." She gestured widely, encompassing the area with her hands. "Can't you see it? Can't you smell it? The vervain. The stink of death. Evil is all over this place. Petro. Black magic. Maybe this is a crossroads." She glanced at Sam, who didn't understand. "You know, a crossroads, a place where the physical earth and the spirit world meet. I can't be sure. But I don't think anybody took this man. He left on his own."

Bear folded his arms across his chest and made a face filled with disgust. "You said that before you even came up here. It's a load of crap. What kind of evidence do you have?"

Rina didn't rise to the bait, but her voice had become tinged with sadness. "What evidence do you have that he didn't?"

"I can't deal with her," Bear said to Sam. "You see anything else before we get out of here?"

Sam, like Rina, did feel something there, something not ordinary. The best she could describe it to herself was as an undercurrent of unease. And she could see something too—a filmy grayness or a dim shadow that danced in the air like northern lights.

But she wasn't about to admit that to Bear. Right now he seemed to think she was the normal one of the two women. She wanted to keep it that way. She realized with some surprise that his opinion of her mattered.

So Sam dutifully looked around at the empty grave, at the trampled grass. Then she did see something, a little rusty spot on top of Barringer's grave marker. "What's that? That discoloration on top of the stone?"

Bear stepped closer to the headstone. It was just a faint smudge, a small smear of something brownish. "I don't know how your people could have missed this," he griped. "Looks like blood. We'll need to get somebody up here to get a sample."

Rina looked over at the two of them. "They didn't miss it. It wasn't there on Sunday. I'd bet on that. Bet too it's animal blood. Chicken or rabbit. Like I said, Petro voodoo. Bad stuff."

16

RINA refused to go to the administration building with Bear and Sam. "Waste of time," she said, and wandered away, weaving her way through the headstones, stopping every now and then to read what was written on them. "I'm going over to the Kennedy Memorial." Her words became fainter as she loped like a young deer down a hill. "I'll meet you later when I'm done."

Sam thought Rina's assertion about how useless going to the administration building would be might prove right. She had a feeling they weren't going to strike gold within the first hour and solve the case. It would have been easy if the three photographers had registered, given their real names and addresses, and turned out to be the body snatchers. But that happened in TV shows, not real life.

As it turned out, Ms. Terrell, an exceptionally sweet woman with soft eyes behind her bifocals, found no permission requests for a film crew to shoot in the cemetery the previous week, not on Wednesday or any other day.

But the security office did have Wednesday's surveillance videos. Bear asked for a place to review them in private. A young secretary, who blushed and giggled when she talked to Bear, led them into a side room that contained a TV monitor they could use.

Sam's spirits sank as soon as they found out that three surveillance cameras had recorded eleven hours each of people walking in and out of the visitors' center from eight a.m. to seven p.m. They also recorded the empty building for the rest of the twenty-four hours.

Sam had become so weary she could barely think straight. Jet lag had left her brain addled. Plus she had gone from baking to freezing. This building was intensely air-conditioned. She put her jacket back on. Shivered. It crossed her mind that going from the intense heat of outdoors into this chill, artificial air was another stressor on her already stressed-out body.

But the biggest stressor of all was this man at her side. Maybe it was her overall, bone-deep fatigue; maybe it was the smell of him, salty and clean; maybe it was the way the stars had lined up in her horoscope. She didn't know the cause, but she did know she reacted to him. She was physically pulled to him.

And she hated that. He was not her dream man. He was her nightmare man: military, overbearing, uncultured, and most likely a man who thought lovemaking was all screwing and no foreplay. Bear Rutledge was Mr. Wrong, not Mr. Right.

"Let's get through these as quick as we can," Bear's no-nonsense voice broke into her thoughts. "I want to get to talk to Bartikowski," he added.

By using the fast-forward setting, they were able to speed through the hours of video, but it made it hard to spot the men Smith had described. Sam focused her attention on the flashing screen, trying not to let her eyes slide closed, but the images soon all became a blur.

So it was Bear who spotted the first guy. He hit the pause button. "There, that's him!"

A man wearing a visor cap was hurrying across the floor in front of the reception desk in the visitors' center pulling along a hard metal studio carrying case on wheels—it looked like a square black trunk more than a suitcase—and he carried a tripod as well. Bear started the picture again and soon a second man appeared in the building, toting a high-end, portable camcorder, a professional model, clearly not the kind of camera a tourist would carry.

The men's visor caps obscured their faces, but Bear felt Rodney Smith should take a look and see if he could identify them. He walked into the other room to ask the secretary to try to find the park service employee. A few minutes later she reported back to them that Smith must have gone out of the park during his break, because he wasn't answering his radio walkie-talkie, and he wasn't down at the service complex or maintenance building either.

Bear shrugged and said for her to try again later. He and Sam went back to reviewing the surveillance video, but Sam knew she wasn't being any help. She touched Bear lightly on the arm.

"I'm not making excuses, but I just got in from Iraq. I haven't slept in over twenty-four hours. My eyes won't focus anymore. I'm going to sit this out for a while." She couldn't read the expression on Bear's face. Did he think she had wimped out again?

Sam moved to a chair on the far side the room, and despite her intentions not to, she dozed off. The next thing she knew, Bear was talking to her.

"Chase? You awake? I'm done here."

"Huh? Oh, sorry. I was just resting my eyes. Did you spot the third man? The guy with the flowers?"

"No. He probably came in with an excursion group. It's like a stampede every time a busful arrives. I must have missed him. I did see the guy with the studio carrying case leave the building. But there're too many hours of surveillance to look at now."

Sam shook herself awake. "What about the rest of the park. Anything?"

"Not that I picked up. The only areas they've got covered by cameras are John F. Kennedy's grave and the Tomb of the Unknowns. Security for the rest of the cemetery—and this place covers over six hundred acres—is from U.S. Park Police guys riding or walking through."

Then Bear said bluntly to Sam that he wanted to take the material back to the DOD and let the technicians there take a look. It was obvious he didn't want to let the agency snatch them.

Sam stood up, uncomfortable with him looming over her. Practically toe-to-toe, she held her ground and shook her head. "No, I can't go along with that. We can't risk a leak of information. Like it or not, the agency needs to handle these."

Anger flared up in Bear's face. He glared at Sam for a moment. Then something changed in his eyes.

Sam stared at the big man who was close, too close. It was a mistake. The handsome face where anger had first flashed was now filled with something else, something like desire. His attraction to her swept Sam's feelings into turmoil. She took in the dark hair tousled by the walk in the cemetery, the strong line of his jaw, the massive chest inches from hers. Her stomach clenched and her breath quickened. She wasn't supposed to react like this; she didn't want to react at all, and yet she did. Her attention was drawn to his lips, his head drawing closer.

I think he wants to kiss me.

She took a step to the side, slipping away from him, increasing the space between them. She raised her hands in apology and smiled to soften her earlier harsh words. "I'm sorry, really. I'm on your side in this. All we can do is put up a fuss to make sure they tell us what they find, assuming they find anything."

Just then the secretary popped her head in the door. "Agent Chase?" she asked.

"Yes?" Sam answered.

"A car will be coming for you and Agent Martus in fifteen minutes. You're supposed to stay put until it gets here."

"Right," Sam replied, and suddenly realized that her fatigue had made her more vulnerable to Bear Rutledge. He wasn't just sexy; he was proving to be a very nice guy, and she hoped he didn't end up putting her in the same category as Rina, which was . . . what? A nutcase? A fraud?

But she *was* in the same category as Rina. They were both psychics. It was crazy to think Bear wouldn't find out about her and why she was really on this case. She brought her hands to her face again, covering her eyes, her fingertips pushing back her hair. "Sorry," she said out loud. "I'm beat. I need to get to bed."

Immediately she wanted to retract the word *bed.* She meant nothing sexual, but the moment she uttered it, she connected *bed* with *Bear,* and it became erotic. A rosy pinkness crept into her cheeks.

"No wonder the heat got to you before," Bear said, regarding her with intensity. "You've got to be dead on your feet. Why don't you sit down again until your car gets here."

It didn't matter how much Sam chastised herself for her physical response to this man; it was happening anyway. It was just the two of them in this room. It was intimate. It was private. Bear sat down on the chair next to hers. He moved his leg so it nearly touched hers, but didn't quite. She slid her foot, accidentally and in all innocence, until it rested alongside his.

For no apparent reason, Sam found herself smiling at Bear, and he was grinning back. She caught herself and stared down at her hands. Bear must have felt as uneasy about what was happening between them as Sam did, because he abruptly stood and asked her if he could get her a drink of water from the dispenser near the far wall. It would be better than the lukewarm water left in the bottle, he said.

"I'm parched," she answered truthfully. "That would be splendid."

He moved away quickly. The connection between them had been getting so strong, Sam felt as if Bear were an emotional magnet pulling the disparate heap of her fragmented feelings toward it.

When Bear came back from the dispenser and handed her a little paper cup, he didn't sit back down but stood some distance away.

Good, Sam thought. *Things are getting out of hand.* It seemed to her they should act like two professionals and talk about the case. She plunged into what had bothered her most. "There's something I wanted to run by you. I'm disturbed that our briefing didn't include the information Smith just gave us. It changes everything, don't you think? What's your take on it?"

Bear gave his head a little shake. "You mean that garbage about the beating heart and squirming brains?

Why wasn't it in the briefing? Simple, it wasn't true. Your people discounted it, just like I am."

"How can you do that? Just discount the information? The man *saw* it."

"No! He *thought* he saw it. He found an open grave. The body had vanished. He's alone up there—and hey, he got spooked. Not unexpected, you know. You could see he was still scared out of his wits. His mind played tricks on him, that's all."

"That's *all*? That's your position even when you add Smith's account to Barringer's body disappearing from the grave without any physical signs of how it was removed? To me that adds up to something beyond the limits of our understanding. I can't believe you still think this crime has a rational explanation."

Bear gave her a look of disgust. "Of course I do. Any sane person would." Bear folded his arms across his chest. "You don't really believe that voodoo stuff, do you?"

Bear's pigheadedness looked like a bigger problem than ever to Sam, but she was determined to keep her mind open and listen to what he had to say. She swallowed her feelings for now. "Tell me how you see it then."

Bear pulled the chair over to him, turned it around, and sat on it backward facing Sam. His arms leaned on its back. That put him close enough to Sam so she could see that his lashes were long and little flecks of green lit up his hazel eyes.

"Look at it logically," he said. "The way Smith tells it he didn't see any signs of a person or a vehicle *that morning*. But Barringer's body could have been removed anytime during the night, or even the day before. How was it done without disturbing the grass? Simple. It wasn't. It was just made to look as if it was.

"And another thing: Don't assume that Smith's telling the truth. Maybe he is, but people lie all the time. Maybe Smith needs to protect himself or somebody else. Maybe Smith is shielding his friend Bartikowski, who knows? Or maybe he or Bartikowski was paid to look the other way. Maybe someone else, one of the night patrols, was paid to look the other way when the body was taken out."

"I didn't think of any of that," Sam admitted.

Bear raised an eyebrow. "How long have you been an investigator?"

Sam's eyes slid away from Bear and stared at the water in her cup. "Not all that long." She glanced up at him, but only briefly before regarding the room beyond his shoulder as she misled him about her experience. "Not for the agency, I mean. I was working for the Foreign Service in Iraq for the past year. Stationed over there."

"So how did you end up with the agency?"

Sam moved one shoulder dismissively and made her voice sound as casual as possible. "Better offer. You know how it is. Anyway the things I worked on in the Foreign Service weren't anything like this."

Bear nodded. "There you have it. I think that's your mistake."

"What mistake?"

"I mean you're looking at this case differently than any other crime, any other theft or homicide you worked on."

"But this one *is* different, now, isn't it?" She dared to look at him directly and found him watching her as if she were a piece of cake and he was very hungry.

"I don't think it's any different," he said, and stood up in a fluid motion that Sam enjoyed witnessing. "Think about it. What pushes people to be violent or devious? Those basic motives are timeless. Human nature doesn't change. The circumstances of the crime vary, but the big picture—since the beginning of humans walking the earth—the big picture is always the same. Love or hate, greed or desire for power. That's what it's always about."

"You think so?" Sam conceded that he might have a point.

"I *know* so. Nothing, not one case I ever worked on, has made me doubt it." Bear was silent a moment. Sam sipped from her paper cup of water, finishing it, then looked around for a place to set it down.

"Here, let me have that." Bear reached over and took it from her, then reached his arm high to lob it into a wastebasket. "Two points," he crowed, and smiled at her.

She smiled back, and there they were, grinning at each other again.

"You know," he said, his voice low, "before you leave, I'd better give you my contact information." He pulled his wallet from his back pocket and took out a business card. "I'll put my home address and phone number on the back." He picked up a pen from the nearby desk. As he wrote, he said, "If anything comes up, call me. I mean that. Day or night." He handed the card over to her.

Sam took it, then pulled her Post-it pad and pen from her purse. She held the pen poised over the yellow square. "I don't have a new business card made up yet. My U.S. Foreign Service one won't help. But I guess I'm going to be living back in Bel Air, Maryland. That's where I grew up.

"My parents live in Tucson now. They signed over the house to me before they moved. It was a perfect arrangement for them. They have a place to stay when they come back east to visit. I get to keep the home I always loved. They said I'd get it anyway, but it was really great of them. I just left all my stuff there when I got stationed overseas—"

She had said more than she meant to. She felt flustered and wrote quickly to cover her feelings. She pulled the sticky note from the pad and handed it over. "Anyway, here's the phone number and address in Bel Air."

Bear took the yellow square of paper, folded it, and put it in his wallet. He was looking at her again. "I don't know what time you're going to be free, but if you're up to it, we can go grab some dinner together." His face reddened and he added quickly, "That way I can fill you in on whatever I find out this afternoon."

Sam found that her heart was racing; she didn't expect this. "Uhhhh . . . I don't know, but, uhhh . . ."

Bear's eyes narrowed and lost their warmth. He was clearly annoyed—at himself or her, she didn't know.

"Hey, it was just a suggestion. Forget it," he said, and turned away. The connection between them snapped.

Disappointment swept over her, as if she had glimpsed the pony promised for Christmas but was told she couldn't have it. She knew it would be a big mistake to see more of this man. She definitely didn't want to have feelings for him. And yet—she wanted to see him tonight. She opened her mouth to tell him she'd try to make it, when the secretary stuck her head through the door again.

"Your car's here, Ms. Chase."

17

OUTSIDE the building, heat shimmering in waves above the asphalt of the parking lot, the Lincoln Town Car was nowhere in sight. Instead Ms. Z sat behind the wheel of a long white van, like the ones that D.C. hotels used to pick up guests at the airport. Through the dark-tinted glass, Sam could see luggage piled in the back of the vehicle. Another passenger sat in the second row of seats.

Bear walked over to the driver's side and rapped on the window with his knuckles. Ms. Z lowered it. He handed over the video memory cards and began saying whatever it was he had to say to her.

Leaving them to their conversation, Sam walked around the front of the van. She spotted Rina coming toward her.

"Good timing," Sam said to her. "Our ride just got here."

Rina nodded. "Kennedy says Oswald didn't act alone. But all the conspirators are dead. He's okay with it."

Nonplussed, Sam blinked. "Oh . . . that's good to know." They stood together outside the van, *together* being a relative term. Rina made sure she didn't get too close. Sam figured Rina's preferred "personal space" was around a mile.

Rina didn't indulge in small talk either. "Should we both sit in the back?" Sam asked after an awkward moment of silence.

"I sure as hell don't want to sit next to the dragon lady." Rina slid open the rear door, gave a little nod to the passenger in the second row, and chose to climb into the empty third row of seats.

Next Sam ducked into the cool interior of the van and slid onto the middle row, next to the woman she had spotted through the glass.

"Hi," the woman inside the vehicle said. Her fair skin, sharp nose, and dark red hair tumbling in wild curls around her shoulders spoke of Celtic ancestors. She sat huddled toward the far door, pulled into herself with arms tight against her body. She looked less like a volunteer than a prisoner. "I'm Frances Corey. Call me Frankie." Her eyes seemed frightened. She loosened up enough to extend a small hand toward Sam.

"I'm Susan Chase. And you can call me Sam," Sam said, and exchanged a brief handshake.

Frankie gave Sam a long look. "I didn't see you at the Rhine Research Center tests. Rina and I met there, didn't we, Rina?"

"Yeah," the gruff voice came from behind them. Sam glanced back. Rina had slouched down in the seat, her eyes turned toward the window. The women all fell quiet.

"I'm from Salem, Massachusetts." Frankie, unable to handle silence, spoke nervously. "The place where they burned the witches. But not all of them, of course." She made a sound that came out between a laugh and a sob. "I'm a witch, and I'm still alive."

Sam wasn't sure what kind of response she should make to that extraordinary announcement. The woman evidently was another member of AngelWay. Was Frankie Corey going to be as strange as Rina? she wondered, but what she said was, "That's interesting, I guess."

"I suppose it is. Interesting." Frankie paused and glanced at the back of Ms. Z's head, as if to check whether the woman was listening. Then, like an uncoiling spring, Frankie's words spewed out, an outlet for her clear anxiety. "To tell the truth, most people don't take us seriously. They figure Wicca is just a feminist thing. Celebrating the power of the female. In a way it is, but that power can—" She cut off the words, changing her mind about finishing the thought.

"I never really thought about it, spells and black magic, that kind of thing," Sam murmured, more interested in hearing the conversation going on between Ms. Z and Bear. She couldn't catch every word, but Bear's voice was angry; she could tell that much.

Not seeming to notice Sam's lack of attention, Frankie said loudly, "*Black* magic? Absolutely not!" She anxiously glanced again in Ms. Z's direction. "I only practice *white* magic. It's dangerous to call on demons or evil spirits. But Rina and I don't see eye-to-eye on that, do we, Rina?"

"You got that right," Rina muttered.

"Where are you from?" Frankie, determined to carry on a conversation, asked Sam.

Sam let go of her efforts to eavesdrop on Bear and turned toward the woman. "Iraq. At least, that's where I was just stationed. I grew up in Maryland, a town called Bel Air. Typical suburbia. It's maybe an hour from here."

"Why, you're practically back home. You married?"

"No. Never been," Sam said, not entirely happy with Frankie's probing.

"Me neither." Sadness washed over Frankie's face. "But then again, being a witch doesn't make it easy to have relationships."

"I'm sure it doesn't," she agreed. *Hiding a big secret doesn't make it easy to have a relationship either.* Sam stole another look at Bear. As far as she could tell, he hadn't glanced her way even once.

"You can say that again." Frankie's fingers nervously picked at the strap of the seat belt.

"I can relate to that," Sam said, and then she was back to staring out the window at Bear.

A heavy sigh came from the seat behind them. "Men are trouble. But if you want one so bad, just cast one of your love spells on him and stop your whining."

"I would *never* do that, not for myself." Frankie's face looked frightened again.

"Save it for the judge," the unpleasant voice from the backseat said, then fell silent again.

Frankie sucked on her teeth as if stifling her anger.

She cocked her head toward the rear of the vehicle. "Rina, here, she's from Savannah; she's a Southern girl, though you'd never know it from her manners."

Sam swiveled her head to look at the prickly young woman in the third seat.

Rina's eyes, as blue and hard as marbles, stared back at Sam. Then Rina leaned forward, laying her thin arms on the back of the seat. She put her face close to Sam's and whispered, "I am a voodoo priestess down there. So remember, don't fuck with the Blue-eyed Snake."

Sam's body jerked away.

Frankie shook her head in disapproval at Rina's behavior. "I embrace the light. Rina here is in touch with the dark forces."

"How the hell do you know?" Rina said. Then she sat back, putting space between herself and the others again.

But this time Ms. Z had finished her exchange with Bear and raised the window. Sam watched as he stepped back from the van. Bear turned abruptly and headed back to the building, his walk stiff and angry. He never once looked back at Sam as the van pulled away.

"I take it you've introduced yourselves," Ms. Z said, talking to the three women but keeping her eyes forward to watch the road. The van left the grounds of the cemetery, but instead of going over the bridge into the heart of Washington, Ms. Z went north, following a route along the Potomac. The river's surface reflected the bright sunlight. The trees along the way were still. Not even a breeze disturbed the stifling heat.

"One of your team is still missing. She'll be joining you soon. She's coming from— It doesn't matter. All of you have traveled some distance to get here. As much as we would prefer you spend today on the current case, I realize you need some time to settle in and get some rest."

Sam leaned her head back on the seat, closed her eyes, and thought, *Amen to that.*

"You can have until tomorrow morning to get your personal things in order. Right now, let me clarify some housekeeping details and set up your working schedule."

Frankie moved in the seat and said in a voice so low

only Sam could hear it, "Do you think she's human or a robot?"

"Robot," Sam whispered back without opening her eyes.

Ms. Z continued talking. "Number one. Martus, listen up. There's a package on the floor next to you. Open it and pass out the contents. Each item is marked with a name."

Sam heard the rustling of packaging being removed. She figured naptime was over and sat up. Dizziness overtook her for a moment. Jet lag had her in its teeth and was rattling her brain. Her energy reserves were registering empty. All she wanted to do was get back to Bel Air and into her own bed. She hoped it would be soon.

"BlackBerries," Rina announced as she passed a clear plastic bag to Sam and another to Frankie. "There's one bag left, marked 'Daybreak,' " she said.

"That's correct," Ms. Z glanced in the rearview mirror quickly. "It's for your other team member. Make sure she gets it."

Sam slipped the BlackBerry from the plastic bag that was labeled with her name. The bag also contained a battery charger and a belt clip.

Ms. Z was speaking again. "Pay attention, all of you. I say things once. Keep these devices with you at all times. Before you ask, yes, even when you sleep. Put it under your pillow, on a bedstand, whatever. You must never be out of contact; do you understand? Say, 'Yes, ma'am, if you do."

Three voices in chorus: "Yes, ma'am."

"I am number one on the speed dial. If I am contacting you, this is the sound you'll hear."

All the phones rang then, playing "The William Tell Overture." It stopped abruptly. Sam resisted the impulse to roll her eyes.

Ms. Z went on. "If you take the time to go over the device's menu, you'll find that each of you has a speed-dial number and a distinctive ring tone. You are to use these devices—*and only these devices*—for all communication with one another and with me. Both text messaging and voice links are encrypted. Security is vital. Do you understand?"

Three voices in chorus again: "Yes, ma'am."

"We've also programmed in some other special functions, including complete GPS capabilities. I'll talk more about them as the need arises. Now, let me get on to something else. For this mission, Agent Chase will be the team leader. She's an experienced government employee and knows how to work within the bureaucracy. Go to her first with a problem or request. She'll bring it to me."

Sam cringed. *Oh, goody, I'm den mother. That should be lots of fun.*

"That brings up the matters of your employment status and living accommodations. This project and you women are on probation. If it doesn't work, if any of you don't work, it will be terminated in exactly one month. If you solve the case before us right now, in all likelihood AngelWay will be given a permanent structure."

Like I care, Sam thought, clouds of fatigue swirling through her brain.

"So we feel, in all fairness to those of you who will be relocating, that until the probation period is over, it is best that you live together, with your team leader—"

What? Sam bolted upright, her eyes wide. "With me?" she blurted out. Sam couldn't believe this.

"—with your team leader in Bel Air, Maryland. She owns a large home there; it is currently unoccupied, and you can easily commute by car or train. Besides that, you will not physically report to Langley on a daily basis. For the most part, you'll be working in the field."

"How can you possibly—" Sam began.

Ms. Z's sharp voice cut her off. "This is not a request, Agent Chase. You will be compensated for any expenses incurred. It is a temporary solution only, so suck it up and soldier on."

Sam slammed her mouth closed. Those were her father's words. She didn't think Ms. Z's use of the phrase was a coincidence. It was a reminder that the agency had vetted her well, and they didn't play fair.

18

AFTER her announcement that the women would be living with Sam, Ms. Z said she wanted to know what they had learned at the cemetery so she could decide how to proceed. Sam started to say that Rodney Smith had given them some new information that wasn't in the report when Ms. Z cut off Sam midsentence.

With impatience like a sharpened knife, Ms. Z snapped, "Look, Chase. I don't give a rat's ass about what Mr. Smith said. You need to get something straight. You're *not* a criminal investigator. That's your *cover story*. Get it? The agency has plenty of *trained* forensic people. That's not your job. Your job—the reason we have you here—is to use your *psychic* abilities to tell us what the forensic people can't.

"So what I want to know, without any more bullshit, is what did you *see* there? What did your gift of 'sight' show you? What did your voices tell you? Bottom line, do you know where the body is? Do you know how it was removed from the grave? That's what we need to know. That's *all* we need to know."

Sam went rigid. "No." She practically spat out the word. "No. The answer to both your questions is no. I didn't get any messages 'from the beyond.' I told you it doesn't work like that with me. I don't know anything." Even while she spoke she was thinking, *What am I supposed to say? That the voices of the dead deafened me and pummeled me with sorrow? That I saw gray shadows in the air? That I sensed evil?*

Sam had never discussed things like that with anyone.

She wasn't starting now. She went completely silent. Then help came from an unexpected quarter.

Reclining in the rear seat, Rina, her voice lazy, almost insolent, spoke up. "So you want answers from the dead? The dead have to *want* to talk to you, Ms. Z. But this guy Barringer was gone. I say that he left that grave himself. I don't even know if he's really dead. His soul is no place. I got nothing from him."

Sam could see Ms. Z's hands tighten on the steering wheel. She saw the tension in the woman's shoulders. "You have no idea where this body is? You're both telling me that neither of you knows anything yet?"

Rina leaned forward, putting her arms on the back of Sam's seat again. Her face jutted forward until it was between Sam's and Frankie's again, but this time Sam thought she detected just the briefest hint of a smile. Then Rina gave her a quick wink and started talking. "Ms. Z, *I* know this: that the guy left the grave, left his coffin, on his own. Nobody dug him out. Somebody called him out of there. *I'm* telling you it's bad mojo. What we call Petro voodoo. Conjuring up the dead."

"Who called him? How did they do it? Why were the heart and brains left behind? Can you tell me that?" Ms. Z spoke as if her teeth were clenched.

"Ha!" The word burst forth from Rina, and her breath again brushed Sam's ear. Sam turned her head just a little, so she could see Rina's eyes closing and her head starting to move from side to side.

Frankie Corey saw it too. Fear had invaded her eyes again. Her hand reached over and grabbed Sam's. It was cold. It squeezed Sam's hard.

Then Rina, her eyes shut, her features slack, began to speak in a singsong, in a patois that wasn't her own voice: "Maman Z, Maman Z, dat is so eee-zee. Dat is what a chile knows. De dead that walk, dey no need no brain. De dead that walk, dey no need no heart. Dey come for yours!" Then she let out a cackle of a laugh that chilled Sam's blood.

* * *

Rina's performance ended all conversation between Ms. Z and the rest of them until the van pulled into the driveway of the worn-out, avocado green split-level where Sam had grown up. The vintage 1950s construction with its faux-stone front, single-car garage, and wide lawn sat placidly under tall sycamore trees on Jackson Boulevard in Bel Air, Maryland.

This was home. It had always been home for Sam—her comfort zone. And now, just when she wanted nothing more than to go in, fill up the tub, soak, then fall into bed, she had uninvited guests who weren't going to leave for a month. Thirty-one days. A new taste of bitterness camped out in Sam's heart and drove in stakes to tie down its tent.

Ms. Z stopped the van, but left it running. She turned around and snapped at the three women, "Get your stuff out of here. I'll send a car out for you tomorrow. Be ready at nine."

Sam was so tired she felt as if her feet were encased in cement when she emerged from the backseat. The heat immediately got her in a choke hold. She heard the sound of a basketball bouncing on a driveway not far away. She wondered how anybody could be shooting baskets in temperatures topping one hundred degrees.

She herself had no strength left. She went to retrieve her carry-on, which had been stowed with the other women's luggage in the rear of the van. She opened the cargo door and stared at the pile of luggage.

Rina reached in and took out one small soft-sided bag. Sam grabbed her carry-on. The three remaining large suitcases, a knapsack, and a Tote Along had to belong to Frankie. "I was told to bring my equipment," Frankie said apologetically. Despite her fatigue, Sam felt she had to offer to help her carry the baggage, but the one suitcase she pulled from the cargo space had to weigh over sixty pounds.

Rina spoke then. "If you can handle that big one, Frankie and I can take the rest. I think the dragon lady wants to get out of here."

So Sam struggled up the walk with Frankie's bag and her own, put her key in the front door, and walked back into the home she had left a year ago. The two women followed her inside. None of them bothered to watch Ms. Z gun the van, back quickly out of the driveway, and take off down the street as if the devil were chasing her.

Inside the bright, airy house, the air smelled like lemon Pledge. Everything was immaculately clean. A friend of Sam's mother's who lived nearby had taken on the job of caretaker while Sam was in Iraq. Sam's reliable Toyota Corolla would be in the garage, kept in working order too.

But something was different. Something had changed since Sam had left. A pall of some kind seemed to hover over everything. Sam immediately thought it must be herself, not the house, that had been irrevocably altered. Maybe she couldn't believe anyplace could be a sanctuary anymore.

She paused to take everything in. A large living room sat to Sam's right. The carpet was a leftover 1970s shag, but it held the grand piano where Sam's father liked to play Broadway hits while her mother sang. A comfortable chintz-covered couch sat in front of a large bow window. The stairs to the second floor stretched upward directly in front of her.

Framed photos covered the wall on the way to the second floor: Sam toothless at seven next to a pony; Sam joyful in a white uniform accepting her black belt from her sensei; Sam unsmiling in a strapless prom dress; Sam sober-faced in cap and gown. Then came a larger photo of her and her father, both grinning, each of them holding a rifle in one hand and holding up a trophy for marksmanship in the other. Her dad was known as one of the best shots in the world; he had qualified for the Olympics that year. Her parents' wedding photo hung there too, next to a large portrait of her father in his dress uniform. But the pictures looked jumbled, all hanging crookedly, not perfectly squared like they used to be.

That's strange, Sam thought.

"It's a lot like my parents' house." Frankie said.

"I didn't change anything when my folks moved to Arizona. It's badly in need of some upgrades," Sam explained, and walked straight ahead into the small kitchen. There would be no food in the refrigerator, but she could run out to the supermarket later—if she had the energy, if she could even lift her head off the pillow once she got it there. She dropped her house keys on the table.

Something tapped Sam on the shoulder. Startled, Sam whirled around. "Oh!" she cried out.

Rina had slipped noiselessly into the room right behind her. "I didn't mean to frighten you. I wanted to say I'm sorry."

"Sorry? For what?"

"For us intruding on you, in your home and all. I'll stay out of your way. I'd get my own place, but they won't let us. I know; I asked."

Sam noticed then that Rina, if one looked beyond the Texas-size chip on her shoulder, was only about her own age. She also had a supermodel's body that she hid under her drab clothes, and was really quite pretty.

Sam suddenly felt bad about her earlier annoyance and unkind thoughts. Rina must have sensed that Sam didn't want the other women there. It wasn't their fault, after all. They didn't choose to move in with her.

"It's okay." She managed a wobbly smile. "It wouldn't make sense for you to get your own place if this whole thing falls through. I understand."

Rina looked at Sam with those strange blue eyes of hers. "No, I don't think you do. You bought that story Ms. Z told?"

"What do you mean?"

"They didn't send Frankie and me here to do *us* a favor, or save themselves a few dollars. Hell, the Defense Department and Homeland Security have *billions* in their budgets. They could have put us up at a Residence Inn for a month, now, couldn't they?"

"So why are they insisting you live here, then?" Uneasiness sent cold fingers across Sam's skin.

"Because they think our living together will put us in synch. Make our powers stronger. You know, like women in a dormitory. Their menstrual cycles get the same. There's been research that putting us all together will intensify 'the sight,' as they call it."

"Rina's right, you know." Frankie's worried voice came from where she was standing in the doorway. "They recruited us because they need us. They know what we can do, but we're not *people* to them. We're tools to be used. They'll push us until we break if we're not careful. I mean, I'm only here because they . . ." She hesitated. "Never mind that . . . but we need to watch each other's backs. Be sisters, you know? We've all got to hang together, as they say."

"Or we'll all hang separately," Sam finished.

Rina nodded. "You got that right."

19

THE board convened their meeting in a lovely home in the best section of Georgetown. The smell of fine Scotch mixed with the smoke from expensive cigars. There were five members of the cabal, besides the balding man. All were businessmen. All were well respected in the community. All had friends in high places—in fact, most of them currently were or recently had been in those high places themselves.

One board member had resigned a few years ago from a spot as the assistant secretary of defense. Another had been an adviser to the Joint Chiefs of Staff and left to form a Pentagon think tank. Another had had a position at NASA before moving on to run a large aircraft corporation.

They all knew the true worth of this "scheme," as their chairman, the balding man, had called it. The billions being made by Halliburton would look like chump change compared to the profits they'd realize. And once they had succeeded they'd possess the biggest oil reserves in the Middle East. They could drive up the prices to five hundred dollars a barrel overnight. And the U.S. would pay. It would have to pay. The economic future of America would be in their hands.

Better than money, this small group of ruthless men would have power. The special soldiers they were creating—killing machines that could not be killed—would let them conquer a small country. But that primitive backwater land was just a beginning. A trial run. A practice for toppling the next government, the true object of this sweet endeavor—the Saudis. Then the board and their minions would build an empire, and who knew? Armed strength coupled with the paralyzing effects of terror had spawned grandiose plans and even bigger dreams.

The board could potentially conquer the world.

Naturally there had been a cost, which they all saw as an investment: the cash wadded together and put in paper bags that went to the right people . . .the flights south to the Caribbean . . . the experiments that hadn't worked and resulted in some unfortunate mishaps that had to be hushed up.

But they all knew that enough money could hush up *anything.*

As for the risk involved . . . for some men with enough connections, the risks were always small. They had all agreed from the beginning: Nothing great was ever achieved without audacity, cunning, and the willingness to gamble everything on one world-changing plan. But stacking the deck put the odds in their favor.

"Gentlemen." The chairman in his Hawaiian shirt with its cheerful blue parrots stood and lifted his glass of single-malt, and its amber color gleamed in the lamp-light. "I wish to report our first success. You might say we have raised the dead. Or at least have learned to use them!"

"Hear, hear!" They clinked their glasses together.

"We should have completed phase one. Charles, we shall have to begin using your warehouse in Virginia tomorrow night. Is it prepared?"

"Of course." Charles had a long, patrician face and he wore a blue pin-striped Savile Row suit.

Then the chairman turned to the man on his right. "Arthur, how is damage control going?"

A wide roll of neck fat made Arthur look as if his head rested on a large kielbasa sausage. He picked up a napkin and dabbed the perspiration forming on his upper lip. "Splendidly. The agency still can find no evidence of how the body was removed or where it might be. I understand they have resorted to a new undercover team, all rookies. They're supposedly experts in microexpressions and fraud detection, something way off the mark, if my sources are correct."

"Excellent. The DOD is also investigating, of course, but the officer assigned to it is convinced this is a mere grave robbery, although one with a rather arcane motive. No one suspects the truth, or anything remotely like the truth."

"And how could they?" the eldest of the men interjected. Age had dulled all the passions of this shaky octogenarian whose head wobbled with Parkinson's, except his love of power. "The truth would not be believable, now, would it? By the time they must believe it, it will be too late."

Arthur blotted more sweat from his lips. "But we do have a small loose end."

"And what is that?" the chairman snapped, not pleased.

"The 'film crew' has been caught by the video surveillance cameras."

"That won't do. That will not do at all. You will take care of this, won't you, Arthur?"

Arthur nodded and reached for his water glass. "Absolutely. What do you want me to do with them?"

The balding chairman waved his hand impatiently. "Send them over to the Bokor tomorrow. He knows how to take loose ends and"—he made a scissors motion with his index and middle fingers—"snip."

20

FOR a little more than two hours Sam slept the sleep of the innocent, undisturbed by dreams for most of the time, although in one she remembered vividly a large black bear stood up on his hind legs and rang the doorbell to her house. She awoke to the bright sunshine of a Maryland summer afternoon filled with the sounds of songbirds, not artillery fire. Her heart felt lighter. Despite her earlier uneasiness about the house, the feeling had passed. Even though she wasn't completely rested, she was no longer mentally numb and swaying on her feet.

Earlier in the day, before she had staggered into her room and collapsed onto the bed, she showed the other women the three empty bedrooms. She told them to decide between them which one they wanted. Sam's room had its own bathroom, but there was another full bath up here on the second floor. A half bath sat off the kitchen. Another full bath adjoined what her parents always called the "recreation room" or the "rec room." Today's Realtors would call it a family room, with its fireplace and television.

One thing Ms. Z got right: The split-level had plenty of space for all the women. Once again Sam decided to accept what she couldn't change.

Too exhausted to bathe before she slept, Sam now took a long, leisurely shower, washing away the last of Iraq from her body and soul. Afterward she toweled off and rummaged around in the clothes she had left behind before her Iraq tour. She pulled shorts and a halter top from a dresser drawer. Barefoot, she padded downstairs, feeling cleansed and whole. She met Rina and Frankie in the kitchen.

"I found cans of soup in the cupboard," Frankie told her. "Hope you don't mind, but Rina and I just had some. How about some classic tomato? You must be famished."

"Sure," Sam said, and started toward the cupboard.

"Uh, uh, uh," Frankie said, and blocked her way. "I owned a catering business back in Salem. I'm a bona fide chef. I graduated from the CIA—oh, not *the* CIA; I mean the Culinary Institute of America. I'm a sommelier too. That's why it's so hard to keep these pounds off."

Sam looked at the woman, who wasn't in the least bit obese, but rounded in an appealing way. "You're not heavy," Sam said.

Frankie sighed. "Thanks for saying that. I guess I look for excuses for always ending up alone. When I am honest about being a witch, it either scares men away or they get turned on by it. I'm always between a rock and a hard place. Do I tell? Don't I tell? Do I lie? Don't I lie?" She put the pot on the stove. "There I am, rattling on about men again. Sorry. But you're hungry, and the least I can do is cook for you—even if it's just condensed soup. You sit down at the table and it will be ready in a minute."

Sam took her usual chair, the one that let her look out the window at the backyard deck with the bird feeder hanging over the forsythia bush and the redwood patio set surrounded by four Adirondack chairs. It was a view that remained exactly the same as it had always been, but shadows lurked out there that Sam didn't remember, and a strange darkness lay over the lawn and trees.

Sam sighed. She realized that her life, so recently shattered like glass, might never be put back together.

"Thirsty?" Rina said, motioning toward a pitcher of iced tea, its sides frosty, that sat on the kitchen table. She pushed a glass toward Sam. Sam took it as Rina's way of being friendly. "Frankie also found some Lipton tea bags. I picked some mint out in the back garden. Have some. It's sweet tea, Southern-style."

The tea was icy cold and delicious. Sam drank one glass and poured another. She glanced over at the new resident cook. "I do believe I am starved."

Frankie smiled a rather sweet, sad smile. "Remember I also can also conjure up spells. That's where my interest in cooking began. You know, 'eye of newt and toe of frog' recipes and all. And I can fly—"

"Yeah, she can fly," Rina interrupted, "after she's had a couple of bottles of that wine she likes so much."

"Can't you ever be nice, Ms. Rina Martus?" Frankie's voice held an undercurrent of pain as she rapped her ladle sharply against the rim of the pot she had on the stove.

"Don't know. Never really tried to be. I'd rather be honest," Rina said, her face serious.

Sam didn't know if the voodoo priestess was kidding or not.

Sam was halfway through her bowl of soup, jazzed up with spices that Frankie had brought with her so that it didn't taste like the canned stuff at all, when the doorbell rang. She put down her spoon. "I'd better answer it. It might be my mother's friend who's been watching the house."

But it wasn't. Outside the front door stood a short girl wearing a fierce look on her face. Long black hair, damp from perspiration, clung to her temples and hung lankly down her back. Her cheekbones were high, suggesting a Native American heritage, as did her dark eyes. In her thin arms the woman was carrying two bulging paper grocery bags with DAYBREAK 981-41608 UNIT B written in bold, slashing black Magic Marker on each one. On the woman's shoulder sat a big orange tabby cat wearing a collar and a leash.

To the question Sam had not yet asked, the woman answered, "I'm Aurora Daybreak. Part of your team. Sorry I'm so late, but something went wrong with the paperwork, and they weren't going to let me out of jail."

"Oh," Sam said. She stared at the cat. The cat stared back with green, unblinking eyes.

"Then, of course, I had to go pick up Miranda. Friends of mine were taking care of her while I was inside, you see."

"Oh," Sam repeated, then recovered enough from her surprise to remember her manners. "I'm Susan Chase. Call me Sam. You'd better come inside." The newcomer stepped into the coolness of the hallway and trailed behind Sam to the kitchen.

"It's our other teammate," Sam announced.

"Daybreak," Rina noted, looking at the grocery bags.

"That's me. In Tsalgi—you'd call it Cherokee—my name is Ug-it-sis-gu Nu-da. Dawn Sun." The girl's words were musical and foreign. "My English name is Aurora Daybreak, which is close enough." Her mouth was generous, her nose small. "If you're all wondering about Miranda. I'm an animal communicator. Miranda helps."

"I see. She's a familiar." Frankie had been leaning her backside against the counter. She stood upright and put out her hand. "I'm Frankie Corey. A Wiccan."

"Pleased to meet you," Aurora said, setting the paper bags down on the floor and shaking Frankie's hand.

Meanwhile Rina was studying Miranda. The cat's green eyes surveyed Rina, narrowing as they did. Then the animal politely jumped from her perch on Aurora over to Rina's shoulder. The cat rubbed her head once against Rina's cheekbone, then purred.

"Sit down and have some iced tea," Frankie offered. "Tell us a little about yourself."

Aurora sank down in a chair and her body sagged, her fatigue obvious. "Thanks. Tea would be great. And you'll have to fill me in on what's going on. I guess all of you are psychics, because that's why they let me out of prison. To be part of this psi project. I have a 'gift,' as the agency put it. They should know. They used what people said about me to track me down." She sighed deeply and went on.

"I do have a gift. I made a living at it when I was on the outside. Mostly people hired me to find things, missing persons or lost pets. Mostly lost animals." Aurora's voice was thin, almost childlike.

"I hope you can find a missing corpse," Sam quipped, and sat back down. She returned to her tomato soup.

"I'll look for used dental floss as long as it keeps me from being locked up," Aurora answered.

Frankie started searching through the cupboard. "You want some canned soup? I think there's still some chicken noodle."

"Can't. I'm vegetarian. Have to walk the walk as well as talk the talk. I believe in animal rights. Like Rina."

Sam raised her eyebrows. "So you two know each other?"

Aurora shook her head. "Uh-uh, I never met any of you before now."

No one spoke for a minute. Frankie recovered first and laughed. "Well, if you're really psychic, you'd know Rina is no animal-rights activist. She's a voodoo priestess. They practice blood sacrifice."

Rina looked away from the group and focused on the wall opposite her. She spoke in her blunt, harsh voice. "You assume a lot. And you don't know anything about me. I don't kill. I won't kill. The dead, human and animal, call out to me for justice. I try to give it them. There is no blood on my hands."

"Of course not." Aurora's voice was kind.

Rina's head snapped in Aurora's direction. "But there is on yours."

The new woman's shoulders sagged, her eyes looked down at the table, and her wide-jawed face became suffused with a grief-stricken sorrow. "I know. But it was all a mistake."

Rina offered no mercy. "If you're looking for sympathy, you can find it in the dictionary right between *shit* and *syphilis*. You killed him. He's just as dead, whether you meant to or not."

Aurora lifted her dark, sad eyes to Rina's. "Don't you think I know that? But . . ." Her face hardened, and she glared at Rina with defiance. "I can't change what happened. I did what I had to do. You of all people should understand that."

Sam watched Rina's pale white hand reach up and gently stroke the orange marmalade cat's fur. The cat began to purr loudly. For the first time since Sam had met her, she saw Rina smile. When she did her face became achingly beautiful. "Yeah, you got that right," Rina said.

A short while later the four women piled into Sam's Toyota, drove to the supermarket, and bought an enormous amount of food at Klein's on Main Street. They stopped for toiletries at CVS. They avoided discussing anything personal during the ride, although Sam wondered if any of the other women had been blackmailed into joining AngelWay, as she had.

Back at the house they dispersed to put away their items; then they all gathered again in the kitchen and sat down at the table.

"I have something to say," Frankie said. Tension pulled at her face; the fear was back in her eyes. "A couple of things, actually," she continued. "First, I need to talk to you, Sam. It's about this house. Something's been here, a presence, and it's not good."

Dread grabbed Sam's heart. The negative sensations hadn't been her imagination. "What do you mean?" she choked out.

"I'm not sure what to tell you, except that as soon as I stepped inside I felt the trace of it, whatever it was. What about you, Rina?"

"Yeah, I felt it. I think somebody put a curse on this place—or had a spell for harm put against the owner. Somebody who lived here made a bad enemy, I'd say." Rina wore a leather cord around her neck. She lifted it to show the small pouch that had been hidden under her shirt. "Gris-gris. To protect me."

Frankie closed her eyes for a minute, then looked at Sam. "I'd like your permission to burn some sage, do a cleansing. It's not a long-term solution, but it will help. Okay?"

"Sure, of course. But do you know what this 'presence' could be?"

Frankie looked down at her hands for a moment and took a deep breath. "No. It could be . . . I don't really know. Like Rina said, evil sent to do harm? I think we all need to be cautious and alert. Aurora, you doing okay?"

Aurora had been staring down at the table during this exchange. Now, when she raised them, her eyes revealed a shrewdness belied by her childlike demeanor. "I'm always okay. I have Miranda."

Sam wasn't sure what that meant, but the cat swished its tail as it sat on the woman's lap.

"Now to my next point," Frankie continued. "We all could use a good night's sleep, but it's not even dinnertime yet. We need to do some work."

"What kind of work?" Aurora's words sounded like a chirping bird.

"Exercise our talents. Ms. Z laid down the law on our way up here. We need to provide some information on the case. That's the work I'm talking about."

"I'm ready." Aurora spoke again in her piping, melodious voice. "I have too much to lose to waste time. If we fail, I'm going back to prison. I'd rather be dead. I really would. What do you have in mind?"

Frankie obviously had a plan ready, as she spoke quickly. "I want to use some of my equipment; after all, I dragged it with me all the way from Salem. I'll try some scrying—that's a reading with my crystal ball. Sam, don't look so skeptical. I actually have one. It's how I concentrate. Focus. I find it effective.

"With all of us together maybe our power *will* be stronger. We can see if anything or anyone comes through. That's what I can do. What do you use to help you find things, Aurora?"

"Something that belonged to the person is best. Without that, I can look at a map of the city where the object might be. That's worked for me before."

"I throw bones." Rina slouched down in her chair and stared into space, avoiding everybody's eyes.

They all looked at Sam expectantly.

What should I tell? How much should I tell? Her mind raced. "Me? I . . . I . . . see things that are happening someplace else."

"You do remote viewing. That's terrific." Frankie sounded like an encouraging parent after a tone-deaf child's piano lesson.

"I don't know how terrific it is. I never tried to see anything specific. The visions just come to me. I don't think I'm going to be much help." Anxiety squeezed Sam's chest. She was talking about things she had never discussed with anyone. And she was standing in her own kitchen with three strangers who claimed they could do things most of the world didn't believe were real.

She wasn't sure she believed any of it herself. Maybe she was just crazy. Maybe they were all deluded. Her breaths became shallow. She felt light-headed. "I don't know if I can do this," she blurted out.

"Sit! I'm going to make you some more iced tea," Frankie ordered. She got busy running water into the kettle and talked while she worked. "Listen, we all have our doubts. But you wouldn't have been brought into this program if you weren't incredibly gifted. You're feeling the pressure; that's all. And you went into the cemetery today. That was very brave. I don't know if I could have done it."

Sam put her face in her hands. She was trembling and on the verge of tears. She struggled for control. She was usually so strong. She let the waves of emotions pass and finally looked out the window at the backyard deck, trying to find comfort in familiar things that had suddenly become less familiar and somehow touched by evil.

"I feel overwhelmed," she said at last. "It's just that . . . everything's happened so fast. Two days ago I was in Iraq. Now I'm home in Bel Air, Maryland. My career is over. Gone. I've been treated like a criminal. I've been threatened. I don't really know what the hell I'm into—this investigation, I mean—but parts of it scare me to death."

"Like what?" Frankie had been pouring water into a pitcher. Now she looked at Sam, anxiety clear in her eyes.

"Rina knows, but you, Frankie, and you, Aurora, don't. At the cemetery Rina and I found out something that Ms. Z didn't tell us, something crazy. The park police guy who got to the grave first said the heart and brains in the coffin were still alive, or . . . or at least they were *moving*. The heart was beating and bloody. I believe him."

The women stared at her, and there was no sound, as if no one dared to breathe. Then Frankie said, "It sounds like magic. Animation. Evil stuff."

Sam nodded. "Evil. I felt that so strongly there. It terrifies me. This *all* scares me."

"You're not the only one to feel fear. I know I do." To Sam's surprise, it was Rina who spoke, her gravelly voice almost gentle. She stood up and moved to the doorway, apart from the others. The cat walked over and rubbed against her legs. "Look at us four. We live with witchcraft, voodoo, and nightmares. We struggle with dark powers other people don't even see. But we have to remember what's stronger than the strange things that are scaring you. That are scaring me. Remember what it is that you have inside you."

"What's that?" Sam asked.

"Light. Everything you can do, everything you can see comes from that place. Not from evil. See with the eye of the heart. Your gift of sight comes from love. From the great Bondye. From light."

21

THEY didn't discuss the cemetery after that, at least not then. Frankie said they all had a lot to think about, but the cleansing couldn't wait. Then, her auburn curls dancing around her head like flames, she went from room to room with bundles of smoldering sage. She moved slowly and deliberately, like a priestess performing an ancient ritual. Sometimes her hand shook and the sage vibrated as if grabbed by an unseen force. Other times her eyes took on a haunted look, as if beholding a thing too horrible to bear.

By the time she finished, the afternoon had gone. Rays of the early-evening sun slanted golden through the bow window.

Sam watched, uneasy. None of this sat well with her nor fit with the outwardly conventional life she had always led. The three other women shared a commonality of experience Sam didn't. She never dabbled in anything remotely counterculture or occult.

She wished Bear Rutledge had been right when he said paranormal phenomena was all bunk, but she had to admit that it wasn't. As the acrid smell of the sage filled the rooms, she experienced a difference in the house. A heaviness had lifted. Shadows lightened. A sense of malevolence had vanished.

Yet seeing and feeling the power of Frankie's ritual, Sam felt worse in another way. Did she want to be part of this, be like these other psychics? She found the possibility disturbing and pushed the thought from her mind.

Meanwhile Frankie finished and put away the sage

and started her preparations for the scrying. She pulled the heavy brocade drapes on the bow window closed to dim the brightness. She asked everybody to mute their cell phones and for Sam to turn off the ringer on the home phone. Next she dragged one of her large suitcases into the living room. She removed thick white candles from it and hummed as she anointed each one with oil from a small vial.

She explained what she was doing, looking directly at Sam as she did. "If I were casting a love spell for a client, I would choose pink. Green for healing. Black for communing with the dead. But today I want white, for truth. There is a waxing moon tonight, which is helpful too."

Frankie arranged the candles in a circle on the coffee table. When she lit them they emitted the odor of lilies. She set up a CD player and put on a disk. Lilting, almost eerie music began.

A Loreena McKennitt album? Sam guessed.

"Please sit around the coffee table," Frankie instructed in a hushed voice. "On the floor." After the women did, she took a long, diaphanous black robe from her luggage. She put it on, and when she did Sam shivered. Where Frankie had been now stood an ancient druid with blazing eyes and long wild hair. She ushered in a smell of earth and trees. She crackled with energy and emanated a muted glow of visible power.

Sam stared, mesmerized, as she witnessed a dark goddess of the faery isles now made flesh.

With great solemnity, Frankie removed a silken white cloth from the suitcase and draped it across the coffee table. She raised a golden chalice in her hands, then set it down. She chanted in a low, singsong rhythm in a language Sam didn't know.

Then this witch, this maker of magic, alchemy, and sorcery, did as witches had done for centuries upon centuries: She opened the lid of an ebony box painted with symbols and signs. She carefully lifted out a globe that sat on an ebony stand. She placed it on the silken cloth. Then she raised her head. "Sam?"

Puzzled at being addressed, Sam answered, "Yes?"

"You are untrained. Let me help you control your gifts. Now. Let me help you release your powers."

"Uh . . ." Sam's mind raced. Had Ms. Z told Frankie to coach her? "Okay. How?"

"Think of Rina's light." Her voice was soft, coaxing, a seductive whisper. "Close your eyes and visualize a white light entering you, filling you, making everything clean and good." She closed her eyes and lifted her hands, palms facing upward.

"*Thig an anthair as an toll, La donn Bride.* 'The serpent will come from the hole on the brown day of bride,' " she chanted. "Brigid, goddess of augury, I ask for your spirit to come forth, and for the sight to come to me. I ask to see what we seek. Let the powers of light chase away all darkness. Let only good come through from the beyond. Help me see what happened in Arlington. Help me right the wrongs that have been done. Help us all to find what we seek."

Then Frankie opened her eyes and gazed at the crystal ball. "Look toward the globe but don't stare at it," she whispered. "Let your vision blur and look with an empty mind. Look with an open mind. Let what will come, come."

She fell silent. All the women became quiet, sitting unmoving in the darkened room. The candles flickered and cast long shadows on the walls. The sounds of ancient Ireland, ageless and alive in the high, lilting voice of Loreena McKennitt, surrounded them.

Seconds passed. A minute ticked by. A candle sputtered. It went out suddenly. Then another died. A draft of wind ruffled the curtains on the windows, and Sam felt cold.

The globe reflected the flickering, sputtering candles. Pinpricks of fire danced within it. Sam, tense, her nerves on edge, thought she saw a mist appear within the clear crystal ball. It swirled and moved like fog. The hairs on her arms stood up. A prickling sensation ran across her skin. She waited, but she saw only the fog, the mist, nothing more. Yet she felt as if she were poised on the edge of a precipice, about to leap into space.

Then the globe began to change. Inside it the mist became like flakes of snow caught in the wind. Then they turned to red, bloody red, and amid the red flakes Sam saw a bright circle—a silver wafer of light. It reminded her of the sun in the Iraq sky when the dust came. She imagined she could feel grains of sand hitting her. She remembered what it was like when the wind blew so hard the red dust scoured her flesh until it burned and burrowed into her pores.

Just as quickly as it came, the circle faded and the red flakes were gone. The mist returned and began fading into a thin, pale wisp. In an instant the globe turned transparent once more.

Sam blinked. Had she really seen what she thought she had? And if she had, what did it mean?

The other women were watching Frankie, who had, like Sam, ceased gazing into the globe. "Ahh, it's done," she said, and gave two sharp claps with her hands. Then she raised them again, palms upward. "Let me give thanks to the light, give thanks to the sight. Thanks for the visions of this day. In humbleness I offer my praise. In humility I offer my gratitude."

She bowed her head briefly, then picked up the globe. She rubbed it carefully with the silken cloth before returning it to the ebony box. Next she folded the silk and put it back in the bag. She took off her inky black robes. Only then did she turn to the other women.

"Did anyone see anything?" she asked.

Sam described the bright circle and the red, bloody dust of her vision. She said she could guess it had to do with her time in Iraq, but she didn't know what it meant or why she had seen it.

Frankie nodded. "What you see within the globe can be symbolic, like the witnessing of a dream. The meaning is arcane; all is unclear. The diviner's art is to understand what is hidden. Let it flow through you." She shrugged. "You will figure it out, or not. Be patient; be open."

Neither Rina nor Aurora saw anything at all, not even the mist inside the globe. "I do bones, like I said." Rina got up and walked over to the CD. "Okay if I turn this off now? Maybe you have some Black Sabbath I could put on?"

Once again Sam didn't know if Rina was serious or just being sarcastic.

Frankie told her to turn off the player. To Aurora she said, "If you haven't done this before, it's not unusual to see nothing. It takes practice to scry." Then she looked at Sam. "I did see something. It was a bit odd too. I saw a black box on wheels. It was rolling across a marble floor. Then it was rolling on grass. On the side of the box were stenciled the words, 'Picture Perfection, Inc.' Does that mean anything?"

It did, of course. Sam said she was positive that the black box of Frankie's vision was the hard-sided equipment case brought into the cemetery by one of the photographers. If Frankie's vision was valid, it provided a real lead to finding Barringer's body and why it had been taken. The four of them, the new team called AngelWay, had had a breakthrough. Their first success.

Excited, Sam rose from the floor. Her first idea was to share the news with Bear. But she stopped. How could she tell him anything? Where could she have gotten the information? A wave of disappointment passed over her. The only person she could call, the one person she would *have* to call, was Ms. Z.

While Sam used her new BlackBerry for the first time to phone in the information, the other women decided to take a break. Frankie wanted to start supper, and recruited Rina as her sous chef. They decided that after the meal Aurora should look at some maps of D.C. and the surrounding states from Sam's road atlas in hopes of getting a location for the missing body.

Rina took a chef's knife from the block on the counter. "Waste of time," she growled, and brought the eight-inch blade down hard on an onion with a *thwack*. "No offense, Aurora, but this body gone from the grave, this Barringer? He isn't lost. He's where he wanted to go. And I have a bad feeling we'll know where that is soon enough."

Sam had walked back into the kitchen in time to witness the exchange. A sick feeling flooded through her.

She shook her head for a moment, and a tendril of hair fell forward into her eyes. She pushed it back off her face. When she did, she felt something gritty. She brought her hand down and looked in disbelief at her fingertips. On them were grains of fine reddish sand.

22

BEAR Rutledge fumed. He wanted to punch a wall or break something. When he was younger he would have. Now he just seethed while rage built up inside him.

After the women left Arlington National Cemetery, he hadn't been able to find Smith's friend, John Bartikowski, to interview him. Smith himself had never returned to his job. That told Bear that his gut instincts had been on target. Now he was sure that the men knew something, and they didn't want to be found.

The giggling secretary gave Bear the men's home addresses and phone numbers. He tried Smith's house first. Smith's wife answered. No, her husband hadn't come home, and she insisted she hadn't seen or heard from him. Maybe she was lying, but Bear thought she sounded sincere.

Then he phoned Bartikowski's home number. The phone rang and rang. The answering machine picked up. He didn't leave a message. Instead he looked at his watch. It was still early in the day. The park police supervisor lived right in the city. Bear figured he'd drive over there. Maybe Bartikowski had gone home and wasn't answering the phone. Even if the place was empty, Bear could question the neighbors. Checking out the house would be all win-win for him.

The sun was high in the sky, pouring down noon sunshine when Bear got to southeast D.C. The run-down neighborhood south of the freeway was baking in the fiery oven of this especially hot July. Vacant lots sprouted white plastic bags like a cotton crop. The asphalt of the potholed streets absorbed the heat and brought temperatures at their surface to over one hundred sixty degrees. Recently repaired sections melted into gooey tar pits.

On street corners jobless young black men with do-rags on their heads stood around drinking beer or passing around a bottle of booze in a brown paper bag. They laughed loudly. They yelled at passing cars and made obscene hand gestures. Emotions crackled like dry sticks just waiting for a spark. It was the season for urban unrest. Looting an air conditioner would be a welcome diversion from their dead-end days.

Bartikowski's house was a sagging two-story wood-frame building faced by faded blue shingles. A stiff wind might blow it down. When Bartikowski's wife answered the door, leaving the security chain on, through the narrow opening Bear could see she wore a white nurse's uniform.

"I'm Inspector Lance Rutledge. Department of Defense. I'm looking for John Bartikowski."

"Do you have some identification?" The woman waited while Bear handed his ID to her. She looked at it carefully. Worry stamped creases in her forehead. She handed it back, saying, "I'm sorry, but John's not here. He's never here during the day. He's at work. At Arlington Cemetery. You can reach him there." She went to shut the door.

Bear put his big hand out to stop it. "No, ma'am. He isn't there. That's why I came here."

The woman paused. The creases in her forehead deepened. "I don't understand."

"Maybe I could come in? I can see you're worried. I'm worried too. We can talk," Bear suggested.

The woman blinked. She seemed to be thinking. "Yes, yes, of course." She closed the door slightly to remove the chain, then opened it for Bear to enter. As she led him into the spotless interior of the little house, she explained that she normally worked the midnight to eight shift at Walter Reed, but she had put in some overtime. "I just came home," she explained.

In the box-shaped living room, a plaster icon of the Virgin Mary stood a foot tall atop a stand labeled

MEDJUGORJE, 1981—GROW IN GOD'S LOVE LIKE A FLOWER. She saw that Bear noticed it. "I made a pilgrimage last year. I saw the Virgin, I did. Just a spinning bright light in the sky, really, but . . . I know some people don't believe it, but she's there. I felt her."

Bear nodded without comment.

"Please sit down. Let me look in the kitchen. Maybe John left a note. I'll check the answering machine too."

She disappeared through a door. Bear sat down on a sagging easy chair, the fabric on its arms threadbare. He heard Bartikowski's wife playing back her messages. The voices drifted in from the next room. Her glasses were ready to be picked up at the optician's; she had a free rental at the video store, good until Sunday. Nothing more. A moment later she returned to the living room.

She shook her head. "No message. I really don't understand where he could be. I didn't see him this morning like I usually do. Maybe if I had, he would have told me. He could have had a dentist's appointment. I just don't know."

"Do you think he went to the dentist? Maybe you can call?"

She sat down on the sofa. Her shoulders sagged. She turned faded blue eyes toward Bear. "No, I don't think he went to the dentist. I make his appointments. What's going on, Inspector Rutledge? What do you want to talk with John about?"

"Something happened at the cemetery, Mrs. Bartikowski. I wanted to ask him about it, that's all."

"Is John in trouble?"

"Do you think he is?"

She sat quietly for a moment and folded her hands tightly together on her lap. A small diamond winked on her ring finger above a gold wedding band. She touched it and stared at her rings, not at Bear, when she answered. "John is a responsible man. A hardworking man. He goes to work. He comes home. Straight home. Every day. Same time. You can set your clock by him. He's . . . predictable. A predictable man. So if somebody asked me if I thought John was in trouble"—she finally looked at Bear—"I would have laughed. John? My John? Except—" She stopped talking.

Bear waited.

"Except lately . . . I don't know. Something . . . something's going on with him."

"Something? Do you know what?"

She shook her head. "John isn't a man for talk. Keeps things in. The past week I knew he was upset. He started avoiding me. He works on repairing old radios. That's his hobby. He has a setup in the basement. Every night he went down there. I've barely seen him for days. I should have guessed it was something at work. He loves that job." She stopped. She gave Bear a beseeching look. "What happened at the cemetery?"

"To tell the truth, Mrs. Bartikowski, we're not sure. That's why I need to speak to your husband. Do you have any idea where he might be? A friend's house, maybe?"

A frown appeared between the woman's eyes. "In the middle of a workday? I just can't imagine it. I suppose he could have gotten sick. . . ." She shook her head. "No, that can't be it. I'm a nurse. He would have called me right away. He'd have come home or met me at the hospital."

"Think. Is there anyplace else? Anyplace at all he could have gone?"

A light seemed to have come on behind her eyes. "There's the crab shack, I suppose, if he really wanted to get away. I can't believe he'd go there without telling me, but maybe—"

"Where's the crab shack?"

"It's a summer rental up in Havre de Grace, Maryland. Just an old shack. But he likes to go crabbing on Sundays. He and Rod go up there."

"Rod?"

"Rodney Smith. They've been friends for years. He works at the cemetery too. Maybe he knows where John is."

Bear nodded. "Maybe he does. Would you write down

the address of the place in Havre de Grace?" He pulled a small notebook and pen out of his pocket and passed it over.

She talked as she wrote, shaking her head a little. "I just can't believe John would go there. Walk out of work and go there. Here." She passed the notebook back.

Bear stood. He took one of his cards from his pocket and held it out. Bartikowski's wife took it. "That's my number. When you hear from your husband, tell him to call me, will you? It's important that I speak to him."

The woman nodded, her eyes wet now. "I'll call around to everyone I know. I'm awfully worried."

"I didn't mean to upset you, ma'am. Your husband probably has a good explanation for leaving work. I'm sure he'll turn up."

But Bear was offering small comfort to the upset woman, not the truth. At some point in the conversation with Mrs. Bartikowski, Bear had begun to suspect that the agency had picked up her husband and Smith. That was why they were missing. They hadn't run. He remembered Allen's warning about being stonewalled. Bear could sense the granite rising all around him.

He cursed himself for not getting a contact number for that iron maiden Ms. Z. As soon as he left Bartikowski's place, he climbed inside his government-issue Stratus and called his boss's secretary, Lily, from his cell phone.

Rutledge saw the pleasant, fifty-something civil servant almost every day. She did his administrative work when he had some. Overall she was fussy, a mother hen, but a good egg. They had a friendly relationship that demanded the niceties of social discourse, something Rutledge would just as soon have skipped. Therefore he inquired about her health—she had a perpetual sinus problem—before he asked if Allen had a phone number for their contact at Langley.

Lily said Allen had left for the day. She apologized, but she didn't have a number for Langley. She assumed Allen did. She'd leave him a message to call Bear.

"Great," Bear muttered to himself, and clenched his

teeth. That and two dollars would get him a cup of coffee.

Having no other choice, he tried the number that Sam Chase had given him. The home phone rang and rang. No one answered. He left a message on her answering machine. At that point, frustrated, his anger on simmer, he figured he'd head home.

Only after he unlocked his front door and walked into the hallway did his rage soar into the red zone. He knew right away that somebody had been inside his house. Bear Rutledge was a man who liked order to the point that he knew to the centimeter how far the pen was from the pad he left on the hall table. The pen wasn't there. He walked down the hall and found that a kitchen drawer was open just a hair.

Worse, Nada was gone. He had kept the little cat inside this morning, not wanting her outside in this heat and fearful of what could happen to her on the streets of the city. She tried to dart through the door when he left, but he knew her tricks and foiled her escape attempts. All the other times when he managed to keep her in, she sat by the door purring when he came home, ready to greet him.

She wasn't waiting today, and she didn't come when he called. He looked throughout the house, but he knew his hunt was futile. Somebody had to have opened the door, and, seeing an opportunity, she ran out.

He could find no evidence of forced entry. After a quick survey of his belongings, he knew he hadn't been burglarized. He concluded with certainty that the CIA had checked him out with a thorough and professional search. What were they looking for? What did they think they'd find? Or was this one of the mind games they were notorious for playing?

The violation of his privacy and constitutional rights infuriated Bear. He wanted to rip somebody's head off. He tried Sam's number again. Still no answer. He left a message again, terse and impersonal: "Rutledge here. Call me. This is urgent." Then he started walking the neighborhood, crying out his cat's name until sweat soaked through his shirt and rolled in rivulets down his face. He didn't find her. All he could do now was hope she showed up at the back door.

The fact that the small cat was missing tore at his insides, stoking the fires of anger already burning. He changed into fresh jeans and a clean shirt. He left the house so worked up he had to grab a pack of Tums to quell the acid burning into his gut. He had made up his mind to drive up to Bel Air and confront Sam Chase. He wanted answers, and if she didn't have them, she could damn well get them.

Bear left the Stratus in his driveway. He went to the garage he rented and got in his own car, a classic Shelby 1968 Mustang GT California Special. He was restoring it, and it ran fine, but it was far from being a show car. The upholstery remained shabby and torn; he planned to work on that next. He had been thrilled to find this rare Mustang. Only 4,118 had ever been made—a "Little Red" with a supercharged 427 engine. The "Green Hornet" movie fans saw in the old Steve McQueen film *Bullitt* came out a few months later.

He loved that car, and driving it usually calmed him down. But as he pushed down the accelerator as far as he dared and headed up Route 295, he got riled every time he thought about the agency and their saddling him with a team of women to work with. It wasn't that he had a problem with an all-woman squad, exactly. He just thought it was odd. Maybe it was some kind of affirmative-action move on their part, but in the back of his mind he had the thought that he was being set up. They wanted to bust him for something—searching his house gave him reason to believe that. And sexual harassment charges would be a natural way to get any guy working with a woman as attractive as his new "partner," Sam.

Just thinking about her did something to him. She affected him; he couldn't deny it. And the fact that she wasn't picking up the phone when he called felt like a knife jabbing in his gut.

When Bear finally turned off the main road that ran through Bel Air onto Jackson Boulevard, the overhanging branches of the old trees arched above him like a

Gothic cathedral. Nothing stirred, not a person, not a tree leaf. The rumble of his 427 engine shattered the hush like a fart at a funeral. This was a neighborhood for suburban soccer moms driving mommy wagons. He didn't belong here.

He slowed to search the house numbers until he came to the address Sam had given him. He wheeled his muscle car into the driveway. He stopped, opened the driver's door and got out, straightened his powerful denim-clad legs, and took off his sunglasses. He took notice of the out-of-date split-level that had refused to change for fashion, that proudly proclaimed its heritage as midcentury, postwar white-bread-and-apple-pie America.

The air around him became absolutely still. The world turned so quiet he could hear his heart pounding in his chest. He had come ready to tear into Sam, but the house caught him unawares. A doorway in the recesses of his mind opened and brought up a memory: This was the house worthy of the Beav and Wally; this was the very house of his time-travel daydreams.

23

THE drapes in the bow window moved. Aurora Daybreak peeked furtively through them at the man getting out of the old Ford Mustang.

"Somebody's in the driveway!" she called out, as if Sam couldn't have heard the thunderous roar of the Mustang in front of the house. "Is it your boyfriend? Holy Mother of God, he's built like the Terminator, and he's sexier than Antonio Banderas. What's he— Oh, he's taking off his sunglasses. . . ."

By this time Sam had joined Aurora at the window. "Bear! What's he doing here?" she cried, her voice coming out a squeal. Her heart bumped against her ribs as she ran to the front door and rushed outside.

"What's wrong?" she said as she reached him and saw the storm clouds in his face.

His jaw muscles tensed; his lips barely moved, his mouth was so tight. "You tell me. You didn't answer my calls."

"Your calls? I didn't get any calls. What are you talking about?"

"Don't act like you don't know." His voice sounded like flint striking stone. "I called you all afternoon. You didn't bother picking up. I left two messages. You didn't call back. I told you it was urgent. You're avoiding me—why?"

Sam's eyes widened. "Avoiding? No. No. We were . . ." she began saying, then backpedaled to change her story, since she couldn't tell the truth. "I was . . . asleep. I turned off the phone. I forgot to turn it back on. I haven't checked my messages. I'm sorry if you thought . . . I wouldn't do that." Sam's face registered her upset at the misunderstanding and his low estimation of her character.

"I'm sorry, really. Please." She gently touched his arm. She felt his warm skin quiver beneath her fingers. "What's happened?"

Bear stared down at her. When he spoke his voice had given up some of the anger. "Smith and Bartikowski are both gone. I think your people picked them up."

"My people? I swear to you I know nothing about this. Let me call Ms. Z and see what I can find out." Sam stood barefoot in the front yard, her eyes riveted on this man whose rage had flashed like lightning but revealed such deep hurt in his eyes.

"I'll get my cell phone."

He gave her a questioning look.

"I just got it today. A BlackBerry. I'll be right back." She couldn't ask him inside the house. She didn't know how she'd explain Rina's being there, or the other women. She improvised. "I'd ask you in, but I have roommates. I was renting out the house to some girlfriends while I was in the Middle East. I won't be a minute." Leaving him standing there in the driveway, the shifting sunlight coming through the leaves of the maple tree dancing around him, she hurried off.

Rina and Frankie weren't in view; they must have discreetly gone to their rooms. Only Aurora and her cat remained in the living room, still peering through the drapes. As Sam started up the stairs to retrieve the BlackBerry from her bedroom, Aurora said softly from below, "He's gorgeous. And he's just standing there, staring. He's got this look on his face like this house is a castle and you're the princess inside. He's crazy about you."

Sam halted midstep. "What? No, you have it wrong. That's not my boyfriend. He's the DOD's investigator. He's working on this case. We don't really get along."

Aurora shook her head, and in her little-girl's voice she said, "No, Sam, *you* have it wrong. His feelings are like a whirlwind. They will sweep you away, and if you can't handle what he has to give, be careful. He's not a man to play with."

Like a butterfly's beating wings, a fluttering began deep inside Sam as she again began rushing upward. She snatched the BlackBerry from her dresser and then flew back down the stairs and out the front door, hurrying to get back to Bear with the odd sensation that she was running toward destiny.

Standing next to the Mustang, Sam speed-dialed Ms. Z, putting the BlackBerry on speaker so that Bear could hear. "I'm here in Bel Air with Rutledge." Her voice came out loudly, as if she were speaking to an old person wearing a hearing aid. "He thinks you have Bartikowski and Smith, the park service employees. They've gone missing."

"Rutledge is with you?"

"Yeah, I'm here." The timbre of Bear's voice was like a file scraping metal. "Where are the men?"

"I don't know where they are. We don't have them," Ms. Z answered quickly, sounding annoyed. "I'll get somebody on this."

"Don't bother. Chase and I will handle it," Bear snapped. He didn't say anything about the break-in of his house. For now, he wanted Langley to believe he didn't know.

"Carry on then," Ms. Z responded, and severed the connection.

"She's quite the charmer," Bear said. "Come on; let's go." He opened the door to the Mustang.

Bear's assumption that Sam would just hop in and take off with him rankled. "Excuse me?" Sam said. "Where am I supposed to be going?"

"Havre de Grace. We need to check out Bartikowski's summer place."

"You assume a lot, Mr. Rutledge."

"Are you *working* this investigation?"

"Of course I am." Her eyes flashed.

"Then what's the holdup? This is the only lead we've got."

"I have to change. I can't go like this."

A look of irritation chased across Bear's face; then he slowly took in Sam's long, bare legs. Desire sparked in his eyes. He shifted his glance away. "Yeah, go ahead." His voice was thick. "You can't run around half-naked."

Sam's cheeks burned with embarrassment but she huffed, "Gee, thanks for giving me your permission." She turned on her heel and headed back to the house.

Ten minutes later Sam reemerged clad in some of the few clothes still hanging in her closet: tight black low-rise jeans, a black halter top that she felt would be cool in this heat (but left her back daringly exposed), and flat sandals. She had grabbed a shoulder-strap purse and stashed her BlackBerry inside. As an afterthought, she folded a jean jacket over her arm to leave in the car. She thought thundershowers were threatening; she had heard heat lightning in the distance. The night air might get cool down by the Chesapeake.

When she saw Bear standing next to the car waiting for her, anxiety warred with excitement, making her jittery, as if she were a schoolgirl on a first date. She chastised herself. But she couldn't deny that Bear Rutledge affected her on a basic, bestial level.

That didn't surprise her, really. Over the course of the last forty-eight hours, the shell of her guarded existence had been smashed, then peeled away. The reality of who and what she was had been exposed. Her trembling, raw emotions left her vulnerable—and Bear had been there at the crisis points, virile, primitively male, and regarding her with unmistakable interest.

As she climbed into the red Mustang, she vowed to act professionally and nothing more.

Bear drove eastward on Route 155 toward the small town of Havre de Grace, where the wide, brown Susquehanna River flowed into Chesapeake Bay.

Bear visibly relaxed as he drove. He glanced over at Sam and explained that he had a hunch that both Smith and John Bartikowski had had a role in getting Barringer out of the cemetery. Maybe it was as minor as letting a hearse into the grounds without recording it.

But they knew something. Now they were spooked, and they ran.

"If they were involved, why did Smith report the missing body? Why did he tell us about the photographers?" Sam nervously pushed a strand of hair behind her ear.

Bear kept one hand at twelve o'clock on the steering wheel and the other lightly resting on the stick shift. He stared at the road a few minutes, and Sam decided his silence meant he was thinking about what she just said. Finally he spoke.

"Okay, okay. Maybe Smith wasn't involved in the body snatching. But here's what could have happened. We talk to Smith. He remembers the photographers, something he didn't mention when your people interviewed him on Sunday. After we leave, he hops in his truck and goes straight to his friend Bartikowski. Bartikowski confesses whatever it was he did. He's in big trouble. Maybe he can lose his job. Maybe he's been threatened if he tells. Smith feels as if he ratted on a friend. Panicked, they take off."

Sam shrugged. It rang true, but it was still supposition. "You think they're going to be in Havre de Grace?" she asked.

"I think it's a good bet. We'll see soon enough."

Sam stayed quiet for a moment before she said, "I have some more information. About the photographer's carrying case. It was from a place called Picture Perfection, Inc. The technicians at the agency pulled it off the surveillance videos." That was the third lie she'd told to Bear within an hour. She added that the agency was going to track down the company and let her know what they found. That much was true; Ms. Z had told her exactly that when she reported Frankie's vision.

Bear didn't respond to Sam's revelation right away. He seemed to mull it over before he said, "Why don't you Google the company on your BlackBerry? We might get lucky."

Sam felt stupid for not thinking of doing that herself. She quickly found the listing. "It's a film equipment rental place out in Reston, Virginia."

Outside the windows of the Mustang, the bright blue sky had faded into a sickly milky tone. Ugly dark clouds piled up in mounds to the east. The summer twilight had lengthened the shadows that reached across the highway.

"It's too late to talk to anyone there today," Bear muttered as if talking to himself. He looked over at Sam, the hardness back in his face. "You know, I don't appreciate your not getting that information to me earlier. Time matters. I could have talked to the rental place people already."

"The agency probably already did that," she answered.

Bear's fingers tightened on the steering wheel. "Yeah. They probably did."

Lying had already complicated her relationship with Bear. Sam didn't blame him for being pissed. He had been excluded; she acknowledged that. Yet his negative intensity drained her. She shifted to look at him. "You're right. I should have called you. In my defense, I have to say I'm still beat from the long flight. I'm not thinking all that clearly. But your anger doesn't help. Do you think we can get past this and start fresh?"

Bear chewed on his lower lip; then he nodded. "You're right. I have a lousy temper. I used to settle arguments with my fists, probably because I didn't have the words. In my defense," he echoed her own words, "I did try to reach you. If you left your phone on, this could have been avoided."

Sam reacted. "You're blaming me?"

"Settle down. I didn't mean that. What I'm trying to say is, we need to communicate better. Agreed?"

Their eyes met and held for a moment; then, embarrassed, they both looked away.

Uncomfortable with silence, Sam fished for a topic of conversation. Her father liked muscle cars, which drove her mother crazy, since she preferred a clean, new vehicle with some status, like a Cadillac. But Sam relished going with him to car shows, and she knew exactly what kind of car Bear had chosen.

So she acted impulsively, a little out of character. She

started singing softly, lightly under her breath, "Good Lord Mister Shelby," a bluesy song about Carroll Shelby, who created the vehicle Bear so loved.

Surprise lit up Bear's face. "I am impressed," he said. "You know about Shelby."

Sam smiled. She didn't reveal that her real interest in the car's designer was not his breakthrough muscle car, but the story that he had dreamed the name "Cobra," woke up, wrote it down, and gave it to the sports car he was building using a Ford V8. When she heard about this dream vision, she saw him as a kindred spirit, and she felt less alone.

What she said to Bear was, "I'm the son my father wanted. It's a terrific car."

All behavior has purpose, whether one is conscious of the motive or not. Sam's knowledge of the Mustang impressed Bear—and delighted him. On some level Sam knew nothing else she could have said or done would have pleased Bear more.

24

BY the time the red Mustang rumbled through the town of Havre de Grace, night had slammed the shutters closed on day and ushered in the towering storm clouds. Bear drove down to the bay and pulled into a small unpaved lot that was mostly crushed shells and sand. Two pickup trucks were already parked there. One lone streetlight illuminating pale green marsh grasses stood straight in the stinking mud all around it.

Sam and Bear got out of the car. The heat of the night folded over Sam as she stood next to one of the other vehicles. While she waited for Bear to remove a flashlight from the trunk of the Mustang, she heard a sound from the direction of the water. She turned and saw an old man with a wire crab trap in each hand trudging up a path from the bay. He came into the parking area and headed toward the pickup farthest from them.

"Hey!" Bear called out. "I'm looking for John Bartikowski. You know his place?"

The man nodded. "Right down thar. Number tin's on the pilin'."

"Thanks," Bear said.

"Yah-up." The man didn't bother looking at them as he stowed the crab traps in the back of his truck.

Sam walked in the flashlight's circle of light in front of Bear as they went single file down the path through the dune grass. Shells crunched beneath their feet. Mosquitoes buzzed around Sam's head. They hadn't gone more than a hundred feet before she spotted Bartikowski's summer rental, which was nothing more than an old crab shack up on poles at the end of a rickety boardwalk.

The windows of the small building were dark. The Chesapeake's water stretched like a sheet of black glass beyond it. The heat lightning near the horizon looked like exploding artillery fire. Thunder rumbled ominously in the distance.

Sam stepped on the boardwalk. It creaked. She started toward the shack. Water slapped the wood below her. Just then a fresh breeze came in off the bay. Sam rubbed her hands on her arms as goose bumps rose on her bare flesh, knowing it wasn't the drop in temperature that had caused them.

She heard a boat in the water near the shack knocking against the pilings. A loose corner of a plastic No Trespassing sign tacked to a pole flapped in the wind. The *wind.* With a roar and a rushing like moving air, the image of a man jumping up from a chair and knocking it over flashed through Sam's mind. She stopped moving forward.

"What?" Bear asked.

"Something's wrong. I feel it."

"Okay, wait here," Bear answered in a low voice, and moved past her, leaving her standing alone on the wooden boards.

Sam saw his flashlight beam hit the door of the shack. She could see that it was standing ajar. She watched Bear reach inside the opening. He must have found the switchplate, because the inside of the shack suddenly blazed with light. Bear motioned to her to come before he disappeared inside.

Sam moved quickly to the open door. "What did you find?" she asked.

Bear pointed to a plate on an end table next to a sagging couch. It held a half dozen white lollipop sticks. Next to it was an ashtray filled with cigarette butts. "Guess Smith started smoking again."

Another image flashed across Sam's mind. She squeezed her eyes shut. She saw a fight in this room between three, maybe four men. She recognized Smith as he caught a punch in the face. She didn't know the others. She heard a yell. A glass broke. Somebody cursed. Nothing else. She opened her eyes and looked at Bear. "Do you see signs of a struggle?"

Bear raised his eyebrows. "Broken glass on the floor. The chair's on its side. And that." He pointed to some drops of what must have been blood on the worn linoleum floor. "I'd have to be blind not to see them. Maybe the friends had a falling-out."

Sam shook her head. "I don't think so. More likely they were waiting for somebody and their visitor or visitors attacked them."

"What makes you think that?"

Sam shrugged. "I'd bet either Bartikowski's or Smith's car is still in the cemetery's parking lot. If they left together, they wouldn't have taken both cars. And there was another pickup where you parked the Mustang. It had D.C. plates and a U.S. Park Police parking sticker on the windshield."

And Sam *had* seen that; she just hadn't realized what she was looking at until now. She kept talking, figuring things out on the fly. "So it's a stretch, sure, but since the pickup's still here, how did they leave? They didn't take the boat. So they left with somebody else, or were taken out of here by force."

Bear gave Sam a look of frank admiration. He removed his cell phone from the clip on his belt. "I'm going to call the men's wives. Find out what vehicles each of them drives." While he made the first call, Sam went to the open doorway and looked out at the dark water, feeling proud of herself and excited too. Behind her she heard Bear talking to Smith's wife.

"Smith drives a silver Pontiac Grand Prix," Bear called out. "I'm calling Bartikowski's house now."

Just then Sam saw a jagged streak of lightning hit somewhere to the north and heard thunder again, louder than before and much closer.

"She's not answering. I'm getting the message machine." He flipped the phone shut and joined Sam at the door. He stood close. She could feel the heat of his body.

"I think I'll pay her a visit before I head home," he said.

Sam turned her head. His face was only inches away. She smiled at him, her gaze focusing on his lips, which were full and sensual. "Didn't you ask me a little while ago if I was *working* this investigation?"

"Yeah, why?"

"I spotted the pickup truck; you didn't. I'm not getting left behind now."

Bear gave her a lopsided grin, clearly pleased. He looked into her eyes. Something moved in Sam's breast, another flutter of the butterfly.

"I thought you were tired," he said.

"I've gotten a second wind. Besides, I think we're getting somewhere. I want to be there."

Just then a blinding flash filled the shack, instantly followed by a deafening crack of thunder. Sam screamed. The lights went out, leaving her and Bear in total darkness.

Then everything happened very fast. Bear pulled Sam protectively into his arms. The heavens opened, and water poured down like a gray wall. A blast of wind blew the drenching rain into the shack. Bear drew Sam into the room and kicked the door shut.

Sam didn't protest. She let herself be pressed against Bear's firm body. Lightning strike after lightning strike lit up the interior of the crab shack. In the white flashes she could see Bear's face, his eyes heavy lidded with desire. He hesitated, as if looking for a sign that she wanted him too. She gave it to him by putting her arms around his neck and standing on tiptoe, raising her lips to his.

Their first kiss exploded into fireworks for Sam. She didn't break their long embrace, but opened her mouth, inviting his tongue inside. He entered hungrily, exploring her and dominating her at the same time.

Sam stretched the length of her torso tightly against him. His hands moved to the bareness of her back exposed by her halter top. He backed her up until she leaned against a counter that ran the length of the shack wall. He picked her up, sat her on it, and stepped between her thighs. His entire body trembled as they continued the long kiss. She believed he was losing control.

He suddenly held her more tightly with his powerful arms and groaned.

For Sam, the primal sound issuing from Bear's throat undid her completely. Her own fragile hold on her feelings broke. She was swept away.

The rain came down, pelting the roof above their heads in a ceaseless din. Lightning periodically lit the darkness surrounding them, striking nearby over and over. Thunder crashed with terrifying force. They kissed without stopping. Sam ran her hands through Bear's hair. She wanted to devour him. She wanted him to devour her. He moved his hands from her bare back to her full, heavy breasts.

Suddenly he stopped, dropped his hands, and broke the kiss. "Jesus! I'm sorry."

Sam lips were still very close to his. She felt confused and whispered, "Sorry? Why?"

Bear backed away, tearing himself from Sam's arms and leaving her perched on the counter. She heard him move across the room and open the shack's door. The rain had stopped. The clouds had gone. She could see him standing there, the waxing moon visible in a clear sky beyond him. Then Bear said loudly, "That was stupid. I was stupid."

25

THE balding man the others called the chairman had driven over to Virginia and was inspecting the warehouse himself. Not that he didn't trust Charles, but the chairman was from the old school: Believe everyone, but always cut the cards first.

Inside the facility a large area had been filled with cots ready for the incoming "guests." Another section of the big open space held crates of weapons and field supplies. But the room in the back of the warehouse, off from the main floor, where the offices had been, was so very special.

That room had been refurbished partially according to the chairman's very own design, although some of the contents had been directed by the Bokor, who had called the room a *hounfort*.

The balding man went through the heavy steel door and looked around. Surgical instruments were lined up neatly on a tray. A stainless-steel gurney with gutters running down each side had been positioned under intense operating room lights.

On one side of the room was a long counter with shelves above it. He could see a primitive rattle, a wooden bowl filled with cornmeal, some black candles, a small drum, and a disgusting-looking paste that the Bokor called *migon*.

At the rear of the room sat an altar covered in red fabric, piled high with candles, and filled with small dolls.

It excited the man just to look at it all, although his eyes kept returning to the steel slab with its straps and gutters. Tonight more "guests" would arrive, and the air in this room would get heavy with the scent of incense—and blood.

The only thing that concerned him now was the time it took to perform the ceremony. The Bokor told him "not to worry, mon." He would bring in others to help.

"Can the others be trusted?" the balding man had asked, concerned.

The Bokor laughed. "Trust de devil, mon. You now his friend, right, mon?"

Then the chairman decided it didn't matter. No one in the government or in law enforcement took these Bokors and what they did seriously. Who would believe them if they decided to tell—and who would they tell? Most of them were illegals anyway. And they knew who was paying their way. They wouldn't bite the hand that fed them.

The chairman looked at the surgical instruments again, and then at the steel gurney. His excitement grew. It surprised him how much the thoughts of blood and violence turned him on. He was here alone. He shrugged. Why not satisfy himself?

He went into the room and closed the door behind him. It was pitch dark in the windowless space. He moved forward until he could touch the smooth, cool steel with one hand. With his other hand he stroked himself as his breath quickened. He thought about what had happened there—and what would happen there.

He thought about the dark dream, the grand design that was coming to fruition; then, with a satisfying rush, he finished, smiling while he did.

26

"WHAT did you just say?" Surprised, Sam pushed off the counter. Her feet hit the floor with a smack.

Bear was outlined in the doorway, facing her. She could see his hands clenched into fists. "Look, I'm sorry. That was inappropriate. It was a mistake. It won't happen again."

The dark of night out here on the waters of the bay left the interior of the crab shack deep in shadows. Sam couldn't see Bear's face, and he couldn't see hers. She was glad. She felt foolish—humiliated, really. "A mistake?"

"Yeah. A mistake. I'm sorry. Let's forget it." He turned around and stared out the door.

"Forget it? Sure. Okay." The setting *was* inappropriate, Sam thought, but the long kiss, his touch, their passion—they had been wonderful. Disappointment blossomed like a black rose inside her chest.

"The rain's stopped. Let's get out of here. I suppose you want me to take you home."

"Like hell." Sam didn't think before she spoke. "We have a job to do. I'm on this case, remember." Anger replaced the painful sting of Bear's rejection. This man wasn't going to get rid of her that easily tonight, Sam thought. The kiss was a mistake? Maybe she'd make him uncomfortable by sticking around. Maybe she'd make him mad, but she wasn't going to be left behind because he couldn't handle his feelings.

She put her hand back on the counter where she had once sat. Her fingertips touched what felt like a small, stuffed rag doll. She felt a stick pushed through it, and short pieces of yarn were attached to the head, which was made of felt. What would a child's toy be doing in a crab shack? She quickly stuck it in her waistband at the small of her back, where it could remain out of sight. As soon as she returned to the Mustang she would find a way to slip it into her purse.

Silence filled the drive south back to Washington. At one point Bear, his voice contrite, said, "Look, I want to explain. Maybe I misjudged what happened back—"

Sam cut him off. "*Nothing* happened, so you don't need to explain anything." She went back to studying the scenery out the side window of the car. She had no desire for conversation.

But finally Bear's stomach grumbled so loudly that Sam realized she too felt starved. She hadn't eaten anything since the bowl of soup earlier in the afternoon.

Bear asked, "You have a problem stopping by my place before we go to Bartikowski's? I have some takeout we can heat up. It's better than the drive-through at Mickey D's." He gave her a tentative smile.

"Yes, sure, if that's what you want," Sam replied, suddenly feeling a little better.

"To tell the truth, I need to see if my cat came back."

"I didn't know you had a cat." Sam looked at Bear with surprise.

"There's a lot you don't know about me." Bear's voice held a hint of sadness. They didn't talk again until they arrived at Bear's row house.

No thundershower had cooled down Washington's inner city. Not one drop of rain had fallen. Hot air rose up as sidewalks released the day's heat. The air lay like a heavy blanket filled with the odors of fried foods and sweat. Young people sat on the stoops of the row houses, rap music blasting from CD players. Old people leaned on their elbows in open windows. Low-riders with loud exhausts drove by filled with teenagers. Cigarette butts arced out of the car windows like antiaircraft tracers and tumbled trailing sparks along the streets.

Like a pressure cooker building up steam, the city of

Washington boiled. Its inhabitants sweltered. Tempers turned ugly and violent. Sam grabbed her purse and jacket and climbed out the Mustang. Bear's neighbors stared, but nobody shouted at her, a white woman amid dark faces.

"My neighbors are mostly nice people." Bear probably saw Sam's worried expression as he came around the back of the car and opened a low iron gate into the postage stamp–size front yard. "The ones who aren't know what I do and that I carry. They respect a gun. They leave me alone."

Inside the row house, which surprised Sam with its elegance, Bear went into the kitchen, opened the refrigerator, and removed a carryout container. He slid it into the microwave and set the timer. Then he excused himself and went out the back door. Sam heard him calling, "Nada! Nada! Here, kitty, kitty. Come on, girl. Where are you? Nadaaaa. Nadaaaa."

When the timer on the microwave sounded, he returned, shaking his head. "She's not back. Let's eat and get out of here."

He plated some fried chicken and corn bread, collard greens on the side. Sam didn't sit down. She laid her purse and jacket on the kitchen counter and stood stiffly at the breakfast bar. She forked food into her mouth amid an uncomfortable silence, avoiding Bear's eyes.

She observed that the kitchen was immaculately clean and orderly. She herself was not nearly so fastidious. That neatness, his surprising revelation about his cat, and his obvious distress at the pet's absence revealed more about the man, who was proving more complex and unpredictable than Sam first judged.

"You done?" Bear asked at last. Their eyes finally met. Feelings surged through Sam. She felt such a wave of desire for this man that it flooded her completely, drowning her reason. With a flash of perception, she became acutely aware that they were alone together, in his house, in complete privacy. She imagined his bedroom upstairs. She imagined them going there. She thought of how his body must look without his clothes.

And even as she did, she reprimanded herself for her

thoughts. It was so unlike her—or, at least, the woman she had been a few days ago—to think such things. But maybe that woman had been as much a facade as her pretense that she wasn't different, that she didn't have . . . didn't have—she had to just admit it, think it, validate it—the gift of sight. But it was hard to come clean. She wasn't used to being so honest with herself.

Then she saw that Bear was staring at her, his own feelings of want showing. He reached his hand out. She put her own in his, and electricity danced across her skin. He smiled. "I wanted your plate."

Color rose into her cheeks, making her blush a dusty rose. "Oh!" she said, feeling embarrassed, but he didn't release her hand right away, so she guessed it was okay. Their eyes locked. Sam could barely breathe. Her lips parted and her breath came out in a sigh. She stepped toward Bear. The very air between them seemed to sing.

Bear watched her hungrily. Then confusion spread over his face, followed by a look of suspicion. His desire seemed to give way to anger. He dropped her hand and reached past her for the plate on the counter. "We'd better get going," he said gruffly.

Sam moved back quickly. She didn't understand what was going on. She thought he wanted one thing—and she was sure he did—then he abruptly shut down. She pressed her lips into a line, clearly annoyed.

"Hey," he said, stealing a glance at her as he rinsed off the plate. His voice had changed again, softer now. "We really do need to get moving, that's all."

She gave him a curt nod. He ran so hot and cold she didn't know what to think.

Bear opened up the refrigerator to put away the unfinished food. A bottle of cranberry juice fell from a shelf to the floor. Its top must have been loose, for a puddle of red began to spread across the white ceramic tile.

Bear jumped back. "Damn it! Watch your feet." He picked up the now half-empty bottle and placed it on the counter, then ripped off a wad of paper towels to mop up the spreading liquid.

Sam froze where she stood and stared at the floor.

What she was seeing was not cranberry juice. She saw blood spreading, running in a gory stream across white marble. She knew where that marble was—in the amphitheater at Arlington National Cemetery.

Although she saw no one in the vision, she heard the sharp crack of gunfire, followed by a man's terrified voice yelling, "Help us, for the love of God, somebody help us."

Her heart started pounding as she continued to view gruesome red streams running down the walls onto the seats in the bowl of the amphitheater. Since she was looking at this from above, she realized her vantage point must be from the walkway that followed the tall columns around the rim of the great theater, fifteen feet above the cemetery below.

Then her vision shifted away from the ghastly rivulets of gore, and Sam was looking out into the cemetery itself, dark under the sliver of moon that was very high in the sky, much higher than it had been earlier at Chesapeake Bay.

She gasped. Pale mounds of dirt gave testament to grave after open grave. Then, directly below the rim of the amphitheater on the wide stone path, she saw a man, only it wasn't a man. It was a corpse, walking blindly with dead eyes and madness in its terrifying face.

"Sam? Sam? Are you okay?"

Bear was talking to her. The vision vanished. Sam shook her head. "I'm okay. Sorry, I thought I heard something." Her mind was racing. They needed to go to Arlington—now, right this minute. She didn't know if what she had just seen had already happened or whether it was going to happen soon. But they had to try to help, or if they could, they had to try to stop whatever was happening there.

But how could she get Bear to go? What could she tell him?

She began talking fast, her lies flowing more easily than earlier in the evening, now that her guilt at telling them had disappeared. "I heard a humming. It just came to me: My BlackBerry's still on vibrate, not ring mode. It's here in my purse. I'd better take the call."

She snatched the phone from her purse and turned

away from Bear. While pretending to answer a call, she hit the speed dial, number one. Ms. Z. Now she had to put on a convincing act.

"Chase here," she said to the sound of ringing. To her relief Ms. Z picked up at once.

Caller ID would reveal who was calling her CIA chief; Sam knew that. The voice that answered asked, "Chase? What's going on? Did you find Bartikowski and Smith?"

"No. I'm in D.C.," Sam answered the question, then kept talking. "What do you mean, something's going on in Arlington?"

Ms. Z didn't respond for a second; then her voice came over the phone, excited. "Are you trying to tell me you had a vision? Is Rutledge still with you?" Ms. Z was quick on the uptake and figured out what was going on.

"Yes," Sam said, and looked at Bear, mouthing to him, "It's the agency."

"What did you see?" Ms. Z asked.

"Maybe an assault of some kind? A report of more empty graves? Do you want me and Rutledge to get over there?"

"Of course I do." Ms. Z's voice became sharp and urgent.

"But you say you're not sure?" She paused, although Ms. Z said nothing, then continued. "No problem, we're not far from Arlington. We'll leave right now."

"I agree," Ms. Z affirmed. "You should check this out, even if you aren't certain. But be careful. I'm going to make some calls. I'll contact security at the cemetery. Phone me as soon as you are able to confirm what you saw. I'll bring in a team just in case we need to get right out there."

"Sure. I'll get back to you."

Sam ended the call. "Ms. Z wants us to run over to the cemetery. There might be a new situation. Maybe more body snatching and a struggle. She wasn't clear."

"How do they know? Security call it in?" Bear's voice sounded suspicious.

"I guess. She didn't say. Just for us to go over and have a look. If we find anything, I'm supposed to ring her back."

* * *

When they left the house Sam tried to see the position of the moon, but she couldn't find it at all.

In the Mustang, driving over to the cemetery, Sam began to feel afraid. She knew the cemetery contained not just the dead, who could do no harm, but something malevolent, something horrible as well. She had felt it this morning. Rina had felt it. Now, in her vision, she had seen something that she knew was evil.

"This might be real bad," she said, taking her eyes off the road ahead to look at him.

Bear returned Sam's gaze, meeting it with more suspicion. "Do you know something you're not telling me?"

"No, just a . . . just a gut feeling. Maybe we should call for backup now. We don't know what we're walking into."

"Which, as your chief told you, might be nothing. That's probably why we're being sent over there. It really doesn't sound serious, but don't worry; you know I'm carrying." He reached down and pulled up the leg of his jeans. He wore a black automatic strapped to his calf. "Can you shoot a gun?" he asked.

She nodded, not mentioning the sharpshooter medals she herself had won, but saying simply, "My father trained as a sniper. In the service. He's a good shot. He taught me."

"Then open the glove compartment. There's a .38 snub-nosed revolver in there. Do you feel comfortable with that?" His voice was skeptical.

"Yes," she said, popped the glove compartment open, and took out the gun. She checked the safety, then tried to figure out where to put the weapon. She opened her purse and nestled it next to the odd-looking doll she'd found in the crab shack. She didn't say what she was thinking: that she didn't think bullets were going to stop what she feared.

"I had an idea this morning," Bear said as he drove, seeming relieved that Sam was talking to him again. She marveled at his ability to really act as if nothing had happened between them. He went on. "I have this theory about this case I'm going to run past Allen, my boss, and this new development fits right in."

I'm sure it's not the same idea I have, Sam thought, but she asked, "What theory?"

"If more graves are open, and *if*—and that remains to be seen—they're also recent burials from Iraq, then I think we're dealing with what I thought all along. Grave robbers."

"What would grave robbers want in a soldier's grave?"

"Treasure. Gold. Jewels. Sent back with the bodies, put in the caskets somehow. Think about it. Millions of dollars' worth of valuables were looted from Iraqi homes and museums, jewelry stores, you name it, when the Americans entered Baghdad. You know that's what happened. We all saw it on television.

"And how much of that stuff was ever recovered?" He glanced over at Sam. "You aren't going along with this? You don't think so?"

"I never heard anything more about the looting after the first days of fighting." He didn't seem to pick up on the coolness in her voice.

"Come on, Sam. Think about history; look at World War Two. The Nazis stashed billions of dollars of gold and art underground in mines so the Allies couldn't get to it. The salt mine at Altaussee alone held looted art from all over Europe, and tons of silver. Hungary's entire treasury was in there. You think that Saddam's people—or others—didn't do that too before we got there?"

Sam shrugged. "Maybe, I don't know."

"And your man Barringer. He was carrying on 'delicate negotiations' when he was killed. Negotiating what? Maybe he had a lead on millions, even billions of stolen gold and gems."

"I guess it's possible. It's a logical explanation." That was what Sam voiced, but what she had seen in her vision wasn't reasonable; it was extraordinary and terrible. It suggested an entirely different reason why those graves were empty—and it was a reason Bear would have a hard time believing.

All of a sudden her own folly in kissing him hit her hard. What if he hadn't stopped? What if things went further? It would have been a worse mess than it already was. This was a man who would never accept her psychic abilities, who would always find a reason to discredit the paranormal. His world was concrete, tangible, measurable. It was the polar opposite of Sam's.

Bear had done her a favor by backing off from the intimacy she found herself wanting with him. She realized that now. So why did it still feel so bad?

27

"WHERE are the security people?" Bear wondered aloud as they drove up to the cemetery and found the gate across the driveway closed and locked. "You know, this just doesn't feel right."

They had just arrived at the service complex. The service building's parking lot held Smith's silver Pontiac Grand Prix and a few other parked vehicles. But there was no one waiting for them. There was no one around.

That was not entirely true. The dead were here. Already Sam heard them, just as she had this morning. The buzzing energies assailing her no longer shocked her. She had expected their presence and hoped to handle it better than she had at first.

But the dark night conjured up terrors as ancient as mankind. Even if the spirits meant no harm, fear of ghosts was a human reaction, and fear of death was even greater. Mortality was tenuous, and life so fragile it could be snuffed out in an instant. The mournful siren sounds of the dead brought with them Sam's dread of joining them before she was ready to.

Sam spoke then, trying to sound calmer than she was. "Maybe the park people went up into the cemetery to investigate?" In truth, she didn't like this either. Ms. Z said she'd notify security that they were coming. Surely she told them to sit tight and wait for Bear and Sam, and the gate should have been open by now.

Bear parked the Mustang close to the building and they got out. A wind had picked up. The tree leaves rustled like stiff satin. A dog howled in the distance. Sam got out of the car and slung the strap of her purse over her head and across her shoulder, bandolier style. Then she scanned the sky. She spied the moon nearly directly above her head. She thought it looked to be in the same position she saw in her vision. A shiver racked her entire body despite the stifling heat.

Meanwhile Bear stepped quickly over to the main building and tried the door. It was locked. He pushed a bell, then rapped on the door with his knuckles. No one answered. He looked around. A few windows glowed with yellow light, but no one seemed to stir inside. Then he returned to Sam, shaking his head.

"Like I said, I don't like this. Let's stay as quiet as possible. I'm going to grab the flashlight, but I don't think we should use it until we find out what's what. No use advertising we're here any more than we already have."

Sam's heart was thudding in her chest. She hugged herself tightly as she watched Bear quietly open the trunk of the Mustang. He pulled out the flashlight, hesitated, then removed a tire iron too. When he rejoined Sam, he handed the flashlight to her. "Can you carry this?" he asked in a low voice.

She nodded yes.

He gestured to her right. "We're going to have to scale that wall over there. I'll give you a boost."

The wall was only about six feet high. Sam put her foot in Bear's cupped hands, and he gave her an assist. She landed on top without effort. He handed up the tire iron, then pulled himself onto the ledge. Then they both lowered themselves into the darkness of the cemetery on the other side.

"Did your boss say where we should look?" Bear whispered.

"The amphitheater. Let's head up there."

Security lights lit the stone walkways as well as the service roads through the graveyard. Bear and Sam followed the roads, but stayed in the shadows on the other side of the low chain along their borders.

The cemetery had clear direction markers for visitors. The signs appeared with regularity, pointing the way to the Tomb of the Unknowns, which sat directly in front of the great white marble amphitheater. But the cemetery covered over six hundred acres, and their destination lay almost on the far side of the vast burial grounds.

Clouds of mosquitoes bedeviled them all the way. Perspiration quickly soaked through Sam's clothes. They headed west on Patton Drive at a run, but by the time they reached the service road marked Eisenhower, where they turned north, she could hear Bear breathing hard. She herself panted and gasped hungrily for air.

Beyond the light from the streetlamps, darkness shrouded the cemetery. The headstones reflected white in the moonlight. No graves yawned open. Nothing moved. The unseen spirits moaned, the wind still shook the leaves in a dry rustling, and Sam could hear her and Bear's own footfalls, a steady rhythm of soft thuds on the grassy verge.

They had reached another intersection and were being directed north on Porter when a terrifying wail came from somewhere ahead of them. Filled with anguish, this voice didn't come from the dead, but Sam believed it might have been the sound of someone dying.

Startled, she stopped jogging.

Bear halted too.

"Did you hear that?" she called out softly.

"Yes," he said.

They both remained motionless and listened. Crickets chirped, a night bird called, but they heard no live voices, no vehicles, no screams.

"Nothing now," he said. "It didn't sound good." With a new urgency the two of them jogged on.

After that Sam detected a distinct voice amid the murmuring of the dead. It was a different moaning, a wail conveying terrible sorrow, bewilderment, and, she thought, perhaps rage.

She wondered if that new voice would have talked to Rina. It didn't talk to her.

The land began to slope upward, and soon the amphitheater appeared ahead of them, looking like an ancient Greek temple atop a hill. When they reached the round building, its center open, its huge white columns holding up only sky, they slowed their progress and looked about. From the direction of their approach, from Porter Drive, which ran to the south of the building, they saw no open graves and nothing amiss.

Sam's uneasiness, however, overtook her utterly, nearly paralyzing her movement with a sudden fear. No voices in her head told her to run, but her every instinct screamed at her to turn back, not to go ahead, not to climb the stairs up to the promenade that followed the circle of columns around the amphitheater's rim. Willing herself to move forward, she put her hand on her purse, ready to grab the gun within.

Bear put his arm out to stop her. He placed his mouth close to her ear. "Something's wrong. It's too quiet. No crickets. Stay close behind me."

He began to climb the stairs, hugging the wall. Sam followed, both of them being as silent as possible. When they reached the top of the stairs and started to walk to their right, Bear grabbed her arm, yanking her behind a column.

A sharp, metallic smell reached them on a sudden breeze. Bear started forward again, but motioned for Sam to remain hidden. She could tell he was using his body as a shield to keep her from viewing what he had just spotted.

But Sam already knew what was there. She had seen it earlier, when the vision came to her in his kitchen: Bright blood would be running across the white marble, forming puddles on the aisle and dripping down the walls.

She popped out from behind the column and started after Bear.

He heard her. "Stay there," he whispered fiercely.

'No," she insisted. "Someone may be injured and need help."

Bear shook his head. "It's too late for that," he said in a low voice, and moved enough for her to see what lay before him. It was exactly what she feared she'd see.

Two men in U.S. Park Police uniforms lay sprawled on the white marble a few columns away. Their chests had been torn apart, leaving gruesome, gaping wounds, as if a beast had clawed them open. Worse was what had happened to their heads. Their skulls had been peeled back like the pop-tops of soda cans. Where the gray matter of brains should have been, only blood so dark it looked nearly black filled the emptiness.

"That's why security cops didn't open the gate—they're dead," he said. "You need to call this in."

But Sam stood immobile as a statue. She shook her head at him and put her finger to her lips for him to be silent. She took his sleeve and drew him into the shadow of a column. She gestured for him to look into the cemetery below.

Sam already knew what was out there. Her vision had told her what she would see next, and she knew with a terrible sense of dread what was coming for them now.

Bear appeared puzzled, since he had heard nothing, but he looked where she pointed.

"Who the fuck is that?" he said under his breath as his body tensed. He pulled Sam down into a crouch next to him. He reached down and got his gun. "We need to get out of here," he said, putting his mouth near her ear.

She nodded. She knew they did; she just didn't know how. They couldn't go back to the stairs they had just climbed, because by now she could hear slow, measured footsteps on them, barely fifty feet away.

Bear grabbed her hand with his free one. They left the shadows of the column, and together they hurried directly toward the bloody remains of the security guards. They had no other choice. Carefully they skirted around the bodies, trying to avoid stepping in the blood and leaving a telltale trail.

Moving as quietly as they could, they rounded the vast circle of the amphitheater, heading for the front of the building, where wide stairs led toward the Tomb of the Unknowns.

Sam glanced back over her shoulder. She could see a figure in a combat uniform—camouflage brown-and-tans, like she had seen so often in Iraq. The soldier, if that's what it was, moved stiffly with a shuffling gait in their direction. Then she took a sharp breath and grabbed at Bear's jacket. She gestured for him to look.

Behind the shuffling figure came two more. One started

in the opposite direction around the rim of the amphitheater, and the other climbed into the pit that held the seats, where red blood ran in thin streams toward the podium in the center of the arena below.

By this time Sam and Bear had reached the front of the amphitheater, where a reception area formed an enclosed rectangle. They shrank next to the wall and sneaked toward the stairs. As soon as they could see that no one waited below, they dashed headlong down toward the plaza, with its tiny kiosk for the changing of the guards, empty now. Then they sprinted toward the path, adrenaline giving them speed, not knowing whether they were being followed and not willing to look back.

28

THE walkway sloped downward, leading back in the general direction of the security complex. They had just reached Roosevelt Drive, perhaps a thousand feet from the amphitheater, when Bear stopped and motioned to Sam to follow him. He crossed the service road, and instead of turning right, in the direction they had come, he went straight into the graveyard, jumping the low iron chain along the road like a hurdle. Sam stayed close behind him, clearing the chain in the same way and plunging deep into the dark, tree-shaded meadows that held the graves of the nation's dead.

Once hidden by the night, Bear took Sam's arm and pulled her down until they knelt on the ground behind some bushes. Sam could see the road they had just left, and understood why they had taken to the shadows.

Coming up Roosevelt Drive under the streetlights, moving toward the amphitheater, came a long black hearse. *Transport for the bodies,* Sam immediately thought.

The hearse pulled to a stop nearly directly in front of them. A man climbed out of the back of the hearse where the coffins were carried. A baseball cap kept his features hidden. He dragged his feet as he walked, moving stiffly and unnaturally. A stench of decay wafted from him and gagged Sam with its odor.

Her heart nearly stopped in her chest. *That isn't a living man,* she thought, as crazy as that sounded.

The hearse pulled away. Once the figure who had emerged from it moved slowly toward the amphitheater, Bear signaled to Sam to follow. They crept away, deeper into the graveyard.

They didn't dare use the flashlight, since unfriendlies were clearly roaming the grounds. The moonlight turned the landscape a monochrome of no color, and their eyes adjusted enough so that they could walk without much difficulty if they took enough care. Even so, Sam stumbled. She fell to her knees, and the unyielding marble of a grave marker grazed the top of her forehead. The sharp stone bit into her flesh and cut her scalp—quite deeply she thought, but it didn't hurt.

She stood up quickly and found she was a little dizzy. She touched the wound with her fingers and felt wetness. *Damn it, I'm bleeding.* She had a tissue in her jeans pocket and stopped long enough to get it and blot the cut. The tissue was soon wet through. *It must be worse than I think.* She applied pressure with the tissue to slow the blood flow.

The whole episode had taken only a minute, but suddenly Sam realized she was standing in the dark alone. Bear didn't know she had fallen, and he hadn't stopped. She could no longer see him in the dim light, although she could hear him ahead of her. She started in that direction. She didn't dare cry out to him, but she was sure he'd notice her absence in a minute. She quelled her fears and hurried after him.

The land sloped downhill. She never caught up with Bear, and she was getting worried. She thought she could still hear him moving ahead of her, but sometimes she wondered whether she was walking in the right direction. In a voice barely above a whisper, she tried calling his name: "Bear. Bear. Can you hear me?"

No answer came. A branch cracked behind her. She spun around. Then she heard a thud in the direction she had been heading. She spun around again. She didn't know where Bear was. Her heart started racing. She had to continue on alone. She had no other choice. She hoped she was heading toward the service complex, where they had come in. She'd know as soon as she reached a road. She made up her mind that she'd risk walking in the open and follow it.

She tried not to think about the dark shadows that fluttered and undulated as the wind moved the leaves in the moonlight. Ahead of her the white tombstones formed a macabre avenue to follow. Bear was nowhere to be seen. She increased her pace, jogging as often as she dared. In a few minutes large trees deepened the gloom. Instead of reaching a road, Sam had entered an older section of the cemetery.

Fewer spirits seemed present here. The energy level felt lower, as if time had helped these fallen men to separate from the bonds of earth that kept the newer dead from moving on. The small white marble slabs of the enlisted men had also given way to larger headstones, some elaborately carved and weighing many tons. Their indistinct shapes formed a corridor of stone on both sides of the rows of graves. Sam could see this was the final resting place of admirals and generals, the grand scale of their monuments testifying to the owners' rank and prestige.

It was an officers' club for the dead.

Suddenly Sam heard something to her right. She froze. Maybe she had found Bear—or maybe something, someone, had found her. "Bear?" she whispered. "Bear? Is that you?" She got no answer. *Oh, God. Who is it?* She thought she should run, but where? She listened carefully. She heard a different sound now, like an animal scratching in the dirt. It was probably a rabbit or a rodent. It was probably nothing. She had just panicked here in the darkness. She began to relax.

Then she smelled a horrible stench. She heard dirt falling, as if being tossed by a shovel. *The grave robbers!* She had to see what was going on.

Sam moved cautiously toward the sound and found herself stepping on something soft. She stooped down to investigate, and her fingers touched leaves and the soft petals of flowers, mounds of flowers with a strange sweet smell. *Is this the purple vervain Rina mentioned? Is someone really calling out the dead?*

Sam put one of the blossoms in a pocket of her jeans, then crept forward, trying to see what was happening. She saw headlights maybe a hundred feet away. She could barely make out a hearse, its motor idling. In a clearing directly in front of her, she could distinguish a mound of pale dirt in the dim light, and she could see clumps of dirt flying upward to land on top of it.

But no one was digging. The dirt seemed to be moving by itself, as if invisible hands were opening one of the graves. Then the dirt stopped. The head of a figure appeared; then hands reached up. *Oh, my God,* Sam thought. *Did I hit my head harder than I thought? Can this be happening?*

Sam slipped the snub-nosed gun from her purse and took the safety off. She had taken a few steps closer to the deepening grave when she heard a rushing in her head. The familiar voice of her spirit guide cried out, *Stop. Don't. Go back. Run!*

Sam halted at once and spun around, as the voice commanded. She started blindly forward in the shadows. Her knees banged into a headstone. She paused, feeling frantic, trying to decide where to go and waiting for the voice to direct her.

Her hesitation proved a mistake. An arm came from the darkness behind a monument and, quick as a striking snake, grabbed her shoulder and jerked her off her feet. She cried out as she was slammed facedown onto the ground. A knee went into the small of her back, and she felt fingers grabbing her hair, pulling her head back as if to snap her neck.

The man holding her smelled of blood. He grunted like a beast. She had dropped her gun when he grabbed her, and the only weapon she had was her will to survive. She exploded in a fury, fighting with all her strength, bucking and twisting, trying every evasive technique she had been taught.

But fighting in a dojo was vastly different from the desperate struggle she waged here in the night. Biting the putrid flesh of his arm until he released her hair, she managed to turn toward the assailant. A hood covered his head, and she couldn't see his face. She scrabbled backward like a crab. He caught her foot and held her fast, then dove on top of her.

He slammed his forearm into her throat like an iron bar. She made an inarticulate sound as her air supply was cut off. She fought to stay conscious, struggling to remove the pressure from her windpipe.

At that moment, when blackness threatened to overtake her, Sam sensed rather than saw Bear appear. She heard the thud of a tire iron slamming into her attacker's body. The forearm left her throat and she hungrily sucked in air, her lungs heaving as she struggled to her feet. She backed up, trying to put distance between her and her attacker, who had turned his attention toward Bear.

She could make out Bear swinging the tire iron again. This time the dark-hooded assailant grabbed it. He wrenched it from Bear's hands and flung it away. Sam saw the bar sail toward a large granite cross. It hit the headstone, metal crashing into stone. Then the attacker launched himself at Bear and knocked him down.

Sam could hear the blows landing as the men fought. She didn't know how to help. *Find the tire iron,* the voice in her head instructed her. She hurried to the large white cross and began desperately groping around on the ground. "Where is it? Oh, Lord, where is it?"

Suddenly her fingers touched metal.

Picking up the iron bar in both hands, she ran toward the fight. Bear was on the ground and the man knelt over him. Not taking time to think, she brought the tire iron down with all her might on the attacker's head. He stiffened, then toppled over like a felled tree.

"Bear!" she cried out.

He was already getting to his feet. "I'm okay. Let's go!"

He grabbed her hand and they ran, racing downhill through the grass blindly, weaving through gravestones, and splashing across a small brook.

At last they slowed. They were in the open. No one seemed to be chasing them. They could see headlights from cars passing by the cemetery along Jefferson Davis Highway. Sam realized she had no reserves of strength left. Her legs had become shaky. Her emotions felt raw.

"You need to call for backup now," Bear ordered, and let go of her hand.

Sam pulled out her BlackBerry. Bear's directive annoyed her. "That's what I was going to do," she snapped, and punched in one on the speed dial. Ms. Z picked up at once.

"Yes, Agent Chase?"

"Two men are dead. At the amphitheater. Six known assailants. We need help."

"A team's already on the way."

"How close?"

"They're crossing the Memorial Bridge. ETA three minutes. Get yourself out of there."

"Right." Sam clicked off. "Backup's on the way," she repeated for Bear's sake.

"Let's get to the car," Bear said. They loped toward the highway, stumbling now and then. "Stay in front of me, where I can see you," he ordered. "I can't risk your getting lost again."

But he didn't take Sam's hand a second time.

29

THE driveway gate had been unlocked and left open by the time Bear and Sam reached the service complex maybe ten minutes later. Ms. Z waited next to a black SUV in the parking lot.

Once the adrenaline rush had subsided as they tracked the final distance to the service complex, Sam had begun limping. She realized she must have gotten hurt during her struggle with the assailant. Now, when she and Bear reached the lighted area, she could barely put any weight on her left foot. Her throat ached. She looked down at her clothing. Streaks of mud and grass covered her palms and dirtied the front of her halter top.

"Do either of you need medical assistance?" Ms. Z asked. She held a two-way radio in her hand.

Bear answered, "I'm okay."

Sam said, "Only scrapes and bruises, I think. Maybe I turned my ankle."

Ms. Z focused on Sam's bloody forehead; then she reached out and tipped Sam's head back, looking for a moment at her neck, her eyes registering something Sam couldn't read. "Get in the vehicle, Chase," Ms. Z barked. "You need to have a doctor check you out." She held the door to the passenger seat open and waited for Sam to get in.

"You," Ms. Z said to Bear. "Write up a report and get it to me by morning."

"I'll write a report and get it to *my* boss in the morning," Bear replied in a hard voice.

Ms. Z gave him an annoyed glance. "Just do it," she spat out.

Sam didn't say anything to Bear before Ms. Z slammed the door between them. She didn't look at him when Ms. Z gunned the engine and pulled away.

Bear wiped sweat off his forehead with his forearm, leaving a dirty smudge. He watched the black SUV drive off. Sam had fought like a tiger and saved his life. But earlier she had tried to set him up for a sexual harassment charge by coming on to him. That was what she had been doing, right?

Or maybe she wasn't setting him up. Maybe she and he had a real connection. Or did. He had put a stop to it, and it was too late now if he had been wrong.

In truth, he didn't know what to think. He wasn't sure exactly what he had lost this stinking, hot night. But, measured in grief and regret, it seemed incalculable.

He took slow steps toward his Mustang. Unless Nada had returned, he had nothing to go home to except his own dark thoughts. He considered driving down to Bartikowski's place in southeast Washington. It was after midnight. Bartikowski's wife should be working her shift at Walter Reed. Either Bartikowski himself would be there or nobody would. Either way, Bear could find out what he needed to know.

Meanwhile the black SUV headed swiftly into the heart of downtown D.C. Within minutes Ms. Z pulled into a well-guarded underground parking garage off Constitution Avenue. Sam thought they had entered one of the many buildings in the vast Department of the Interior complex, but she couldn't be sure.

During the drive, Ms. Z told Sam to wait until she had gotten medical attention before going over everything that had happened in the cemetery. She said the agency's people were on the scene. She already knew what they had found.

She kept shooting anxious glances at Sam. A few times she asked how Sam was feeling.

"Mostly numb. A little dizzy," she said, then added, "There's something I saw—"

"Don't bother talking. We found the open graves."

"No, no. You can't let visitors can go back into the cemetery." Sam was finding it harder and harder to talk.

"Don't worry; there will be no trace of what happened in the amphitheater," Ms. Z assured her.

Sam pushed herself to speak. "No, listen; I had a gun. I dropped it when I was attacked, when this—my neck—happened. It's still out there somewhere."

"I'll call it in to a team in the cemetery. Where should they search?"

Sam explained as best she could that she had been in an older part of the cemetery among monuments for officers. She described the monument carved to look like an American flag draped over a boulder that she had seen near the place she had been attacked. "The groundskeepers should know where it is," she said.

"I'll tell the team to search the area thoroughly. See what else they can find. Did you see the man who attacked you?" Ms. Z asked.

Sam went to shake her head, but that didn't feel too good. It didn't feel so good to keep talking either, so she just said no, then paused, and even though the world had started to spin, she decided to say something else. "He was big, bigger than Bear. He smelled bad, like blood and rot. To tell the truth, I don't even know if it was a man."

"Are you saying that you think you were attacked by a woman?"

"Uh-uh," Sam choked out, and made an effort to say what she had been thinking. "I mean I don't know if my attacker was human."

The young Asian doctor was very kind and didn't ask any questions about the source of Sam's injuries. She might have a mild concussion, he said. Her ankle had a slight sprain, but no tendons had torn. He said to stay off it for a day or so, and wrapped it in an ACE bandage.

He was most concerned with her neck injuries. He spent a very long time examining her. Ms. Z told him to take some digital photos "for the files."

Then he had a nurse push Sam down a long hall in a wheelchair for X-rays. Sam heard him say to Ms. Z that an MRI would be better.

A long time later, with Sam dozing on and off, the doctor walked back into the examining room with the X-rays in his hand. He put them up on a lighted box and sat on a swivel chair looking at them for a while. Then he told Sam she had been lucky. From the visible contusions on her throat—Sam herself wouldn't learn how bad she looked until much later, when she got in front of a mirror—it was clear she had narrowly escaped having her hyoid bone crushed. "You took quite a blow to the throat," he observed. "It came close to killing you."

Sam remembered the feeling of the man's arm against her neck and looked toward the wall.

Ms. Z, hovering nearby, looked grim.

The doctor shook his head. "I'd like to put you in the hospital, but I understand from your boss that that's not an option. If you're in a lot of pain tomorrow, you should come back so we can send you for an MRI. I don't see anything on the X-ray, but I'd like to be sure you don't have a fracture." He swiveled back to the lighted box, studying it again. "That bone is at the base of your tongue. You might have some trouble talking for a couple of days. Maybe not."

He gave Sam a little paper cup of water and a Darvocet. He handed her a white paper packet and said she could take another pill before she went to bed. After that she should take one every four hours, or as needed. She also got a crutch to help keep the weight off her foot, and a couple of ice packs, one for her ankle and one to try to keep the swelling down in her neck. "I guess I'm not going to be moving around much," she whispered, and gave him a wan smile.

He patted her on the shoulder and looked at Ms. Z. "I suggest that she doesn't move around at all for the next twenty-four hours, at least. She should spend tomorrow on bed rest."

Ms. Z nodded noncommittally.

* * *

On the ride back to Bel Air Sam's neck felt stiff and her throat ached, but the Darvocet made the pain bearable. In a whisper she told her tale of what had happened in the cemetery.

"We found those open graves," Ms. Z replied. "Most were over in Section Sixty again, the new burials. Soldiers who had been stationed in Iraq. Ten, maybe twelve newly opened graves."

"Rutledge's theory is that this is some kind of grave-robbing ring, gold and gems stolen in Iraq and shipped over in the bodies or something."

"I know that's what he thinks. What do you think?" Ms. Z asked.

"Not that. It makes sense and all, but the . . . whatever they were that came after us in the amphitheater were more like, I guess, zombies than men. Then I saw a grave opening. Nobody was doing it. The dirt was flying out by itself. I guess that's nuts, but maybe Rina's right: The dead are walking out of their graves. But why? I don't know. And who killed the security guards? Do you think they saw something or somebody they shouldn't have?"

"I don't know if we'll ever know why those men were killed. I never reached security at the cemetery. They had already gone up to the amphitheater, I guess. Maybe the surveillance cameras picked up something. One is right up there by the Tomb of the Unknowns. We'll take a look."

Sam didn't want to talk anymore. She put the ice pack on her neck and leaned her head back on the headrest.

But Ms. Z had one more question. "What you said about zombies, Chase. Is that your own opinion or did you . . . I mean, did you hear from your spirit guides about that?"

Sam took the ice pack off her neck and turned her face toward Ms. Z. "If you mean did I get a message from the great beyond, no. I just mean that the guys in the combat uniforms moved as if they were in a trance. Maybe they were on drugs or something. Their being the living dead? That seems far-fetched. But do you know something I don't?"

"Well, somebody removed the security guards' hearts and brains. We were trying to figure out why."

Ms. Z helped Sam out of the car and up to the house. Despite the late hour the outside light was on, and Rina opened the door.

Ms. Z handed Rina a brown envelope. "That's for Daybreak, something from Barringer's personnel file. It's a photo he provided, so he touched it. That's the best we can do."

She gestured toward Sam. "Agent Chase won't be coming with you tomorrow. She's on leave for the next twenty-four hours. If she gets any worse, don't wait. Call it in to us. Help her up to bed, will you?"

"Sure," Rina said, and took the plastic bag containing the ice packs.

"That must have been some date," she said to Sam, and closed the front door after Ms. Z left.

Sam gave her a dirty look.

"I was making a joke! Look, I threw the bones tonight. They warned of death. I asked them if that meant you. They said no. But I figured you were headed for trouble. I wanted to wait up and make sure you were okay."

"Thanks," Sam croaked, her throat really hurting now. She not only felt physically sick, she emotionally hurt to her core. She balanced on one crutch and fished the packet of Darvocet out of her purse. She held them out toward Rina. "I need one," she whispered. "Now."

Rina went into the kitchen and Sam followed, hopping along on one foot and using the crutch for balance.

"Just sit down," Rina said in the kindest voice Sam had ever heard her use. "I'll get you some water. Or would you rather have hot tea with some honey and lemon?"

Sam nodded.

"You want tea?"

Sam nodded again. Rina filled a mug with water and put it in the microwave. She leaned against the counter. "I can see you can't talk, so let me just fill *you* in. The others went to bed hours ago. Bad things were going on out there tonight. I could feel them.

"Then the boss called around ten. I told her about throwing the bones. I told her Aurora tried to locate Barringer by simply using a map but had no luck. Aurora thought she'd do better if she had something of Barringer's to hold." Rina held up the envelope. "So here it is."

The microwave buzzer went off. Rina took a box of herbal tea and a jar of honey out of the cupboard. "Lemon Zinger," she said, then took out a tea bag and fixed the cup for Sam.

"Anyway, I have been ordered to look into any voodoo activity in this area. So that's what I'm going to be working on tomorrow. I imagine that's got something to do with what happened to you tonight, am I right?"

Sam nodded.

"I figured something swung their opinion that way. Aurora's going to try to do her 'finding things' parlor trick using the photo, and they're sending Frankie out on another case."

Sam made a surprised face.

"Yeah, I wondered about it too. Some Arab diplomat says 'a baby' robbed his house. He's blaming the CIA for sending in a robot or a midget to get hold of his secret stash of who knows what. He's causing a big flap in the State Department. Frankie's been elected to deal with the guy. Lucky her."

"A baby thief?" Sam wondered if she heard right. Her brain was muddled, and that sounded bizarre.

Rina shrugged. "Yeah, I know. Even to me, a baby thief sounds weird. But according to Aurora the breach of diplomacy could become a major incident. And the guy controls a lot of oil in his country. Ms. Z wants her to get in there, fix the problem or find the kid, and get out."

"Oh, boy. I guess I really didn't know what AngelWay could get us into."

Rina allowed one of her rare smiles to brighten her face. "You can say that again."

Sam took the Darvocet and drank a little of the tea, but not much. The pain of swallowing was too great. She hoped the pill kicked in soon. She pointed upstairs.

"Yeah, let's get you to bed. You need anything, rap on the wall. I'm right in the next room. I'll hear you."

Sam thought how she had misjudged Rina. She had the hardest shell on the outside, but seemed the softest inside. Then Sam remembered what she'd found on the counter in the crab shack. She held up her index finger to tell Rina to wait a minute. She took the purple flower out of her pocket and passed it to Rina.

"Vervain. The conjuring herb. You found this at the cemetery?"

Sam nodded. She held up her finger again and took the doll from her purse to get a look at it in the light.

Squat and crudely made, the doll had brown yarn glued above a face made of white felt. A stick had been pushed through the shoulders horizontally to form the doll's arms. Sporting a badge made of foil, the figure was dressed in a rough approximation of a U.S. Park Police uniform.

Rina put out her hand, and Sam passed the doll to her. She ran her thin fingers down the figure. "Petro voodoo," she murmured. Then she turned the doll over and pointed out what Sam hadn't noticed: Stuck through the figure next to where a person's spine would have been was a cruel-looking pin. The doll had been stabbed in the back. "Black magic. Someone made sure this man was betrayed by a friend."

30

RUNNING on raw nerves and discontent, Bear stopped off at his house to change his dirty clothes and pick up a couple of items he figured he might need. He took off his gun, checked it, and then, instead of putting it back in his ankle holster, he grabbed a shoulder holster and strapped it next to his skin. He found a clean cotton shirt in his closet. He put it on and didn't bother to button it, leaving his chest bare.

He also looked for Nada. She wasn't outside the back door. Worry twisted violently around in his stomach like a trapped beast. Then he spent at least ten minutes calling for her and walking around behind the house before he gave up and decided to get going.

He had already returned the Mustang to its rented garage. A classic muscle car in southeast Washington would draw too much attention. Instead he drove the Dodge Stratus with all the windows down and a hot breeze whistling through them. As he turned down Bartikowski's street, he could hear Snoop Dogg rapping on somebody's radio.

Smog and the weak illumination of grime-covered streetlights shrouded Bartikowski's house in a gray haze. The night brooded around it, hot and still. Bear passed by and saw it was dark. The curbside in front of it had cars parked bumper-to-bumper. Bear himself had to drive another two blocks to find an empty space to pull into.

Then he walked back to the house, watching for any movement in the shadows as he did. The humid, fetid air smelled of asphalt, rotting garbage, and ganja. Breathing didn't come easily.

Or maybe his breath came hard because of the tight bands that had formed around his chest the moment he saw how badly Sam had been injured. She had gotten into the black SUV and left before he could say . . . what? He was sorry? That was lame. *Sorry* didn't even begin to express the remorse that had opened a chasm filled with pain inside him.

Now he needed distraction. He needed to forget what an asshole he had been.

He stood on the sidewalk and surveyed Bartikowski's house. No vehicle was parked on the cracked cement driveway that led to an empty carport. The windows stared out dark and blind, as if the occupants were in bed. More likely Bartikowski's wife had gone to work, and Bartikowski himself had never returned home.

Bear slipped down the driveway to the back of the house. He took a rubber glove from his pocket and slipped it on before he tried the door. The knob turned in his hand. A red flag started waving in his brain. An unlocked door in the city wasn't normal. Somebody had been careless; maybe Bartikowski's wife had left in a rush, been upset, and forgotten to lock it. Yeah, that was probably it. But still Bear hesitated. He had another thought: Somebody else, not Bartikowski or his wife, who didn't have a key could have left the house, and without one they couldn't lock it again.

His senses sharpening, taking care to move quietly, Bear opened the door just as wide as he needed to slip inside. He closed it silently behind him. He took out a penlight and flicked it on. He found himself in the kitchen. Nothing stirred. The house seemed empty. The message light was blinking red on the answering machine. Bear wanted to play it, but decided he had better check out the house first—because all of a sudden his nerves started to dance. He got a funny feeling that something wasn't right.

Bear paid attention to his gut feelings. He stopped moving through the kitchen. He took out his gun. He listened again. He heard water dripping from the kitchen faucet. He heard a car engine rumble as it started up, then the noise faded as the car pulled away from the front of the house.

It was quiet again. He heard nothing else, but he smelled something: the sharp tang of copper. Bear made sure the safety was off his gun. He knew what the copper scent meant: fresh blood. That was what it smelled like when someone bled out.

He held the penlight cupped in his hand, allowing just enough illumination to make sure he didn't bump into any furniture. He inched his way to the door into the living room.

Bear had been wrong in thinking that Bartikowski's wife was working her shift at Walter Reed. She was right there in front of him, sitting in the chair he had occupied earlier. Her eyes, wide-open and staring, seemed to look right at him. Her mouth hung open in a soundless scream. Blood, black in the dim light coming through the windows, had burst from a bullet wound in her chest and run down to make a dark stain on the carpet.

Damn, Bear thought. *Did Bartikowski do this?* Bear's heart gave a hard squeeze, and anger poured like hot lead through his veins. She was a nice woman. A decent woman. She didn't deserve to die like this.

Staying where he was so he wouldn't disturb the crime scene or risk stepping in blood, he shone the penlight around the room. He didn't see a weapon. He didn't see signs of a struggle, except that the Virgin's statue had been knocked off or fallen from the stand. It lay shattered on the floor. Its plaque, saying GROW IN GOD'S LOVE LIKE A FLOWER, had landed beside it.

Bear shook his head. Mrs. Bartikowski wouldn't have the chance to grow anymore.

Bear turned away from the dead woman and let his penlight dance around the kitchen again. He saw that the door to the cellar was ajar. He decided to check it out and moved through it. Below him the basement was a formless void. He flipped on the switch he found to his left, and a fluorescent light flickered on. He went down the stairs, keeping close to the wall, his gun at the ready.

Once he got to the bottom, he looked around warily. The basement had been finished with the kind of cheap brown paneling popular in the 1970s. The low acoustic-block ceiling pressed down from above and barely cleared the top of Bear's head. Bartikowski's workbench sat against the far wall. Old vacuum tubes filled a cardboard box on top of the bench. Some tools—needle-nose pliers and a couple of screwdrivers—had been left haphazardly nearby. A vintage Philco table model lay on its side with its back removed.

Bear glanced at them, then noticed a shoe box below the bench. He edged it out with his foot and used his gloved hand to open the top. Nestled inside was a blue muslin bag next to a wrapping for Mystic Brand Evil Eye Gris-Gris. He also saw two blue candles, a small vial of what looked like oil, and a hand-carved and painted wooden pipe. In a crumpled paper bag next to the box he discovered a half dozen used black candles, a satin scarf, and a rattle painted in bright colors.

Guess Bartikowski was playing with more than old radios down here, Bear thought. He didn't find anything else of interest in the basement, gave a quick search of the rest of the house, and then left by the back door.

It was clear that nobody had broken in to shoot the woman, so she probably opened the door for the intruder. Bartikowski could have returned home, although if what Sam thought happened in the crab shack was accurate, Bartikowski might be as dead as his wife.

Bear crept back down the driveway, then jogged toward his car. He stopped short when three young white boys, barely in their teens, stepped onto the sidewalk in front of him. All of them held knives.

"Gimme your money." The biggest of the three was tall and scrawny and wearing shorts with the crotch down to his knees. He also wore a bandanna in his gang colors tied around his head. He moved closer to Bear.

"I don't think so," Bear said. "You'd better go home to your mama."

The skinny kid stuck out his chin. "What you say?"

One of his partners got brave. "Go on, Antony. Stick da wiseass."

The skinny kid, now identified as Antony the fearless leader, waved the knife. "You crazy? I'll cut you."

Bear reached for his gun in a practiced movement and pointed it at the teen. "Not if I shoot you first. Now get the fuck out of here."

The boys ran.

Bear shook his head. *Gangs. Kids looking for trouble and headed to the morgue,* he thought. He got to the Stratus, drove a while, and found a pay phone to make an anonymous call to 911. He figured the agency would have liked to cover the murder up, but the hell with them. This was a homicide, Mrs. Bartikowski needed some justice, and as far as anybody knew, Bear was never here.

31

SAM slept fitfully. She dreamed of being chased through dark streets by zombies. Then she was driving through a gray fog. She couldn't see to steer. She felt lost and afraid.

She whimpered. The dream changed. She was back in Iraq. The red sky was filled with sand, blowing, ever blowing, getting on her skin. She saw the glowing disk of the sun, her vision in the crystal ball returning. She cried out, *No, no.* The disk floated above her. It disturbed and frightened her. She didn't know why. She cried out in her sleep again, moaning. Then the sun exploded into a thousand shining fragments that fell toward earth through the terrible red sky.

Sam returned to consciousness when the dawn light came creeping through her bedroom window. Not just her throat and ankle hurt; every muscle in her body ached. Even her scalp felt sore from the guy grabbing her hair. She needed to take another Darvocet.

She sat up and discovered that somebody, maybe Rina, had left a glass of water on her bedside table. She tapped a pill out of the white packet, took it, and returned to a drugged sleep, barely aware when one of the women came into her room and stood over the bed, asking, "Are you okay?"

Sam made a sound. She tried to say yes, but it came out as a hoarse *eh.*

She also heard a car pulling into the driveway, followed by the women going out the front door. The house got very quiet. She dozed on and off through the morning hours. The bedsheets tangled around her legs.

She felt sweaty and feverish. She heard her cell phone play its annoying tune a few times, and, sounding very far away, the house phone rang.

Finally she opened her eyes and stared at the ceiling. Then she forced herself to get out of bed. She put on some loose shorts and an old T-shirt. Her home phone rang again. The message light was blinking. She didn't listen to them. She lay back down with her clothes on. She must have fallen asleep for a few minutes, because the next thing she knew, Aurora was again standing in the doorway of her bedroom.

"Ms. Z brought me back early. To check on you." She had a glass of iced tea in her hand. "You need your painkillers?"

Sam's thoughts moved sluggishly, mired in quicksand. She tried to figure out the right answer. If she took one, it would knock her out again. If she didn't, she'd be in pain. She nodded yes. She might as well sleep. Aurora walked over, picked up the packet, and dropped a white pill in Sam's palm. She handed her the glass of tea and waited until Sam took it.

"Mind if I talk a minute?"

Sam gestured with her hand toward the desk chair. Aurora went over to it and sat.

"I tried to locate Barringer this morning, using his photo," she said. "The important thing was that he had touched it. Psychometry is what the researchers call what I do. I hold an object and sometimes I can see a place real clearly, with a street number and everything. Or I can look at a map and point to the exact location. This time . . ." Aurora sighed deeply. "I had flashes of images. A bedroom. A white sheet. I saw a chair. I saw a van. I saw a big gray building. Not a lot of detail. It was almost as if his body were being transported or something. He was moving around, anyway, so I guess someone else was moving him. The dead can't walk, can they?"

Sam pushed herself to a sitting position. Dizziness set the room spinning. "Rina . . ." she croaked.

"I know, Rina says they can. She thinks they're zombies, like in *Night of the Living Dead.* But I've never encountered anything like that, and I've seen . . . awful things.

"Anyway, I didn't get anything helpful from holding the photo. I'm worried. I need to show the agency I'm valuable. Otherwise . . ." She sighed again. "They'll probably send me back."

Tears welled up in the woman's eyes.

"Maybe you're trying too hard," Sam whispered.

Aurora nodded. "I think so. I've thought about taking Miranda out to the cemetery this afternoon. It's possible a squirrel or a bird saw something. The problem is interpreting what they've seen. I think it's worth a shot, though, don't you?"

To Sam, Aurora's going out to Arlington to chat with a squirrel or bird sounded crazy. She had mixed feelings about Aurora anyway. Something didn't ring true. Not able to agree with her, Sam just shrugged.

"Okay, maybe not." Aurora stood up and turned to leave. Sam closed her eyes and leaned her head back on the bed pillows. But with her lids opened just a slit, she could see Aurora moving things around on her desk and quietly opening the desk drawer. The woman was a snoop, she thought. *I wonder why she was in jail? Aurora killed a man. Isn't that what Rina said? Is she also a thief?*

Wondering about Aurora, Sam dozed off, falling into a medicated slumber. She began to dream. She was in a plane's cockpit. She didn't know how to land and started to cry. In another dream she got on an elevator that went sideways instead of up and down, and suddenly she found herself pressed against Bear. They were kissing. He fondled her breasts, then called her a whore. She slapped him and the elevator doors opened. She ran away.

Sam stirred. She felt herself getting uncomfortably warm and kicked off the covers. She couldn't have been very deeply asleep after that, but she wasn't sure what woke her up—the noise at the window or the voice in her head insisting, *Wake up*.

Sam's eyes flew open. A roar was in her head. The voice cut through her mental fog. *Wake up. Shut the window. . . . Hurry.*

Feeling disoriented, Sam tried to stand. The room started to spin. Her stomach heaved. She felt faint. She sat down heavily on the bed.

Shut the window! The voice came again.

Fighting against the drowsiness that tugged at her heavy eyelids, Sam raised her eyes. She saw that the window by the dresser was open. She made another effort to stand. She got to her feet and swayed. She grabbed the headboard of the bed and steadied herself. Then she hobbled across the room toward the open window.

A gust of wind made the curtains dance. The blinds rattled like old bones. The temperature in the room plummeted.

Sam pitched forward and grabbed the windowsill to keep from falling. Outside she could see the trees bending. Their leaves turned over and showed pale green undersides. Maybe a thunderstorm was coming.

She slammed the window shut and locked it. The room stayed eerily cold. A gray cloud passed over the sun. Sam squinted and tried to see whether a thunderhead had formed. It was then that she saw the darkness wasn't a cloud. It was more like a shadow in the air, like she had seen at the cemetery.

The shadow started to thicken, to take on shape and form. It moved until it filled the space in front of the window, blocking the daylight. Sam backed away, her blood racing. The pane began to shake, as if something had grabbed it from the outside and was trying to push the window back up. Next a scratching sound began. It wasn't the sound a tree branch made. It was more like sharp claws pawing at the frame around the window. Suddenly pieces of wood splintered and flew off. The window started to shake again, violently this time.

A howling began, and Sam could hear the words, *Want you . . . Want you.* Her heart pounded. She backed farther away, thinking of running for the door. She could see now that the gray shape had long arms and a bulbous head. It pulsed and swirled outside the window. The pane rattled harder. The whole window began to vibrate, and then . . . the walls of the house began to shake.

Sam's eyes grew larger. Terror washed over her like a wave. Suddenly the lower notes of the piano sounded from downstairs, as if hands had crashed down on the keys. She screamed out in fright, "Oh!"

An instant later Aurora burst through the door. "Sam! What's wrong?"

Sam pointed. The gray shape had become huge and menacing, with glints of sharp teeth in the macabre head. It battered against the glass, which shook and rattled. Frankie's white-witch cleansing must have still been working, because the glass held and didn't break. Loud thuds pounded the walls, and the floor beneath Sam's feet shook.

Waaaant YOU. Waaaaant YOU. The words echoed and repeated.

The cat, Miranda, leaped off Aurora's shoulder and jumped to the sill. Her ears went flat against her head. She arched her back, hissed and spat, then began to yowl.

Aurora's face turned deathly pale. "Miranda says it's something evil. A beast."

"I think she's right," Sam whispered. "It was at the cemetery, in the air near Barringer's grave. Rina saw it too. What should we do?"

"Fight it! We have to fight it. Call the light, Sam. Call your spirit guide."

Sam felt panic. "I can't."

Another great thud hit the bedroom wall from the outside. One windowpane cracked. The big orange cat hissed, her tail rigid, her hair bristling.

"Sam, you have to! That glass is going to break. Miranda says the beast is too big for her to kill. She'll give her life to try to protect us, but she's not strong enough. Sam, call your spirit, please!"

"I . . . I . . . don't know. I never have."

"Do it, Sam! Hurry!"

Sam thought of light, white light, like Frankie had described before the scrying. She called out in her hoarse voice. "Guide! Help me, please. Stop that darkness out there. Please."

Suddenly a blast of brightness filled the room, like the

terrible whiteness of a magnesium flare. It rotated in a spire of blinding radiance, sending rays streaming from wall to wall. Sam lifted up her hands to shield her eyes. As she did she thought she glimpsed a strange woman near the window, but she couldn't bear the intensity of the light. She had to look away.

From outside the house she heard a strangled call, followed by a high-pitched scream like the cry of an eagle. The thuds abruptly stopped. The window stopped rattling. The cold vanished and the room became warm again.

Then the pulsating light faded and went out. Sam took down her hands from her eyes. She looked toward the window. The gray cloud was gone. Sunlight streamed in. The sky was a perfect robin's-egg blue.

32

FRANKIE Corey let out a deep sigh. She felt relieved to be out on her own, away from that dreary suburban house and the other women. She turned up the air-conditioning in the government vehicle Ms. Z had assigned her. She was wearing a golf visor on her unruly hair to deal with the glare of the pitiless sun. It didn't really bother her, though. Driving in solitude seemed a treat. It was a new day.

But within a few minutes she tasted bitterness in her mouth, the same bitterness she had felt inside for weeks. Her catering business was gone; her Salem home was gone. Her Wiccan community had cast her out. Okay, she had made a mistake, an error in judgment, maybe, and she still wasn't sure how it had happened.

She blinked. No, she had to stop lying to herself. She knew exactly how it had happened. She had gone through a rough breakup, a nasty situation, really. All her insecurities had converged in one fell swoop. She felt used, pushed aside, and betrayed. So she had cast a spell she knew could be dangerous and it backfired. A sob started up from her chest. She gritted her teeth and pushed the memories away.

Salem, the man called Bobby, that terrible night when everything went wrong. That was then. This was now, her membership in AngelWay, her chance to make a clean start of it again.

She glanced over at her BlackBerry in the holder on the dashboard. Ms. Z had programmed in the address where she was going today, a posh Georgetown mansion belonging to an Arab diplomat, the prince of Oman.

Frankie didn't know the area yet, but Georgetown didn't seem too far from Langley. Frankie looked at the distance and estimated driving time on the BlackBerry's screen. She wasn't sure she liked using the map function on these devices. They dumbed a person down. No thinking required. Just do what the voice told you to. That wasn't Frankie's style. She liked to be in control.

She sighed again. She worried that particular personality trait of hers would make living with the other women difficult, no matter how temporary the situation was. The woman named Sam seemed like an okay person, although she was the only one of the team who hadn't been a professional clairvoyant or medium to start with. Frankie thought it was odd that the CIA had brought her into the project. After all, she and Rina had undergone a battery of tests to prove how good they were.

And they were good. She and Rina had outperformed hundreds of other mediums. Rina and she had tied in nearly every area of testing when the results came out. But that Rina! She wore her suffering like a badge of honor. And what she did—working with demons, calling out dead spirits—carried a lot of risk. Playing around on the dark side was no joke. Frankie had learned her lesson about that. The one time—the only time she had . . . The sob started upward in her throat again. She cut off the thought.

By this time Frankie had reached her destination. She parked in front of the beautiful old Georgetown home. Even after she turned off the engine, she kept sitting in the driver's seat and peered over the steering wheel at the house. She had been given a dossier about the prince, his staff, and this so-called robbery. She had questioned Ms. Z about why she was being sent here. Could the strange incident she was supposed to investigate have anything to do with the missing bodies at Arlington?

Ms. Z had been evasive, but didn't say no. "Find out for yourself," she said. "See what you think. Use the talents we recruited you to use." Then Ms. Z's pasty white face turned sour. "I'd like to see some results from you people."

Frankie climbed out of the car and nearly choked on the hot, humid air. She hurried up a flight of stone stairs to the front door. A middle-aged housekeeper let Frankie into the house and escorted her to a large, professionally equipped kitchen.

"You call yourself a chef?" The words flew out of Frankie's mouth before she could stop them.

"Just who might you be?" A handsome man in his late twenties set down the jar of mayonnaise he had been ladling into a bowl of what looked and smelled like canned tuna fish. His accent was pure Dublin. From his ruddy cheeks to black eyebrows that arched like a raven's wings, his face was a map of Ireland.

"Frances Corey. Are you Liam Mahoney? I was told to talk to you about a robbery." She extended her hand.

"Liam Mahoney, that's me." He picked up a towel, wiped his hand, and took hers without enthusiasm. "If you're here about the robbery, why is my cooking any business of yours?" His eyes weren't friendly.

Frankie frowned. "Your cooking isn't. But I was told you trained with Wolfgang Puck. You're using prepared mayonnaise. No real chef would. So who are you really?" Her voice was sharp. She had never felt comfortable with really good-looking men; her usual defense was to verbally attack any fault she could find.

The red crept up the young man's neck. "Listen, Sherlock Holmes. This *real chef* is preparing lunch for an indulged five-year-old who won't eat any mayonnaise but Hellmann's. And he does know the difference."

Frankie felt stupid then, but refused to back down. "How was I supposed to know that?"

"You could have asked before calling me an impostor." The young man went back to fixing a tuna sandwich.

A flash of intuition hit Frankie. This man *was* lying about something. "If I misjudged your behavior, I beg your pardon," she said carefully, paying closer attention to him now.

"It was none of your business." Liam avoided her eyes and opened up a large bag of potato chips.

Frankie glanced in the direction of the potato chips. "Perhaps," she said. "Look, I need to ask you some questions. About the robbery."

"Ms. Corey, if you will excuse me, I will answer your questions in a minute. His majesty, the young Prince Brat bin Sultan, is waiting." His voice had turned bitter. He picked up a Hostess Twinkie as if it were a dog turd. He added it to the tray now containing the sandwich, chips, and a can of Coca-Cola, and left the kitchen.

When Liam returned, his angry look had gone. He put out his hand again. "Ms. Corey, let's start over. I be owing you a wee bit of an apology meself."

He knows how to turn on the charm, Frankie thought, *and lay on his Irish accent with a trowel.* She took his hand and shook it. She'd be lying if she said she didn't feel something when she touched him. She did. He was a gorgeous young male.

For his part, Liam may have noticed her reaction. He preened like a man who knew women stared at him. Then he went on talking. "I don't like feeding junk food to a child either. But I do what I'm told if I want to keep my job."

"And his mother wants you to feed him that?"

"I really don't know what his mother thinks. She's not allowed to talk to me. His father, Prince Abdul bin Sultan, ordered me to give the boy what he wanted. He wants crisps and soda pop. At least he's not asking me for cocaine, don't you know."

Frankie smiled. When she chose to show them, she had dimples that changed her face from plain to one that men liked. She showed them now. "That's one way to look at it."

Liam stared at her with interest. His voice changed in the slightest way, becoming friendlier, nearly flirtatious, giving their conversation a sexual undercurrent. "Now, you wanted to ask me about the robbery. Come sit over here, so I can work while we talk. The prince is having some businessmen over this evening. He wants hors d'oeuvres."

Frankie sat at the breakfast bar on a stool as close to Liam as possible. "I hear you are the one who saw the 'baby' stealing . . . what was it? A diamond watch?"

"First off, I wouldn't say it was a baby, exactly. It looked sort of like a baby, but it wasn't a child a mother could love, I will tell you that." Liam began bathing asparagus in some ice water.

"Describe to me what you did see, okay?"

"It was small, maybe a foot and a half or two feet high. Big head. Small hands and feet. Grayish skin. Its eyes were covered in a cloudy film. The damned thing looked right at me. It sort of hissed at me. Then it ran on by, carrying the watch."

"Where were you when this happened?"

"Standing right here, doing pretty much what I'm doing now, except I was talking on my cell phone at the same time. It went through that door over there, after scooting across the kitchen, and ran out the back door.

"I yelled, 'Hey! Where you going with that?' I had a knife in my hand and I ran after it. But when I got in the back garden I didn't see anything. I looked around. It was small enough to hide itself under a bloody cabbage leaf, you know. But I didn't find anything."

"And Prince bin Sultan believed you?"

"He probably wouldn't have. Hell, he might have blamed me for the missing watch—and the other jewelry that's gone. I may be a Mick, but a dumb Mick I am not. I turned around my phone and took a picture of the wee, ugly thing. Here, take a look." Liam picked up the phone, which had been lying on the granite countertop, pushed some buttons, and passed it over to Frankie.

She looked. She recognized the thief immediately. "It's a toyol."

"A what?"

"A Malaysian child spirit. An Indonesian witch doctor can make it from a dead fetus. You can buy them if you have the right connections. But they don't let most people see them. I'm surprised it let you glimpse it."

Liam hesitated just a fraction of a second, then said, "I'm Irish. We all have a touch of the sight, you know."

Frances Corey's nose twitched a little. She supposed he was Irish, but he overplayed it. *Why?* she thought. "That probably explains why you could see the creature. They're used to steal things from wealthy people. Any Malaysians work for the prince?"

"The gardener. Or at least, he did. He and one of the prince's cousins had an argument. It came to blows beginning of last week."

"And it was about . . ."

"I think the cousin dug up some flowers, very rare ones evidently. He said he was burying a dead rat. The gardener about had a fit, started screaming in Malaysian, so I don't know for sure what he was saying, but it wasn't a rat that got buried. That's why the gardener was so upset—that and he really liked those flowers."

"Hmmmm. That's interesting. You have his name?"

"Ramli Adnan. He lives right off the Red Line someplace, Takoma Park or Silver Spring. You'll have to get the address from the housekeeper, Mrs. Doyle."

"By the way, if this cousin didn't bury a rat, do you know what he did bury?"

"I think it was some kind of animal entrails. A heart, maybe."

With the alarm bells going off, Frankie understood why Ms. Z had sent her out here. But what was the connection with the missing bodies? Did the prince fit into the scheme? Did Liam? She decided to hang out in the kitchen for a while. As long as she played on Liam's ego he didn't seem to mind, so she asked him about how he cooked for a large group.

He said he had to make a couple of vegetarian dishes, but most of the hors d'oeuvres he had to produce were simple—and expensive. The prince preferred caviar. His current favorite was a caviar shooter, a spoonful of fine Beluga accompanied by a shot of vodka or aquavit. Bin Sultan also had a penchant for edible gold and silver.

"The guy's got more money than God, or should I say, Allah," Liam said, and showed Frankie how to gild the rim of a martini glass with Oro Fino. Then he put some thin strips of silver on black caviar, which was piled on points of toast.

"But he's always wheeling and dealing. Trying to make even more money. He's from Oman. Never heard of it, right? If you check a map it borders Saudi Arabia on the Arabian Sea. Plenty of oil, of course. The prince meets with a lot of defense contractors. I think that's who's coming tonight."

"Hmmm. Liam, if you get the opportunity, pick up a name or two for me, will you?"

He looked at her shrewdly. "Why should I do something like that?"

"It might be worth your while, one way or another. Besides, you do want to cooperate with the authorities, right?"

"Are you asking me if I have a green card?"

Frankie shrugged. "Not really. But call me if you get anything, will you? Here." She handed over a business card she used for her most discreet consulting work, the kind she did with clients looking for love spells or revenge. It revealed nothing but her name and now, written in carefully over some Wite-Out, the number of her new BlackBerry.

Liam thought he caught her meaning and put the card in his back pocket. He almost leered. "I'll do that."

Then Liam got busy and Frankie said her good-byes. She went to find the housekeeper. She glanced back as she left the kitchen. The chef was bending over, getting something out of a low cabinet.

Nice ass, she thought, and wondered if she was getting herself into something she couldn't handle.

33

WANT you . . . Want you. The words echoed in Sam's brain and chilled her blood.

She left her bedroom, wondering if she'd ever feel comfortable there again. She headed for the kitchen and sat at the old red Formica table. She stared out at the backyard. The sun shifted in and out of the leaves, making the shadows move on the grass. Nothing looked amiss.

But the macabre apparition trying to get through the window had murdered Sam's desire for sleep. Her nerves had taken over. Her thoughts raced. She wanted to flee this place. The house that had been her refuge now felt like her cage.

Her BlackBerry rang. Since it was playing "The William Tell Overture," she knew without glancing at the screen that the caller was Ms. Z.

"You sound better," Ms. Z said.

"Somewhat." Sam's throat still ached, but it wasn't all that bad. She could bear it.

"Good. Look, Chase, we couldn't locate the gun. Are you certain about where you dropped it?"

"Yes. No doubt."

"It wasn't there. Signs of a struggle, yes, and we found the tire iron. Someone, probably your attacker, took the weapon with him."

"Okay. I wouldn't want some kid to pick it up, that's all."

"We had to let the public into the cemetery this morning, but the gun's probably gone. . . ." Ms. Z paused. "Anything? Any new information?"

Sam felt a flash of anger. The pressure to produce visions made her feel like a sideshow freak. "No."

"I'll be in touch." Ms. Z clicked off.

Sam sat for a minute debating whether she should listen to her messages on her home phone. She couldn't keep running away from the situation. She decided to listen to them.

They were all from Bear: First message, he had something he needed to tell her. Second message, he had gone out to Reston to Picture Perfection, Inc., and found out the equipment case, lights, and a camera had been rented to a Jamal al-Fayeed. Third message, al-Fayeed lived in Baltimore. Bear was on Route 295, driving out there. Fourth message, he need to speak with her. He really needed to speak with her. Call him . . . *Please.*

Sam's feelings about Bear weren't just mixed; they had been tossed around in a Cuisinart blender. She couldn't sort them out. She thought for a moment. She didn't know if she could drive with the Darvocet in her system, but Bel Air would be only a short detour for Bear on the way to Baltimore. She made the call.

Sam limped out of the house and slipped into the passenger seat of the Stratus. She had put on the same khaki slacks and jacket she had worn on the plane. She had few things to wear, with most of her wardrobe still in transit from Iraq, but still folded neatly in one of her dresser drawers she had found a pretty white cami with thin straps of satin ribbon. The lacy edge scooped down low, revealing the swell of her breasts, and the thin fabric was nearly transparent. It might not be work-appropriate, but no one would really see it anyway if she kept on the light cotton jacket.

She also had tried to disguise the bruises on her neck with makeup. The blemish stick didn't hide the injury completely, but it was the best she could do.

As far as Bear went, it didn't really matter what Sam wore. His face paled when he saw her. He studied her with worried eyes. "You up to this?"

Perspiration had broken out on her forehead just from walking the fifty feet from her front door to the car. The heat wave had continued unabated. Bear reached over and turned on the air conditioner full blast.

"I'm okay," Sam croaked. "Thanks for picking me up."

"Yeah, sure." Bear studied her again. Sam turned her head away and got busy watching out the window. He backed the car out of the driveway and headed toward Baltimore. They didn't exchange another word. Bear put a news station on the radio and let the announcer's voice fill the silence between them.

A special report talked about street gangs breaking shop windows in southeast Washington and looting some electronics. Police had beefed up patrols in the area. Until the heat broke, authorities agreed tensions would escalate. The mayor threatened to impose a curfew. Then the discussion switched to global warming and whether the heat would batter the nation's capital for the rest of the summer.

Meanwhile al-Fayeed's address led Bear and Sam to a brick house in one of Baltimore's westside neighborhoods not far from the old B&O Railroad yards. A short, built-like-a-tank African-American woman opened the front door. A blast of cold air escaped from the interior into the furnace of the day.

"We're looking for Jamal al-Fayeed," Bear said.

"He's not here." The woman wore army fatigues and combat boots. Her voice was clipped, military, suspicious. "Who are you?"

"Lance Rutledge, working out of the inspector general's office of the DOD." He pulled out his wallet and showed her a badge. "You are . . . ?"

"Staff Sergeant Robinson, Army National Guard, Fifth Regiment. What's this all about?"

"We need to ask Mr. Fayeed a few questions. Do you know where he is?"

"No. He's crashing here until he gets his own place. We don't keep tabs on each other. We were stationed together in Iraq."

"Is he still in the military?" Sam's voice was hoarse, but audible.

After Sergeant Robinson studied Sam's bandaged

scalp, she looked at Sam's bruised neck before meeting her eyes. "Jamal do that?" she asked.

"What? No. Why would you think so?" Sam asked.

"He's not good with women."

"What about with you?" Bear asked.

Robinson snorted. "We're buddies, that's all. Anyways, you asked me if Jamal was still in service. Nah, he got discharged a couple of months ago. I'm not here most of time. He watches the place for me. Works out okay."

"Do you know where he is now?"

Robinson took her time before she answered, probably thinking about what to say. She pulled a pack of cigarettes and a Bic lighter from her shirt pocket. She lit up, took a deep drag, exhaled, then lifted one shoulder dismissively. "I don't know where he is. He didn't come home last night. You should ask his mother. Jamal's a mama's boy. If he's not there, she'll know where he is. She *always* knows where he is." She laughed again.

Robinson gave them an address in College Park, Maryland.

Back in the Stratus, Bear turned to Sam. "You want to go home or come along?"

"I'll come along. I need to be doing something besides sitting."

"Okay, then."

Sam looked down at the tiny woman who had answered the door of a new town house in College Park. Behind her glasses, al-Fayeed's mother had sad eyes that seemed to have lost all hope. A black scarf covered her white hair, and her shoulders stooped under a black dress. She remained standing in the doorway of the house. She didn't ask them inside.

"You want to know where is Jamal? With Allah. My son is dead," she said in a thick voice.

This news caught Sam by surprise. "When did he die?"

"Who knows? But I know he is dead. He hasn't called me. Two nights. He's a good boy. He's always been a good boy. Never in trouble. Always good to me, always calling home every night. Seven o'clock. He must be dead."

Before she and Bear got out of the car, Sam had said she wanted to do the questioning, despite her throat. Now she talked to Jamal's mother in a kind voice. "I hope that's not true, Mrs. al-Fayeed. My partner, Mr. Rutledge, and I, we're trying to find him too."

"Are you the police? You don't look like police." Her voice was suddenly guarded.

"No, we're not the police. We both work for the federal government."

"Ah, yes, so you work with my son?" The woman's eyes narrowed.

"No, we don't. He didn't work for the government, did he?" Sam wondered what was going on.

"He said he did. Top secret work, he said. And that car you have . . ." She pointed at the street toward the white Dodge Stratus, the government vehicle that Bear used. "They picked him up sometimes in a car like that."

"That's a pretty common vehicle, ma'am," Bear cut in. "Why did you think it was from the government?"

"The license plate. It had a government plate."

Sam looked at Bear with a question in her eyes. He shrugged; then Sam turned back to the small, sad woman. "We know your son was taking photographs out in Arlington National Cemetery about a week ago. Did he tell you about that?"

She shook her head and for a brief moment squeezed her eyes shut as if overcome by pain. "No. He never tell me nothing about his job. Not like when he was in the service. He always tell me what he was doing."

Sam tried to prompt her. Surely the woman knew something about what her son did. "We know he was filming in the cemetery with two other men. Could they have been friends of his? Do you know who they were?"

"I don't know nothing about that. If he doing his job, they were just men he worked with. His friends, from before the military, not many still live around here. They all move away."

"Did he tell you how to contact him at work? Do you know what government agency he worked for?"

She nodded, seemingly anxious to prove that what she had said about her son's job was true. "He *did* work for the government. He gave me card. I get for you." She disappeared into the house. She returned a few moments later with a business card. She handed it to Bear. He looked at it and showed it to Sam. In expensively embossed letters it read:

USEI
United States Enterprise Institute
229 L Street NW
Washington, D.C. 20024
Arthur Bilderberg, Chairman

"You know anything about Bilderberg or USEI?" Sam asked Bear when they got back in the car.

Bear started the engine and turned on the air conditioner, but didn't pull the car away from the curb. "Bilderberg? The name sounds familiar. I'll do some digging." He paused. His eyes studied Sam's face, looked at the white adhesive over the wound on her scalp, then moved to the bruises on her neck. A muscle twitched near his temple. "I'd like to clear the air, Sam. Apologize."

Sam's heart sank. Her face got rigid. "Please don't."

"I need to explain. And there's a couple of things you should know." He spoke quickly, before Sam could say anything else. "Bartikowski's wife is dead. I went back there last night. She'd been shot. I found voodoo items in the basement. Under Bartikowski's workbench."

Sam's eyes widened. The dots were starting to connect, but the picture they were making didn't make sense. "Did you tell your boss?"

"No. I called the D.C. cops anonymously from a pay phone I found still working near a liquor store."

"I should tell Ms. Z." She started to pull her BlackBerry from her purse.

"You want to wait on that?" Bear reached over and stopped her hand by covering it with his own. His touch sent electric sparks shooting up Sam's arm. She briefly closed her eyes. She did not want to react. She did not want to feel anything for this man, let alone a flood of desire.

"Why wait?" she asked, and disengaged her hand.

"I have trust issues with you people. It's part of what I wanted to explain. Something's going on, and yeah, I felt like you were part of it. Trying to set me up."

Sam looked stunned. "Set you up? Why?"

"I don't know. Keep me from getting too close to the truth? Keep me out of the loop? I don't know yet. But you people broke into my house and searched it. That's how my cat got out."

"The agency searched your place? How do you know it was us?"

Bear turned away and stared out the front window. "Look at it logically, Sam. Nobody else had any reason to. Nothing was taken. Just snooping around. I don't know why. Hoping to find something that might compromise me? Porn? Who knows?"

An image flashed through Sam's mind. She saw a hand opening a drawer and putting a thick brown envelope inside it. "Bear, how thoroughly did you look around your house? After the search, I mean."

"Well enough to see that nothing was missing. Why?"

"Maybe somebody wasn't searching your place. Maybe they were planting something."

Bear's whole body jerked. He hit the steering wheel with his fist. "Son of a bitch! Son of a bitch! That's it. That's got to be it."

A sudden realization also flooded through Sam. Somebody *was* setting Bear up, but was it the agency? "We'd better get to your place. And, Bear, something else you should know . . ."

He pulled out into the street, focused on getting back to Washington as fast as possible. "What?"

"Bartikowski's wife was shot, right?" she asked.

"Yeah."

"You see the murder weapon anywhere?"

"No. The perp took it with him. She wasn't a suicide, so there wasn't a gun." His comments were offhand, unsuspicious.

He really didn't know, Sam thought. "Are you sure there was no gun there?" Sam persisted.

"Huh?" He glanced over at her. "I didn't see one. I wasn't really looking. Why would the perp leave it behind?"

Sam didn't answer right away, still thinking things over. Finally she said, "You know that gun you gave me? The .38 snub-nosed?"

Bear's body tensed. "The one you told me you dropped in the cemetery during the fight?"

"Yes. Ms. Z said they couldn't find it where we got ambushed. She said the attacker must have taken it with him. Now you tell me Bartikowski's wife was shot to death. Do you really think that's a coincidence?"

Bear's hands tightened on the steering wheel. "I don't believe in coincidence. And if my gun's at the crime scene somewhere, it won't take long for the cops to find it's registered to me." Then he shrugged. "But it won't prove anything. You reported the gun lost in the cemetery. It's no big deal."

Sam gave her head a little shake. "No big deal, Bear, unless . . ."

"Unless what?"

"Unless they think I'm lying about dropping the gun. To protect you."

Bear frowned. "That's pretty far-fetched, don't you think?"

"I don't know. Maybe. But it won't look far-fetched if whatever they planted in your house implicates you too."

34

THE breeze in the branches of the trees along the cemetery wall made a whooshing sound. Aurora thought it could be Oonawieh Unggi, the oldest of the Cherokee wind spirits, talking to her. She stopped to listen.

Rina waited respectfully at a distance. Aurora, having been incarcerated, no longer had a driver's license and was grateful that Rina agreed to the excursion when she returned to Bel Air from Langley with a government vehicle.

When Rina drove up to the house, Sam had just left with Bear. Frankie was still out. But even if the other women had been there, it seemed natural to Aurora to ask Rina to go with her. Aurora felt more comfortable with the voodoo practitioner than with the other two team members. Sam and Frankie were very *white* women, she thought. Aurora wasn't prejudiced. Her mother's grandfather had been Welsh, and her father's mother had been French. It wasn't that. The two women lived lives a world away from hers, that was all.

Rina wasn't so different. The cat, Miranda, had gone to Rina right away, which meant that Rina connected with animals like Aurora did. And Rina's high cheek bones and dark hair made Aurora think she had some mixed blood herself, although Aurora was too polite to ask.

In general, Aurora observed that Rina didn't talk much. Like the Cherokee, Rina used words sparingly. She talked only when she had something that must be said. That suited Aurora just fine too. In the car, on the drive to the cemetery, Aurora had told Rina what had happened at the house.

All Rina did was make a "huh" sound in her throat. She listened to Aurora describe the strange demonic intruder, but didn't ask any questions. Afterward they rode in silence toward D.C. Finally Aurora ventured to ask why Rina had joined AngelWay. After all, everybody knew why Aurora was part of it. It was her get-out-of-jail-free card.

"I was told to join." That was Rina's answer, leaving even more questions unexplained. Who told Rina to join? Why had she agreed to do it?

Aurora had considered asking them, but Rina had turned on the car radio at that point and cranked up the volume on an old Bruce Springsteen song. She made it clear she didn't care for any more conversation.

Now, standing here in the parking lot, listening to the wind, Aurora expressed her thanks to the spirits for her freedom. She thanked Yowa the Great Spirit, of course, but she called on Sint Holo, the horned serpent, for special help. She thought Sint Holo might bring her even closer to Rina, who had a snake totem too, because Aurora badly needed an ally. For one thing, Aurora was not a loner. She grew up as part of a tribe. She appreciated having a new sister to watch her back. But more than that, if she failed in this project, this AngelWay, and if Ms. Z tried to send her back to jail, she might need someone to help her run.

Aurora completed her prayers and beckoned to the voodoo woman. Together they went into the visitors' center and passed through the building into the graveyard's grounds beyond.

Aurora and Rina walked quickly toward the amphitheater. When they got there, the area was largely deserted. Newly erected fencing screened off much of this section of the cemetery. A poster with ATTENTION VISITORS in letters four inches high had been affixed to the tall wooden boards. The official announcement informed the public that the changing of the guard at the Tomb of the Unknowns had been suspended until further notice. The amphitheater was closed. Emergency repairs were under way to curtail "severe and dangerous environmental damage."

Aurora had kept Miranda out of sight, making her ride in a large shoulder bag, but an occasional meow issued forth from her hiding place.

"Miranda hasn't picked up anything disturbing. I don't sense anything more than the spirits of the dead. Do you hear voices calling to you?" Aurora asked Rina.

"No, not yet. But they will," Rina answered. Her face wore a pinched look. "Even if you hadn't decided to come here, I needed to. After the murders last night, this is now a crime scene. This is what I do."

"So do it," Aurora urged.

Rina walked away, following the fence that encircled the building. Her shoulders rocked back and forth; her body swayed. Her odd behavior made the few visitors in the area stand and stare. Parents took their children and hurried away, wary of the woman behaving strangely.

Meanwhile Aurora scanned the tree branches, soon realizing that neither squirrels nor birds would be helpful. They were active in daylight. The killings and emptying of the graves had happened at night. She needed to find a nocturnal creature. A mouse would do; a rat would be even better. They were far smarter.

Aurora looked around. Where there was garbage, there were rats.

Litter bins sat in the middle of the walkways in this high-traffic area, since normally the changing of the guard drew a crowd each hour. But where would the rats be hiding? Aurora knew rats didn't like crossing open ground. They preferred to slink along walls and follow established trails.

She didn't see any evidence that the creatures had been active here, and she didn't have the nose to find a rat's nest, but Miranda did.

She lifted the cat out of her shoulder bag and set her down on the ground. The big orange feline began sniffing a litter bin, then strolled in the direction of the temporary fencing. When she reached it, the cat hunched down and easily walked through the six-inch space between the bottom of the boards and the ground.

Aurora looked around. Every now and then a person walked up to the poster, read it, and quickly left. No one paid any attention to her. She began to follow the fence, looking for a way to slip inside. She didn't want to go too far from where Miranda had disappeared. She found an area near the flagpole where a dip in the lawn left a greater width under the bottom of the fence.

She got down on her back, pushed her shoulder bag through the space, and then scooted under the boards. Once inside she saw Miranda sitting calmly in the sun, waiting for her. As soon as she stood up and brushed herself off, the cat walked off toward a grate near the ground at the base of the marble wall. The cat reached it and sniffed.

Aurora went over and hunkered down next to the grate. She could smell the acrid, musty odor of rodent droppings. She closed her eyes and concentrated. The rats were at home—rats, plural, quite a lot of them. Male and female rats formed couples, raised families, and congregated in large colonies. Aurora hoped one of them would be willing to "talk."

Immediately she sensed that the rats were agitated. The forensic men with their noisy vehicles and equipment had surely upset them. The smell of blood might have bothered them as well. Rats weren't carnivores, although they'd chew on a dead carcass if their preferred diet—packaged processed cheese on wheat crackers was a favorite—wasn't available.

But since the crowds that showed up with food and beverages every hour had been turned away, the litter bins were empty, and so were the rats' stomachs. Aurora could do something about that. She had become a snack-oholic in prison. Nutritious food wasn't readily available, but inmates could buy just about any high-fat edible in the prison commissary. Carrying around chips and candy bars had become a habit, and she had amassed a new stash of goodies when the women had taken their trip to the supermarket.

Aurora rummaged in her bag. She came up with a box of Cheez-Its, a couple of energy bars, and a box of Dots. She opened the Cheez-Its and started pushing them through the grate until a little pile grew inside the opening. She opened an energy bar, broke it up, and added that to the pile. The Dots followed.

She sat there and waited. Finally a young, not-so-cautious rat approached the free lunch. The rat grabbed a Cheez-It and ran off, but soon came back.

Squatting by the grate, Miranda, with her mind, not her voice, asked him to talk with her. He stopped. His nose twitched. His button eyes glared at her. She understood he was hungry. He was impatient to eat. She felt discouraged but asked him if there had been a fight in the amphitheater. A fight was something animals understood.

In her mind she saw images of the park service men, who had been working security that night, their feet, the legs of their uniforms. These things were familiar to the rat. He saw the feet running and the two men falling down, then being set upon by their attackers. He became very frightened and ran. He hid in the shadows under a bench in the amphitheater. He saw the men eating.

Men eating? Aurora questioned him about that. The rat showed her what the men with the combat boots were eating. Gray matter. Brains.

Aurora asked where the attackers went when they were done.

The rat had crouched trembling under the bench until he saw a chance to move. He wanted to reach the grate near the ground so he could get to his nest. He dashed under a bush and hid. The big noisy nest that moved came. Aurora got the image of a long black hearse. The attackers got in it and left. The rat ran back to the grate and felt safe under the amphitheater with the others like him. He had been hungry since then.

Aurora opened up another energy bar and pushed pieces through the metal mesh. It wouldn't feed many rats, but it would help them survive until the visitors' tasty garbage returned.

She straightened up, stiff from squatting. She called to Miranda, and the two of them went back under the fence. Aurora didn't know if what she had learned would be helpful, but it was something, more than she expected. But since she had gleaned the information from a rat, she didn't know how much credence it would hold with Ms. Z.

While Aurora talked to the rodents, Rina had given herself over to the voices of the dead. She had heard them at last, two men—the murdered men. They called to her to come inside the fence too. But Rina didn't shimmy underneath it. She found where a door in the boards was held shut by a length of chain. She wedged her thin body through the narrow opening. The dead led her inside, demanding she climb the stairs to the rim of the amphitheater, insisting she look at the place where they died.

She stood there, on the walkway above the seating, while a breeze tugged at her loose cotton trousers. A deep pain coursed through her body, the pain of the dead. They showed her what had happened to them. She walked over to where they had fallen. She would rather not have seen their last few minutes on earth. They hadn't fought very long. They had been terrified. They had fallen to their knees and begged for their lives.

The men who killed them had no mercy. They wore the combat uniforms that Sam had described. The murdered security guards didn't know their killers. They repeated that the killers were soldiers and told her over and over that these soldiers had dead eyes.

Rina nodded. All she had believed from the beginning had been confirmed. She went to find Aurora and her cat. They needed to get out of here. She'd drive Aurora back to Bel Air. Then Rina would contact people in the voodoo community. Someone had called out the dead. Zombies had come to Washington, D.C. She knew they would kill the living and desecrate the land unless she acted. And acted soon.

35

BEAR squealed the tires of the Stratus as he careened into the parking place behind his house and braked fast. He took off at a run to get inside. Sam followed. He had already flung open the kitchen cabinets when she walked in.

She wanted to tell him to examine the drawers, but didn't. How would she explain that she knew it was there? But he started searching them quickly enough. He pulled the thick envelope from the back of a utility drawer. "What's this?" He tore it open. One-hundred-dollar bills spilled out. He stared at the cash, perplexed. "There must be ten thousand dollars here. And wait, what's this?"

He picked out a white paper, a piece of torn wrapping with the words MYSTIC BRAND EVIL EYE GRIS-GRIS printed on it. "Shit. I found the same thing at Bartikowski's."

"Give it to me. I'll keep it in my purse until you decide what you want to do." She put out her hand.

"Why?"

"Because if I've got it, when the cops show up with a search warrant, they still won't find it."

"You think they're going to show up?"

"I have a strong hunch they will," she said, and she did.

"You're probably right." He passed the envelope over to Sam. "Let's talk about this, what you think is going on, but give me a minute. I need to look for the cat."

But Nada was not at the front door waiting. She wasn't anywhere in the small backyard. Bear called her name a few times, but his heart wasn't in it. She didn't come running. He finally turned to Sam, his voice flat and pained. "You probably haven't eaten. I'll order some Chinese if you want, or a pizza."

Sam took a deep breath. What she was about to do might be a mistake, but she had to try. "Never mind the food. Let me call one of my roommates, Aurora. Maybe she can find your cat."

Confusion appeared in Bear's eyes. "What are you talking about? How can she possibly find Nada? I called all the animal shelters. I walked the neighborhood. At least I didn't find a body in the street, so there's still hope. I can put up some posters. There's nothing else to do."

"Yes, there is. Please, Bear, give this a try."

"I don't know what you're talking about. Try what?"

"Aurora is . . . is . . . what they call an animal communicator. Wait, don't just turn away. She specializes in finding lost objects. She's found dozens of lost pets. Honest to God she has. What do you have to lose?"

Bear shook his head. "I don't understand why you believe in all that paranormal stuff."

"That's not the point. You have to give Nada this last chance. You risk nothing. Do it for her."

Bear exhaled hard. "I'm at the end of my rope. You might think it's dumb to care so much about a cat, but . . . but I love that little animal. She's . . . I don't know. She represents a part of me, I think." When he looked at Sam there were tears in his eyes. He blinked them away. "Yeah, go ahead, call your friend."

Sam quickly got hold of Aurora. She was back at the Bel Air house. Sam explained the situation.

Aurora listened so quietly Sam could hear her breathing. Then, in a soft voice, she said she'd ask Miranda what she could find out.

Sam fidgeted impatiently while she waited for Aurora to come back on the phone. When Aurora did, her voice came through high-pitched and urgent: "Put your fellow on the phone, quick."

Sam handed Bear the phone, but Aurora was talking loud enough so that Sam could hear what she said.

"Miranda contacted Nada. She's trapped in a garage.

Some kids have her. You have to hurry. They've doused her with gasoline. She's terrified."

"Garage? What garage? Where?" Bear yelled frantically into the phone.

"It's . . . Let me see . . . I can't see a street name. But the garage is one of those old cement-block types. Single-car. Folding door in front. There's a white door in the side."

"There are hundreds of those garages. What else can you see?" Bear got his voice under control, as if he knew exploding wouldn't help. But while he listened, he was tearing around the kitchen, pulling a large towel out of a drawer and opening the cellar door to retrieve a cat carrier.

"Let me concentrate. Please be very quiet." Bear stopped moving entirely. After what seemed like an eternity to Sam but was only seconds, Aurora finally said, "I can see a narrow cement walk. It leads to the house in front of the garage. A funny colored house. Deep purple with blue trim."

"Got it!" he yelled. "I'm on my way." He dropped the phone on the counter and grabbed the carrier and towel in his big hands. Then he tore out the back door, leaving it wide-open. Sam retrieved the phone and went after Bear, but made sure the door closed behind her.

Sam could see Bear ahead of her, running flat out. He headed down the long communal driveway that led behind the houses to the next street. He turned left when he reached its end and raced down the sidewalk. He barely slowed in front of a Victorian house, purple with blue trim, before he vaulted over an iron fence and disappeared down a walkway between the house and its neighbor.

Sam reached the walkway in time to see Sam fifty feet away alongside a garage. He was trying to open the white door in its side. It must have been locked. He didn't hesitate. He took his foot and kicked it hard, splintering the frame. The door flew open with a bang.

Sam saw him rush inside. She heard him yell, "*Police!*" Two teenage boys came bolting out through the open white door, ran toward her, and forced her to flatten herself against the building as they rushed past.

Then she darted down the walk to the garage, praying all the while that the cat was alive, that it hadn't been set afire. When she got to the open door, Bear was holding something in the towel. "Is she . . . ?" Sam could barely speak while the fear crawled up her throat like a living thing.

"She's okay, I think. Soaked in gasoline, though. She may be in shock. I can feel her shaking through the towel. Let me get her into the carrier. Here." He reached a hand into his trouser pocket and pulled out his car keys. He tossed them to Sam. "Get the car, will you? I need to take Nada to the vet."

At the emergency veterinary clinic, Sam passed the time leafing through magazines in the waiting room. Bear bought candy bars from a vending machine and a couple of cans of soda. They didn't talk about Aurora or how she had located the cat. It was the six-hundred-pound gorilla in the living room that Sam knew they'd have to acknowledge sooner or later.

Finally Nada was pronounced uninjured and taken somewhere in the back of the offices to be cleaned. Since the terrified cat had tried to bite the vet tech, they were going to have to sedate her to do it. The idea of anesthesia and its risks upset Bear, and he paced up and down the linoleum floor of the waiting room for a while. When he sat down again, Sam asked him what he wanted to do about the boys who had taken the cat.

"Kill them."

Sam's eyes grew huge. "You wouldn't!"

Bear shook his head. "No, of course not. That's just what I feel like doing. I'm so angry. The veterinary clinic is going to file a report on this. Meanwhile, I'll find out who the kids are and talk with their parents. I'll threaten to take legal action if they don't get those kids into therapy." He sighed. "I wouldn't hurt the kids—they're still children—but, Sam, you need to understand something: I might be doing the world a favor if I did. You look shocked."

"That's a pretty radical thing to say."

Bear regarded Sam with glittering eyes. "I'd like to

think that therapy is going to help those boys. But I know—I've been in this business long enough to understand that abusing small animals is a warning sign of serious criminal behavior. Child abusers start off that way. Worse than that can happen too. Serial killers always, and I mean always, start off killing people's pets. Society would have been better served if somebody had stopped them at that point."

Impulsively Sam reached over and took Bear's hand. "But you are stopping them, Bear. You're making these parents recognize they've got troubled kids. You're going to force them to get help—and to know they can't get away with that behavior."

Bear curled his fingers around hers and didn't let go. He stared without seeing at the opposite wall. "They were going to set Nada on fire, Sam. That's a very sick thing to do."

"I know." She gave his hand a reassuring squeeze, and for a long time afterward neither one of them let go.

"Let me call up for that Chinese food." Bear reached for a menu from a holder next to the kitchen phone when they got back to his house. "Here. Pick out what you want. Nada's pretty out of it. I'm going to lock her up in the bedroom with the litter box. I'll leave her food and water up there. After we eat, I'll run you back to Bel Air. It will give me enough time to make sure she's doing okay before we leave."

The cat had yowled loudly all the way back from the vet. To Sam Nada seemed on the road to a speedy recovery. "Sounds good," she said. In truth she felt worn out. Maybe she would feel better if she ate something.

While Bear was upstairs, Sam's cell phone rang. It was Frankie.

"When are you coming back here?" the witch asked.

"In another hour and a half, probably, maybe two hours. Why?"

"I have something to tell you when you get here. And . . ." She paused. "I heard what happened in your bedroom this afternoon. We need to deal with it."

A frisson of fear ran across Sam's skin. "Can you?"

"We can try. Get here as soon as you can."

"Okay." Sam clicked off as Bear came back into the kitchen.

"You know, I really need to get back to Bel Air. Can we skip the food?"

Bear's disappointment showed on his face. His voice was brusque when he answered, "If that's what you want."

Then his eyes caught Sam's, and what he really felt was nakedly apparent: Bear didn't want her to leave. Sam could see that. The world shifted beneath her feet, and a bolt of desire hit her like a lightning strike.

"No." The word came out carried on her breath, somewhere between a whisper and a sigh. "No, that's not what I want."

Bear reached out his hand. Sam took it. He pulled her against his broad chest and enfolded her in his arms. His mouth came down and covered hers. The room began to spin as if Sam were on a crazy carousel, the horses cantering up and down, the calliope playing, her heart racing. She held tight to Bear's waist, losing herself in the sensation of his body touching hers, his lips caressing her, his hands slipping up into her hair.

And as the carousel of passion spun her around and around, Sam knew this was nothing like she had ever felt before. "Oh . . ." A sound came up from deep inside her. "Oh, Bear . . ."

The big man broke the kiss and put his forehead against hers. "Sam, I need to say I'm sorry. You wouldn't let me say it before. But I am. I'm sorry."

Sam felt herself trembling harder now, listening to Bear's emotion-laden voice.

He went on: "I didn't trust you. I didn't know you. I was wrong about you. About a lot of things." His eyes searched her face.

"Bear, it's okay. Everything's okay." But Sam was shaking from head to toe, her body quaking like a leaf caught in the wind, being swept away.

"I know we shouldn't be doing this—"

"But we are," Sam said. "Do you care that we shouldn't be doing this?"

Bear put his hands on either side of her face. "I'd

care if we *didn't* do this. I have never wanted a woman so much."

She believed him. She knew he was telling the truth. He kissed her, and the carousel began turning again. Her desire was building fast, much faster than was wise. Yet all the while they were standing in the kitchen, her back against the granite counter, and the edge digging into her spine made her squirm and shift her weight.

Bear noticed. "Let's go into the family room. The couch would be more comfortable." He hesitated and added, "I mean, if that's okay."

The kitchen was a well-lit place, all hard edges and highly polished surfaces, not a setting for making love. Sam understood that if she said yes to moving away from here, she was saying yes to something else too.

Her eyes glittered. Her face had become flushed. A fire had begun to burn in her belly. "Yes, that's okay."

Bear took her hand and led her through a door into a room with the blinds drawn, the light dim. They stopped near a long, wide couch.

"Would you be more comfortable without your jacket?" he asked.

She nodded and slipped it off. His breath caught as he saw the full, soft mounds of her breasts above the lace of the cami. The ribbon strap slipped down from one pale shoulder.

"My God. You're so beautiful." He reached out for the jacket, then dropped it on the recliner, not taking his eyes from her, adoring her as if she were something precious, something almost sacred.

Sam stood there, her legs steadier now. She lifted the cami up over her head and let it slip from her fingers to the floor. Then she reached out and caught Bear's hand, urgency in her touch, bringing him to her as she moved his hand to one of her breasts.

His fingers teased her nipple, making it stand erect. Then he explored her curves, stroking her slowly until she wanted to purr. She leaned her cheek on his shoulder, savoring the sensations of his caresses. She relaxed against him, her will fleeing. "Do you want me?" Her voice was soft, almost pleading.

"Want you? I want you. I want you so much. But are you sure?" he whispered into her hair.

In answer she unbuttoned her slacks. She told him to wait a moment until she stepped out of them and then removed her panties. She kicked the clothes aside. She felt bold; she felt brazen; she felt as if she couldn't wait another moment before they took the last step across the chasm of the dark abyss of desire.

She heard Bear swallow hard. Now his breath came fast and heavy, and when he spoke, his voice was hoarse with desire. "Should I get a condom?"

"Yes. Yes. Please. Please hurry."

He stepped away, hurrying from the room, leaving her naked and alone there. She thought one last time, should she do this? But she knew the answer. She wanted this; she wanted *him* like she had never wanted anyone before.

Bear came back quickly, the condom unwrapped from the package in his hand. He unsnapped his jeans and unzipped his fly. He wore no underwear. His shaft stood tall, hard, and thick. He put the condom on. Sam watched his every move, mesmerized by his maleness.

He pulled off his shirt. He removed his jeans. He stood there facing her, pausing for a moment before he came back to her. Then his lips descended and lights exploded behind Sam's eyes. He gently pushed her backward, and she sank down on the couch. He followed, positioning himself above her. He carefully lay atop her, belly to belly, keeping some of his weight on his forearms. She encircled his neck with her slim arms. She buried her face against his shoulder, her eyes closed. She could barely breathe in anticipation of what was about to happen. She didn't want to wait. She didn't want more foreplay. She let him know by spreading her legs wide.

Bear wedged himself between them. His erection touched her then, and Sam held her breath. He found her dark center with ease and pushed hard. She exhaled with a gasp as he slid into her.

She was tight; he was large. She felt a burst of pain as the length of him filled her, stretching her open to admit him as far as he could go. She mewed like a kitten, then bit her lip as he drew the length of him out of her, only to ram himself into her again. He ground his hips against her, making her moan. She held on to him fiercely, digging her fingers into the flesh of his shoulders.

And then Bear began a rhythmic pumping that Sam's light, happy sighs soon matched. She was lost in pleasure as he touched her exactly right, moved exactly right, inciting her desire. Then Sam wrapped her legs around his hips, and he penetrated deeper still, touching high up inside her where a burst of feeling made her gasp. He made a noise something like a growl deep in his throat.

"There, right there," she begged, feeling frantic for him to hit the same spot again. "Push again there."

That pressure, their wild hungers, and the total entrapment of her body beneath his released everything she had been resisting. She came, arching her back and flinging her head back, overwhelmed with feeling. She cried out while waves of sensation took her—and with one mighty push Bear shuddered inside her, coming too.

Then they were both quiet, stilled. Bear raised his head to say something—and they heard a pounding on the front door.

"Police! Open up."

"Ah, shit!" Bear pulled away from Sam suddenly and jumped off the couch. He grabbed his clothes from the floor and hurried toward the kitchen as the pounding started again.

"Just a minute!" Bear bellowed. He glanced back at Sam from the doorway. "Get dressed!" he hissed at her, his voice urgent. Before Sam could answer, she heard water running in the kitchen sink, some splashes, and then a paper towel being torn from the roll.

Her mind understood Bear's rushing away, but her emotions didn't. It wasn't his fault that they had been interrupted, but Sam still had an unaccountable urge to cry. The lovemaking hadn't ended right. There had been no time for tenderness, no time to be reassured that sex hadn't been a mistake. With a sinking feeling, Sam wondered if she had been foolish, if it *had* been a mistake.

I'm being oversensitive, Sam told herself as she dressed. She made herself as presentable as possible before walking into the hallway, where Bear glanced over at her before he opened the front door.

Two men stood on the stoop. One was Asian; the other was a hugely obese African-American who was sweating heavily. Both wore wrinkled cotton suits and black tie shoes, the kind with a perpetual shine. They identified themselves as D.C. homicide detectives. They asked if he was Lance Rutledge.

"I'm Assistant Inspector Rutledge, Department of Defense," he barked. "What's this all about?"

"We just want to ask you a few questions, Inspector." The men acted respectfully, even apologetic that they were there. "Mind if we come inside?"

Bear opened the door wider. The two men walked in. Sam was standing in the hall. "This is Agent Susan Chase," Bear said. "Now, what do you men want?"

"Do you know a Robin Bartikowski?" The Asian cop, the shorter, much thinner of the two men, did all the talking. His voice was less pleasant now that he was inside.

Bear stood tall, making himself look even bigger than he was. "I questioned a Mrs. John Bartikowski in the course of an open investigation. Is that who you mean?"

"Yes, sir. When was it that you interviewed Mrs. Bartikowski?"

"Yesterday, around noontime. Why?"

"This interview took place inside her home in southeast Washington?"

"Yes."

"What did you talk about with her?"

"That's classified. It involves an ongoing investigation; that's all I can say."

"Did you have reason to go back there last night?"

"No."

"Did you know Robin Bartikowski is dead?"

"No."

"Do you own a .38-caliber snub-nosed Smith and Wesson revolver? With a pearl handle?"

"Yes."

"Can you explain to us how it ended up in Bartikowski's house? At the crime scene?"

"No. The gun was lost during an attack on myself and Agent Chase in Arlington National Cemetery last night."

"Can you prove that?"

"I reported it to my superior," Sam said.

"So you were not at Bartikowski's house last night? And you don't know how your gun got there?"

"No and no. Is that all, gentlemen?" Bear started to open the door.

"Actually, no, Inspector Rutledge. We're going to have to ask you to come back to the precinct with us."

"Why?" Bear's voice was suddenly guarded. "Am I under arrest?"

"Not if you're willing to come back with us voluntarily. We want you to take part in a lineup."

"A lineup? What for?"

The fat detective's voice came out with a trace of disgust. "*Three* witnesses put a suspect matching your description in the vicinity of Bartikowski's house around two a.m. last night. All of them say you were carrying a gun."

After that, Bear insisted on calling his lawyer. The attorney said he'd meet Bear at the police station. Sam said she'd come too, but Bear said no. She needed to go home. He offered to let her drive the Mustang, since he wasn't authorized to let her operate his government vehicle.

Sam didn't feel comfortable with that. She told him she'd get her own ride back.

He nodded and added that he'd phone her later as soon as he got this situation straightened out. He sounded in control and not upset.

Sam didn't think getting the "situation straightened out" was going to be as easy as Bear thought. As soon as he left with the detectives, she called Ms. Z.

"I have a problem," Sam said. "Can you come pick me up at Rutledge's house?"

"What's going on?"

Sam felt a prickling sensation at the back of her neck. Maybe Bear's house had been bugged by the same people who planted the evidence against him. "Let's wait to discuss it. Can you come?"

"I'm on my way," Ms. Z replied. "I'll be there in twenty minutes."

Then Sam waited, trying not to think about making love with Bear and how good it was before the knock on the door. But that interruption had changed everything. She didn't know if she had done a good thing or made a very dumb move. And until Ms. Z arrived, she tried to keep busy, checking on the cat, straightening up the kitchen, and doing everything she could to chase the lingering sadness away.

"It's his own fault," Ms. Z complained after Sam climbed into a black SUV and explained what had happened. "The damned fool should have contacted us as soon as he found the body. Unless, of course, he did shoot the woman."

"Of course he didn't shoot her! He said he didn't contact you because he had trust issues. Did you have anything to do with planting that evidence in his house?" Sam asked.

"Are you having 'trust issues' too?" Ms. Z snapped.

Sam didn't flinch. "Somebody put the money and that gris-gris wrapper in his kitchen drawer."

"It wasn't us. It wouldn't be in our interest. Give me that envelope and I'll have the lab look at it. Stick it in the glove compartment."

Sam did as she was told, then looked at Ms. Z. "So, who's setting Rutledge up, and why? What can they hope to gain from it?"

"Let me think about that. Meanwhile, I'll get somebody down to the precinct to get him out of there before he says too much. Hopefully his lawyer will make sure he shuts up. The damned fool," she said again.

36

THE chairman didn't like caviar. He thought it was disgusting stuff. Fish eggs. Black fish eggs. People would eat any kind of crap if it cost five hundred dollars a pound.

The slightly built, balding man stood near the wall and surveyed the gathering of people in the large room. He watched Arthur downing the caviar shooters. How many was that? Four? Arthur talked too much when he got drunk. Perhaps it was time to have a word with Charles about Arthur. They were too close to their goal to have a loose cannon on deck.

He also saw the prince standing in sunlight streaming through the French doors that led to the pool. He was drinking gold martinis. Alcohol was forbidden in Islam. But the prince's father was the absolute ruler of Oman. The prince did what he wanted. The chairman smiled. Soon the prince would do what *they* wanted.

The magnitude of the whole brilliant scheme filled the chairman's mind like champagne bubbles. It almost made him giddy. Those stupid, shortsighted neoconservatives like Perle and Wolfowitz only wanted to invade Iraq and Iran. Those neocons wanted a Pax Americana in the Middle East—and plenty of defense contracts to line their pockets. They didn't dream big enough dreams.

Not like the chairman and his board. In just a few more weeks their big dream would become a reality. They would make billions, even trillions of dollars, and a stranglehold on the world's supply of oil in Oman would be their own foothold in the Arab world. Their own "base." He smiled at his own pun on the Arab word *al-Qaeda.* But they were not a ragtag group of idiot terrorists like bin Laden and his crew—they were organized.

And they had an entire country as their base. Their growing force of "terrorists" gave new meaning to terror. Then they would march on with their unstoppable army of the dead. Napoleon hadn't had what they did. Neither had Attila the Hun.

The chairman nearly laughed out loud. The world truly was theirs for the taking . . . including America. Hell, the U.S. already had a kind of zombie for eight years in the White House. Why not put a real one there?

The little balding man sipped his mineral water and became lost in thought. Last night he had seen that this scheme would go forward, and it would succeed spectacularly. It worked. The mumbo jumbo of the Bokor really damn well worked! Cutting into the brains helped speed up the process. They soon could turn out zombie soldiers by the thousands. It was inevitable that a little blood had to be spilled in every great endeavor, now, wasn't it?

He remembered how the warehouse had looked last night. Fifteen cots—no, with Barringer in residence, sixteen cots were now filled. In eleven of the beds were soldiers who had become perfect killing machines. A new praetorian guard. The means to assassinate a king. The others in the cots? Loose ends like Smith and Bartikowski. Or experiments. Expendable experiments. The chairman was sure he could think of something amusing to use them for.

No one investigating the grave openings had even come close to figuring out what was happening. By next week it wouldn't matter. It would be too late.

The prince was walking over. The chairman pasted on a smile.

"You must have food, my dear friend. If nothing pleases you, I'll have the chef prepare something else," Prince Abdul said.

"My indigestion." The chairman held up his glass of mineral water. "I'll stick with this."

"I do hope it won't keep you from enjoying the entertainment. The very best erotic dancers from my country are here. And they have other very special skills. They train these girls for years, you know."

"I had heard about it." The chairman nodded.

"Ah, hearing is nothing. You will see for yourself. Or, rather, experience for yourself. What use is it being the son of a mighty king if I can't provide pleasure for my friends?"

"You are more than kind, Prince. And thoughtful."

The prince laughed. "All men, in your country, in my country, have the same desires. I know what men want."

The chairman smiled and thought, *If you knew what men really want, you'd be running for your life.*

Just then the music started to play, and the prince put his arm around the chairman's shoulders. "Come, sit. Enjoy the dance. Then pick out the girl you want—for later. To experience her special skills." He winked as he led the small balding man into the other room.

37

WHEN Ms. Z drove up to the Bel Air house, Sam saw the curtains move in the front window. Aurora must be watching. She was, and once Sam got inside, all the women wanted to know why Bear hadn't brought her home. Weary and worried, Sam put them off, saying she'd tell them later. Fatigue had seeped into her bones. Hunger made her weak. The heat had sapped her energy. She wanted only to eat something and go to bed.

But the attempted "break-in" had to be addressed. Sam joined the others in the kitchen to discuss what could be done.

Frankie insisted she needed to cast a protective spell for the house.

Rina's strange blue eyes glittered. "Witch," she said, her voice harsh. "White magic doesn't have enough power to stop this."

"What are you saying?" Frankie countered.

"I need to use my magic. Black magic. My voodoo spells."

Frankie stared, not answering right away. Then she said, "Do it. Do what you have to. I don't want to know. And I'll also handle this my way."

Sam picked nervously at her fingernails. "What was it? The beast outside the window. Do either of you know?"

Frankie's eyes took on a haunted look again. "Something ancient. Something evil. Someone definitely sent it." She looked shrewdly at Sam. "Do you know who'd want to put a curse on this house?"

"I have no idea," Sam answered.

"Your parents lived here. What about your father? Does he have an enemy who'd do this?" she persisted.

"I don't know. He'd never discuss anything like that with me. And I was in Iraq for the past year. I e-mailed my parents a lot, but there's no way I'd have known if anything was wrong."

"Ask him," Frankie ordered. "You need to know. It may have wanted him, but you are his blood, so it came for you. And we need to know. In this house, none of us is safe."

Meanwhile Rina seemed to disappear into herself, lost in thought. Finally she looked around with fierce eyes. "Evil has always been here. At war with good since time began. But it's beginning to win." She abruptly left the room and went up the stairs.

"I need to cast the spell right now," Frankie insisted. "We can't wait. It has to be done before night falls. Aurora, help me with this. Open all the windows. Open the flue to the fireplace. Slide open the doors to the deck. We'll have to raise the garage door and open the front door as well, but we'd best leave those two until the last moment. While you do that, I'll get my materials together."

"I can help." Sam rose and immediately pulled back the kitchen slider. She stood for a moment in the doorway, leaning against the jamb, looking out into the backyard. The sun had sunk low on the horizon. The sky had become marbled with orange sherbet and flamingo pink against the faded blue. A dove cooed while it sat on a wire. Two crows lifted out of a tree and flew off, calling to each other. The air smelled of mowed grass and blooming roses.

Whatever evil had come this way earlier seemed to have vanished.

Maryland, my Maryland. Sam sighed, wishing for a past that had gone, perhaps forever.

Aurora hurried downstairs to the rec room. Sam could hear the sounds of windows being raised. Sam roused herself and moved through the dining room and living room, flinging open the windows in this part of the house. While she was busy with that, Aurora emerged from the lowest level and climbed the stairs to the second floor.

Meanwhile, Frankie reappeared in the living room wearing her black robes. Her eyes had changed again, taking on a wise, wild, and almost cruel look. Holding three sticks of patchouli incense, she lit them and handed one to Sam. When Aurora returned she was given one too.

Then footsteps clattered on the stairs. Rina rushed by them, a small paper bag held in her hand. She went directly out the front door without speaking.

In the living room, the witch sat cross-legged on the carpet. "I need to call my energies," she explained. "Once I do, if you two would simply accompany me and hold the patchouli, that would be all the assistance I need."

She closed her eyes and chanted something softly, too low for Sam to hear the words. When she had finished, she stood. "Open the front door, please."

All three women moved into the entryway, and Frankie stretched her arms in front of her, made her hands into fists, and put them one atop the other. She aimed her arms at the front door, which Aurora held wide.

"Fair Brigid! Spirits of light! Come. Hear my prayer. Bar this door against evil. Let no harm pass its sill. Let no demon step over this threshold. Barrier, come! Barrier, come! This is a place made safe!" Fists still together, she moved her arms through the air in the shape of a pentacle, or five-pointed star.

When she had completed the ritual, she nodded at Aurora to shut the door. The three women made their way through the house, and at each opening to the outside Frankie repeated her spell for protection. Then Aurora shut and latched it.

Curious about what Rina was doing, Sam moved to a still-open window and peered outside. She saw the voodoo priestess sprinkling something from the paper bag on the ground around the perimeter of the house.

Rina's head swung back and forth as she worked. Her

body swayed like a snake standing on its tail. She was singing or chanting. Sam was sure that even if she called out to Rina, the woman would not have heard her.

While Sam didn't know the particulars of the spell Rina was casting, it must have been powerful. Sam felt a wall of energy rising around the house. She sensed that if she stretched out her hand, she would touch an invisible shield. She decided, since the spell was not finished, that she had better not try.

By the time Frankie had finished with every room, Rina had come back inside. Night had fallen. Jackson Boulevard had become dark, but a soft lightness suffused the house. Miranda curled up contentedly atop the grand piano and went to sleep. Sam herself felt a new sense of security.

After the spell casting she had witnessed tonight, Sam had begun to believe that the four of them and this new sisterhood did possess a growing power. She would not have believed it just a few days ago, but these women and their gifts were transforming her consciousness. They had changed the way she viewed herself and her world.

Yet a hard knot of uneasiness within her remained. Could Rina's and Frankie's spells protect them if that twisting gray shadow—or something far worse—returned? A shiver of dread passed over Sam. *When it returned,* she thought, for she felt certain it would.

Frankie prepared dinner, a simple meal of soup and salad. After the spell casting, the four women sat down to eat around the red-topped Formica table in the kitchen. Frankie recapped her discovery of the toyol at the Arab diplomat's Washington mansion. She explained what she had learned from the chef, Liam Mahoney, about the cousin burying animal parts in the garden.

"I reported the name of the gardener to Ms. Z. I did *not* tell her about the men gathering at the prince's tonight, or that Liam promised to call me if he discovered any of their identities. Perhaps I should have, but . . ." Her hands turned palms up, as if to say, *So what?*

"I agree," Rina broke in. "We need to hold back information, the same way they do with us." She began eating the soup Frankie had made. "Look what happened to Sam. We're out there, in harm's way. Yet we have not been given access to what they know."

"Do you have any theories about what we're really up against?" Aurora asked.

"I told you from the start." Rina put down her spoon with a clatter. Her eyes shone. "Someone is calling out the dead."

"Why?" Aurora persisted.

"For gain of some sort. Always for gain." She nervously ran her thin fingers through her chestnut brown hair. "Power, greed, perverse pleasure. Men do these things. Men destroy. Men kill. But behind these men? Something else." She searched each of their faces. "I have something to ask of you."

All eyes looked at her.

"Come with me tomorrow night."

"If you need us to, of course," Frankie said, then cleared her throat. "Do you mind telling us where are we going?"

"To a voodoo ceremony. A Bokor, a voodoo sorcerer, much feared by the people of Haiti, arrived here recently. A week ago, maybe. They call him Le Rat Noir, the Black Rat. He brought with him his followers. They're thugs, *tonton macoutes.* Some say they are juju zombies. I think if anyone is calling the dead, this Bokor is doing it, or he knows who's behind it. He will be there. I need to talk with him."

"Will they let us in there?" Frankie asked.

Rina nodded. "I put out word through friends in New Orleans that I would be attending. The Bokor will know I am coming, but he'll guess I am not coming alone." Rina looked around. "I can stand up to him. The snake against the rat. But the four of us together are even stronger magic. He will not be so willing to play his tricks." She paused. "There is still some risk."

"We go together," Frankie said.

Sam had a sick feeling in her stomach, but after Aurora nodded yes, she also agreed.

* * *

Later, Sam sat staring at the BlackBerry's screen for a long time before she punched in the number for her parents' condo in Tucson. She didn't know how she'd question her father about an enemy or someone with a grudge. But aside from that, Sam had to speak with them, The news of her return stateside needed to come from her, before her mother's house-sitting friend who had waved at Sam from her doorway a few times got them all upset by telling them first. She hoped she could put a positive spin on the situation. She crossed her fingers and listened to the phone ring.

Her mother picked up.

"Hey, Mom, I'm back in Maryland."

"Susan Ann Marie! That's wonderful! Are you out of Iraq for good? I haven't had a good night's sleep since you were sent there. Do you have a cold? Your voice sounds hoarse."

"I'm fine, Mom. Yes, I am out of Iraq for good. I think I am, anyway."

"When will you be going to Paris?" her mother asked.

Paris, Sam thought. Her hopes for a posting in France belonged to someone else, someone she had been a lifetime ago. She picked her words with care when she answered her mother. "That's the thing: I'm not going to Paris. I'm going to be living in Maryland. I've left the Foreign Service. I got a better job offer."

"You've moved back to Bel Air? I don't understand, dear." Her mother was clearly puzzled. "I thought you were so excited about being stationed in Paris. Your father is right here. Let me put him on the phone."

Sam steeled herself. This was not going to be fun.

"Susan, this is your father."

Sam rolled her eyes. "Yes, Dad, I know."

"What the Sam Hill is going on? What's this about a new job?"

"Yes, um, I left the Foreign Service. I'm working for a different government agency. The really terrific part is I can live home again, in Bel Air. Isn't that great? I have plans to fix up the house already."

"Which agency?" Her father was a bulldog, and he didn't let go of a topic until he was satisfied.

"*The* agency. You know, the Central Intelligence Agency. It's a big promotion, Dad. A good career move."

Her father's response was dead silence. When his voice returned, it held a tremor, as if he were trying to keep his emotions in check. "Those SOBs recruited you."

"Yes, of course they did, but, um, it's still a good move."

"Are you out of your mind? They're a bunch of unscrupulous bastards who have dumped the Constitution right in the toilet!" His voice bellowed, then became muffled as he whispered, "What am I going to tell your mother? It's been her daughter the diplomat this, her daughter the diplomat that. I can't tell her you're working intelligence. It would kill her."

"Tell her . . . ummm, tell her I'm working for Homeland Security as a liaison, doing something, um, impressive. I know, I'm a liaison with the White House; that sounds good. Tell her I'm practically living with the president."

"Let me think about this, Sam."

"Everything's fine. There's nothing to think about. I'm doing great."

"I'm not going to comment on that right now." Sam knew her father was watching what he said in front of her mother.

"There's something else."

"What's that?" He sounded as if he were speaking through gritted teeth.

Sam made her voice sound upbeat. "I have some girlfriends staying with me at the house. Just for a couple of weeks. Until they get a place. It's been a lot of fun to have some company."

"Susan, what aren't you telling me? What's really going on here? What the hell are you mixed up in?" Her father always picked up every nuance in her voice, and his radar was working well. Just then Sam heard her mother's voice in the background asking, "Hilton, what are you talking about? What isn't she telling you?"

"It's okay, Beth. Sam's going to get the house painted.

She's getting somebody in to give her an estimate. I think she's overspending, that's all."

"She never was very good with money, Hil. Can't you fly home and help her?"

Oh, God, no! Sam thought. "Dad, listen to me. Go somewhere Mom can't hear and call me back. Can you do that?"

"I'll give your love to your mother," he said, and hung up.

Sam paced back and forth, her anxiety climbing with each passing minute. Not more than five minutes later, the house phone rang.

"Susan." Her dad's voice was serious. "What's really going on? What have these people gotten you into?"

"Dad, what I'm doing is classified. Really, that's not the problem. It's something here at the house."

"What?" His voice vibrated with alarm.

"An incident. A couple of incidents. This morning, um, an intruder tried to get in. Not a robbery. Something else."

"What do you mean? Did somebody try to harm you?"

"It didn't go that far. But, Dad, does anybody have a grudge against you? Do you have an enemy who wants to hurt you or pressure you?"

Her father didn't answer right away. His voice was heavy when he finally did. "You think this is personal? Against me?"

"Yes, I do. From what I've been able to figure out, this . . . this stuff, ah, vandalism and threats, started before I got back."

"I don't want you mixed up in this, Sam."

"I'm here, Dad. I'm in it. Help me out. Do you know who's behind this?"

"I think so. I never thought he'd go this far, though. I retired and moved away. I figured that would end it."

"Dad, tell me. I need to know."

"A bigwig, Sam. In the Pentagon. He pulled off a lot of sweetheart deals with some defense contractors. I started keeping tabs on him. Found out he had some offshore accounts. Was taking kickbacks. I blew the whistle, and the Justice Department was going to indict him. Somehow he wriggled out of it, but he lost his job. Swore he'd get me."

"Give me a name, Dad."

"I don't want to do that, Sam. Let me make some calls. I'll take care of this."

"In the meantime, I'm here like a sitting duck. Dad, give me a name."

Silence again. Then, "Charles Rothrock. Sam, don't do anything stupid. He's a dangerous man. Listen to me, Sam. I *will* take care of this. *My* way. Do you understand?"

Fear of a different kind gripped Sam then. She knew her father would kill to protect his family if he had to. She heard the resolution in his voice, and a terrible foreboding washed over her. "Dad! Please! Don't do anything crazy."

Her father didn't answer right away. His voice was steel when he spoke again. "Susan, listen to me. Rothrock won't bother you again. But you must stay out of this. Don't go near him. Promise me."

As Sam hesitated, her father's voice broke through, impatient, charged with urgency. *"Promise."*

"Okay, Dad. I promise."

Sam immediately sensed his relief. His voice, gruff as always but without the sharp edge of a moment ago, came again over the phone. "And about this job you took—"

"The job's great. It's a good move. I like it so far. Don't worry about me."

"Sam, stop lying to me. I know what those people in the agency are like. If you need me to get you out of there, tell me. I can do it."

"Thanks for the offer, but really, I'm just fine." *Famous last words,* Sam thought, and hung up.

About the same time that Sam was on the phone downstairs, Frankie was upstairs lifting a wineglass and sipping a nice California chardonnay she had bought during their first shopping trip. She glanced at the bottle sitting on her dresser. Most of it was already gone. She had a comforting buzz in her head while she thumbed through *Food & Wine* magazine.

When the BlackBerry rang, she didn't recognize the number. She answered anyway.

"Corey, here."

"I have a name." She heard Liam's voice.

"The name is?" she asked.

"Arthur Bilderberg. He got drunk. Took a swim with his clothes on. I had to fish his wallet out of the pool. It just happened to open up when I did."

"How convenient."

"Convenience had nothing at all to do with it. I needed an excuse to call you."

That pleased Frankie enormously, but she stayed cool. "Thanks, Liam. I'll be in touch." She hung up, but her smile lingered for a long while afterward.

38

THE next day, clouds moved across the Mid-Atlantic region, blowing in from the Caribbean. The temperature moderated into the mid-nineties, while the humidity seemed to worsen and the smog reached record levels. The media warned the elderly and asthmatics to stay indoors.

Lethargy coupled with exhaustion slowed Sam down. She had slept okay, surprising herself that she didn't have a problem going back into her bedroom. She conked out the moment her head hit the pillow, and she didn't get up until nearly seven. She went downstairs, found coffee made, and called Ms. Z as early as she dared to find out about Bear.

"No, we didn't get him out yet. The police are holding him as a material witness. Haven't charged him. But you do know three teenagers put him at the crime scene with a gun, don't you? Maybe he did shoot her."

"That's not possible. I told you I dropped the gun in the cemetery. He's being set up. You know that. I know that. The question is why."

"Chase, don't get yourself all worked up. Call me in a couple of hours. I have some arm-twisting to do, Meanwhile, take it easy. You were supposed to be on bed rest yesterday."

Take it easy. Sam thought that was just what she'd do. From a practical perspective, she could use a day to locate her belongings in transit from Iraq and take care of mundane things, like laundry. She had to contact her mother's house sitter too and give her an explanation for being back—with roommates. Sam's mother would have called her the moment Sam got off the phone.

Frankie also told Sam about Liam's discovery, the name of one of the defense contractors.

"Arthur Bilderberg? Are you sure?" Sam asked.

"That's what he said."

"He's the guy the photographer at the cemetery worked for," Sam said.

"So do we tell Ms. Z?" Frankie asked.

Sam thought for a minute. "Not yet, okay?"

"It's your call, Sam. Just keep me in the loop." Then she asked to borrow Sam's car to do some shopping. The other women went along. Sam checked in with Ms. Z, who said Rutledge would be home in a couple of hours. Sam said okay, then, still feeling ill, went to bed and fell asleep.

The other women returned and kept to themselves most of the day. At one point, after Sam woke up, she heard them talking downstairs. Snippets of the conversation ebbed and flowed.

"It's discrimination," Aurora complained at one point. "Seeing Eye dogs get to go everywhere. Miranda's my Seeing Eye cat."

"You're not blind," Frankie pointed out.

"We're all blind," Rina said.

Late in the afternoon, Bear finally called. Sam's heart thumped when she saw his number on the screen of the BlackBerry.

"You okay?" she said.

"Yeah, fine. Look, I wanted to thank you—"

Thank me? Those words weren't the ones Sam wanted to hear. She interrupted him. "Not necessary." Her heart shut down. She closed off her feelings.

"I'm heading home now," he said. "Look, do you want to meet tomorrow? We should go see this Arthur Bilderberg."

Sam hesitated. Bear definitely was acting as if nothing had happened between them. If anything, his voice was impersonal and cold. Sam made her own icy too. "Meet? I suppose we should. What time?"

Bear named a time and suggested a Starbucks downtown.

"Okay, then," Sam said stiffly.

There was a moment of silence. Sam thought Bear might have hung up, when he spoke again, his voice softening. "Sam? I . . . Oh, never mind. I'm just beat. I need to get some rest. You . . . You get some too, you hear?"

"Sure. I will. I'm not doing anything except going to bed early."

Then he was gone.

Sam didn't know what to think about Bear. She also didn't know what to think about her own lies. They came too easily. In her heart, deception didn't sit well.

39

DRUMS beating, palms slapping—the rhythm was fast, driving, and hypnotic. Sam could hear the drummers even before she and the other women entered the narrow brick alley that led to the back of an apartment house in southeast Washington. A crude tent had been erected in a cement-paved yard in front of some garages. A half dozen dark women wearing white came and went, fussing and speaking in rapid French while they set up the area for the voodoo service.

A group of men and women had already gathered there. Most of them were black, but a few Asians and whites sat on the folding chairs as well. The four the agency had dubbed AngelWay now entered the tent, Rina in the lead.

The air had remained so acrid it invaded people's lungs and scalded them with acid. It blanketed the city, hot and thick with humidity. Sam had worn sandals and a simple white cotton sundress, another leftover from college that she had left behind before going to Iraq. Her long honey-colored hair, which she had left loose and flowing, stuck to her perspiring skin. She blotted her face with a tissue. Between the heat and smell of burning incense, she found it difficult to breathe.

Although nothing looked frightening, not even the altar with its strange voodoo dolls, Sam felt uneasy, her nerves tight. Her body moved stiffly, rigid with tension. Her emotions had become ragged, thin, ready to bleed. Too much had happened in too short a time.

Sam made a white-knuckled effort to hold on to her inner control. She was there because Rina had asked them to go with her, insisting she needed the women's strength to back her up. But if Sam had her way, she'd turn around and leave. She had to push herself to be a team player, to hang tough and do what needed to be done.

From the moment they had stepped into the alley filled with shadows and dark alcoves, Sam didn't like the "vibes" of this place. For one thing, the music had her agitated. When the women had arrived at the tent, the handheld drums evoked the rhythm of heartbeats. But they quickly increased in tempo.

Energy built until it seemed to sizzle under the dirty canvas that formed the roof above them. Some people clapped and sang. Others had gotten up to dance. Someone rang a cowbell, discordant and ghostly.

Earlier Rina had explained that the purpose of the service was to call forth the *Iwa,* or spirits. During the ceremony the *Iwa* "mounted" those present, taking them over temporarily and delivering messages. Sam had no intention of letting any *Iwa* inhabit her, and she didn't think the spirit guide already present in her life would permit it. At least, she hoped not.

As they all stood under the tent for a moment, Aurora touched Rina's arm. "Are they going to kill an animal here?"

Rina turned. She had a pouch called a gris-gris hanging on a cord around her neck. She nodded. "Maybe a chicken, yes."

"Then I can't stay. I'll wait out on the street. I'll come running if you need me, but I won't witness the senseless killing of an innocent creature."

"No," Rina said. "You can't leave. I don't like the sacrifice, and I personally wouldn't do it, but the blood releases life into the spirit world."

"I'm not arguing the point. You do what you have to do. I'll do what my conscience insists I do."

"No," Rina said again, her blue eyes boring into Aurora's dark ones. "We're in this together. We stay together. If you go, you don't come back."

Aurora's face looked stricken. "You'd throw me out? You know what that would mean."

Frankie, the loner of the team, suddenly understood more than she ever had what Rina was saying. "Aurora!" She put her hand on the shorter woman's shoulder. Her voice grew tight with urgency. "We can't separate. We can't go our own ways. Even though you don't like what will happen here. Even though it's tough to do this. We need to count on one another absolutely. If we don't—"

Sam spoke then. "We won't survive." Sam herself would have liked to leave. Every fiber of her being urged her to rush out of the tent, but she shook her head no. "We stick together, as agreed."

Aurora looked from face to face. Tears filled her eyes. Then she nodded okay. "I'll stay."

Rina spoke again. "I need to warn you, warn all of you. I have been told this Bokor, the Black Rat, practices Petro, not Rada, voodoo. Petro—that means death curses, zombies, sexual orgies, all kinds of bad shit. None of those negative things are supposed to be part of this service. But I can't promise he won't bring in some evil spirits."

Then Rina's intense blue eyes glittered. "I think he'll try to kill me if he can. He knows I believe that he is robbing graves and making zombies. It will come to a showdown between him and me, snake and rat. That's why I need you with me."

"What do you want us to do?" Frankie asked.

"Stay close. If you see danger, put your hands on my shoulders. Summon the Bondye, the good god. Focus on the light and pour it into me."

"Danger? What danger? How will we know?" Sam asked, her uneasiness spiraling into fear.

"See that man up there? He is the priest, or *houngan*. Behind him is a pole, the center one. See that?" Rina asked.

Sam nodded.

"That's the *poto mitan,* representing the center of the universe. The service will bring the two worlds, the spirit world and the world of flesh, together. This place becomes a portal where the spirits cross over. Watch carefully for the appearance of Kalfu, the dark spirit, or Papa

Ghede. Sometimes he looks like a clown; sometimes he takes other forms. But he is both the Lord of Death and the Lord of Desire. Beware if you see him." She looked hard at Sam. "Don't let him separate you from us."

"Me!? He'd have to drag me away kicking and screaming."

Rina's blue eyes burned into Sam's. "You *think* that. But you don't know yourself. You are vulnerable. So beware."

Rina turned away, shifting her focus to watch for the arrival of the Bokor, Le Rat Noir. She left Sam shaken and newly afraid, not just of what might happen here tonight, but of herself.

Sam felt that Rina's assessment was accurate. She'd had strong feelings for Bear within hours of meeting him. She had become intimate with him quickly. She had never envisioned herself doing something like that before. What did that say about her? That she didn't know herself. She'd take Rina's warning to heart and watch out for Papa Ghede.

The *houngan* carried two machetes and crossed them in front of his chest. Then he laid one down on the altar. A woman came up with a squawking chicken. With a quick motion he grabbed it and chopped off its head. Then he sprinkled the blood around the altar. When he had finished, he lit a candle and began to dance.

Soon he threw his arms up over his head. He began speaking in French, spinning around and yelling out names. He went from one person to another, as if haranguing them about something. Sam figured an *Iwa* had mounted him, and he was spirit-possessed.

Other dancers were taken over by *Iwa* too. The tent filled with cries and shouts. People fell to the floor, writhing in ecstasy. The drums beat faster. The noise, the crowd, the heat, all became chaotic.

By now a column of sick people had approached the *houngan* to be healed. Sam watched for a while, then looked around at the dancers. Occasionally one of them would collapse, overtaken by a spirit entity.

As the minutes passed, the tent had become packed with worshipers as well as curiosity seekers with nothing else to do. Sam was jostled from both sides. She kept Rina in sight and tried to watch Frankie and Aurora, who stood close together, but a half dozen women had stepped between them, stamping their feet and clapping their hands, increasing the distance until Sam couldn't see the other members of the team.

Sam fought to remain where she was until another dancer slid by, pushing her toward the rear of the tent. As she made space to accommodate a few more of the spinning worshipers, she realized she was standing near the outer edge of the group.

She had moved quite a distance from her original position, but she wasn't worried. She caught a glimpse of Rina toward the front of the crowd. She felt better about that, and realized it was cooler back here. She relaxed a little.

The drums didn't bother her anymore, and the hostile feeling she sensed earlier seemed to have disappeared. Any spirits that came through must have been good ones, she thought. But the sheer number of bodies in this small space had made it stiflingly hot under the canvas, and the heat embraced her once more.

Feeling almost faint, Sam moved again until she stood at the very back of the crowd. A breeze ruffled her hair and fluttered the hem of her dress. She took a deep breath of the fresh air. *This feels much better,* she thought. She looked toward the dancing, clapping people. Her fear had vanished. No *Iwa* had approached her or tried to possess her. She was glad about that.

She didn't notice the young white man who came up next to her until he spoke. "Aren't you going to dance?" he said, and smiled.

"No," Sam answered, "I'd rather not." She found herself returning his smile. "I'm just watching."

"Then you will miss the whole experience," he said. Sam looked at him more closely. He was younger than she was, a teenager really, and only about her height. He had long blond hair tied back in a ponytail and soft brown eyes. She could see how well built he was; his white shirt was unbuttoned to his waist, showing six-pack abs. His jeans were low-cut and tight.

He saw her look at his open shirt. "It's really warm in there." He laughed. "I'm about ready to take it off."

Sam laughed too. "That's why I moved back here. It was getting too hot under the tent."

"I take it you don't practice voodoo."

"No, I came with friends." She glanced at the crowd but couldn't see any of them.

He smiled. "You're really very safe at these services, you know. You have to want an *Iwa* to possess you before he will. So why not dance?"

"That's okay. I prefer watching," Sam said, and found herself not looking away. His eyes were mesmerizing. She noticed he was holding an unopened can of orange soda.

He popped the tab and extended it to her. "You look like you could use a drink. This isn't very cold, but it's wet."

Sam took it and drank. It was very sweet. She wondered if she should hand the remaining soda back to him, so she asked, "Do you want to finish this?"

He took it, not minding at all drinking after her. He poured it down his throat, tipping his head back. Sam really enjoyed watching him. He was so young and alive, almost innocent.

He tossed the can toward a litter basket. He winked at her and held out his hand. "Come on. Join me. Let's walk over here, where we can talk without trying to yell over the drums. You're such a beautiful woman. You'll have to tell me why you are here without a husband or a lover."

Surprising herself, Sam took the proffered hand. It was warm and strong. He seemed so nice, and such a handsome young man. He pulled her toward the back wall of the tenement. She moved as if she were in a dream. It occurred to her that maybe there was something in the soda.

But fear exploded inside her as the boy suddenly pulled her through a screen door into a dark empty room. Sam tried to back away. His hand clamped over her wrist like a vise.

She heard her spirit guide's voice say, *Wake up! Get out of there!* But the voice sounded very soft and far away. She could hear the drums too. They were beating, throbbing in the tent, and somehow echoing in her mind.

Her tongue felt thick in her mouth, but she managed to say, "Let me go."

"No." The boy was gone. In his place stood a creature with green skin and terrible lizardlike eyes. Sam began to shake all over.

"You and your friends must be stopped. You must die," the ugly thing hissed at her.

Sam saw the creature raise something in his hand. A machete, sharp and deadly, flashed silver. Sam felt frozen. She wanted to fight, but she couldn't move. She watched the machete start to move. She prepared to die.

Just then the screen door yanked open. "Get away from her, Ghede." It was Rina's voice, and it was angry.

Rina's hand gripped Sam's arm and physically tore her through the doorway. The machete vanished. The creature disappeared. The room behind the screen door was empty again.

Sam collapsed against Rina, who held her up. "My God," she said. "He . . . he . . . nearly—"

"I know. It's okay. I told you to be careful!"

"I thought he was only a boy," Sam began to explain, and felt as though she were going to cry.

"Look, it's not your fault. He's an *Iwa.* He took over your will. My fault. I should have kept you close. Come on; hold on to me from now on." Rina took Sam's trembling hand and pulled her back into the crowd. They found Frankie and Aurora. Rina told them to come to the front of the tent.

Tears had welled up in Sam's eyes. She had nearly died because she had been stupid. She hadn't stayed with the others even though she herself had said they must stay close together. Rina stopped and faced her, gripping Sam's arms. She brought her lips close to Sam's ear and whispered urgently, "Listen to me. That wasn't your fault. You were in his power. Forget it. I will never mention it. It never happened. And *nothing* did happen."

Sam nodded. But she knew she must never forget what had happened. She had made a terrible mistake. Had she been with the other women she would have been safe. The team must be united. The women must stay together. Sam had survived only because of Rina's vigilance. She owed the voodoo woman her life.

40

THE drums suddenly went silent. A few people screamed, and a woman fainted when a shirtless man with a broad muscular chest strode to the *poto mitan.* Gray-white ashes had been smeared across his dark skin. Strips of palm fronds had been woven into a headband and draped down over his shoulders. He was a striking-looking figure, appearing from the darkness outside the tent into the light like some sort of primitive vegetation god.

Four young men followed him into the center of the tent, robotic and dead in the eyes—the *tonton macoutes.* They stood like bodyguards beside him, crossing their arms across their chests.

"I am Le Rat Noir!" the ash-smeared man stretched his arms toward the crowd and called out. "I have the power over death! Are you with me?"

The crowd shrieked, "Yes!" They began to clap and chant; the drums started again.

But at that moment Rina threw her own hands up in the air. A deafening bang made the canvas vibrate. People screamed. Sam suspected that Rina had tossed a cherry bomb toward the top of the tent.

"Bokor!" Rina yelled out.

The crowd went silent.

"Who seeks me?" the ashy man asked.

Rina answered in a loud, high voice that sent shivers through Sam: "The Blue-eyed Snake."

"Go away, white witch," Le Rat Noir said.

"Why have you been calling out the dead of Arlington?" Rina demanded.

The powerful man covered in ashes began to laugh. He stamped his feet and danced around the stage. Finally he stopped his antics and pointed his finger at Rina. "Why I make the zombies? You so smart! You tell me!"

"Money. You raise the dead for money."

"Ha! You want my new Cadillac, witch? You want my gold watch? You want my diamond ring?" His head went back. His body shuddered. He called out, "I deal in the science of resurrection!" He swayed and opened his arms. "I conquer the Lord of Death. I will conquer you!" His head snapped forward. His eyes were blazing. He snatched a machete off the altar, brandished it above his head, and started toward Rina.

Sam's instinct was to run, but instead she put her hand on one of Rina's shoulders. She saw Frankie and Aurora move in close, gripping each other. Rina outstretched one arm in front of her and pointed her hand at the voodoo sorcerer. "No!" Her arm quivered but did not fall. *"No!"*

The tent pole, the *poto mitan,* began to shake. The canvas above their heads flapped and shook. The Bokor stopped, seemingly unable to come forward. Surprise came over his face, then a terrible anger. He threw the machete down. The candle on the altar blew out, and the earth beneath their feet trembled. The pole tipped sideways and the canvas collapsed on top of the participants below.

People started screaming. Many of them tried to hold the canvas aloft with their hands. Sam strained to keep the heavy material above her at the same time the voice in her head insisted, *Run.*

Fat chance of that! Sam thought, as Rina whispered, "We have to get out of here. We need to get to the car. He's going to come after us."

Making sure they stayed together, the four women groped their way to the edge of the collapsed tent and broke into the open air. They ran down the narrow alley without looking back.

"Get to the car!" Rina cried. They dashed down the block to Sam's Toyota and piled in. Sam fumbled around to get the key in the ignition and pulled away from the curb as fast as she could.

"Are they really coming after us?" Sam cried as she

frantically looked at street signs and mentally figured the fastest way to Route 295 and out of D.C. Frankie was in the passenger seat next to her. Rina and Aurora were in the backseat.

Rina twisted around so she could watch out the back window. Frankie kept watch to the side. They had gotten about four blocks from the voodoo site when Rina called out, "There! The Bokor said he had a Cadillac. One is careening around the corner we just passed. It's coming up fast. There's a car pulling out between us—good! But I'm sure the Bokor is after us. Go!"

Sam drove with every skill she had. She made desperate turns and ran red lights. When she pulled onto Route 295 she floored the accelerator, wishing she had a Mustang's 470-horsepower Shelby engine instead of the Corolla's puttering four cylinders. She couldn't outrun a Cadillac, so she'd have to outdrive the Bokor. She also had the advantage of knowing where she was going; the Cadillac had to anticipate her moves.

She hit the Beltway still in the lead. She prayed they wouldn't hit a traffic slowdown, but she needed enough cars on the roadway to allow her to dart in and out. Even so, her heart sank. The situation looked hopeless. The Cadillac holding the Bokor and the fearsome *tonton macoutes* would soon overtake them, and then . . . She didn't know what would happen, but she suspected the larger vehicle would force hers off the road.

The possibility of death opened its bloody maw before her. She saw her car going out of control, spinning, tumbling end over end. She heard screams. She saw fire. *No!* she shouted in her mind. *I will not let that happen.*

"Frankie," she cried out, "do something! Cast a spell!" She kept her eyes on the road, but her teeth had started chattering, she was so scared.

"Sam, I'm trying! I keep trying to call in protection. This Bokor has strong magic. My powers aren't working!"

"We'd better do something, because on this open road we don't have a snowball's chance in hell of staying ahead of this guy. He's coming up fast." She glanced up in the rearview mirror. The black Cadillac was only about ten car lengths behind them.

Aurora called out from the backseat, "The Cadillac's moving into the left lane. He's going to come up on that side. Oh, crap! The one guy has a gun out the window. Get down! Everybody get down!"

A series of pings hit the trunk of the Toyota. Sam had the accelerator to the floor. She couldn't go any faster.

Sam's mind raced. Fragments of a dream came back to her and she understood. "We need to work together. All of us," she shouted. "Call up a fog."

"All right, everybody focus," Frankie ordered. "Think of a thick fog sweeping in from the east, from the warm bosom of Mother Ocean." She gestured in the air, making the sign of a five-pointed star, and chanted, "With this pentagram that I do lay, I call the mist this time, this day. Cover us from sight, let us fly into the night, deliver us safe from harm. Mist, come! Mist, come!"

Hunched down over the steering wheel, Sam suddenly saw tendrils of fog crawling like snakes along the roadway. Then she shuddered. A gray cloud approached, so dense it looked like a solid wall. The Toyota cut into it and it closed over them, swallowing them up.

Even with the fog lights on, Sam had to fight to see the road. As desperate as she was to outrun the Cadillac, she felt blind, nearly panicked, driving without being able to see anything. She slowed down, praying she didn't smash into any vehicles in front of her.

For a few miles they crept along through a pea soup of fog. Sam's familiarity with a road she had driven a thousand times helped her keep her bearings. Within minutes she spotted an exit and turned off the interstate onto a narrow, unlit secondary highway, where darkness made the fog an inky black.

"Fog, go!" Frankie cried, and clapped three times. The fog vanished. The night was clear again. No one was behind them. Sam's hands slipped, covered with sweat from grasping the wheel with a death grip. She let go and wiped each of them on her dress. She sighed with relief.

A half hour later she pulled into her driveway on Jackson Boulevard, activated the garage door, and pulled the Toyota inside.

"I'm glad this night is over with," Aurora said tiredly.

She opened the back door and started to get out; then she screamed, "Close the garage door, quick!"

Sam had already hit the garage-door button as soon she as she stopped the car. The heavy door slid down just as the women saw a black Cadillac pull up in front of the house. "How did they find us?" Sam cried.

Rina's breaking voice answered as the women spilled out of the car and ran from the garage through the connecting door to the rec room. "The Bokor's magic found us. Fate . . . fate . . . no one can outrun it."

Inside the rec room, through the garden-level windows, Sam could see the Bokor and his henchmen getting out of the Cadillac. The five men started toward the front door of the house, but then stopped, looking perplexed and not moving forward.

Sam and the other women kept running, scampering up the stairs into the kitchen, pulling the curtains shut, and checking the locks on the doors.

"Will the protective spells hold?" Sam cried to Frankie.

"I hope so, but you know what you need to do?"

"What?" Sam said, feeling a moment of panic.

"Call nine-one-one!"

In a few minutes a police car siren screamed its approach. A moment later the police pulled up in front of the house. Limp with relief, Sam dared to open the front door. The Cadillac had gone; so had the witch doctor and his *tonton macoutes.* The officers carefully checked around the house and took down all the information Sam gave them about the men in the Cadillac. She warily provided them with very little beyond a physical description of the car and a vague impression of the occupants. She withheld revealing that she knew who they were. In the story she told, she and her roommates must have been followed back from a party in D.C.

The Bel Air police knew Sam's father—and that helped. They promised to send patrol cars past the house at intervals throughout the night.

As soon as the cops had left, Sam phoned Ms. Z. She gave an overview of the voodoo ceremony and the Bokor's public admission that he had created zombies. Although the sorcerer didn't say specifically that he had engineered the removal of the bodies from Arlington, it appeared likely that he had. Sam suggested that someone needed to check his arrival in the United States against the disappearance of Barringer's body, but Sam had no doubt the Bokor had "called out" the dead man.

Ms. Z agreed it was a real breakthrough in the case, and the fact that Le Rat Noir had pursued them seemed to confirm their suspicions. After Ms. Z listened carefully to everything Sam said, she promised to get the INS to arrest the Bokor. That agency already had connections in the Haitian community and should be able to locate him. The CIA would step in at that point.

Sam could hear Ms. Z's excitement. AngelWay had been successful. The women had proven themselves. She considered the case solved; it was just a matter of getting the Bokor to say where they could find Barringer and the other missing bodies.

But Sam didn't agree. Not at all. Somebody had set up Bear. Somebody had murdered Robin Bartikowski. Sam believed that the voodoo witch doctor was only one head of the dragon. The other heads, the most deadly ones, were still out there—and they had very sharp teeth with which to bite.

41

LIKE a locomotive roaring ahead with an open throttle, Bear stormed into his boss's office at the DOD first thing the next morning. He had spent nearly twenty-four hours in a jail cell. He didn't know who had set him up. He had to believe it was the agency, although Ms. Z showing up at the precinct herself now gave him doubts. But all in all, he had no intention of telling Allen about his arrest. He didn't want to be diverted from what he wanted from the man.

The secretary, Lily, looked startled when Bear burst through the door. "Where's Allen?" he said.

The fierceness of his face must have frightened her. "Inside . . ."

Bear didn't slow down. He didn't knock. He pushed through the half-open door. Colonel Allen was in front of his computer, absorbed with something on the screen. His head snapped up. "Rutledge? What the hell! What's going on?"

"Plenty," Bear barked. "This case is now personal. I want to interview Barringer's wife. She only lives in New Jersey. I can drive up there and be back the same day."

Allen's face sharpened. He gave Bear his full attention. "You told me yourself that the CIA put her off-limits. They're calling the shots. It took all my juice just to get you part of the case. Your seeing Barringer's wife is not a battle I'm willing to fight. So give me a good reason to go to war with them."

Then Allen, a smoker for forty years, started coughing and grabbed a bottle of water from his desk to take a drink. To Bear, his mentor looked like an old man. He was close to retirement and obviously not willing to rock the boat.

"Because they're off in la-la land on this. They're focusing on the voodoo angle. But I just don't put any credence in it. That stuff is a bunch of baloney. Somebody—and who else but the agency?—wants to hamstring me. Keep me from looking too close."

"Looking too close at what? At who? What's your theory about all this?"

"I still think it's basically good old-fashioned grave robbery, but with big money thrown in. The other open graves were also Gulf War casualties. To me that's a big red flag."

"What about the killings in the amphitheater?"

"Simple. The victims stumbled into a crime: the perps getting the bodies out of the graves. What else? First thing yesterday I got the agency's forensics people to talk to me. They came up with a couple of tire tracks and a boot print. They're still looking for DNA from fingernail scrapings of the two night security cops. They might come up with something there.

"The crude wounds in the chests could have been caused by animal claws, but most likely by a human using large claws in some kind of homemade weapon. Cult stuff, who knows? But the removal of the tops of the skulls . . . he's saying the murder weapon was something like a machete."

Allen shook his head. "It's strange. Any other leads turn up?"

"Not leads, only bits and pieces of information. The blood smudge on the tombstone turned out to be chicken blood, so someone must have revisited the grave. There's the voodoo angle again."

"If not voodoo, what's your theory?"

"The way I see it, the voodoo is a smoke screen. It's there to throw in some woo-woo aspect so we miss the obvious motive."

"I wouldn't disagree with that." Allen nodded. "Any names?"

"I got one. It's a long shot, though. Arthur Bilderberg. Know him?"

"Can't say I do. You think he's mixed up in this?"

"He runs a company called USEI. One of the photographers spotted at the cemetery works for him. I'm going to check him out today."

"Sounds like the thing to do," Allen said, and picked up some papers on his desk.

"But we're up against the clock. That's why I want to go right to Barringer's wife. We can't waste any more time. The CIA has hushed up the killings. But empty graves, gory murders, zombies, for God's sake—that's too juicy a story to keep a lid on for long. Sooner or later it's going to hit the media. The public will go crazy. With this insane heat, the whole city's on the verge of a riot out there anyway. Fear would spread like a wildfire. It could spark a rampage the likes of which we've never seen before."

Allen put down the papers. He grabbed a bottle of mineral water from his desk, leaned back in his chair, and lobbed the twist-top cap into a trash basket. "Cover your ass, Rutledge. But let the media be the CIA's problem. Stay away from Barringer's wife."

42

FOR Sam, the sun came up on the new day with a vengeance, bringing another blast from the furnace of this strangely hot summer. Deeply disturbed by her brush with death and the terrifying flight after the voodoo ceremony, she hadn't gotten much sleep. But, as her thoughts battered her heart, she kept coming back to Rina's statement that she didn't know herself. And connected with that was her powerful attraction to Bear.

She ended up wrestling with her feelings about him most of the night. She couldn't deny the passions Bear aroused in her, yet she couldn't accept them either. Finally she gave up trying to legislate her own feelings. She had strong and often contradictory responses to Bear. She just didn't know what to do about them.

She got out of bed with her muscles aching and her eyes bleary. She showered and dressed simply from the meager stash of leftover clothes in her closet. When she came downstairs, Frankie was waiting for her. She wanted to borrow Sam's Toyota.

Sam had no problem with that. She just asked Frankie to drop her off at the Starbucks where she was meeting Bear.

At nearly nine thirty a.m. to the second, Sam pushed through the door into the coffee shop. Bear sat at a table, waiting. His jaw was tense, his eyes hard. Sam knew something had happened.

When she reached him, Bear handed her a latte along with the greeting, "What's this crap that the case is closed? We're done? Because Barringer's body was stolen by some Haitian priest?"

"Uhhhh, I guess." Sam was taken aback. She sat and pulled the top off the latte container. She noticed that her fingers trembled a little. "You put some sugar in this?"

He threw some packets of sugar and sugar substitute on the table. "Didn't really know how you liked it, so I brought these over. Now what's this voodoo bullcrap?"

Sam busied herself with opening the sugar packets and fixing her coffee, avoiding Bear's eyes when she answered, "Is that what you heard?"

"I think everybody on our floor at the DOD heard it. I had just finished an early-morning meeting with my boss, Allen, when he got the call from your people. He blew up big-time. I was right there at ground zero. They told him they were wrapping up the details as soon as the INS brought in this Le Rat Noir. He's about to go to the secretary of defense on this, let me tell you."

"Uhhhh, why?" Sam asked a little disingenuously, since she too had her own misgivings about closing the case. "I mean, if the bodies are found, this is all over, isn't it?"

"Excuse me?" Bear's face was a thundercloud. "Have we forgotten logic? What about a plain old-fashioned reality check? *If* this guy has these bodies, okay. But what connects a Haitian priest to a Congressional Medal of Honor winner? Why did he take them? What was he going to do with them?"

Sam squirmed uncomfortably. "Uhhh, make them into zombies?"

A line of red moved straight up Bear's neck and colored his face a livid puce. "There's only one thing wrong with that answer," he growled.

"Which is . . . ?" Sam didn't find any pleasure in being this close to Bear's anger. Her father had sometimes exploded in rage the same way. It was not a trait she admired.

"Zombies don't exist. There are no goddamn zombies!"

Sam could see people at nearby tables peering around their editions of the *Washington Post* and staring.

"So, you're not open to the possibility there could be zombies?"

"No! Are you? Come on, Sam! Don't tell me you're really into this paranormal claptrap. You're too smart for that."

"Let's just say I try to keep an open mind about everything. And you should too. Look at Aurora; she did find your cat."

"That was different, a lot different," Bear said, his voice harsh.

"I don't think so," Sam persisted. "And what did you make of those guys who chased us in the cemetery the other night?"

"What did I make of them?"

Sam gripped her latte cup so hard she almost caved in the sides. This conversation wasn't going the way she wanted it to. She exhaled and plunged ahead. "Yeah, make of them. I mean, they moved funny. They looked . . . they looked sort of dead didn't they? And I saw a grave with the dirt coming out of it all by itself. And the security cops in the amphitheater, they didn't have their hearts or brains. Doesn't that kind of say 'zombie' to you?"

"Hell, no, it says these killers were *fucked-up* in some way, pardon my French. Maybe they were in a trance or in some drug-induced state. That's a lot more likely than their being what? The walking dead? As for the mutilation of the victims . . . the killings were brutal, but not out of the ballpark when it comes to anything I've seen before. You don't want to know what people do to one another." He leaned forward and went on. "Listen, Sam, a machete had been used on these two men. Now, *that* might make me consider this Haitian priest as a serious suspect."

Sam looked at Bear, her eyes beginning to glitter with her own building frustration and anger. If only Bear would listen, put aside his preconceptions, and not be so pigheaded. "Rina Martus seems to think—"

Bear's hand smacked the table hard. "Rina Martus! Sam, please, the woman is a whack job, not a professional crime-scene investigator. I don't know how somebody like that got hired by the agency. You cannot give any credence to what she says."

"I don't think you need to insult her." Sam finally found some backbone in this conversation.

"For God's sake, Sam, what I just said about her isn't personal. I don't care if she practices voodoo or thinks she's talking to dead people. I do care if she influences you and your agency into closing this case. That's just plain nuts."

Sam finally sounded as prickly as she felt. "I suppose we have to wait until this Bokor guy is questioned. But as a matter of fact, if you'd stop yelling for a minute, you'd hear what I'd really like to say. I agree with you—at least partially—and I don't agree that the case should be closed. Here's why . . ."

Sam told Bear what Frankie had found out about the robbery at bin Sultan's, editing out the part about the toyol, but describing the fight between the cousin and the gardener over the buried heart.

"Was it a human heart?" Bear asked.

"I don't know. The cousin insisted it was a sheep's. That just doesn't make sense. And we, my colleague and I, felt the appearance of a heart was too much of a coincidence."

"And this bin Sultan is a prince from Oman?"

"Yes. So there's the Middle East and oil involved. I just have a gut feeling on this."

"What does your boss say?"

Sam was silent a moment. "I haven't told her—because she won't listen unless we have some convincing evidence. But listen, this bin Sultan had a group of businessmen over at his house. Some kind of meeting. My colleague believes they were defense contractors. One of our people on-site was able to come up with a name."

"I'm interested," Bear said.

"You're going to be very interested when you find out who it is." Sam took a final swallow of latte and put the cup down. "It's Arthur Bilderberg."

Bear's face lit up. "No!"

"Yes, for a fact it is."

"Interesting, more than interesting. Let me tell you what I found out about Bilderberg. I did some digging when I couldn't sleep last night. I made some calls. I used the computer. Bottom line is he used to work for—get this—the secretary of defense."

"You're kidding."

"Dead serious. Remember the card we got from al-Fayeed's mother? He's currently a member of the board of USEI, United States Enterprise Institute. I found out that they're a group of ex-government bigwigs who broker deals between countries and defense contractors. They engineered a big sale of Patriot missiles to Turkey a while back. Megamillions of dollars involved. They move that kind of money."

"So what's the connection between USEI and what happened in Arlington?"

"I don't know. But I damn well know there is one. Is it in any way connected to what USEI has going with the prince of Oman? I can't imagine how, but I think it's time we made that call on Mr. Bilderberg."

Sam stood up. "Let's go."

43

A few miles from where Sam met Bear at Starbucks, Frankie was sitting at a table across from Liam. She had quickly put her dark red curls into a ponytail because of the heat, but she had taken care with her makeup. She wanted Liam to think she looked good. She was the one who had engineered the meeting, but her motives were mixed.

The night Liam had called to give her Arthur Bilderberg's name, Frankie had become teary and maudlin once she had finished off the bottle of wine. Although drinking alone had become a bad habit, it chased away the nightmares—for a while, anyway. After Liam's phone call she felt really sorry for herself. She felt lonely. She knew she shouldn't let herself be sidetracked from her work at AngelWay, where she was determined to make a good impression. But she was only human. Being a witch didn't change that.

She saw what was going on with Sam and Bear. The two of them were so hot when they got near each other, they nearly burst into flame. So Frankie kept thinking about Liam. Yesterday she had retrieved his number from the BlackBerry and called him, suggesting they meet to talk about the prince's situation.

She did want to discuss the prince and his defense contractors, despite its being largely a convenient excuse to call him. She also wanted to dig for some truth. At Abdul bin Sultan's house Frankie's sharp perceptions had picked up that Liam was lying about something. With men Frankie was never wrong. He also made that remark about having a touch of the "sight" himself. It aroused her curiosity while it deepened her suspicions that Liam wasn't a real chef. If he was impersonating one, she intended to find out why.

Liam had suggested that they meet at Le Madeleine on M Street and Thirtieth. His choice surprised Frankie and pleased her. The restaurant chain was one of her favorite places. Now they sat across from each other, each sipping a French roast while classical music played softly in the background. She waited for him to say something.

Liam put down his cup and fiddled with a napkin, not meeting her eyes. He had on a black T-shirt and jeans, moccasins with no socks, and wore a Claddagh ring on his right hand. He wore a chain around his neck, but if it held a pendant Frankie couldn't tell, because it lay under his T-shirt. Young, lean, handsome, Liam was eye candy, and Frankie knew she shouldn't even look.

Finally Liam looked up. "You don't talk about your job. I'm not sure what law enforcement agency you even work for. But you were sent out to investigate that bizarre robbery—and you nailed it in minutes. So I need to tell you, the whole situation at the prince's is really bothering me."

"Bothering you? Why?"

"I'm not all that fond of the prince and his kid—*spoiled* is an understatement—but I got a phone call early this morning from the housekeeper. Mrs. Doyle's a grand old dame, really."

"I think she's only about forty, Liam," Frankie said, and took a sip of coffee.

"Well, she's grand. She rang me up because she doesn't know what to do. She wanted my advice. The prince and his son went missing. At least, it seems that way. The prince took off around noon yesterday with the kid and never came back to the house last night. The housekeeper found his wife crying her eyes out."

"Have they called the police?"

"That's not going to happen. The wife thinks the prince took off to fool around with one of the exotic dancers they had perform at that meeting with the defense guys. The housekeeper says the prince and his wife had a big fight over his bringing the girls there in the first place. She heard the whole thing. The wife locked him out of the bedroom. They had stopped speaking after that."

"But why would he take his son?"

"Yeah, that's weird. It's true he takes the kid with him everywhere, so maybe he did take the boy along."

"But you don't buy it—why?"

"Because late last night, well after midnight, Mrs. Doyle heard noises in the garden. She found the prince's cousin burying stuff again. The housekeeper asked him if he knew where the prince and his son were, that they had been gone for hours and the boy was only a wee lad.

"He told her to mind her own ferking business. Really rude. Then he said something like, the prince was getting what was coming to him, and if the housekeeper wanted to keep her job when *he* took over, she should shut up and stay out of what didn't concern her."

"It really sounds like a palace coup," Frankie said, again wondering about Liam. He intrigued her, partly because she was attracted to him and partly because she wondered if he was working uncover too—or if he could be someone like her, someone with a secret.

Liam kept talking. "That's what I thought. What if this cousin has killed the prince and the child? I can't stomach the thought of that. What do you think? Are you willing to poke your nose where it doesn't belong?"

"What do you have in mind?"

"I thought after we finish eating we should take the Red Line out to Silver Spring and talk to that gardener. Then do you think you can check out the cousin? His name is Mohammad Mohammad bin Sultan."

Frankie didn't answer right away. She was thinking. She didn't have any doubts that the voodoo priest Le Rat Noir had had a role in taking the bodies from Arlington, but she, like Sam, didn't think they had found all the answers either. She kept wondering about the connection between this prince of Oman, Bilderberg, and the missing photographers. Now the prince was missing too?

Frankie didn't believe in coincidence. What happened

in the world always had a cause, a prime mover of some sort. "We should go talk to the gardener. But I'd like you to get something for me too."

"What's that?" Liam's eyes were curious, excited, interested.

Frankie's heart quickened. "I need an object that belongs to the child, something he touched recently. And something from the prince too. Can you do that?"

For the briefest of seconds a look of understanding seemed to flash across Liam's face; then his expression returned to a careful neutrality. "I'll call Mrs. Doyle. We can stop by the mansion and pick them up. Why do you want them?"

Frankie looked at him, watching carefully as she responded. "I have a friend who has this . . . this talent for finding people. I want to see what she can do."

Liam's poker face remained in place as he asked with all innocence, "What is she, a psychic or something?"

"Or something," Frankie said, and drank the last swallow of her French roast.

44

ONCE they were back in the car, Bear passed Sam his cell phone. "Call the number on the USEI card, Sam. Pretend you're Lily. She's the secretary for my boss, Col. George Allen, the inspector general at the DOD. Say Colonel Allen is sending over Lance Rutledge to talk with Arthur Bilderberg about an important matter. It's urgent."

Sam did as Bear asked. The secretary she reached immediately responded, "Oh, of course. I'll tell Mr. Bilderberg that Mr. Rutledge is on the way." When she hung up, Sam said to Bear, "That seemed almost too easy."

"I don't know. My boss has a lot of clout. If Bilderberg has been a defense contractor for a while, he's got to recognize the name."

But when they got to Bilderberg's office, a high-rise building in downtown D.C., the man himself wasn't there.

"I don't know what happened," the secretary said. "He was on the phone in his office; then he ended the call and literally ran past my desk. 'I've got to leave right now, Mary,' he said. He seemed terribly upset. He was probably going down in an elevator when you were coming up. I'm so sorry you missed him. It must have been an emergency."

Bear, his voice clearly conveying that he was annoyed, said he'd call to reschedule. Sam just stood there rigidly, a scene flashing into her mind. She envisioned a heavyset man running through a lobby, terrified. She saw him pushing through glass doors into the street, then . . .

then a geyser of dark red blood making a gruesome splatter against the glass doors.

Sam turned to Bear, keeping her voice low so the secretary couldn't hear. Her words were excited, urgent. "We need to catch him. I think he's bolted, scared. He knows."

Bear didn't hesitate. He dashed toward the elevator they had just left. Sam was right behind him.

"Yes, maybe if you hurry, he'll still be downstairs!" the secretary called out after them.

Bear stabbed in frustration at the DOWN button. The doors opened; after they stepped inside, Bear immediately began pressing the button that closed the doors. "We should have taken the stairs," he muttered.

"We're on the fourteenth floor." Sam was anxiously wringing her hands. "It would have felt better, but it wouldn't have been faster."

"Yeah, you're right . . . this time," Bear said.

Sam gave him an astonished look.

"I'm kidding!" He gave a half smile. "Come on, elevator, come on."

When they reached the lobby and exited the elevator car, Sam saw a group of people gathered outside the glass doors that led to the street. A siren wailed in the distance.

"Let's see what's going on," Bear urged, and took Sam's arm. But Sam already knew.

She and Bear hurried over to the knot of onlookers and tried to get through them. After they worked their way toward the front of the crowd, the building's security people stopped them from getting close enough to see anything.

"Everybody move back!" a guard ordered. "There's a street exit on the opposite side of the building. This exit is closed!"

Bear let go of Sam's arm and said he'd use his ID to try to talk to one of the security people. He moved away, leaving Sam standing next to a man carrying a large attaché case and wearing a conservative blue suit. She guessed he was a lawyer.

"What happened?" Sam used her sweetest voice.

"Just what I thought might happen. I've been complaining about the security in this building since our firm moved in," the man answered. "We ought to sue the management company. It was only a matter of time; that's what I said."

"Matter of time for what? What happened?"

"A fellow was attacked right there, going out the front door. In broad daylight." The guy pulled out his cell phone. "Excuse me; I have to make a call."

"Wait! Is the man okay?"

The lawyer shook his head. "No, he's not okay. He's dead. Shot in the face. Right there on the street."

Just then Sam spotted Bear weaving his way through the growing crowd of bystanders in the lobby. When he reached her, he took her arm again and pulled her away from the crowd. When they couldn't be overheard, he said, "Bilderberg's been killed. I don't think it was a random street crime. To me it looks like an assassination."

45

TO Frankie, the Malaysian gardener appeared to be a raving lunatic.

Liam had called the gardener from his cell phone when they were on their way out to Silver Spring. Ramli had reluctantly agreed to see his former coworker. When he opened the door for them, he began shouting, "I know nothing! Nothing! I take nothing!"

"We're not accusing you of anything, Ramli," Liam said in a soothing voice. "I came to see how you're doing. Let us inside, will you? Thanks. You don't look too good, buddy."

Ramli's T-shirt was dirty. His long hair hung in greasy strings. A dirty bandanna had been tied around his forehead. His dark eyes darted back and forth. "I am not a thief! I take nothing! The police try to find me. They keep pounding on the door. Why? Why!"

His movements were jerky. His head hung down, and he swung it back and forth like a beast's. He began to pace frenetically in the small living room of his apartment in Silver Spring. And the apartment was filthy, littered with newspapers and take-out food wrappers.

Liam kept talking to the man. "Ramli, buddy, I'm on your side. Even if you did take those things, that guy deserved it. You got a royal screw job, you did."

"A royal screw job, yes!" Ramli punched the air. "I receive the royal screw. That filthy dog. That bastard."

"You mean the prince?" Liam asked.

"Not the prince. That dung monkey, that piece of shit,

his cousin. I should have killed him. I should have taken the garden shears and stabbed him in the heart!"

"No, no, Ramli. You would have ended up in prison. But look, I need to ask you about that fight. You said the cousin buried a heart, a sheep's heart, right?"

"Sheep's heart? Sheep's heart!" the man shrieked. "It was a human heart. That filthy piece of shit put a human heart in my begonias. I should kill him."

"Are you sure? I mean, did you get a good look at it?" Liam asked.

"Do I, Ramli Adnan, look stupid? I dug the thing up. I saw it. He said it was a sheep. Bullsheet. He defiled my garden. To ruin me."

The gardener began shaking, trembling from head to toe. His eyes rolled back in his head. "I think he's going into some kind of fit," Liam whispered.

Frankie whispered back, "I think so too. He bought that toyol. Now he's paying the price. The spirit is still here. It's tormenting him."

She reached out and put her hand on the shaking man's shoulder and gripped it tight. He stopped shaking. His head hung limply. "Mr. Adnan," she said. "You must go back to the witch doctor who sold you the toyol. Do you understand?"

Ramli Adnan shook his head yes.

"You will have to pay him more money to take the toyol back. Do you understand?"

He nodded yes again.

"And ask the witch doctor for a cleansing spell and a protection spell. That's very important. Do you understand? Buying the toyol was a very bad thing to do."

"Yes," the gardener answered. Sweat dripped from his face onto the carpet.

Frankie looked at Liam. "I'd like to get out of here now."

In downtown D.C., Sam also wanted to get out of the place she was in. She was pacing back and forth in the lobby of USEI's building. She needed to work off the agitation she felt at being left to wait and do nothing while

Bear tried to learn something about Bilderberg's attacker. He had cut her out of the questioning of the security people. Sam bristled at his male dominance and assumptions that he was in charge.

Finally she watched Bear come striding back across the lobby like a gladiator, his strength evident, his unfulfilled need for action clear in the tension of his near-perfect body. She thought that she didn't care how good-looking he was. She didn't care about their former chemistry. She knew now that he was not the kind of man she wanted. Her face took on an annoyed look.

"Nobody saw anything." Bear's voice was a hard growl. "Some passersby heard shots, saw Bilderberg fall, and watched a car speed away. It was a black car. That's helpful, isn't it? A black car in Washington, D.C.—and that's all anybody remembers. No plate numbers. No description of the occupants. I think we're done here."

He looked at Sam then, his entire focus on her, as if he had forgotten to really look before. "How about we go back to my place for lunch? I'll crank the air conditioner up, and we can figure out what to do next." He seemed clueless that his overbearing ways could have upset her.

The thought crossed Sam's mind that being alone with Bear again could be compromising. She quickly discarded the idea. He hadn't said anything at all about their intimacy. It was as if it had never happened. Surely he didn't have sex on his mind. Sam felt miserable, and her spirits slid downward into darkness.

And Bear himself remained quiet during the drive through the city, preoccupied with something. Sam stole a glance at him. She didn't know if he was thinking about her or who killed Arthur Bilderberg.

It was neither. Bear must have seen Sam look at him. He took his eyes off the road for a moment and looked back at her. "Smith's wife doesn't work. His address is only a couple of blocks from mine. Let's stop off and see her on the way home."

46

LEANING back in a chair, the chairman folded his hands across the bulge of his small potbelly. He had heard the news that the INS was looking for the Bokor. It nearly drove him to do something monumentally stupid. But he just couldn't believe that group of nitwits at the CIA had actually stumbled on a connection between the sorcerer and the open graves in Arlington.

Thank God—or more likely Satan, or whatever out there was in charge of the ways of the world—the Bokor hadn't been found. The Haitian had one more job to do; then he too would be expendable.

That final transformation of human into zombie brought up another small problem. This one didn't bother the chairman very much. He had expected some last-minute situations before the plan was set in motion and the company's Gulfstream took off for Muscat.

But this setback made the chairman realize he had been lulled into complacency. The whole audacious plan had been going like clockwork. Even getting Prince bin Sultan out to the warehouse had been ridiculously easy. He thought he'd be inspecting the huge cache of matériel ready to be shipped to Oman. With Saudi Arabia rattling swords on one border and the United Arab Emirates determined to take over Oman's enclaves of Mahda and Musandam, the prince couldn't resist the deal USEI had brokered for him, which included ten of Boeing's C-17s and five Sikorsky helicopters.

Why should the prince hesitate? He had no reason to be suspicious and every reason to be satisfied, since the Pentagon was paying the bill for the aircraft. Congress had approved the whole pork-barrel package, recognizing that U.S. bases in Oman were seen as strategically important. That Oman's military would soon be under the chairman and his board's control, with the prince as their puppet, was a delicious irony, the icing on the cake, so to speak.

A wave of anger crashed down on the chairman again. Nobody expected that stupid, vain, and self-indulgent prince to bring his kid along to the warehouse. What were they supposed to do with the bawling little cretin? There was no point in making a kid into a zombie. Now they had to dump the brat somewhere. If it were up to the chairman, he would just throw the kid into the Potomac. But it wasn't up to him, and he had to admit that drowning the child would bring too much attention to the Abdul bin Sultan household.

In the end he agreed that it was better just to leave the kid somewhere. When the prince showed back up at his house to collect his wife and valuables before the flight, he could use the excuse that he had been searching for his son. But things had to move quickly. Charles was supposed to bring the Bokor in tonight and get this thing done.

The chairman leaned back in his desk chair. In forty-eight hours he would be living like a king, safe and untouchable in Oman. He wasn't going to let anything get in his way. If he had to eliminate a few more "loose ends," it didn't matter to him.

In fact, secretly he hoped it came to that. He could have some fun doing it his way. He could use that nice secure room in the warehouse, the shining stainless-steel table, and all those lovely surgical instruments. He could ensure that the end for his victim could come as slowly and painfully as possible. The arousal caused by such an act could not be matched by mere intercourse. It was always so satisfying when the chairman brought in Eros as a willing handmaiden in that irresistible, ancient marriage of sex and death.

47

CARS filled Smith's driveway and lined the street in front of his house.

"Somebody having a party?" Bear wondered out loud.

"Or a wake." Sam was only half kidding.

A large black woman wearing a caftan opened the door and looked at the two white people on the stoop with suspicion but no hostility. "You cops?"

"Federal investigators," Bear said, and showed his badge. "Are you Patricia Smith?"

"No, Patty's my sister. I'm Penny. O'Neal, not Smith. She in the parlor. We just got back from the emergency room."

"We were hoping to ask her some questions."

"Guess she want to talk. For cops, you got here right quick, that for sure." The woman let them in and led them into a side room crowded with middle-aged women. A heavyset black woman, nearly identical to the one who answered the door, lay on the couch. A white plaster cast covered her arm from the wrist to the elbow.

"Why are all these women here?" Sam asked Penny.

"They came over from the church soon as they find out."

"Find out what?"

"The devil been here."

Bear pulled a wing chair closer to the sofa and sat down. He leaned forward. "Mrs. Smith, what happened?"

She turned wide eyes on him. "Rodney came back. Early this morning."

"Did he do this to you?"

Tears rolled down her fat cheeks. "We been married thirty years. That man never lifted his hand to me before. But it weren't him this time neither. No, Lord. The devil had got him." She rolled heavily on her side toward Bear and clutched his arm with her healthy hand. She looked at him with wild eyes. "Satan was in this house with him."

One of the church ladies cried out, "Jesus! Jesus! Save us!"

"Tell me exactly what happened," Bear said in a kind voice.

"He come in through the back door real early. Seven, seven thirty. I be in the kitchen boiling up some grits 'fore it gets too hot outside, you know. I say, 'Rodney Smith! Where you been? I been half out of my mind worryin' 'bout you.'

"He look at me like he don't even see me. Then he walk on past me without saying a word. And he smell like a slaughterhouse. Real nasty.

"I get mad then. I go after him and hit him upside the head with the spoon I been using to stir the grits. I figure he's drunk, you know?" New tears spilled down her face.

"He stops all of a sudden-like and turns around. He stares me right in the face and I scream. His eyes is flat, no light in 'em at all. Dead. A corpse's eyes. He takes his hand and smacks me in the face so hard I see stars. I scream again and he pick me up like I don't weigh nothing and throw me 'cross the room. I swear he did.

"That when I knew. The devil got him. It weren't my Rodney, no, Lord, it weren't. He starts toward me, and I yell out, 'Jesus! Help me now!' That devil man grab my arm and twist it. . . ." She sobbed.

Her sister said, "There, there, Patty. You safe now. He not coming back here. No, sir." The heavy woman in the caftan looked at Bear. "She all tuckered out. You through?"

"Just one or two more questions," Bear said. He turned to Patricia Smith. "What happened then?"

"He let go. He seem all drugged up. Dazed, I don't know. He smell so bad I like to have gagged when he come so close to me. He never said nothing, not one word. He turn around and walk right through the house. He open the front door and go out. Don't close it or nothing. I try to get off the floor. The pain in my arm hit me so hard I pass out. When I come to, he gone."

"So you didn't see if he came with anyone? If he got in a car? How he left?"

"No, sir. But it still smell in here when I woke up. The devil's stink. That's what it were, no doubt about it. I crawled to phone and called my sister. She got an ambulance."

After Bear and Sam got back in the car, he turned to Sam and said, "Don't you say one word about zombies."

Sam's eyebrows arched. "Why? How else to explain what happened?"

"Just like the lady said. Drugs. He's all doped up."

But Sam kept thinking Rodney Smith smelled just like the man who had attacked her in Arlington.

Hunger made Sam ravenous by the time they returned to Bear's row house. She'd only had the latte at Starbucks early that morning.

"How about I order a pizza?" Bear said.

"Sounds great."

He picked up the phone and called Papa John's. Then he said to Sam, "I'm going to my computer and see what I can find out about Oman. You want to come?"

"Sure. Maybe we can find a link with USEI. I've got a feeling we're close to figuring this out."

Bear led the way upstairs. The computer had been set up on a desk in his bedroom. Sam stopped at the door. Her eyes fell on the queen-size bed covered with a black satin coverlet. Heat crawled into her face. She felt awkward about going into the bedroom.

Then she shook off her hesitation. Bear had been keeping his distance from her. Why would it change now?

Bear sat down in front of the screen. Sam walked up behind him as she pulled up a Wikipedia entry on Oman. She read over his shoulder. The country bordering Saudi Arabia had huge oil fields. The king, Qaboos bin Sultan, ruled as an absolute monarch, allowing no private agencies to operate in his country, not even a Red Crescent or Red Cross. There wasn't even the pretense of a democracy, no parliament, and the judiciary was the Muslim court, the Sharia.

"One man controlling an entire country. An obedient citizenry," he mused. "A coup could put his son in charge easily."

"You think that's what this is all about?" Sam asked.

Bear turned his head to look at her. His face was very close to her breasts. "It's an idea." His voice changed in the middle of the sentence, becoming lower and hoarse. "Just an idea, that's all."

Suddenly the air was charged with electricity. Bear tore his eyes away from her and back to the computer screen. "Let me make another search for USEI."

His fingers fumbled with the keys. Sam knew she should move away, excuse herself, go back downstairs. Their having sex had been a mistake. She didn't intend to let it happen again. But she stayed where she was, just inches from Bear, able to hear his breathing and feel the warmth of his body.

"Well, look at that." He had pulled up an article from the *Washington Post* dated a month ago. USEI had brokered a multimillion-dollar deal between Lockheed Martin and Prince Abdul bin Sultan of Oman for five new F-15 fighter jets.

"Wow," Sam said, moving a few steps from the computer chair while Bear stood up. He moved toward Sam, his voice excited. "We're getting there, Sam; we really are."

"But there are still so many unanswered questions. Who set you up, Bear? Why was your gun at Bartikowski's?"

"I don't know yet." He was staring at her, his eyes becoming smoky with desire. "Sam . . ." His lips lowered toward hers.

The kiss took her breath away. A hard knot inside her loosened. She melted against Bear. Whether this was right or wrong didn't matter anymore. No other man had ever affected her so strongly. She wanted to touch him. She wanted to get under his skin, inside his very blood and bones.

The kiss lengthened. Her head was spinning. His arms tightened around her. His tongue pushed into her mouth. His fingers went into her hair. She felt overcome with longing, with desire. She slipped her hands under his to touch his hard-muscled back.

Time disappeared. They stood there embracing, joining together in a world that contained only them. He leaned down and put a trail of kisses on her neck. She tipped her chin back and felt her flesh tingle every place he touched.

It was Sam herself who sank down on the bed, her legs all shaky and unwilling to hold her up. She drew Bear down next to her.

Bear's eyes beheld her with wonder. His big hand gently stroked the side of her face. "Beautiful. Beautiful Sam." He lowered his lips to the top of her shoulder. She encircled him with her arms and pulled him on top of her.

He raised his head. "Sam? Do you want . . . ?"

"Yes." She sighed and pulled her cotton top over her head. Then she unfastened her bra and lay bare-breasted on the black satin cover. He made a guttural sound deep in his throat and ran his fingers down the sides of her breasts. She shivered and watched him touch her.

He opened the top of her slacks, unzipped them, and slipped them off. She was wearing a red silk thong underneath them.

"God, Sam." His voice was hoarse. With one swift motion he slipped his finger under the elastic of the thong and pulled hard. The thin band gave way easily and tore from her body. He held the wisp of silk and then wrapped it around his hand.

Then, with her white flesh exposed completely, he lowered his lips to suck on a nipple.

Sam moaned. She grabbed his head with her hands. She tugged at his dark hair as sensations poured through her. She begged him to suck hard. She groaned as she felt the sharp nip of his teeth. She pressed against him, hungry, so terribly hungry for his touch.

He suddenly pulled away. With a little cry she protested, "No."

"More to come," he promised in a hoarse whisper. He stroked the side of her face with his hand before he quickly stood and began to remove his clothes. She watched him like a hawk eyeing its prey. There was nothing about him that wasn't gorgeous. The muscles of his chest were cut like a bodybuilder's. His waist was narrow, his legs powerful.

And his member . . . it was long and thick. Sam stared at it shamelessly and with desire clear on her face. She watched him go to the bed table drawer and take out a condom. She watched him put it on. Her eyes were greedy.

He came to her then. He tongued her neck and she threw her head back, nearly overwhelmed with an all-consuming hunger.

"Would you get on the floor, on your hands and knees?" he whispered. His words made her tremble.

"What are you going to do?" she asked.

"Pleasure you," he said, nuzzling her chin. "Fuck you. Make you scream."

With that she could wait no more. She rolled off the bed and sank down to her knees on the bedroom floor. She leaned forward. He turned her smooth white ass toward him. He stroked it. Her breath became ragged. She still didn't know exactly what he meant to do, and a small fear shook her as she thought about giving herself up to his will, to his desires, whatever they were. She had heard about what some men liked to do, to mix pain with their pleasure. She didn't know if she would want that, if she could let him—

He clapped one huge hand on her shoulder, holding her firmly. "What are you—" A wave of panic overwhelmed her, and she cried, "Oh!"

All Bear had done was reach around her body and find the cleft between her legs with his fingers. He probed into her with them. He rubbed her and she moaned. She wriggled and pumped against his hand. His fingers teased her unmercifully.

Then he pulled his hand away and pushed her stance wider. She was panting. She had become mad with wanting him to enter her, impatient with longing.

Just then she felt the hood of his shaft touch her anus. She tensed, but he did not enter there, as she thought he might. She would have let him. She would have denied him nothing, but she wasn't ready for that, for it was something she had never done.

Instead his shaft moved on to her dark, familiar center. She moaned and arched her back, opening for him to enter her. He came into her from a sharp angle, pushing forward as he plunged into her wetness. She cried out as he slid inside her.

Then he rocked against her, putting his hands around her waist and pulling her to him, taking her body under his power so absolutely that she had to give up control to him.

It excited her that he possessed her that way. He thrust into her again and again, able to penetrate to the point where, yes, some pain mixed with her pleasure. She attempted to pull away, suddenly afraid. He would not allow it.

That drove her wild. It excited her to heights she had never felt. She cried out again loudly as he pushed again, holding her immobile. He began to increase his pace, rocking into her. She hung her head as perspiration formed on her face. Sweat made her entire body slick. She wanted more.

But suddenly he stopped, and before she realized what was happening he slipped out of her. She cried out, "No! Don't stop—oh, please, don't stop."

He loomed over her, a giant of a man. "Yes," he said. "Yes, the best is yet to come." He turned her, his strength allowing him to lift her like a child. He laid her on her back. The wood floor was cool against her flesh. He parted her knees with his hands, and before she realized his intention he had hunched down and buried his face between her thighs.

His soft mouth encircled her womanhood. "Oh!" she

screamed. He sucked hard there in that sensitive place. "Oh! Oh! Oh!" Sam cried again and again, grabbing his hair and coming in a rush. A violent orgasm rocked her, taking her higher. And just as she climaxed, Bear lifted his mouth away and spread her lips with his fingers.

The next thing Sam felt was his turgid member, huge and hard, entering her again.

Without warning, Sam climaxed a second time, the orgasm sweeping her away. She gripped him tightly as her body throbbed, her lips frantically seeking his. She was on fire. She was burning up. Her body was shaking on the floor. She couldn't seem to stop coming. He thrust inside her, pushing hard, pulling out, pushing in.

Then he exploded within her. He groaned with a deep, bestial sound. His body shuddered and his shaft filled her, making her open her legs completely to let him take her, possess her, own her.

Insensate with a passion greater than anything she had ever felt before, she quivered uncontrollably as another powerful wave of pleasure tumbled over her. Glittering stars fell all around her. She heard herself saying, "Uh, uh, uh" in a hoarse, sex-drenched voice. She writhed and bucked beneath him. He put strong hands on her backside then and lifted her hips to press against his. He bore down hard, his member massive inside her, his pubic bone grinding against hers.

She could not have escaped him even if she had wished to. He dominated her completely. She could only receive him, open to him, let him capture her and force her complete surrender. From the minute they had first met, she had been waiting for this. She understood that now. She screamed in wild ecstasy as a powerful wave of feeling took her. It carried her far, farther than she had ever been. She knew paradise in that moment, and she did not want it to ever end.

48

THAT same afternoon, when Frankie and Liam finally arrived at Abdul bin Sultan's huge stone mansion, Mrs. Doyle opened the door. "Still no word from the prince," she said. "The princess hasn't stopped crying. I hope you can help the poor lamb."

"We're going to try," Liam assured her. "Did you get what I asked for?"

Mrs. Doyle handed him a white plastic grocery bag. "The little fellow's favorite teddy bear is in there. And a shirt of the prince's out of the laundry. It's a Ralph Lauren pullover. Will you be bringing it back?"

"Definitely," Frankie said. "I'll know very quickly if they'll work. But, Mrs. Doyle, I wonder if you'd help with something else."

"If I can, of course, I will."

"I want to dig in the garden. Can you get me a few more plastic bags?"

"I don't believe we're doing this," Liam said as he knelt next to Frankie in a bed of trampled and half-dug-up begonias. Rain had begun to fall. The loamy earth was fast turning to mud. "Shouldn't we have called the police?"

"I don't think they could have gotten a search warrant. The prince has diplomatic immunity. But it's important that we get what's buried here back to my department. Forensics there will handle it."

"Are we committing a crime by doing this?" Liam wanted to know.

Frankie had absolutely no idea about the legal ramifications of their activity, but she said, "I don't think it matters, as long as we don't get caught. I think our biggest worry is if the cousin shows up while we're still out here."

"And then what?"

"I have the feeling he'd try to kill us."

"Then for God's sake, woman, dig faster."

Seconds later the big stirring spoon that Liam had given her from a kitchen drawer to dig with struck something a few inches under the surface. "I've got it," she said. "Hold your breath; this really stinks."

She cleared away the wet dirt, trying not to take a breath.

"What is it?" Liam asked, his voice muffled because he was speaking through the shirt he had pulled up over his mouth.

She poked around in the hole she had dug with the spoon. She nudged something wrapped in clear plastic. Then she gingerly scooped it out and dropped it into one of the white grocery sacks. "It's a bloody heart and something even more disgusting. It looks like wiggly worms, but I think it's somebody's brains."

49

IN the golden afterglow of lovemaking with Bear, Sam had forgotten what life had already taught her: Real life rarely lived up to one's expectations.

By the time the Papa John's deliveryman showed up, Sam had her clothes back on and wore them along with a feeling of immense satisfaction. She and Bear dug into the hot pie that dripped with melted cheese and drank from bottles of ice-cold Amstel beer that Bear had in the fridge. Sam felt ridiculously happy. What had started out as a dreadful day had ended up to be one of the best.

While they ate, they tossed ideas back and forth about what to do next. Bear thought they had to check out other members of USEI.

"I think we'll find this whole case hangs together in a logical way," he said. "I haven't given up the idea of the missing bodies being used to smuggle in stolen valuables. The Oman thing ties in somehow. We'll figure it out. Nothing paranormal about this. No zombies," he said, and expected Sam to agree.

That annoyed Sam; it also helped her make up her mind. She had to tell him the truth and let the chips fall where they may.

"Bear, I am positive there are zombies involved in this. Whether you believe in them or not, I know what I saw in the cemetery. I know nobody took those men out of those graves. And look at what happened to Smith's wife."

Bear threw down the piece of pizza he was eating. "Why do you have to ruin this? I just don't get it. Nobody as bright and educated as you could really believe in this paranormal crap."

She took a deep breath. "Bear, I need to talk to you about something. Now that we've . . . Now that we have . . . you know. About me."

He misunderstood completely where she was going with the conversation. "What? Is it about your past? How bad could it be? Were you married? Are you married? You didn't do prison time or you wouldn't be working for the agency."

Sam thought about Aurora. "You are probably wrong to assume that. I think they hire whoever they can use. But no, I was never in jail. It's entirely different—"

Bear cut her off again, expressing his own train of thought. "You know, Sam, I probably have some things in my past you ought to hear. I *was* arrested as a kid. I almost went to jail, but the judge let me go into the military instead. I was engaged to a girl not long ago. It didn't work out. But I'm glad about that. And there are other things too. My family—"

"Bear, it doesn't matter about your family. Family is something we get just by being born; we don't choose how we come into the world. But I need to get this off my chest, okay?" Sam's hands had started sweating, and her stomach was churning. She plunged ahead. "We haven't talked about what Aurora did. You didn't think she could help, but she used her cat, Miranda, to find Nada. She saw where Nada was. She told you. She really did it, and you know she did."

"I thought this was about you, Sam. I'm confused. Why are you talking about your roommate?"

"Because she has this gift. Some people call it the gift of sight. Other people say the people who have it are psychic. Bear, I have it."

"You've lost me on this, Sam. Are you telling me you're a psychic? What, do you read tarot cards or something?" He made an attempt at a laugh.

"It's not a joke, Bear. I see things. I hear voices too. That's why I'm working for the agency."

Bear's eyes looked troubled. "I really don't understand. You think you hear voices? You have hallucinations? Are you mentally ill? Do you take medication?"

"Damn it, Bear! I told you, I have the gift of sight. I'm not crazy. It's not an illness." Sam hadn't realized she would get so angry so fast. But he didn't believe her. He just flat-out didn't believe her.

"Look, I'll prove it to you. The other night, when I said I got that phone call from the agency about going out to the cemetery? I faked it. I called Ms. Z; she didn't call me. I stood right here in this kitchen, and when the cranberry juice spilled, I saw what was happening up in the amphitheater. I saw it all!"

"How could you have? That's crazy, Sam."

"It's *not* crazy. I'm not crazy. And another thing: There are zombies. You're so wrong when you say they don't exist. The Bokor and his juju zombies chased me home last night from Washington."

"Wait a minute. Hold up. You told me you were staying home last night. How were zombies chasing you in D.C.?"

"Rina asked me to go with her to a voodoo service."

Bear's face got rigid. His voice got loud. "So why did you lie to me about it? You could have just told me the truth about going out. What else have you lied to me about?"

"What are you talking about, Bear? I haven't lied to you. I didn't tell you I was a psychic working with a team of other psychics for the CIA. It's supposed to be classified information. I'm not supposed to be telling you anything. But I didn't *want* to lie to you. Don't you get it?"

"I don't get anything except that you're not who I thought you were." Bear's face was a thunderstorm.

"Who did you think I was? I'm Susan Ann Marie Chase. The same person right this minute that I was a half hour ago when we were upstairs screwing our brains out."

Bear stood up abruptly and turned his back on Sam. He put both hands on the breakfast bar counter, leaned his weight on his arms, and hung his head. Finally he said, "I have to do some thinking about this. It's a hell of a thing to just drop on me." He turned his head and looked at her with eyes shot through with pain. "I don't even know if you're sane."

He pushed away from the counter. He picked up her purse off the chair and handed it to her. She took it with a shaking hand.

"Come on; I'll drive you back to Bel Air."

"Just a minute, Bear. I have something I want to say. I just told you my deepest secret, something I have never revealed to any other man. And you slapped me in the face with it. You don't even know if I'm sane? I'm not only sane; I'm kind, and loving, and damned smart. But you know what? You just blew it. You just lost the best thing—and that's *me*—that you *almost* ever had."

Sam turned around and walked to Bear's front door. "And I wouldn't drive home with you if I had to walk all the way back to Bel Air. Fortunately, I have a cell phone and I have friends. I'll get home—and I'll get by—without you."

With her spine rigid and her head held high, Sam opened the front door of Bear's elegant Georgian row house. She walked out into the summer afternoon, where a sudden rain had begun to fall like silver tears onto the green grass of Washington.

50

FRANKIE pulled up in the Toyota within fifteen minutes of Sam's exit from Bear's house. Sam managed to contact the white witch just as she left Langley. She told Frankie where she'd be, walking north on Bear's street. The sudden shower drenched her clothes; then when the sun came out, she believed the heat seemed worse. She felt faint and unwell, but she had managed to gain control of her emotions by the time Frankie spotted her, pulled over, got out, and let Sam take the wheel.

Sam gave Frankie points for not asking why she had been walking the Washington streets in the rain, her eyes puffy and her nose red. Sam figured the woman probably could guess even if she weren't psychic.

On the ride back to Bel Air, Frankie's chatter helped keep Sam's mind off Bear and the devastation of her emotions. Frankie filled in Sam on what she and Liam had found in the garden and on the prince's disappearance, which, to Frankie's disgust, Ms. Z had shrugged off. Langley was more interested in the organs Frankie dug up and the bin Sultan cousin, a shady character the agency had been watching for some time.

"But we have to find the prince and his boy," Frankie said.

"We? Us? The team?" Sam asked, trying to pay attention to Frankie's narrative and not let her mind drift off to think about Bear.

"Yes. I already called Aurora and said we were on our way." Frankie fiddled with the radio, trying to find a good station. "What do you have the buttons set on for this?" she asked.

"NPR is the first one. I don't know what the others are. Go ahead and fool around with them," Sam said, not really caring.

"You want to talk about anything?" Frankie asked.

Sam shook her head. "No. Not now anyway. Maybe later. You say Aurora's going to try to find the missing prince and his child?"

"Yes, as soon as we get back to the house. Like I said, Ms. Z isn't interested. She asked if I had picked up anything of the cousin's so Aurora could try to find *him.* I said no, that I didn't even think of it. She seemed pissed off. First she loves us because of the Bokor; now she's making faces and acting disappointed. Hell, we cracked this case, or almost. It's like you can't do enough to please her, ever."

"Speaking of the Bokor, did they arrest him yet?" Sam asked, a little worm of anxiety coming alive inside her.

"Not yet. I guess they'll find him, but you know, Sam, we need to be careful. I'm not saying he's going to come looking for us with his *tonton macoutes*, but he's probably really angry. These voodoo sorcerers are very into revenge. He may be sticking pins into voodoo dolls with our names on them this very minute."

Sam glanced over at Frankie, the little worm now becoming a strangling rope of fear. "Do you really think that? Can you do anything?"

Frankie smoothed her denim skirt with a nervous hand. "I do think that, and I'm going to perform some spells the minute we get back to the house. I'm hoping Rina has already been working some of her own, though. She knows better than any of us what he's capable of."

Back in Bel Air, Rina had been throwing up for the past several hours. She had a high fever. Her body was racked with pain. She did know what the Bokor was capable of. He was attacking her with everything he could. She was fighting back, the snake against the rat. She intended to win against this violent and demented Bokor, but there were moments when she feared he would kill her, that all her magic couldn't withstand the evil he was sending to destroy her.

Aurora took Frankie and Sam up to Rina's bedroom as soon as they arrived at the house. Frankie said to the thin, groaning woman lying on the bed, "I hear you're not feeling well."

"Never been this sick," Rina muttered.

"Our combined energies might help. You think so?"

Rina nodded and struggled to sit up. Her face was paper white. The women entered the room and surrounded her, each putting one hand on a shoulder or arm. As soon as they did, a healthier color came into her face. Her breathing became less labored.

Frankie said for the women to join hands and make a circle around Rina, who stood on trembling legs in the middle. Frankie began to chant:

"In night, in darkness, evil hides,
Coming to take you from our side,
But together we will be strong
And join our hands to stop all wrong.
Never can the Bokor find you.
Never can he smite or harm you.
For from this day, not one nor two,
nor three, but four forevermore.
We stand together a solid shore
Sisterhood's power will endure.
Be gone, Bokor!
Be gone, Bokor!
It is done."

And it was. Rina straightened up and grimaced. "Most of the pain's gone."

Frankie added wryly, "At least for a while. We're supposed to eat something to restore our energies after that kind of spell, so let's head for the kitchen. I'll make us some omelets while Aurora does her own magic and finds the missing prince of Oman and his child."

51

BEAR had sunk into the nadir of his existence. A blackness had opened up inside him and threatened to swallow him whole. He felt he had screwed up. He felt Sam had betrayed him. He felt alone. He felt stupid. He felt miserable. He felt everything at once.

And feeling that much for Bear Rutledge was unacceptable, unbearable, unmanly. He pushed what had just happened between Sam and him out of his mind. He shoved it down inside him.

As soon as he did, what took its place was outrage at this case the CIA was trying to close. That in part had caused his explosive reaction to what Sam had told him. It had pushed him off the edge. Psychics? Woo-woo visions? Walking dead? Had the whole fucking world gone crazy?

Rutledge had investigated a lot of crimes. Humans—living, breathing Homo sapiens—had committed them every single time. This whole zombie angle was a smoke screen. It had to be. He didn't understand why the agency was buying it.

But then again he was dealing with the CIA. They probably weren't buying it. They were just playing their games and leaving him out there twisting in the wind.

They had picked the wrong patsy this time, he thought. He wasn't going to lie down and let them ride over him. He wasn't going to take the weight when everything blew up and everybody started pointing fingers. Big Bear Rutledge wasn't going to be the fall guy for those scheming, slippery bastards.

"Fuck it!" he yelled out loud in the empty kitchen. "I

just don't give a shit anymore. If I get fired, I just don't fucking care."

Bear figured he might as well finish off this day by giving himself some satisfaction, at least. He picked up the phone and placed the call he had wanted to make for a week.

"Mrs. Barringer? Mrs. Michael Barringer?" he asked.

The woman at the other end said in a weary voice, "Yes, who is this?"

"My name is Lance Rutledge, ma'am. I work for the Department of Defense in Washington, D.C. I'm investigating your husband's . . . your husband's death."

"Why would you be investigating that, Mr. Rutledge? It happened months ago in Iraq."

"Yes, ma'am. But he was working an intelligence mission at the time, and it's come to our attention that someone had a grudge against him. That person may have been involved in . . . in wanting revenge. Do you know if he had received any threats prior to his death?"

There was silence from Mrs. Barringer.

"Ma'am? Are you still there?"

"Yes. Yes, I'm sorry. I just didn't expect you to say that. I've always felt there was something wrong about the way Michael died. I asked at the time; I did. All I was told was that he died a hero's death. That he had thrown himself on a grenade and spared the lives of others. They gave him the Congressional Medal of Honor, you know."

"Yes, ma'am. I know. In no way am I questioning his sacrifice or courage. By all reports he was an exemplary soldier with an outstanding record. But you said you felt something was wrong. Can you explain? I'd appreciate it, ma'am."

"I'll have to go back a few weeks before Michael died. He called me and said he had an opportunity to leave the army and make a lot of money. A fortune. We'd be set for life, he said. He was very excited. He was going to work for a company called USEI."

"USEI? Are you sure?"

"I'm positive. But the catch was, we'd have to live in Oman. He didn't know how long we'd have to stay there.

Years, I think. I . . . I didn't want to go. I told him that. We fought about it for days. Finally I gave him an ultimatum—if he took the job, he'd have to go to Oman alone. I'd file for divorce." Her voice broke. "I think that's why he's dead. If I hadn't—"

Bear was soothing, understanding. "You can't blame yourself, ma'am. You had every right not to want to uproot your family and move to an Arab country. Your husband had to know that."

"I suppose he did, but he said this was the opportunity of a lifetime. He'd never get another chance like this. But after I . . . after I threatened to divorce him, he agreed to turn down the job."

"What happened?"

"That's when I began to sense that something was terribly wrong. Michael sounded nervous the next time we spoke. He said the company, that USEI, was putting a lot of pressure on him to take the job. I think 'pressure' meant threats. I asked him if he had signed a contract with USEI or anything. He said no, but that he had already started working for them, in a way. I didn't know what he meant by that, and he didn't explain."

"How long was that before he was killed, Mrs. Barringer?"

"About a week. I talked to him one more time after that. He sounded . . . he sounded preoccupied, worried, not himself. I don't know. Frightened, I think. He told me he was sending me a letter with information in it. If something happened to him, anything suspicious, I should keep it as 'insurance,' he said. He said it wasn't something he wanted to tell me, but there might come a time I'd need to know it."

"Did he send the letter, ma'am?"

"Yes, he did."

"What did it say?" Bear felt his pulse speeding up. This was what he wanted. This was what his gut told him would happen. Here was the information that would break this case with the truth, the real truth.

Mrs. Barringer sighed; then she said in a sad voice, "I never opened it. When Michael died, and his commanding officer told me about him falling on the grenade and all . . . it just seemed like reading it . . . I don't know. Like I wouldn't like what he wrote in there. Michael was dead. I wanted to hold on to the memory of him as a good man, as a hero."

Bear had a sinking feeling. *Don't let her tell me she burned it.* "Mrs. Barringer, that letter is very important. Tell me you still have it."

"Yes, of course I do. Michael told me to keep it, so I have."

"Is it possible for you to get it and tell me what it says?"

Again there was silence.

"Ma'am, are you there?"

"I-I find this very difficult, Mr. Rutledge. I don't want to know the contents of the letter. I don't want to open it, not now. Not ever."

Bear's frustration soared. He wanted to explode. But he knew that this emotionally fragile woman would hang up on him if he pushed too hard. He had to play this right and improvise a story fast.

"Mrs. Barringer, I need to tell you something in confidence. Please listen to me carefully. Your husband was helping the Central Intelligence Agency. He was in delicate negotiations with the Iraqi government. This company that tried to recruit him . . . we here in Washington feel they are highly dangerous to our nation's security. I can't reveal why. But what your husband learned about them is of vital importance.

"I understand your reluctance to read the letter. I respect that. So I am about to ask you to do something, not for me, but for this nation that your husband loved. This country that your husband gave his life for. Will you do it?"

"Yes, of course. What is it? What is it you want me to do?" Mrs. Barringer was clearly on the verge of tears.

"Give me the letter. Or at least let me read it and make a copy. I will drive to your home right now, today. That's how critical that information is. Do you understand?"

"Yes. Yes, I do." Mrs. Barringer's voice was quavering.

"All right, I am going to drive there from Washington.

You live in Willingboro, New Jersey, correct? That's the address I have."

"Yes, that's correct."

"I'm going to leave right now. I'll be there in under three hours. Do not, I repeat, do not tell anyone about that letter. Do not call anyone. The men your husband feared are still out there. If they know that letter exists, they wouldn't hesitate to kill you to get it."

"Are you serious?" Mrs. Barringer's voice shook violently.

"I am dead serious. Please do as I ask, Mrs. Barringer. Your country's future depends on it. I will be there as fast as I can."

52

BARELY able to finish her omelet, Sam forced the last few mouthfuls down. Then she set the plate on the coffee table and sank wearily onto the sofa in the living room. Her muscles ached from the fight in the cemetery, but her heart hurt infinitely more. She didn't know a person could feel so much pain inside and not die.

She noticed that Rina didn't eat at all. Sam watched her pick at her food, then droop, exhausted, in one of the wing chairs.

A wave of worry washed over Sam. Rina had become thin to the point of emaciation. She looked ill. And Sam realized she now cared very much for the mysterious Rina. In fact, she had begun to care about all the women, despite not knowing exactly what had brought them here, to this crossroads, to this strange curve in the paths of their lives.

Just then a lusty alto started to belt out a song in the kitchen about country roads. Keeping on pitch, Frankie sang the words loudly enough to be heard above the running water. She seemed to have gained the energy Rina lost. Something or someone had charged her batteries.

Aurora too had lost any vestiges of frailty. Her body looked small, sturdy, and strong. Wearing a loose white cotton top and shorts, she sat cross-legged on the floor with her cat, Miranda, at her side. Maps sat in a pile next to her. Frankie turned off the water in the kitchen. She walked briskly into the living room carrying a white plastic grocery bag. She handed it over to Aurora.

Aurora peeked inside and took out a brown teddy bear that was wearing a plaid vest. One ear had been ripped nearly off and one button eye was gone.

"A little boy loves this bear very much," Aurora said. "It's his one true friend."

"The prince's son?" Frankie asked.

"Yes. He's a spoiled little boy, but not a very happy one."

"Can you see where he is? Is he all right?" she said.

Aurora smiled. "He's fine. A little hungry, though. He's in some kind of maze, a boxwood maze. Let's see if I can figure out where it is." She closed her eyes. "Hmmm, what's that building? Let me see if I can move around it. Yes, I can see a bronze plaque on the side. Dumbarton Oaks?" She turned to Sam. "Is there a park near Dumbarton Oaks?"

Sam nodded. "Sure. Montrose Park is right next door. It's off of R Street in Georgetown. You think that's where he is?"

"I know that's where he is."

"Let's go get him then," Frankie insisted. "What about the prince? Can you locate him too?"

Aurora reached into the bag and pulled out a Polo knit shirt. "No!" she cried when she touched it. "It's bad. I'm sorry. It's very bad."

"What do you mean?" Frankie asked.

"There's something very wrong with this man. He's hurt, I think. He's not with the child; that's all I can tell."

Suddenly a roar of wind blotted out all sound for Sam. She grabbed her temples. Pain racked her head. She could see a room; it looked like an operating room. The prince lay on a table, the top of his skull open. She cried out, "I see him. He's having surgery. I don't know. Blood running across a shiny table. It's horrible."

"Can you figure out the location? Can you see anything?" Frankie urged.

Sam shook her head. "It's confusing. It's not a hospital. The man operating . . . it's the Bokor, I think. It's terrible. The prince's brains are . . . spilling out of his head." The pain behind her own temples was becoming unbearable. Tears began to run down her cheeks. She raised her eyes to look at the other women. "That's all I see. I'm sorry. I don't know where he is."

Clearly concerned, Frankie stared at Sam. "It's okay. Maybe something else will come to you. The important thing is that we can find the little boy. Sam, you don't look well at all. Will you be able to drive us into Washington?"

Sam hesitated. She really didn't feel in any shape to get behind the wheel. "You go. Take my car. I'm going to go to bed. I feel pretty awful."

Rina pushed herself up from the chair. "I'll come along for the ride. I feel like crap too, but I'd better stay close to Frankie right now. She's got the good mojo for me tonight. Le Rat Noir is still out there, and he wants me dead. I feel him trying to get to me. He probably stuck a thousand pins into a voodoo doll with my name on it."

Rina grimaced and took the gris-gris bag from around her neck. She tossed it over to Sam. "You wear this. The Bokor's after me, not you, but you'll be here alone. So just in case, you know."

Sam caught the small leather bag that hung on a cord. It emitted a strong odor. She could detect the smells of licorice, bay leaves, citron, and eucalyptus. She didn't think she'd be able to sleep wearing it. She put it down on the coffee table. She smiled at Rina. "The house is safe, remember? And the police are still driving by. I saw a squad car go by a few minutes ago. I'll be fine. But thanks. I appreciate it."

"Let's get going," Frankie said. "That poor kid is out in that park by himself."

"Bolt the door behind us." Rina's voice was stern. "Wear that gris-gris. The Bokor has strong magic. Hard to stop. This has been a bad-mojo day. It's not over yet."

"A bad-mojo day," Sam repeated as she walked behind the women to the front door. Once they left, she shut it and locked it. "You can say that again."

Then she gripped the banister and pulled herself up the stairs. All she wanted to do was take a shower and crawl into bed. The gris-gris bag sat where she had left it. She never gave a second thought to putting it on.

* * *

After showering, Sam lay down on top of the sheets, not bothering to put on the T-shirt she usually wore when she slept. Although it was still early in the evening and too soon to turn in for the night, Sam hoped a short nap would revive her. The events of the day had flattened her emotionally and physically.

She glanced at the bedside clock. Not even six yet. After she rested, she thought, she'd get up, dress, and make a list of some things she needed until her belongings arrived from Iraq.

Her eyelids closed before she even realized it. She fell into a deep but fitful sleep. She moaned and pleaded, crying out as she dreamed of zombies chasing her again. She couldn't seem to run fast enough. She couldn't escape. She tossed on the bed, wanting to awaken but caught by her vision, trapped in her unconscious.

Then the red sky appeared in her dream. A hot wind blew. A silver disk of light penetrated the dust-filled air. She lifted her arms to shield her face from the blowing sand. In a rerun of what she had dreamed before, the disk exploded in a terrible burst of light. Silver fragments rained down through the air. They sparkled and shone as they fell through the red sky and disappeared in a flat expanse of blue sea.

Wake up.

Sam heard a voice call her. Her spirit guide was back in her head, commanding her. *Wake up.*

Sam sat bolt upright, her eyes flying open. "What? What's wrong?"

She looked toward the window, fearful that the gray miasma would be there. Nothing. A summer dusk had fallen. The brief showers earlier had cleared. A weak ray of light from the sun, now low on the horizon, flickered through the windowpane.

She rubbed her hands over her face. *Maybe I was just dreaming I heard the voice,* she thought. She swung her legs off the edge of the bed.

Right then she heard a thud somewhere at the back of the house. She strained to listen. Footsteps, she thought. She froze for a moment. Then came a loud bang from downstairs. She jumped up. Another bang reverberated through the house. Something was hitting the glass of the slider leading to the back deck.

Get out! the voice in her head ordered sternly.

Naked, Sam rushed out of the bedroom and down the stairs. She paused on the bottom step. She saw the gris-gris bag on the coffee table in the living room. Should she take it?

She took a step toward it. Suddenly the slider's glass exploded, sending fragments through the air. She heard thuds. Two of the big men she recognized as the *tonton macoutes* came lumbering toward her from the kitchen. The gris-gris bag forgotten, her nakedness ignored, she leaped toward the front door, yanked it open, and screamed at what she saw.

The Bokor stood there, huge and menacing. She backed up. She whirled around to run, but the men who had broken into the rear of the house were already upon her.

Sam kicked out desperately. She lowered her head and butted the one closest to her, and wrenched away from their clutching hands. The other *tonton macoute* threw a punch, and she blocked it with her forearm. Her own fist lashed out and connected with the nose of one of her attackers. Blood spurted, spraying her with red.

From behind her someone grabbed her hair, yanking her off her feet. She found herself flat on her back on the wooden floor, the air knocked out of her in a sickening whoosh. The Bokor loomed over her. "You're not the snake. But you'll do for now," he said, and smiled showing very white teeth in his dark face.

Then his ham hock of a hand formed into a fist. Sam tried to squirm away, turned her head as fast as she could, but the cruel descending fist slammed into the side of her jaw. Pain burst through her mind like an exploding grenade, the world turned white, then black, and then she knew no more.

53

BEAR saw the front door of Barringer's Jersey ranch-style home open the minute he pulled into the driveway. He climbed from the Mustang and stood on the warm black asphalt, waiting.

Barringer's wife came out of the house and walked toward him. Tracks of tears stained her cheeks.

"I won't ask you in. I have kids in the house, Mr. Rutledge. I don't want them asking questions about this." She clutched the white envelope in her hand. "You can have this on one condition."

Bear nodded.

"I don't want to know what's in it. I don't ever want to know. Whatever Michael did, it's between him and God. Our kids think he was a hero. Don't let anything change that."

"I give you my word," Bear said.

She handed over the envelope, folded up three times and damp from her hand. He took it. Without a good-bye, she turned away and walked back to the house.

Bear lowered himself into his Mustang and stuck the unopened envelope in the sun visor. He slammed the door shut. He pulled out of the driveway and drove a short way. As soon as he was out of sight of the house he pulled over. He took down Barringer's letter and ripped it open.

Barringer's statement was handwritten and nearly three pages long. He leaned the papers against the steering wheel and read, the words making everything that had happened in Arlington and afterward click into place—and shaking him to the marrow of his bones.

Dearest Ceci,

It's not easy to write this. I know it won't be easy for you to read it—and if you are, it means I'm dead. I'm sorry. I'm sorry for everything. You need to know I love you. I have always loved you, even when I did some very stupid things.

But stupid or not, you need to know—the authorities need to know—what happened. Because, honey, if I'm dead, somebody killed me. Maybe they did it clever-like and it didn't look like murder. But it was.

So here's the whole story. All the stuff I never told you.

Back in the fall, back when I started my second rotation in Iraq, I was in the officers' club over in the Green Zone listening to some music and having a drink when in walks one of my old army buddies, Al. You remember him. Short guy, cocky as a bantam rooster. We had him over a couple of times at Christmas. He's the one who always brought me the Scotch.

I was sure surprised to see him. He had another guy with him. Looked like a diplomat or something. Too classy for the military, I'd say. They walked right over to me. Al, you know, was always a straight arrow, a stand-up guy. I asked him what he was doing in Baghdad. He said he had come looking for me. He was in the private sector now and wanted to talk to me.

I thought, That's weird. I hadn't seen the guy in a couple of years, but okay, I'd listen to what he had to say. He told me he had formed a consortium called USEI. He introduced the white-haired fellow with him as one of his partners, Charles Rothrock.

Bear looked up from the pages. *Rothrock?* Bear thought. He knew Charles Rothrock. The man wielded a lot of power in Washington. He had recently resigned from a job in the current White House. Bear had once delivered some materials from the DOD to the man's posh estate in Virginia's hunting country. It wasn't far from Washington. *Interesting,* Bear thought, and returned to reading.

> Now Al tells me USEI is into something big and he wants me to get in on it. They needed someone who could run the military part of the operation. Somebody with a lot of combat experience but administrative stuff too. I was perfect.
>
> As the story went, they had hooked up with an Arab named Mohammad Mohammad bin Sultan. He was the son of the brother of the king of Oman. Sorry if that sounds complicated, but to cut to the chase, Oman has got some of the richest oil fields on earth. It's ruled by one man. And USEI and this Mohammad had decided to take over.

And so the prince of Oman and the cousin plotting to betray him enter the picture, Bear thought.

> I thought it sounded nuts and risky as hell, but Al said the old king was just like Saddam Hussein, a murderous, greedy bastard. He had a son who was the same way. And now the king had gotten pissed off at the U.S. He threatened to kick us off our bases there and give them to China. They'd sell their oil to China too. Screw the good old USA. Al and his people intended to secure America's interests in the region. He made it sound like it was a black op, you know, military but secret, so secret it couldn't be connected to the U.S. government.
>
> Not my kind of thing anymore, right? Maybe when I was younger, but that was before we had the kids. So why did I say yes? The money. Honey, they offered me millions. Yeah, millions.

So I lied to you. I told you I was going to quit the military and work for an oil company. You got real mad. You wouldn't ever consider moving to the Middle East. That woke me up to how crazy Al's offer was. Especially when he started giving me the details about the old king having a fatal "accident" and his son, the prince, going mental. The prince would sit on the throne but would be just a puppet. The cousin Mohammad would be the real ruler—and USEI would rule him.

Now listen, Ceci, 'cause here's where things got really weird. Al was putting together this squadron of supersoldiers. He called them a "praetorian guard." Only they were coming in from Haiti. Haiti? What the hell? The whole thing started to go sour in my gut. I wanted to get out of it.

I didn't know what to do, so I went to the CIA station here in Baghdad. I worked with them before, some low-level intelligence work. I told them everything—except I didn't give them Al's name. I mean, he's a friend. He was trying to do me a favor; that's how I looked at it. And I'm no rat, you know. I did give them the name of the cousin, Mohammad bin Sultan. They didn't like that, but I wasn't going to do Al wrong.

Al was plenty pissed when I told him I wanted to quit, though. He said if I backed out of the deal I'd become a "dead man walking." I didn't know what he meant, but I figure I'm between a rock and hard place now. The CIA's pressuring me, and the consortium like as not thinks I know too much to stay alive.

One more thing I got to say, Ceci. If you hear anything about me and a woman named Fatima, don't let it bother you none. She was just a bar girl over here. I never even knew her last name. It wasn't right for me to see her; I know that. But it wasn't anything you should let get to you. I wouldn't even bring it up, but I know how people are. Sooner or later somebody will throw it in your face.

Again, I'm sorry. I'm sorry more than I have words to say. And if I'm dead, I'd have to say USEI killed me. And if I'm dead, I guess Al did it. So you might as well tell Langley his name. Give them this letter, so they know it. Col. George Allen.

Bear's hand began to shake. He had some trouble folding up the letter and putting it back into the envelope. He now understood why the heart and brains had been left as a message in Barringer's grave. It was to tell the world that Barringer didn't have a heart or a brain—no loyalty, no intelligence. How sick was that?

Bear shook his head. But what got his stomach churning was the identity of the man who'd contacted Barringer in Iraq. Bear wanted to believe that Barringer made it up, but everything fit now. It was true.

The man who approached Barringer about the Oman scheme, the man Barringer ultimately betrayed even if he didn't give the CIA his name, was the same Col. George Allen who was Bear's old friend and mentor, his boss at the DOD.

Bear drove his Mustang south down the interstate, heading back to D.C. as the sun went down in the west, casting the last long shadows of day across the highway.

He drove with the roar of the Shelby engine soothing him as it always did. His mind wandered, and he wondered what the hell he should do. He should probably turn the letter over to the agency, to that dragon lady who was Sam's boss.

Sam. The thought of her twisted inside Bear like a knife. Did it really matter if she called herself a psychic? Did it matter if she had "visions"? He'd thought it did when she told him, but maybe he was wrong. He had been attracted to her since the first minute he saw her. The sex with her took his breath away. It had never been like that with any other woman.

Plus, he could not ignore that she had helped him find Nada. She never hesitated, never said that he shouldn't care so much about a cat. He didn't know how her roommate was able to tell him where Nada was, but he had to admit she did tell him. If she hadn't done that, Nada would be dead, having endured terrible suffering first.

Maybe, Bear thought, he'd overreacted to Sam's confession. Maybe the human mind was more complex than he ever understood it to be. He shouldn't have been so ignorant. He should apologize. But maybe Sam meant what she said and it was over.

Sadness opened up a dark void inside Bear. He knew he had blown it. He had lost the best thing he *almost* ever had.

He pushed down on the accelerator and the Mustang responded, surging forward effortlessly until the needle of the speedometer climbed past one hundred and ten miles per hour. Bear managed to smile. He didn't have the pedal on the floor either. This car had more juice in her. He needed to take her out on a track to see what she could do without blowing the engine.

He backed off on the gas and the Mustang slowed down to about eighty. At this rate he'd be back in Washington in two hours, and he still didn't know what he should do about the letter, Colonel Allen, or Sam.

54

WHEN consciousness returned, Sam found herself in darkness. Her jaw throbbed with excruciating pain. She was lying naked on metal that was hard and cold beneath her back. She tried to move. She couldn't. Metal restraints held her wrists bound to the table sides. Cold shackles were clamped fast around her ankles. She struggled against her bonds as a burst of fear exploded in her chest.

She heard herself screaming.

Suddenly a door opened and someone turned on a light above the table so intense it blinded Sam. She squeezed her eyes shut. She heard someone approaching, but the light was too bright. She couldn't keep her eyes open long enough to see who it was.

She heard a man's voice say, "You're a pretty chickadee, aren't you? Working on you will be a pleasure. Oh, yes, a pleasure. But one I must defer for a short while. I have a previous appointment. But soon enough, my little bird, soon enough."

She felt fingers lightly stroke her across her stomach and move to her breast. She struggled with all her might to pull away. But a hand grabbed her upper arm hard, the fingers digging into her flesh. She felt the jab of a needle as its point slid through her skin deep into her muscle.

"No!" she screamed *No!*

The overhead light stayed lit, but a different kind of darkness overtook her. Within seconds Sam couldn't hear her own screams or stop herself from sliding downward into a pit of blackness and endless night.

* * *

Bear was halfway through Maryland on the interstate, nearly to Baltimore, when his cell phone started ringing. He picked it up and saw it was coming through as Sam's BlackBerry. Relief flooded over him. He answered, "Sam! Sam I'm so glad you called—"

A woman started speaking. He had heard the voice before, but it wasn't Sam's. "Bear Rutledge? This isn't Sam; it's her roommate Aurora. I was hoping Sam was with you. Obviously she's not."

"What do you mean? Where are you? You're using her BlackBerry, aren't you?" Worry grabbed him hard. He knew something was wrong, very wrong.

"I'm at the house. In Bel Air. We—the other women and I—borrowed Sam's car to drive into Washington. She didn't want to go, so she stayed here. That was a couple of hours ago. We just got back. We found the glass slider that leads out to the deck shattered. There's some blood on the floor by the front door. Sam's gone. Her BlackBerry was next to her bed. We're afraid the Bokor took her."

"The Bokor? That voodoo guy? Why? Where?" His voice shook with tension and fear.

"Bear, we don't know. The Bokor was probably after Rina. The INS is looking for him. He blames her, we think. I'll try to see where Sam is, you know, like I did with Nada."

"That was a cat! This is Sam we're talking about! My God, don't you people have any idea where she could be?"

"We don't. I'm sorry. I'm going to do my best. I'll call you back if I get anything." Then Aurora hung up.

Bear couldn't wait around for some kooky woman to try to get a vision. His first thought was to get hold of Allen. Hold of him? He'd break the guy's neck. A lightbulb lit up in Bear's brain. And there was the damned Haiti connection. Allen had to be working with this Bokor.

Bear took a deep breath and dialed the office, not holding out much hope that Allen would be there this late. He wasn't. Then Bear tried Allen's home number.

An answering machine picked up. He didn't leave a message.

Bear didn't know what to do. Then he remembered that he had a home phone number for the secretary, Lily. He called her. When she picked up, Bear worked to make his voice sound normal, not to reveal the turmoil coursing through him. He apologized for bothering her, asked how she was, and then said he had been trying to reach Colonel Allen. He couldn't locate him. It was urgent. It had to do with the case Rutledge was on. Rutledge had critical information to get to the colonel. "Remember how upset Allen was this morning?" he asked her.

Of course, Lily said she did. Everybody within hearing distance had heard Allen's yelling. Lily wanted to be cooperative; she would do anything to help.

In the calmest voice he could, Bear asked her if she knew where Allen might be. Right this minute. He wasn't at home.

Oh, yes, Lily answered quickly, she did know. She had made the note in his day planner herself. Right about now he was meeting with Charles Rothrock at Rothrock's home in Virginia. Then he was going out of town. He was leaving the country, she believed. It was all hush-hush, she said.

"I don't have a phone number here at the house for Mr. Rothrock; I'm sorry," she added.

Bear felt a surge of adrenaline. "That's okay, Lily. You've been a tremendous help. Thanks."

Bear put the accelerator of the Mustang to the floor. He would risk a state policeman trying to stop him. *Trying* was the operative word. Bear knew the Shelby could outperform even the hyped-up engine of a police vehicle, so he had no intention of pulling over even if a cop did come after him.

He raced toward northern Virginia, averaging well over one hundred miles an hour. Bear knew how to drive. He wasn't going to waste a minute. Sam was in trouble. He didn't need a psychic to tell him that. As far as the consequences if the police gave chase, right now Bear didn't give a good goddamn.

55

"NOTHING very helpful. I'm sorry." Aurora looked worriedly at Frankie and Rina. She had a map of Maryland and another one of Virginia spread out on the floor in front of her. "Virginia. I'm getting northern Virginia somewhere, but no town. No map coordinates. When I try to contact Sam herself all I'm seeing is darkness. I think she's unconscious."

"Or dead," Rina dared to say.

"No! I'd feel that. I don't. Sam's in a dark place. That's not death. Death is different." Aurora folded up the maps. "I felt so good about finding the little boy, and he's home safe. I had gotten all my powers back, and strong. Stronger than they'd ever been. But I'm failing with Sam. I'm just failing." She put her arms around her legs and rested her face on her knees. "Maybe I'm not really very good at this. When it matters, I'm a failure."

'Don't be ridiculous, Aurora," Frankie said. "Stop the self-pity. What you can do is extraordinary. If you can't see where Sam is, there's a reason. Maybe a spell has blocked access to her."

Aurora lifted her head, her eyes widening. "That's it. I think you're right. We're pretty sure the Bokor took her. There must be voodoo involved. Rina, that's your specialty." Her eyes became animated. "You have to throw the bones. Throw the bones!"

Rina sat down on the carpet too. She opened a leather pouch and poured the bones into her palm. There were six small pieces of vertebrae, crudely cubed into six-sided dice. Some sides had numbers written on them;

others held symbols on their sides. Rina spoke more to herself than the other women. "I'm going to ask for a name. The location where Sam is."

She threw the dice. All numbers came up. She studied them. She picked the bones up and put them between her hands, as if warming them with her body heat. Then she threw them again. She took note of where they landed and how close to one another, as well as what symbols appeared. She muttered, "Okay, okay." She threw the dice again.

Then she stopped. She turned to Aurora. "Look on the Virginia map. Along Route Four Ninety-five. I'm certain about the highway number. Then look for a town named Happy Meadows, Joyfield, or Happyfield. Something like that."

Aurora ran her finger down the blue highway. "It's Merrifield. In Fairfax County." Her voice was very worried when she said, "It's a distance. It's going to take us over an hour to get there."

Frankie grabbed the car keys. "Then let's get a move on."

The three women were in the car in minutes, not knowing exactly where in the town of Merrifield to find Sam, but sure they'd be able to locate her when they got closer. While Frankie drove, Aurora put the location into the BlackBerry, and directions came up on the screen.

They were driving south on Interstate 95 when Frankie got a phone call.

"It's Liam," she said out loud after she spotted the number. "Aurora, answer that. Put it on speaker. I have to drive."

"Hey, Liam," she said. "I'm in the car with a couple of colleagues. What's going on?"

Liam's voice was excited. "Okay to talk about . . . you know?"

"Talk. They know about the situation."

"Okay," Liam said, and explained that Mrs. Doyle had just called him. Prince bin Sultan and another man had come back to the Georgetown mansion a short time ago. The prince came slamming through the front door and stood there, while the man with him shouted for bin Sultan's wife. When she came running downstairs, the man told her they were boarding the prince's private jet for Oman that night, and she should get packed.

But the prince's face was all distorted. He was lurching around and knocking over furniture. The princess took one look at him and ran back upstairs screaming. Mrs. Doyle said bin Sultan looked as if he were on drugs or hypnotized, or like one of those zombie creatures you saw in the cinema.

The prince went after his wife. She fought him, but he dragged her back downstairs. While the strange man watched, he started to drag her down the hall toward the front door.

The princess screamed for Mrs. Doyle to help her. Mrs. Doyle didn't hesitate; she figured she was dealing with a devil.

Liam laughed. He could barely get the words out when he told Frankie that Mrs. Doyle ran into her bedroom and pulled her crucifix off the wall, the one that she kept the fronds from Palm Sunday behind all year round and that was "blessed by the Holy Father himself." She clutched the crucifix in one hand and pulled an old German Luger pistol out of her bedside table with the other.

"I don't know which one scared the prince and his companion more, an enraged Irishwoman rushing at them with a cross or the fact that she was waving around a big gun," Liam said, "but they left the house. I'm going there to stand watch. Can you get over here? Where are you headed?"

Frankie told him about Sam being missing and that they were driving to Merrifield to search for her.

He was quiet for a heartbeat or two. "I hope you find her okay. I don't have a good feeling about any of this."

Sam woke up still surrounded by darkness. Her jaw hurt, but it was more like a bearable ache if she didn't open her mouth . . . if she didn't scream. When she raised her head, dizziness overtook her. Her mouth was dry. She desperately wanted a drink. It didn't take long for her to realize she was still shackled to the steel table. Panic started to flood through her again.

At least the man hadn't come back. But he would. The thought of his return made Sam start shaking with terror. He was going to kill her; she was certain of it. That didn't frighten her as much as what she imagined he'd do to her first, because even if he planned to kill her, he wasn't going to make it quick.

She had to do something, she had to get free, but there seemed to be no way and no hope. But she wasn't going to just lie there. She had to do something despite being imprisoned on this table, in this dark room.

Then she realized that her mind . . . her mind was free. And her mind was strong.

As the car carrying the women continued southward, the cat, Miranda, let out a cry from her perch atop Aurora's shoulder. Aurora cried out, "It's Sam! She's trying to contact us. I can hear her clearly. She's chained to something and she can't escape."

"Tell her we're coming. Tell her to be strong," Rina said.

"I am. I am. I'm asking her where she is," Aurora answered. "She says she's in the dark. A room. She doesn't know where."

"Just keep reassuring her. We'll find her somehow," Rina urged.

Frankie drove on as fast as she dared, heading toward Merrifield. She held on to the hope that Aurora or Miranda would sense Sam's location. She was sure they could. But they were still forty minutes away. She just wasn't sure they'd get to Sam before something dreadful happened.

Bear raced against time too, risking his life on the roads into northern Virginia. Finally his Mustang roared into Rothrock's driveway, its headlights illuminating the figure of a white-haired man loading suitcases into the trunk of a black BMW sedan. Bear slammed on the brakes and barreled out of his car.

Feet crunching on the white gravel, he ran toward the

startled Rothrock. Bear grabbed the man by the collar of his suit jacket and slammed him against the side of the Beemer. Then Bear put his big hands around Rothrock's throat.

Part of him wanted to go ahead and squeeze the life out of the man. He could feel his fingers tightening on Rothrock's neck, but he gained control of his rage and screamed, "Where's the girl? Goddamn you. Tell me, or I'll break your fucking neck."

The man's eyes were wide with terror. He choked out his answer. "I don't know anything about a girl. What girl?"

"The girl the Bokor snatched out of Bel Air. Don't play games, Rothrock. You've got thirty seconds before you're a dead man."

"I don't know! I don't know! Maybe the Bokor took her to the warehouse. That's where we kept them."

"Them? Who?"

"The dead men. The zombies."

"I don't give a fucking shit about zombies." Bear tightened his hands around Rothrock's throat and thought for a second. "Where's this warehouse?"

"In Merrifield. Right off of Route Four Ninety-five."

"I need more than that, you son of a bitch."

The man gasped. "It's called Safe Storage. Big sign. You can't miss it."

Bear loosened his grip and asked in a quieter but menacing tone, "Where's Allen?"

"Allen? He left. He's already gone."

"If you want to take another breath, Rothrock, tell me where the fuck he's gone."

"He . . . He . . . He's going to the airport. Dulles."

"Are you sure? You don't sound so sure."

"He's stopping . . . stopping at the warehouse, I think. He said he forgot something. I don't know why—"

"You do know, Rothrock, and I should kill you right now. But I don't have fucking time." Bear drove his fist into the man's face. He didn't stick around long enough to watch Rothrock slide slowly down the side of the black Beemer and sprawl unconscious on the ground.

Bear was already in the Mustang and backing down

the driveway, spitting stones as he careened back onto the highway. As he drove, pushing the muscle car for every ounce of speed it had, he pulled his gun out of his shoulder holster. He set it on the seat beside him. He intended to go into that warehouse and get Sam out. Whoever got in his way was going to die.

Lying alone in the dark, Sam clearly had an image of the women in her car, Frankie driving, Rina in the backseat, Aurora and the cat on the passenger side. She heard Aurora's voice. She knew they were coming for her. Aurora kept asking her where she was. Sam could have cried with frustration. She didn't know. She couldn't tell her; she just didn't know.

Then a slice of light bit into the darkness. The door had opened. She knew it wasn't the women. She began to shake. She looked and saw the silhouettes of two men standing in the doorway before the overhead light flashed on, and she had to snap her eyelids shut because of the blinding pain.

"Ah, my pretty one. You're awake, I see," the man's voice said. "That will make it so much better."

Sam heard him move closer. She felt his hand on her arm. She tried to jerk away.

"You don't like my touch? You'll pray for me to touch you once the Bokor here begins his work. He says he is ready to help me play my game. Aren't you?"

Another voice answered. "Yes, mon. We must hurry. We get started now."

Sam turned her head and opened her eyes. The man she recognized as the Bokor was standing in front of an altar, lighting a black candle.

"No, please," she whispered despite the pain in her jaw. "Let me go. Just let me go."

The other man said, "We'll let you go, you pretty thing. After. Of course, you won't know it anymore. You won't know anything anymore, once he takes out your brain!" The man laughed a horrible laugh. "But women don't need brains, do they? You'll still be beautiful."

Rage filled Sam then. She blinked against the light and saw an older man with white fuzzy hair like a dandelion top standing next to the steel gurney. "And you will still be a disgusting old man," she spat out.

He lifted up his hand and hit her hard in the face. Her injured jaw hurt so much she nearly fainted. Tears coursed down her cheeks, but she wouldn't made a sound. She wouldn't give him the satisfaction. And she had to think. She had to do something.

She saw the Bokor approaching where she lay. She saw him pick up a hypodermic needle.

"No, do it without that. I want to hear her screaming," the older man said.

"Whatever you say, mon," the Bokor answered. He put the needle down. He took his hand and pushed back Sam's hair, probing with his fingers along her temple.

Sam was on the verge of panic, but she fought her fear. She focused all her energy on the light. She concentrated on bringing in the light. She called to her spirit guide to come to her, to bring the light. Nothing happened, but Sam kept focusing, concentrating all her energy on the light.

The Bokor picked up a small electric saw. He positioned it above Sam's forehead. He moved his thumb to switch it on when the older man suddenly interrupted, "Turn it off. Keep quiet."

Sam heard a door bang against a wall. The sound of footsteps walking on concrete echoed in what sounded like a large space. "Sam! Sam! Are you in here?" It was Bear's voice. Sam started to cry out when the older man's hand clamped down over her mouth, silencing her.

She had to tell Bear she was here. He had to know she was right here. She screamed out to him in her mind. *Bear! Bear!* She called to him in her thoughts. She thought she heard the footsteps going away. She called again, *Bear, in here! The door! Behind the door!*

She couldn't hear anything now. She kept calling out, her hope fading. He must not hear her. A sickening feeling filled her chest. She thought she heard a door close. All was quiet now.

The older man nodded at the Bokor. He flipped the switch and the saw began to hum.

Sam's eyes grew huge with terror.

Just then the door flew open and there was the sound of a gunshot. A red hole appeared dead center in the middle of the Bokor's forehead. He dropped the saw and his body fell like a downed tree to the floor.

"Rutledge!" the older man said. "You!"

"Turn her loose, Allen, or I'll shoot you next," Bear said.

56

AT Dulles airport, five long black limos pulled up to a VIP entrance, apart from the main terminal and used for diplomats and heads of state.

An entourage of men wearing turbans and robes emerged from the first two. Some women heavily veiled in black burkas followed along behind them. Soldiers in combat uniforms climbed from the others. They walked slowly and stiffly as they moved toward a white Gulf-stream V turbojet. It was readying to take off for Oman. Its tail carried the number N379P painted in green.

From the last of the limos emerged four white men, one very old. He turned to the others. "Allen and Rothrock aren't here."

Another of the board members made an unpleasant snort of impatience mixed with disgust. "They must have gotten caught in traffic. Not our problem. They'll have to come over on a commercial flight. We can't delay our takeoff."

The aged man nodded in agreement and started toward the steep steps leading to the plane's hatch. He moved well for his age. He didn't even need a cane.

In a way, the board member was right about the traffic problem. Cars had backed up for miles on the Beltway. Drivers craned their necks to try to see what had caused the massive jam. Helicopters roared overhead. Police sirens screamed in the distance. Stopped with their air conditioners running, vehicles quickly overheated and left their drivers standing on the highway, cursing and miserable in the hot night.

On one of the access ramps to the Beltway, a black BMW huddled like a wounded animal next to the cement barrier. It must have been moving slowly when it crashed. While the front fender sported a major dent, overall the car looked undamaged and intact.

But the white-haired, elegantly dressed man inside was dead. His hands still gripped the steering wheel, and his head had fallen forward, depressing the horn. Its earsplitting noise blared unceasingly into the night. The glass of the driver's window had shattered, and a single, perfectly round hole had marred the thin white skin of Charles Rothrock's temple.

While one statie put out flares to warn other drivers away from the wreck, another highway patrolman stood outside the BMW studying the dead man inside. He looked at the bullet hole, then glanced around. He couldn't figure out how anyone could have made the shot that killed this guy.

Then he spotted a grassy knoll at eye level with the access ramp, but several hundred feet away. The cop shook his head, having to admire the killer's marksmanship. *That's where the sniper must have stood,* the state policeman thought. *That had to be one amazing shot. Even with a scope, the shooter must have been one hell of a marksman. Somebody with that kind of ability? He could qualify for the Olympics.*

Back in Merrifield, three young women came running across the empty warehouse's floor and rushed through the open door of the room on its far side. Frankie, Aurora, and Rina saw Sam wearing Bear's shirt as he held her cradled in his arms like a child.

An older man was shackled to a metal table. He was cursing, incoherent, and mumbling something over and over. "Rutledge. Supposed to be in jail, not here. Not here. The patsy. The dumb cracker Rutledge was supposed to be in jail."

The Bokor's inert body lay where he had fallen on the floor.

"Is she okay?" Frankie asked Bear.

"I'm fine," Sam answered. "Bear, you can put me down, really."

"I'd rather keep holding you," he said, but set her gently on her feet.

Sam turned to her friends. "Somebody should call Ms. Z. She needs to send somebody out here to arrest Colonel Allen."

Frankie nodded. "And she needs to stop the prince's plane about to take off for Oman."

Bear's eyebrows rose in surprise. "They're going to pull a coup," he said. "Yeah, somebody needs to stop them at the airport. Once they take off, they'll be out of reach."

But nobody had to call Ms. Z.

At that moment, three black SUVs pulled up at the Safe Storage warehouse. Ms. Z got out of one. A dozen men in black piled out of the others. They swarmed into the warehouse. Two of them came and got Allen and took him away.

Ms. Z walked over to Sam, Bear, and the women. Even at this hour of the night in this heat, she wore a black suit. A Bluetooth device was in her ear. She was smiling her crocodile smile.

"Well-done," she said. "Well-done," she repeated. "We'll take over from here. You can go home."

"Wait!" Sam said. "You need to get some people to Dulles. You need to stop a plane from taking off to Oman. That's what's behind everything."

Ms. Z looked impatient, not pleased. "Don't worry about that. It's been taken care of. This case is closed."

"So you stopped it from taking off?" Frankie said. "The prince is a zombie, you know."

Ms. Z let out a deep sigh. "We know. Of course we know. We know everything. You did your job, and you did it well. You can go. I'll talk to you all in the morning."

Sam still had questions, though. How did Ms. Z know about the plane? How did she find Sam at the warehouse? She wanted to ask, but Ms. Z said, "Our forensic people need to get busy. Go on, get out of here."

"But don't you want to ask us questions? We found out everything," Sam said slowly, feeling as if something had happened and she didn't know what.

Ms. Z gave her a level look. "I said we know everything. But you"—she turned to Bear—"give me the letter from Barringer's wife."

The three women got back in Sam's Toyota and headed back to Bel Air. Sam said she wanted to go home too, but Bear asked her to ride with him. He had some things he needed to say to her, if she'd listen.

She did.

Bear drove with one hand, and despite the awkwardness of the seats, Sam managed to sit as close to him as possible. He swallowed whatever was left of his pride and apologized—he did more than apologize; he begged forgiveness.

"Sam, I don't know how to ask. I know I don't deserve it. But give me another chance. Let's start over. I think we can make it. I really do. You're everything I've always wanted. I mean that."

He put his arm around her and pulled her even closer.

"Can you accept me, Bear? As I am?" Sam asked the one thing she had to know.

His arm tightened around her shoulders. "Sam, when I went into the warehouse and found it empty, I thought I had failed. I called out. I didn't know where you could be. The place was silent as a tomb.

"Then I heard you—in my head. You told me where you were. I pretended to leave, but what I did was take off my shoes and go straight to that door. You know the rest. Look, I can't pretend I understand it. I still think zombies are a crock. But, Sam, it doesn't matter whether you're a psychic or not. It really doesn't."

Those were the words Sam wanted to hear. She snuggled close and closed her eyes. She had never before felt such joy, such unmitigated happiness.

But after a few minutes of savoring Bear's words, Sam spoke again. "What do you think? About Ms. Z showing up like that? How did she find me that fast? How did she even know I was missing? The women didn't tell her. And how did she know that you had that letter, anyway?"

Bear let out a deep sigh. He hugged Sam to him. "Sam, sometimes I think you're too innocent for this work."

Sam tensed. "What are you talking about?"

"You're working for the agency. They're spies, remember? And they're not just spies. They're as good as Israel's Mossad, maybe better. The agency is at the top of the heap. The best. It's their business to *know*." Bear kept his voice light, as if he were joking, but Sam knew he wasn't.

"Are you telling me they spied on me? On you? With what? How?" A dark feeling moved around in Sam's stomach.

"Surveillance, Sam. Your house is probably bugged. Mine too, probably. Your car must have a tracking device underneath it somewhere. Then there's your phone—and where did you get the BlackBerry, anyway? I'm sure Ms. Z heard every word you ever said."

"Oh. I should have known." Sam's voice got very small.

"You do now." Bear's voice was grim. "I learned a long time ago, it sometimes hurts to know the truth, but the truth is all you've got in the end. So never back away from it, Sam. Ignorance can get you killed. The truth will keep you alive. Once you know it, you can deal with a situation."

Sam nodded. "But I never thought . . . I mean, I'm one of them."

"Are you, Sam?" Bear said. "Do you think the way Ms. Z and others in the agency do? For them, the ends justify the means. They're fighting for this country in the way they know best—with nothing out of bounds. They feel that's what they have to do to keep America safe. To protect us. But where will you draw the line, Sam? Do you think it's okay to use torture? To kidnap people. To murder?"

The Mustang rolled up the dark highway toward Bel Air, Sam lost in thought, pondering what Bear just said. Could what he said about the agency be true? Finally, having no answers, she dozed off and began to dream. In her dream she saw a red sky with a silver disk glowing through air filled with dust. Then the disk exploded in a flash of flame. Silver pieces fell from the red heavens, drifting down, down, down until they disappeared into a wide blue sea.

She sat upright with a gasp, realizing exactly what she had seen.

"What's the matter?" Bear asked.

"Bear, you were right. Everything you said was right. Ms. Z didn't stop the plane," she said. "Before it took off, they didn't stop it."

"The plane to Oman?"

"Yes. Ms. Z said it had been 'taken care of.' " Sam looked at Bear with sad eyes. "She didn't stop it. She never intended to stop it. It was the agency's plane. It was booby-trapped. She blew it up, Bear. It took care of the problem for them." Grief washed over Sam. "All those people, Bear. Not all of them were bad. Not all of them were guilty. What about the pilot? What about the women? But she blew up the plane and killed everybody on it once they left the ground."

Epilogue

TWO D.C. policemen, both of them African-American and longtime veterans on the force, were on patrol in southeast Washington when they spotted ten or twelve young men—a gang of whites, Hispanics, and blacks—smashing the window of an appliance store. The cops called for backup, then got out of their vehicle with their guns drawn. One of the gang, a teenager, pulled a gun out of his belt and aimed at the cops.

Another patrol car arrived at the scene just as the shooting started. When it was over, one of the cops had been badly wounded and five people were dead, including the teenager who had first pulled the gun. He was fourteen years old.

The rioting started in southeast Washington an hour later, when news of the shooting hit the local television stations. It spread northward like a wildfire, devouring block after block.

And above Bel Air, Maryland, a filmy grayness or a dim shadow danced in the air like northern lights at the same time that Rina climbed from the sturdy Toyota. Aurora and Frankie went into the house, but the thin, chestnut-haired woman gazed for a moment out of the still-open garage door at the quiet neighborhood.

"Bad mojo out there tonight. Bad mojo," she said. Then she left to join the others as the garage door slid down.

ACKNOWLEDGMENTS

I would like to express my deep gratitude to Iraq veteran Shawn Bose, who answered my questions about serving in the Middle East and shared with me his photos and memories of his time in Iraq. If I got any of it right, it's to his credit.

Also thanks go to Hildy Morgan, manager of the Dietrich Theater in Tunkhannock, Pennsylvania, and member of Penn Writers Group, who generously gave her time to read this work in manuscript form.

More Undead Action and Sizzling Romance
from

Savannah Russe

BENEATH THE SKIN

Book Three of the Darkwing Chronicles

To get over a recent break-up, Daphne must throw herself into her work, joining her colleagues to chase down a ruthless enemy. Mysterious, cruel, and unstoppable, this assassin is dead-set on killing a certain presidential candidate. Now Team Darkwing has to find him before it's too late. But soon, Daphne finds herself drawn back into the life she once rejected: a secret vampire underworld, where all pleasures—like human blood—can be found.

Available wherever books are sold or at penguin.com

FROM

SAVANNAH RUSSE

Under Darkness

Book Five of the Darkwing Chronicles

The terrorist threat to America continues, but this time it's so top secret that only those in the highest circles of government know about it. One of America's most important symbols of liberty has been stolen. But that's nothing compared to the terrorists' chilling plan for the next attack on America. And as it unfolds, Daphne Urban and the vampire spies, the Darkwings, become the first—and only—line of defense to save a city...

Team Darkwing's assignment: figure out and defuse the terrorist plot. But Daphne gets distracted when vampire hunters storm the city. Is Darius, her hot-and-cold lover, behind their reappearance? This time, will he return to love Daphne—or to commit the ultimate act of betrayal?